A Way of Life, Like Any Other
Patrick Kavanagh
W. R. Rodgers
The Conscience of James Joyce

THE
SILVER SPOONER

DARCY O'BRIEN

SIMON AND SCHUSTER/NEW YORK

Copyright © 1981 by Darcy O'Brien
All rights reserved
including the right of reproduction
in whole or in part in any form
Published by Simon and Schuster
A Division of Gulf & Western Corporation
Simon & Schuster Building
Rockefeller Center
1230 Avenue of the Americas
New York, New York 10020
SIMON AND SCHUSTER and colophon
are trademarks of Simon & Schuster.
Manufactured in the United States of America

10   9   8   7   6   5   4   3   2   1

Library of Congress Cataloging in Publication Data

O'Brien, Darcy.
    The silver spooner.

    I.   Title.
PS3565.B666S5   813'.54   80–22971
ISBN 0-671-25264-X

The author wishes to thank the University of Tulsa, the John Simon Guggenheim Memorial Foundation, and Charles B. Clement, Jr., for generous assistance and encouragement in the writing of *The Silver Spooner*.

TO GEORGE O'BRIEN,
BOB GREGORY AND
GAILARD SARTAIN

"How did I end up like this?"

—Seamus Heaney, at
Wheeler Dealer's, Tulsa

ONE

In the Choctaw language, Oklahoma means red people. But this is a story about white people. They live in the eastern part of the state among the Choctaws, Chickasaws, Cherokees, Creeks, Seminoles and Osages, but they do not see much of the Indians or of the black people, many of them the descendants of Indian slaves, who live there. In this part of the country people have their own distinct ways of life and death, or prefer to believe they do.

It must have been back in the summer of 1957, when A.G. Kruger and Ramsey Hogan were twelve years old, that they heard the story about the woman who drank Falstaff. Out near the Coyote pasture on the Sunrise Ranch on that summer day some twenty and more years ago, the heat rose up in waves off the ground and poured down from the sky, and the air was heavy with invisible moisture. This was not the flat, dry Oklahoma of the plains but a green land full of lakes, woods and fat cattle, the Oklahoma of which Will Rogers said that if it was not the Garden of Eden, it would have to do until something better turned up. The men sweated as they stacked the hay.

They had been stacking all day. It seemed to get hotter by the minute, and they had even stopped talking about all the beer they would drink that evening. The only sounds were the swish of the hay, flies, locusts and the occasional bird. A.G. and Ramsey worked along with the men, dreaming of ice cream, feeling ready to drop, but they would sooner have died than show it.

Everybody paused at the sound of a pickup drawing near. Over the top of a hill from the direction of the big house came old man Kruger, A.G.'s father Earl, bringing a load of watermelons to his men. They straightened up and cheered. Little A.G. threw his big white hat at the sun.

"It's too goddamned hot to work," Earl Kruger said, descending from his truck. "I heard on the radio it's a hundred and eight in Tulsa. Here's a couple knives, A.G. You and Ramsey slice up them melons. Jesus Christ, boys, I'm sweatin like a nigger on election day."

That was the way it was, working for Earl Kruger on the Sunrise Ranch. You could break your ass for him, and his wages were low. You would get to hating him and cursing him, and then he would do something to make you grateful, and you would work twice as hard. A lot of people hated Earl Kruger, especially the small ranchers he had squeezed out, bullied out or burned out. "You know how that son of a bitch got all that land, don't you," people would say. "Grabbing, that's how. Just grab and grab." But everybody feared him, some respected him, and some even loved him. His cowboys stuck by him. He got them indoor plumbing and paid their doctor bills.

The men spread out under a tree as A.G. and Ramsey passed out the watermelon slices. Earl stood over them, big-faced, hog-gutted. Except for his silver belt buckle shaped in the form of the Sunrise brand, he was dressed like the cowboys in jeans and an old shirt and well-broken boots, but there was no mistaking the boss. He was six feet and two hundred pounds and he looked even bigger. He chatted about the heat, how the cattle were looking good, how he was going to do a deal for another five hundred acres. "I'm not talkin about some kinda pussyfootin bullshit. By God, I mean closure. When I want closure, I get it. That deal will be signed, sealed and delivered before the poor son of a bitch knows what hit him." His red face pulsed with alert inscrutability. A.G. sat down off to the side to enjoy his melon and admire his father.

"Your daddy is the biggest man in the county," Ramsey said.

"In the state," A.G. said. "Nobody beats out my dad."

"Mr. Kruger," one of the cowboys said, "I'd say you was the meanest man I ever met."

"Well thank you," Earl said. "I'd like to think so. I never met a man as mean as me and I don't expect I will. You know what they say. When Earl Kruger says it's Easter, you better hide them eggs. Sam," he said to a small, old cowboy, "give us a story."

"One time there was this old gal," Sam began, right off, as he always did, stories flowing out of him like whiskey from the bottle, "she must of been fifty or more, she come into this bar ever night and she would order a Falstaff. Just one Falstaff and then she lies her head down on the bar and passes out. She does this ever night and they have to wake her up when it's time to close. Well, after a couple weeks, the bartender says to some of the boys, hell, let's fuck her. So they did. They drug her into the back room and go after her one after the other, and she never does notice a thing. After a while, word does get around, and what do you know, there must of been fifty boys back there ever night a-fuckin away at her, and she never does notice, they just stick her back up on the bar stool afterwards and wake her up when it's time to go.

"Well one night, after about a month, she come in, sits down at the bar, and she orders a Coors. 'A Coors?' says that old bartender. 'A Coors? Hell, I thought you always ordered a Falstaff.' 'Well, I know I did,' she says. 'But you know? I found out somethin. That Falstaff makes my pussy sore!' "

Everybody just about died laughing, so they asked for one more. Sam went on about the blacksmith who told his young wife that he was the only man in the world with two peckers, but that he had given one away to the postmaster. The wife came back from mailing a letter one day and told her husband that he had given away the better pecker. The men had heard the story before, but they laughed anyway and went back to

work in a good mood, thinking that working for old man
Kruger was a pretty good life. Some of the men had very little
choice in the matter anyway, because Earl Kruger had made a
deal with the sheriff to spring them from jail if they would
work on the Sunrise at whatever wages Earl Kruger set.

Ramsey Hogan was staying with the Krugers for the summer, and that night he and A.G. lay in their beds in A.G.'s
room on the second floor of the big house, listening to the
comforting whirr of the attic fan, feeling tired, full and content
from a big dinner.

"That Falstaff made my pussy sore!" Ramsey said, and he
and A.G. shook their beds laughing.

"Sam's got a million of 'em," A.G. said. "What about that
other one?"

"Imagine a feller havin two peckers."

"That's just a joke."

"I know it," Ramsey said. "It could happen though. I remember hearin about it happened over in India or some place
like that."

"Don't be stupid."

"Sure it could be. There's cows born with two heads, ain't
they?"

"That's true," A.G. said. "I wonder where it would be,
though."

"What?"

"The other pecker. On top or side by side?"

"Stickin out behind," Ramsey said.

They laughed and drifted into private thoughts.

"I was wonderin," A.G. said. "Couldn't the blacksmith tell
his wife was fuckin the postmaster? I mean, wouldn't there be
some way to tell?"

"You should ask Vicki Martin," Ramsey said.

"Vicki Martin! She does it for everyone."

"That's what they say. She'd know all about it. I'd like to ask
her. Maybe she'd give me a demonstration."

"Would you?"

"Sure I would. I'd like to ask her right now. My cock's stiff as a board. It's like a jungle flashlight."

"Mine isn't yet. I can't think of anything. I think I'll think about Vicki Martin. You ask her about it and then I'll ask her."

"Okay. Let's both ask her."

"Okay. She sure would know."

"You know," Ramsey said, "the first time I jerked off, I thought I was the only one doin it. I thought I invented it."

"Maybe you did. You taught me."

"You gonna do it now?"

"Yes."

"So am I. You know what they say. It's your soap—you can wash it as fast as you want."

Ramsey and A.G. had been friends since the first grade. They had few secrets from each other, and they were together so much that the other boys sometimes called them Frick and Frack. Ramsey had always been bigger and stronger than A.G., but A.G. was smarter, or did better in school, and he carried about him the prestige and power of the Sunrise, so they made a good team.

Before meeting Ramsey, A.G. had been a lonely child. His mother and father had been in their forties when he had been born, their first and last, and they had doted on him like the unexpected gift he was. They had just about given up hope for an heir when he had arrived. There had never been a thought of adoption, for as Earl had said, the Sunrise was going to go to a Kruger or it was going to hell, and that meant a Kruger by blood. A.G.'s birth on V-J Day had been a big event in that part of the state in 1945. It had seemed to signal a continuation of the prosperity that the war had brought to the ranch, and it ended finally speculation about the future of the Sunrise. It also disappointed many who had hoped that with Earl's death in twenty or thirty years, they would see an end to the Krugers.

A few of the neighboring small ranchers hated the Krugers so much that they had hoped to be around to watch Earl's widow be forced to sell off parcel after parcel of land, because no one believed that she would be willing or able to carry on so vast an operation herself. That would make the old man turn in his grave, they said. He held onto land like a tiger onto meat. But with A.G.'s birth there was no telling how long the Krugers would carry on, maybe forever.

Certainly A.G. was treated from the first as though through him a dynasty would be extended. One servant did nothing but care for him, and his mother, Margaret, fussed over him endlessly and made sure that he had every toy a boy could possibly want. His earliest years were spent in a world of adults. He hardly ever saw another child, except at Christmas, when the Krugers always threw a party for the cowboys and their families, and even then he was set apart, not out of snobbery or fear of contamination but simply because he was a Kruger. He spent his days with his mother and the servants, and in the evenings Earl would hold him in his lap, telling him stories and exciting him with descriptions of all the wonderful things father and son would do together when A.G. got a little older. Usually A.G. would crawl up on one of Earl's big shoulders and examine his father's bald spot, which fascinated him. "Daddy," he would say, "you have a hole in your head." Earl would always laugh and tell his son that he was the only man he knew who could get away with saying that.

When he was old enough to wander around, he would sit for hours in a pasture dreaming, watching the wind touch blossoms or wondering what the cows were thinking. One of the cowboys carved little wooden boats for him, and he would take these to a creek and send them on imagined voyages, staring at them as they bobbed and swirled against rocks, imagining sailors on their decks, loading them with tufts of grass. He had his own horse by the time he was six and he would ride all over the ranch by himself, thinking that he was a real cowboy while city boys could only pretend. He was lonely, but he did not know that he was lonely. He knew only that after a couple of hours by himself he would always feel like going back to the house to see where his mother was and to hear her voice. Sometimes he would make up something to say to her, just to hear her respond to him.

Gradually he came to sense that he was somebody, and he began to like it. He came to know that the Sunrise was his and that it was more than any other boy had and that even the cowboys were, in a way, his. When he would ride into town he knew that he could buy anything, candy or an ice-cream cone or a pair of gloves, on credit, and he heard people saying, "That's the Kruger boy," or "That is Earl Kruger's son." He realized that he was different, maybe even better, though he was reluctant to be sure about that. Sometimes it occurred to him that he might be something like a prince, and he liked that, but there were times when he had the urge to put on a disguise and sneak into town to mingle with everyone else.

That was why he enjoyed Ramsey so much. Ramsey lived like every other boy, and being with him made A.G. feel natural, somehow, because he knew he was better off than Ramsey and yet, with Ramsey, he could do all the things every other boy did. He could be above Ramsey and yet the same as Ramsey all at once, and that was a good feeling. A.G. knew that his father wanted him to be able to rope and turn a herd and mend fences and shoot as well as the other boys, or better, and with Ramsey he could learn these things more easily than when his father, often so impatient, was trying to teach him. "Goddamnit, son, can't you do anything right?" his father might shout if A.G. missed a target, and A.G. would miss again, but with Ramsey everything was so relaxed, so natural. He grew so attached to Ramsey that there were times when he thought it might be fun if they could exchange identities for a day or a week. Ramsey could see what it was like to be him and he could see what it was like to be Ramsey. The only real drawback to the plan, A.G. thought, was that Ramsey didn't have a father.

It was with Ramsey, when the boys were about eleven, that A.G. really learned to shoot.

"Let's go get us some turtles," Ramsey said one morning.

A.G. had never shot a turtle up to that time. He had shot a few birds, crows mostly, and he knew that turtle shooting was a great pastime among the cowboys, but he had never had the urge to shoot the creatures on his own. He had always liked the turtles and for years had watched them along the creeks and by the sides of ponds, sunning themselves and plopping into the water. They made him think of noble dinosaurs grown small. He had a private theory that when the dinosaurs had been threatened by fiercer beasts, they had made themselves tiny and had grown shells to survive, and now they were called turtles. He knew that there was no way to prove the theory, so he kept it to himself, but he chose to believe in it, and when he saw a turtle disappear into a pond with small splashes and ripples, he imagined that it had once been gigantic enough to make a river spill its banks and flood a town.

So when Ramsey said they were going turtle shooting, A.G. had misgivings, but he knew that it was something that had to be done, because everybody did it. They rode out a mile or two from the big house and found a pond with two turtles resting on its muddy slopes. I wonder if they are husband and wife, A.G. thought.

The boys took their .22s from their saddles and loaded up.

"You go first," A.G. said.

"Wait a minute," Ramsey said. "You got to give 'em a sportin chance." He explained how you didn't shoot a turtle in cold blood. It would be like shooting a man in the back. You waited till you spotted one swimming. They swam with just their heads sticking out, or sometimes they would bob up for air and you would aim for the head in just the few seconds it surfaced. Hitting them in the shell or while they were taking the sun was chickenshit. Ramsey picked up a rock and threw it at the pair on the bank. They scrambled into the water.

"They got to come up for air," Ramsey said. "Just wait." He readied his rifle, his freckled face against the butt, his red hair bright in the sun. When one little green head bobbed up, he fired and hit it square.

A.G. was glad when he saw the turtle sink out of sight. It might surface later, but at least for now he didn't have to look at it. He managed to stop thinking about whether it had been the husband or the wife Ramsey had killed and waited his turn. When a head showed, he shot and missed, his bullet skittering into the mud bank beyond.

"Try again," Ramsey said. "We got all day."

Now A.G. was all concentration. He knew he didn't have to pretend he was as good a shot as Ramsey, yet, but he knew he had better hit one soon. He focused all of his body and mind on the pond and imagined an invisible line between him and the turtle's head that he knew would soon appear, a line connecting the barrel of his gun with the target. It was just like throwing a football or a punch. You had to feel yourself connected to the target. When the next head appeared, A.G. pulled the trigger and didn't even notice the slight kick from his .22 as the bullet hit home.

"I bet you hit that little son of a bitch right in the eye," Ramsey said. "Nice goin."

A.G. got caught up in the shooting after that. He hit six more turtles that day and a squirrel, and when he told his father about it, he reveled in the old man's praise. A.G. and Ramsey went shooting all the time. Once in a while they would check into school, just to make the roll call, and then sneak off for a day of glorious shooting freedom. In the fall they accompanied Earl when he went after duck, goose, quail or the pheasants he bred on the Sunrise. And they went after poachers, too. A.G. had been thrilled when he was old enough to ride out for the first time with Ramsey and three or four armed cowboys to scare poachers and run them off. Word had come to the big house that a couple of poachers had been spotted, and Earl had chosen a search party and told the boys that they could go along. It was never absolutely certain whether hunters were deliberately poaching or not, because the Sunrise holdings were so vast that you could easily be trespassing without knowing it, but Earl felt that every poacher had to be made an example, no matter what his intentions, because otherwise things could get out of hand.

There was little trouble locating the poachers after a search of an hour or so. The sound of the guns gave them away. They were after quail in some bottomland four or five miles inside the Sunrise borders, and Earl's men surrounded them before they knew what was happening. Two poachers against four cowboys and the two boys.

"Don't you know this land is posted?" one of the cowboys said. "This is Earl Kruger's land. You're on the Sunrise Ranch."

The poachers said nothing, looking as though they knew they were in for it. Their dogs, two fine English pointers, seemed to want to make friends. A.G. held his breath as the cowboy said that somebody was going to have to be taught a lesson. He told the boys to hold their guns on the poachers while he tied the dogs to a tree, disarmed the captives and started shoving them around. The other cowboys dismounted and took turns slapping the poachers and taunting them.

"Hunt your own land, whistle-dick, if you got any."

"You think we should kill one of 'em? Which one?"

A cowboy held one of them while another cowboy punched hell out of the poacher's gut. The dogs yapped and whined and tangled themselves with the ropes.

"You boys want a go at 'em?"

A.G. thought his role was probably to sit on his horse and watch, more or less supervising the action, and he found himself feeling a little sorry for the poachers and for their dogs, though he knew he should not have such feelings. He thought the lesson had probably been taught well enough already. But Ramsey dismounted and got in a few licks. His blows were feeble compared to the cowboys', but to A.G. it looked like the poachers were pretty sore by that time and could have done without even a kid beating on them.

As he rode away, A.G. glanced back and saw that the poachers lay on the ground unmoving. He hoped that they would get up soon and untie their dogs.

"Those guys won't be back," A.G. told his father.

"They goddamned better not," Earl said. "What do people think I am? Givin it away? I am not the government!"

One November, Earl, Ramsey and A.G. went after a trophy whitetail buck that had been spotted on the ranch over near the Arkansas line. Under his father's guidance A.G. placed in his rucksack a short-bladed, round-edged knife, a whetstone and a compass, and from his belt he hung a light ax. His gun was a gift from Earl, a Weatherby 7mm Magnum that would shoot flat at two hundred yards. A.G. had been practicing with it for days and was almost confident with it. It was more accurate than Ramsey's old Winchester and it narrowed the gap between their skills.

They took a pickup to the hilly, wooded country where the deer had been seen and set out, enjoying the wet freshness of a typical Oklahoma autumn morning, the sun rising on a clear, still day. By ten o'clock Earl had found the buck, stalked him into a meadow and downed him with two shots to the head at a hundred and eighty yards.

It was A.G.'s first deer hunt, and he was shocked to see the big buck, which had looked so proud and defiant, fall so quickly and so easily. He figured his father must be one of the best shots there was. He was secretly glad he had not been quick enough to shoot first: he might have missed, for one thing, and there was special satisfaction and a chilling thrill in seeing his father do the job right. That was the thing about his father. He would say he was going to do something and then he would do it, every time.

Earl, the boys trailing him, walked up to the buck and pressed his gun barrel into one big eye.

"Got to make sure he's dead," Earl said. "You can go for a pretty wild ride if you're not careful. All right, A.G., get out that knife. I'll show you boys the right way to dress out one of these sons of bitches."

The buck lay on a small rise, and Earl grabbed the points, rolled the animal over on its back and pulled it around until the head was uphill. With one light stroke he slit the belly hide from the breastbone to the anus, just missing the penis and testicles to one side.

"Now look here," Earl said. "That there is the stomach, and you see it ain't punctured at all. You don't want to slit the stomach, see. Spoils the meat. Now watch me get that liver."

A.G. held his breath as his father reached in and pulled down on the liver and severed the diaphragm from the ribcage. Then he got down on one knee, reached up into the chest cavity, grabbed hold of the windpipe and severed it and, in turn, the gullet and large blood vessels, bringing them out with bloody hands and hurling them into the woods. A.G. was too entranced by his father's skill to give in to the nausea and horror that rose in him.

"Somethin'll eat that," Earl said. "Quite a buck. I bet he's over two hundred pounds easy. Give me that whetstone, A.G. Be quick about it, would you?"

Earl sharpened the knife for a full minute and then plunged it in around the buck's anus, making a deep circular incision. He tied off the rectal tube and cut the sex organs free, pulling them back into the body cavity. A.G. felt weak, and when Earl rolled the carcass over on its side and all the remaining organs and entrails spilled out onto the ground, A.G. thought he would throw up, but his pride kept him from it. He knew this was all part of hunting and life and being a man, and he

would learn to love it no matter what. He could almost sense
himself inside the body of his father, shooting like a champion,
cutting like a surgeon, owning the world. It was very few boys
had a father like that. Poor old Ramsey didn't even have a
father at all.

That night everyone ate fresh deer liver and onions and Earl
said:

"They ain't many white folks eatin like this tonight. And no
niggers."

"Don't say that, Earl," Mrs. Kruger said. "Edward might
hear." Just then Edward appeared with another bottle of wine
and poured some into Earl's glass.

"Well why shouldn't I say it?" Earl said. "It's true, ain't
it?"

When A.G. found himself enjoying the deer's liver, he figured he had come a long way in a day, although he wondered
whether he would ever be able to dress out a deer the way his
father had, calm and skillful as an Indian. I think I will always
take someone along to do that, A.G. thought. Ramsey could do
it.

"I showed the boys the right way to dress out a buck, now
didn't I?" A.G. figured his father must have been reading his
mind.

"You sure did, Daddy," A.G. said.

"You got to learn to do it right. Down in Texas I know these
ranchers, they got these wetbacks will take one on and have it
in the freezer in twelve minutes. They might have three wetbacks for the one animal. I believe that takes the sport out of
it, don't you, boys?"

Ramsey and A.G. agreed.

Often when he found himself alone A.G. would head for an
old abandoned water well that he was drawn to for some
reason or other. He had asked his father about the well, and
Earl said that he had no idea who had dug it but that it must

be pretty old. The stone foundations of a house, or a shack, really, were visible in the grass nearby, and A.G. liked to imagine some pioneer family living in the house, maybe sleeping six to a bed and drawing their water from the well. He made up stories about the family to himself. The father was a terrific shot, but so were the sons, and many was the time they had saved their lives and those of the womenfolk by gunning down hordes of bloodthirsty Indians who would descend on them from the plains in search of scalps. A tornado had leveled the house one night and nothing was ever heard from the family again. They had huddled together in a corner, hugging each other and trembling at thunderclaps. Through the window they saw a tree struck by lightning—the explosion of thunder was deafening and the struck tree blazed up, incandescent with white and blue flames leaping from it, subsiding to a red glow. Then silence, and finally a distant roar, low at first but growing louder. In seconds the tornado tore through the house, carrying the family to where no one would ever find them.

The well was just deep enough to have a slight echo, and A.G. would call down to hear himself call back. The well would become overgrown in spring. A.G. would spend an hour clearing it, pulling out long roots and, when the light was right, kneeling to catch glimpses of himself in the shallow water, his face framed by a wreath of clouds, then tossing in a stone to blur his reflection in ripples. He loved going to the well. He thought it would be a fine place to be during a tornado. If only the family living in the shack had known that, they might never have been blown away.

TWO

Earl liked to make sure that A.G. toed the line. He figured that if he was going to give the boy everything a young man could wish for, A.G. had better be ready for it and had better learn responsibility sooner than later. When A.G. did not behave up to snuff, Earl had a wooden paddle with his son's initials carved on it that could help make the boy understand what his place was and what his obligations were.

"You get that brush hoggin done, stud horse?"

"I forgot."

"You what?"

"I just forgot it. I can get to it tomorrow."

"What was you doin that you forgot?"

"Me and Ramsey, we—"

"Let me tell you somethin. You got certain things to do around here that is yours to do 'em. Now I don't like to see this. Get me that paddle. You startin to bawl? You gonna bawl? I'll give you somethin to bawl about. Get that goddamned paddle. I am gonna beat you like a redheaded stepchild. If I'd of done what was right I'd of pinched your damn head off when you was born."

And A.G. would have to drop his pants right there and take six or eight good whacks. For the most part he accepted the punishment as his due, but as he grew older, he wondered how many years more it would go on. By the time he was ten he figured he was still too little to challenge Earl, not that he thought he would really want to, but he was sure he could outrun him, and so he decided that the next time Earl got out the paddle he would put his speed to the test.

"Get them pants down!" Earl said, after going through his customary admonitions, with digressions on the state of the nation, California dope addicts, lazy Indians, soldiers who refused to obey orders and cost the lives of good men. He swished the paddle about and rubbed its surface as if to warm it up. "Get them pants down and take it like a man."

His legs were trembling but A.G. bolted, out the front door, down the driveway and along the dirt road that stretched five miles from the big house down to the highway. He had a vague plan. When he had put enough distance between himself and his father, he would crawl through a fence, head across a pasture and disappear into the woods to spend the night. His parents would be so worried about him that by the time he returned the next morning, the cards would be in his hand and he just might be able to see the paddle put away forever.

He ran on, not looking back, down the road in the twilight, until he began to feel short of breath, when he stopped and checked back to figure whether he had gone far enough. What he saw puzzled him at first and then made him light out again as fast as he could. About a hundred yards away, Earl was coming after him. Backwards. All A.G. could see was Earl's back, his elbows and his heels pumping away at him, the big form running at him, gaining on him, backwards. There was something extra frightening in the sight. A.G. stumbled as he tried to start up again, losing more ground, and in less than half a minute Earl had caught up to him, grabbed him by the arms and lifted him into the air.

"You thought you could run away from your daddy?" Earl shouted at him, panting, his face red and enormous. "I'll tell you somethin! Your daddy can catch you runnin backwards! You better believe it and you better not forget it! Now you get the hell back to the house and get those pants down real quick!"

That night as he lay in bed with Margaret, Earl said: "I got to admire the spunk in that boy."

"Maybe you could let up on him some," Margaret said. "He's a good boy. Maybe you could let up on him. It does seem like he's learned his lesson."

"Maybe so," Earl said.

Earl and Margaret had named their son August Grant after Earl's father, who had staked the original land of the Sunrise, and Margaret's father, Simon Grant, who had been forced to sell his land during the Depression and had shot himself to death. Earl had himself bought his father-in-law's land at the rock-bottom price, and relations between the two had been icy right up to Simon's suicide, although it had been Earl's position that Simon Grant ought to have been grateful to get what he could during a time when a lot of piss-poor farmers were getting nothing but a foreclosure notice. Margaret had seen her father's death coming, had seen that his spirit had been broken by his wife's early death, by the rough times and by his sense that the dreams he had had for himself would never come true. She knew that the same thing had happened to many men in those days and thought that it was all summed up the first time she had heard Bing Crosby on the radio singing the song that went I built a railroad, made it run on time, brother can you spare a dime, and she never heard that song without crying. But she had Earl, and Earl was a different sort of man from her father. You felt that nothing would ever break Earl down and that if the world were coming to an end he would be there until the last, protecting her. Just by being there, Earl had made it easier for her to accept Simon's death. You had to accept it and to go on. Some men survived and others did not. That was all there was to it.

Earl never ceased reminding Margaret, A.G. and himself that every head of cattle and every hog pen and every fence post was there for one reason only, and that was to give A.G. the best damned operation that it was possible to give him, so that he in turn could pass it on to his children and his children's children, debt-free, all the struggle behind, a cattle kingdom growing more prosperous by the year. The future belonged to A.G.

With his father A.G. lived the life of the boy becoming a man, but with his mother he could sometimes indulge his boyish fantasies, and Margaret loved to encourage his speculations on what it might be like to be an airline pilot or President of the United States. She read him stories from the Bible, telling him that he could believe them or not, as he chose. And when he asked her whether she believed them, she said she did, but that his daddy did not, because that was the way it was: some people believed and others didn't. Believing didn't necessarily make you a better or a worse person.

"Why doesn't Daddy believe them if you do?"

"Well, he wasn't brought up that way."

"Does Daddy believe there's God?"

"Why don't you ask him?"

So he did, and Earl said:

"I look at it this way, son. What a man does, he does by himself, for himself. If there's something up there, I'll believe it when I see it. You're holding the ace, show me. I'll tell you one thing, all the goddamned Baptists ever did for this state was keep a man from havin a drink when he wants it, and all the goddamned Catholics did was root for Notre Dame."

A.G. never did make up his mind about God, one way or the other.

She taught him to read, and as a little boy he had been known to spend days by himself in his room, reading away, emerging to tell the stories in his own words to his mother. They talked over the *Arabian Nights* together again and again and agreed on the advantages of living in a jeweled city with slaves and endless riches and beautiful women who obeyed commands.

"You can be anything you like and go anywhere you like," Margaret would say to A.G. "All it takes is the will to do it. That's what your daddy always said, and it was true. Look at the Sunrise."

"Sometimes I don't know what I want to be or do," A.G. said. "I think I want to be like my daddy."

"That's a wonderful idea," Margaret said. "But just remember, you can be anything you want."

"Sometimes I think I'd like to be like Captain Nemo. Live under the ocean and travel around where nobody else goes."

"Well, you could do that, too."

"Or shoot tigers in India."

"Yes."

"Or discover the pyramids."

"Discover something else. The pyramids have already been noticed, sweetheart."

"Well then I'll discover a city hidden away in the jungle, like Tarzan did. Only my city will have skyscrapers like New York and instead of being green like Oz it'll be bright red."

"My God, A.G. You have the imagination of an elephant!"

As he grew older and went more and more about his manly pursuits, A.G. read less, and this was as it should be, Margaret supposed, although she missed their crazy talks. She knew that her boy would always be a dreamer in some way or another, and she was glad of that.

Sometimes A.G. would dream of soaring across the plains and living like an eagle in Colorado. He would dance on the tops of mountains while crowds looked up at him with terror and amazement on their leaden faces. A.G. sometimes believed he actually could fly. Sometimes he knew he could. He imagined that one night he would leap from the window of his room and fly out over the Sunrise. All he would have to do was move his arms slightly, that would be enough; his legs would follow, floating along like a kite's tail. He would fly away from the big house and look back at it with its lights burning, and then he would head out over the barns and corrals, their dark angles indistinct in the moonlight, and go visit the cattle and the horses. They would take no notice of him. Perhaps they always knew he could fly. When the dawn broke he would ascend to a great altitude and survey the thousands and thou-

sands of acres of the Sunrise, going from black to green in the
spreading light.

His conviction that he could fly grew so strong that sometimes he would wake from these dreams and believe that they
had been revelations, that some power was trying to tell him
that he had already flown and could fly again. He decided,
vaguely, that one day he would put his secret skill to the test.

He began by skipping steps as he ran out of the house down
to the barns. His legs felt like springs and gave him hope. Out
riding, alone or with Ramsey, he would surreptitiously move
his arms slightly, just to see whether his power was great
enough to lift the horse, too. One day he and Ramsey were
chasing each other around the bunkhouse, and A.G. climbed to
the roof with Ramsey in pursuit. He let Ramsey get close to
him at the edge and then jumped.

It was only a one-story building, but he hit the ground hard.
One knee shot up and popped him in the eye and gave him a
good shiner.

His mother wondered why he would do such a thing. Earl
said that every man has to jump off a roof once to find out
what a ladder's for. A.G. had a lot of time to think about his
failure as he lay in bed recovering. He could not quite bring
himself to believe that his power had deserted him completely.
It may have been that he was not supposed to fly in front of
other people. His mother stayed close to him, bringing him ice
packs and trying to tell him that there was a difference between being brave and being foolish, and Ramsey told him he
was crazy.

I am not crazy, he said to himself, I am A.G. Kruger. He
contemplated himself. He was not as big or as strong as Ramsey, but then he was not as fully developed as Ramsey either,
in any way, but that would change, no doubt. He could ride as
well as Ramsey and shoot almost as well, and he knew he had
to be smarter than Ramsey. Ramsey could hardly read, and his
handwriting nobody could read. A.G. could cut a herd with

anybody, and he was better with a rope than Ramsey. It could
happen that there would come a day when suddenly he would
be taller and stronger than Ramsey and could take him out
with a quick combination to the head, not that he would ever
want to. He would end up as big as his daddy, and nobody
tangled with Earl Kruger.

When A.G. was over his fall or his jump, Ramsey reminded
him that it was only six weeks or so before school started again
and suggested they go on an adventure together.

"We could set out and just ride. Stay off the highways. Just
ride and ride. Take our stuff with us and camp out. We'd
probably have some adventures. Hunt our dinner. You know,
stay out a while."

A.G. thought that was one hell of a swell idea, and he went
to his father to ask permission.

"What about those fences?" Earl said. "Who you think's
gonna fix 'em? I suppose you'd send your mother. Well, she's
got better things to do."

But A.G. begged and pleaded and promised he'd work twice
as hard when he got back. They'd only be gone a few days.
Earl gave in and offered the boys plenty of advice about how
to follow streams so they'd always have water and what equipment they would need. Old Sam liked to go out by himself and
had a tent the boys could probably use.

"Don't get into trouble like Tom Sawyer and Huck Finn,"
Margaret said.

"We won't," A.G. said.

Margaret's remark gave A.G. the idea that he and Ramsey
should call themselves Tom and Huck while they were on the
trip, although A.G. couldn't decide whether he wanted to be
Huck or Tom, and Ramsey had not read the books anyway, so
A.G. dropped the idea. They set out at dawn and by evening
figured they must have been thirty miles or more south of the
Sunrise. A.G. had decided that if they headed due south one

way and due north on the way back, they were bound to end
up where they started.

"I wonder where we are," A.G. said. They had camped beside a stream and were waiting for the sun to go down before
starting their fire.

"I heard a highway this afternoon," Ramsey said. "I didn't
want to mention it."

"I feel like Daniel Boone."

For dinner the boys ate a couple of cans of Dinty Moore
stew, which they heated over the fire, and they thought it
tasted great out there in the woods, surrounded by blackjack
oaks and pines.

"Tomorrow we'll stop early and shoot something," Ramsey
said.

The boys fell asleep easily and awoke with the July sun.

But it was in the middle of the next afternoon that they
happened on something that was to change their plans. They
had ridden steadily, stopping only occasionally to rest and
snack, and A.G. had begun to think he could go on like this for
days and days. It was so peaceful being borne along in his
horse's rhythm, hearing nothing but birds and the creak of
saddle leather, thinking about Daniel Boone and Hopalong
Cassidy and the story he had heard about Tom Mix being
arrested for horse stealing once up in Osage County. There
was nothing like this riding out in the woods to let your mind
wander, and it was good to get away from the ranch chores.

"Hold it," Ramsey said suddenly. He was in the lead and he
held his hand up and stood up in his stirrups, and A.G. thought
of John Wayne in *She Wore a Yellow Ribbon*. "There's a
bunch of cars up ahead."

"What do you mean, cars?" A.G. was disappointed. They
had managed to avoid civilization this far.

"Cars parked," Ramsey said. "Come up here and look."

Among the trees maybe a hundred yards ahead they could
see the glint of cars and pickups, and they heard voices.

"Let's go and see what it is," A.G. said.

"Tell you what," Ramsey said. "We'll leave the horses here and sneak up. You never know what we might find."

They hid behind trees as they went, until they were close enough to see that some kind of a meeting was going on, way out there in the woods. There were sixty or seventy cars and trucks parked at all angles but more or less in a circle surrounding what looked like a cleared campground. Seven little wooden huts formed an inner circle, with a big fire burning in the middle.

"Indians!" A.G. said.

"Yeah," Ramsey said. "Keep down and keep quiet."

Indians, two or three hundred of them, men, women, and children, sat around the fire, some of them in the huts, which were roofed but open on the sides, and the rest casually in folding chairs and on the ground. Near the fire an Indian wearing boots, jeans, a fancy western shirt and a straw cowboy hat with a feather stuck in it was delivering an oration. Next to him on a battered card table lay seven brightly colored wampum belts. The Indian paced back and forth, speaking and gesturing, but A.G. and Ramsey could not hear or understand what he was saying.

"Let's move in a little closer," A.G. said.

They crept within hearing distance and realized that the Indian was speaking in his own language, in long syllables and grunts that sounded, A.G. thought, the way Indian language was supposed to sound. After a while, the Indian began picking up the wampum belts, walking slowly around the circle to display them to the crowd, talking and pointing at their colors, patterns and figures.

"What the hell is this?" Ramsey said. "Listen to that mumbo jumbo."

"I wish we hadn't of left our guns on the horses," A.G. whispered.

The boys watched quietly as the Indian continued his talk.

His audience was attentive but relaxed, some of the men smoking or chewing tobacco, young children wandering around from time to time but keeping quiet. One by one the speaker picked up the wampum belts, and when he finished with the seventh and last, he walked over to one of the huts, which had several framed photographs and one oil painting tacked up on it. The Indian pointed to each of the pictures in turn and talked about them. Suddenly his talk was finished, and as he sat down, the crowd let out a subdued shout.

"That must mean 'Amen,'" Ramsey said.

"Here comes another one."

A second man, also with a feather, but a smaller one, in his hat, now came forward and began addressing the fire, which had been built atop a carefully packed pile of ashes some three feet high, suggesting many fires before this one. This speaker spoke only to the fire, pointing at it and touching one by one four logs, one each pointing east, west, north and south, which had been placed around it. His speech was short. The shout went up again at its finish, and this time everyone got up and began milling around and talking and laughing freely.

"Well that's over," A.G. said. "What do we do now? Let's see what else they do."

"What if they find us?" Ramsey said.

"We're goners."

A.G. didn't know whether he really believed this, but it seemed the right thing to say at the time. After all, he knew from his Oklahoma history at school that the Indian wars had been over for some time. Still, there was something so strange about coming on this ceremony or whatever it was in front of him, with that big fire burning in the heat of the day in the middle of July and the strange language. At least the Indians were wearing regular clothes and not skins and war paint.

The crowd moved over to a long, long table piled with food. The man with the big feather in his hat stood at the eastern end, with the women lining the south side and the men the north. He said a few words over the food, pointing to the sky and to the earth, and then they all heaped their plates and dispersed among the trees to eat and talk. It was beginning to look like an ordinary picnic. A.G. was not close enough to see what they were eating and he was wondering whether it was some secret Indian mixture of nuts and wild plants when he felt a hand gripping his shoulder. It was not Ramsey's.

THREE

A.G. and Ramsey were frightened when they were discovered and propelled along toward the center of the grounds by a fellow they took to be a strong young warrior, with enough muscle in his grip to tell both of them that there was no point in struggling and trying to escape. The boys knew little about Indians except that there were more of them in Oklahoma than in any other state, but what they thought they knew was enough to make them doubt that they would ever see the Sunrise again. A.G. was convinced that Indians were generally drunk and violent, and as he passed by the big fire, it occurred to him that he might very well end up roasted in it. They would probably scalp him, cook him, and eat him or tie him to the ground on stakes and let ants devour him, or drag him around and around from a horse until he died, although he did not see any Indian ponies about. He tried to take comfort in the idea that these Indians might have left some of their un-civilized ways behind along with their tribal costumes, but when he found himself standing before the man with the big feather in his hat, his elbow still gripped by the warrior, he figured this was it. The man with the feather must be the chief, and it was up to the chief to pass sentence. His fate was sealed.

"Hello, boys," the chief said. They managed a hello them-selves, and A.G. thanked God that the chief spoke English. Maybe he could be reasoned with. Maybe they could make some sort of deal with him. He might need rifles. Horses. Maybe the chief would demand a ransom. A.G. figured his father would pay, but he would probably try to rescue him by force, and there would be a lot of bloodshed.

"Out for a ride?" the chief asked.

A.G. and Ramsey looked at each other. They had no cover story, but then again, A.G. thought, maybe they didn't need one. He replied, since Ramsey seemed tongue-tied, that that was it exactly. They had been out for a ride and a camping trip. They meant no harm. They had come here by chance and had seen the fire and the chief talking and had decided to watch. It had been very interesting.

"I'm glad you thought so," the chief said. "We figured you were just curious when we saw you come in."

"You saw us come in?"

"Sure. We have to be careful, you know. For a long time we had to have our meetings and practice our religion in secret. Some people tried to stop us. It's better now, but there are still a lot of people who'd like to make trouble. We don't let our own people make trouble either. See that sign? No intoxicating beverages. No rowdiness. No littering. That goes for our own people, too."

A.G. noticed that the chief spoke slowly and rather formally, like a chief should, he thought. All of a sudden he was not very worried. There was something calm and reassuring in the chief's manner. It looked as though there might be a chance for a treaty of friendship.

"What are your names?" the chief asked.

"This is Ramsey Hogan and I'm A.G. Kruger. My daddy owns the Sunrise Ranch. He's Earl Kruger."

"I've heard of him. My name is William Red Bird Smith. I am chief of the Katuba Cherokees. On this day, July nineteenth every year, we celebrate my grandfather's birthday. My grandfather brought us here from Georgia and saved us from dying out and preserved our religion. I'll tell you about it if you want, but first why don't you have something to eat. The women have prepared good food. We want you to have some.

Just go up to the table on the north side and help yourself. There's plenty lemonade over there in that barrel."

The boys filled paper plates with fried chicken, corn, peach pie and chocolate cake. A woman dipped their cups for lemonade and the chief motioned for them to come sit by him.

"What d'ya make of this?" Ramsey whispered.

"I think we've lucked out," A.G. said.

"Could be a trick."

"Could be."

As the boys sat beside Chief Red Bird Smith in one of the huts, other Indians wandered up and chatted with him, some in English and some in Cherokee. They talked about their families and jobs. Some of them complained about sheriffs and Bureau of Indian Affairs agents.

"There was an agent here this morning," the chief said. "He must have thought we were pretty stupid. He sat over there by the fire and he kept throwing stuff into it. He looked like a beatnik. You know we don't throw anything into the fire unless it's a funeral. I asked him what he was throwing into the fire, and he said it was sacred food some Indians up in Montana had given him! Can you imagine that? We asked him to leave."

"A sheriff over near Apache," one Indian said, "he was askin my brother, he said to him, 'Hey, I hear you Cherokees can turn into dogs at night, man. Is that right?' My brother told him, 'No, sir. You got it backwards. The dogs, they turn into Cherokees. See, it's the other ways around.' That sheriff, he was pretty spooked."

A.G. found himself laughing. He looked over at Ramsey, who was eating and pretending he could not hear anything. Ramsey is still scared, A.G. thought, but I'm not.

A man came up to the chief and began talking about family troubles. His children were getting out of control. He felt that his oldest son was turning against his parents and was probably hanging around with bad characters and would get into trouble. His wife was depressed and his youngest children would not learn the Cherokee language. He was becoming nervous about the situation and was having difficulty performing his job. He needed the chief's advice.

"Come to my house a week from today," said the chief. "We need to talk about these things. Bring all your family. Tell your son that I ask especially for him to come. He's not here today?"

"I'm the only one."

"Bring them all a week from today. I will pray very hard and I will have something to tell you then."

After the man went away, the chief turned to A.G. and said:

"That man who just spoke to me, did you listen to what he said?"

"Yes," A.G. said.

"He has a lot of problems, don't you agree?"

"It sure sounds that way."

"Well, that man is a Baptist minister. He's a Cherokee but he's also a Baptist minister."

"Is he?"

"Yes, and yet he still comes to me for advice. And when his family is sick, he comes to me for medicine. What do you think of that?"

"That's something," A.G. said. He did not know what to think of it.

"Do you believe all that?" Ramsey asked him quietly.

"I guess so," A.G. said. To him the chief did not seem like the type to make things up.

As twilight came on the stream of visitors to the chief never stopped. Most of them simply chatted, telling stories, bringing him up to date on their families and doings, some seeking advice. Across the campground A.G. and Ramsey could see men, women and children playing a strange ball game in a cleared area. About twenty-five or thirty people grouped around a tall wooden pole that had a fish carved at the top of it. The males each wielded two small sticks with nets at the end of them. They would scoop up the ball with the sticks or catch it in the air and then fling the ball up toward the wooden fish. The women used no sticks but simply caught the ball with their hands and threw it at the fish. When someone hit the fish with the ball, a man would make a mark on the pole, and everyone would cheer. A.G. studied the game and noticed that the Indians did not seem to compete very fiercely with one another. It was hard to believe that they cared who won. He concluded also that the women had a big advantage, because they didn't have to use sticks, and he wondered whether the men realized this.

With the coming of darkness the visitors to the chief ceased. The fire blazed higher and, after telling the boys that they would enjoy the next part of the celebration, the chief stood before the fire and announced, in Cherokee and in English, that the dancing would now begin. He reminded everyone that absolutely no drinking was permitted and that he had the power to enforce the law. Anyone found with liquor would be thrown out. Six men lined up behind him. Chanting, they began hopping and skipping counterclockwise around the fire, chanting in Cherokee, circling the fire three times, until other Indians, men and women, children, women and men with children and infants in their arms, joined in, following behind the chief. Many of the women wore clusters of shells around their legs, chinking the shells in rhythmic unison, snaking around and around the fire. The sounds of singing and the shaken shells rose into the hot night.

"Our stomp dance," the chief said to the boys as he returned to the hut. The dancing went on without him. He had begun it, but it had achieved its own momentum now, around and around, the chinking and singing constant, speeding up and slowing down, dancers joining and dropping out at will but the dance never stopping. No one seemed to take the lead. Everyone seemed to be following everyone else. A.G. looked at the faces of the dancing Indians and saw that most of them were singing and smiling, except for the littlest children, bounced along happily in their parents' arms.

"Do you like it?" the chief asked the boys.

"Oh yes," A.G. said, and Ramsey nodded. A.G. asked Ramsey if he was still afraid, and Ramsey said no, the dancing looked like a lot of fun. It was sort of like the bunny hop they did at the high school. As the boys watched the dancing, sitting silently, they relaxed and felt oddly at home, and Ramsey, his fears at last drained, began dozing off. A.G. was calm but strangely excited. For a moment he wished that he could be out there dancing, too, but he knew that you had to be an Indian to do that.

"I'll tell you the story of this celebration," the chief said. He had moved up close to A.G. "Do you want to know it?" A.G. said he did. "You are only a boy," the chief said, "but there is a reason you came to us today. I don't know what that reason is, but your father is an important man. Maybe I should tell you the story so you can tell it to your father. Maybe you need to hear it yourself. Do you know about the Trail of Tears?"

A.G. said that in school he had learned that the Trail of Tears was when the Cherokees had come to Oklahoma from the east.

"Why did the Cherokees come here?" the chief asked.

"Well," A.G. said, "I guess the white men, I mean, I guess we made you come. Isn't that right?"

"Not you," the chief said. "Some white men. Long ago, when my grandfather was alive. You are another generation. But you are wrong on one thing. Not all the Cherokees came on the Trail of Tears. We, the Katuba Cherokees, we came before that."

"Why was that?"

"Because my great-grandfather had a vision. Or a dream. The dream told him to take his people out of Georgia and to go west, before they were driven out, before there would be the terrible Trail of Tears. Not all the Cherokees listened to him, but some did, my ancestors. My great-grandfather settled in Arkansas, in Fort Smith, where my grandfather was born, Red Bird Smith. But my grandfather was very young when his father was dying, so his father told a man named Crooked Sam the story of the dream vision, and he gave Crooked Sam the sacred wampum belts you saw this afternoon, and he told Crooked Sam the meaning of the wampum belts also. All this Crooked Sam passed on to my grandfather, when he was old enough, and then my grandfather led his people here, where they were given land by the United States Government. We have been here ever since, through my grandfather's and my father's time, and here we will stay, forever."

"How do you know that?"

"Because the dream says so. Do you want me to tell you the dream that came to my great-grandfather?"

"Yes!" A.G. was excited. He was glad that Ramsey was asleep, because he felt privileged hearing about the dream from Chief William Red Bird Smith himself.

The chief told of how one night his great-grandfather had dreamed that he was out hunting with two other little boys. They each shot a bird with their arrows, but as each of the three birds fell to the ground, it was eaten by a huge white diamondback rattlesnake. After it had eaten the three birds, the white snake was tired and full, and it crawled around the eternal fire of the Cherokees, the same eternal fire that A.G. saw everyone dancing around tonight. The people were frightened, but the snake was tired and seemed friendly, and when the snake yawned and opened up its enormous mouth, the people thought that that looked like a nice, inviting place, and so they crawled inside the snake's mouth, and one by one they were swallowed up and trapped inside the snake's belly.

All except the three little boys. The little boys were terrified, but an angel appeared to them and told them to shoot the white snake with their arrows. If an arrow fell in the seventh diamond of the snake, the people would be saved.

The first boy shot his arrow, but it fell short and hit the ground. The second boy shot his arrow, but it too fell short and hit the ground. The third boy now shot his arrow, and it fell short and hit the ground. But it ricocheted and landed right in the middle of the seventh diamond. The arrow did not penetrate the snake's skin, but the snake was so full that he belched when the arrow hit, and all the people were vomited forth and were free.

"That is the story of my great-grandfather's dream," the chief said. "Can you tell what it means?"

A.G. hadn't a clue, he confessed. He thought it was a beautiful story and an exciting one.

"I'll tell you what it means," said the chief. "First of all, you see all my people dancing out there around the eternal fire. They are celebrating their freedom from the snake. We call it our stomp dance, but it's a snake dance, too, around and around. They will dance until dawn, and the end of the dance will celebrate the new day. They will spend the dark night in the belly of the snake, and then the light will come, and they will be free.

"You see, the third little boy in the dream was my great-grandfather. He set his people free. The white snake was the white people, who killed my people and their religion and took away their hunting grounds and made them silent and trapped them. For a time the Cherokee people tried to live with the white man and like the white man. That is when we climbed into his mouth. But then my great-grandfather listened to the angel, who told him to follow the old ways of the Great Spirit. He freed his people not by violence. You remember, the arrow did not penetrate the snake's skin. He hit the snake in the right spot by listening to the old ways. The snake was so full because of his greed. He ate so much, much more than he needed, and that was how my people fooled him. By following the old true ways of his faith. Grandfather brought my people here, where they could practice their religion and keep their language. Not fight with the white man, but keep to themselves. Live in friendship, but respect their God and the ways of their ancestors. All this is explained in the sacred wampum belts. Do you understand?"

"I think so," A.G. said.

"Follow the right way and you will be all right," the chief said. "That's what we teach. If you stray from the way, you're in darkness. You can only get back to the right way by listening to the Spirit and following the light. The way is through love and friendship. Not by greed or violence."

At this point the chief put out his hand, and A.G. shook it.

"Now," the chief said. "Wake up your friend there. You can't just sit all night. You have to dance with us."

The chief led him and Ramsey single file to the head of the line. At first the boys were awkward, but they fell into the rhythms and dared imitate the chanting. Round and round the fire they followed the chief, and when they sat down again, they were happy. Someone brought them more lemonade, and they were content, dozing off and on, watching the dancing till dawn.

FOUR

When A.G. told his parents about the adventure, Margaret was delighted, but his father was unimpressed.

"I can't think of a goddamned thing the Indians have done for this country," he said. "I'd trust a Jew before I'd trust an Indian. I'd trust a nigger before an Indian, even if they do drop the ball on the five-yard line. You give those Indians twenty dollars and they'll drink it."

"That was one thing," A.G. said. "There wasn't any drinking allowed at all."

"That's an Indian first," Earl said. "You should of been around in the twenties when them Osages come into all that oil money. Why you couldn't drive down a road up in Osage County without you saw a brand-new Cadillac just left there because some crazy Indian run it out of gas or into a tree. What they didn't spend on cars they drank it up. What Indian ever did somethin for this country, answer me that."

A.G. believed what his father said about the Osages, but, while he felt uncomfortable holding any opinions different from his father's, he decided he would continue liking the Cherokees. Before he and Ramsey had left the campground, the chief had told him that if he ever needed anything, advice or medicine or anything like that, he should feel free to come and ask for it, and that he would always be welcome to come and celebrate Red Bird's birthday.

In the months that followed, A.G. thought often of the white snake and the eternal fire. These were his secrets. There were some things, he concluded, that you could share with people and some that you could not. It made him feel good to think about the Cherokees' salvation.

Life on the Sunrise drew him along. "Have a goal," his father would say, and whenever A.G. wondered what that goal was supposed to be, he could remember Earl's words: "I built this son of a bitch up from nothing. Your mother and me. I couldn't of done it without her. But the key to it was, nothing would stop us. Remember that. Set your sights and go get it. Find out where that goal line is and go for it with all you got. Anybody dumb enough to stand in your way, knock them down. Look at Texas Tech last season. Undermanned. They had no offensive line at all to speak of. But goddamnit, they won eight games, didn't they? Be a winner, son. Losin don't take nothin."

Under his father's tutelage, A.G. discovered some of the pleasures of winning. He emerged from his dreamy ways long enough to taste small victories here and there, and he began to savor them. He learned that he could whip any of the local boys at poker, and he won so consistently that sometimes he would have trouble scaring up a game. He might have two eights showing in a game of five-card stud and keep raising and raising until he drove everyone out. That way his pair could end up beating a straight or it didn't matter what. The other boys could not keep up with his betting.

"How much did you win, son?" Earl would ask.

"Fourteen dollars. Would've been more but they pulled out. Scared, I guess."

"That's right. You are learnin somethin. And learn this, too: they won't like you any better for it."

"Yes."

"You are not in this game to make 'em love you. And here's some advice. Next time, bankroll Ramsey. That way you can both sucker 'em in."

By the time A.G. was sixteen, he would accompany his father up to Kansas City for the cattle sales, and Earl would get his son into some high-stakes games. Here his technique of raising did not work. They would play all night and Earl would keep supplying A.G. with money, but A.G. noticed that when he did not have the cards, he lost, sometimes hundreds of dollars at a time. One night A.G. lost fifteen hundred backing a straight that was beaten by a full house. "That's all right," Earl said. "You're learnin. Sometimes you got to fall on your ass to learn to get up. You'll get 'em next time. I hate a cautious man, anyhow. I didn't get where I am countin pennies. Shit. Let's go buy your mother some rings." It made A.G. feel better about losing the fifteen hundred to see his father spend five times that on diamonds for Margaret.

But it was the McAdoo High football program that really built up A.G.'s confidence and made him begin to believe that whatever life threw at him, he might just be able to whip it. He was only five foot nine and a hundred and forty-eight pounds as a sophomore but with Earl's guidance he decided to go out for the flanker position, and he made the starting squad. The practices turned out to be rougher than the actual games, because in practice the coach made everybody do everything including blocking and tackling, and they would practice every afternoon and Wednesday evening under the lights until nine. Sometimes, when the coach was in an especially tough mood, they would spend the first hour or two doing nothing but calisthenics, and A.G. would fall asleep that night hearing the coach shout, "On your belly! On your back! On your belly! On your back! On your belly! On your back!" A.G. hated it but knew it was making him tough.

Earl attended most of the practice sessions faithfully and, during whatever drill, A.G. could hear his father shouting at him, "Keep that shoulder down!" or "Keep those knees high!" or "Get that son of a bitch!" and sometimes, especially when he missed a tackle or dropped a ball, he wished his father had stayed home; but when he had done well, it was satisfying to hear his father's praises and analysis as they drove home in the

silver Coupe de Ville: "That was one hell of a catch you made
there on the thirty-five, A.G., but if you'd of juked right just
after you brought it in, you would of been gone."

A.G. found out soon enough that he would never get anywhere trying to run through players or over them. His worst
moments came during practice when the coach had him get
down in a three-point stance and try to run through two linemen. Sometimes one of the linemen was Ramsey, who played
guard, and his buddy would show him no more mercy than
anyone else, because after all, when you played football, you
meant business, and A.G. would invariably take a beating and
get nowhere but on his ass. But he excelled at running pass
patterns. He was no Crazy Legs, but he was fast enough, and
by the time he had learned the head fakes and how to make
the top part of his body lean one way and his feet go the other,
he could get clear more often than not. His best move, he
decided, was to run right at the cornerback, run right up to
him until he took just a half step backwards or to either side,
and then streak right by him and look up for the ball, which
was usually there, once he and the quarterback had worked
out their timing. At his father's suggestion, he began carrying a
football around with him all the time, except when he was
doing his ranch chores. Some of the other boys on the squad
picked this up, but not all of them could afford their own
footballs.

A.G. worked at his pass patterns until he could do them in
his sleep, and he studied the moves of all the wide receivers he
saw on TV. His diligence paid off during his senior year in the
big game against Pawhuska, when he ran right past the de-
fender and got loose for a forty-yard gain that turned out to set
up the winning touchdown. Running down the field and looking back over his shoulder for the ball, he felt his legs weaken
under him but swore to kill himself if he fell. The ball seemed
to hang up there for minutes and he had time to think of every
possible disaster, like letting it bounce off his fingers or having

it hit his shoulder pad, but as it finally descended he gathered it in and kept on running until he was hit from the side. If that son of a bitch hadn't of had an angle on me, he thought as he went down, I'd of been gone. He bounced up quickly and the cheers made him feel like a million. He thought he could hear his father cheering above all the others. Somehow catching that ball against Pawhuska made all his mistakes, and like everyone else he had made his share, vanish. "It's things like that will stick with you for a lifetime," Earl told him. "You will face tough decisions and you will feel like you're beat, but you will remember what you did against Pawhuska and you'll be a winner again."

In spite of his triumphs on the football field, and the Pawhuska game was not the only one, A.G. did not exactly become a school hero. The quarterback and the running backs were idolized more than he, and besides, there was the fact of the Sunrise, which would never quite go away. No matter what he had accomplished, everyone else figured that he had it made anyway and withheld from him the full credit that a boy from another background was given freely. A.G. sensed this but was determined not to let it stand in his way. It even made him put out more effort, knowing that it might not be fair but that he was fated to have to prove himself precisely because he had no reason to prove anything. "The only good fighter is a hungry fighter," he heard people, especially coaches, say over and over, and he said to himself that even though he might never go hungry, he would be a hell of a fighter nevertheless.

Once a month on a Friday during the spring, that other-worldly time in Oklahoma when the weather can change from soft to fierce in twenty minutes, hail following sun, tornados rushing in like unscheduled freight trains, A.G. would race his red Thunderbird down to the fairgrounds for the informal rodeo. All the local boys were in on it, and a lot of them wanted nothing more than to beat A.G. It was sweet to win against the boy who had everything. They did not like his

hundred-dollar boots and they did not like the fancy trailer he
brought his horses in, and A.G. knew it, but what was he
supposed to do, borrow some old clothes and drive a wreck
just so he wouldn't make people mad? Screw 'em, his father
said. If they don't like it, let them get rich.

Some of the boys would have enjoyed getting at Ramsey,
too, for acting like A.G.'s second, but nobody in his right mind
tangled with Ramsey. He had the reputation of being toughest
of the tough, and that was a distinction among a bunch of boys
who favored carrying a small-caliber pistol in one boot and a
half-pint of whiskey in the other. Ramsey had become the kind
of boy the others tell heroic tales about. There was the time
Ramsey had been playing catch with Mike Brewer, who was
supposed to be pretty tough himself. They had been throwing
the ball back and forth at twilight, and it was obvious that
they were trying to catch each other off guard in the fading
light, because they kept throwing harder and harder, and you
could hear those balls hitting the mitts with a terrific smack. As
A.G. would tell it:

"Old Ramsey he had this steely in his pocket, only Brewer
didn't know that, and it was dusk anyway, and nobody could
see real good. So Brewer hummed one in and Ramsey caught
it, real casual, and then Ramsey just switched the steely for the
baseball. They were only about fifty feet apart or so, and Ramsey wound up like he was gonna strike out Ted Williams, and
he threw that steely about ninety mile an hour at Brewer, and
you know what happened? That steely broke right on through
the webbing on Brewer's glove and hit him in the teeth. Must
of knocked out a dozen. Sure, Ramsey said he was real sorry."

And every time he told the story, A.G. felt good that he had
Ramsey on his side, because he had come to realize that a lot
of the time it was going to be himself against the world, and it
was good to have an ally. At the rodeos A.G. won the quarter-
horse races time after time. He had the best horses money
could buy, and he rode as well as anyone, although it was not

the way of the other boys to give him credit for that much. To them it was his money pure and simple, and when he would win something like the calf roping too, they would hint that he must have fixed it so he drew a sick calf, just to make the best time. A.G. sensed how they felt, but he was not about to lose just to give them satisfaction, if he could help it.

One Friday the boys hatched a scheme to get A.G. There was a big black horse on a ranch over in Rogers County that everybody said was the fastest quarter horse in the state, but nobody could control it.

"You ought to get A.G. to ride that black horse," the boys told Ramsey.

"He's got his own damn horses," Ramsey said. "He don't need nobody else's. Ain't nobody can ride that black horse anyhow."

"A.G. couldn't ride it? I thought he was pretty good."

"I'll tell him," Ramsey said.

A.G. figured this was a challenge he could not pass up. Otherwise everyone would say he was chickenshit.

"What if he throws you?" Ramsey asked.

"He won't. And what the hell, nobody else can ride him. I got nothin to lose."

A.G. decided not to enter any of the other events that evening. He spent all his time with the big black horse, talking to him and walking him around. He could sense the energy in the animal, but he hadn't been thrown since he had been a child, and he knew that if the horse felt confidence in his rider, there would be no trouble. He did have confidence. He was also nervous as a cat, but he did his best not to show that.

At the start his white hat flew off and it looked as though the horse was going to shoot right out from under him and leave him riding thin air. I would rather be on a bull than this son of a bitch, he thought, and I wouldn't have as far to fall. But he stuck to the saddle, and in seconds he had pulled away from the field. He let out a yell of triumph and won by ten lengths.

But the black horse would not stop. A.G. pulled in with all his might but the horse kept right on going. When the boys saw what was happening they began to shout and jeer, and Ramsey took off after A.G. on foot. The horse headed straight for a barbed-wire fence. A.G. tried leaning down and pulling hard on the right rein to force the horse into a circle, but it was too late and the animal was too headstrong. He tried to jump the fence, caught his legs and fell. A.G. was thrown clear, but when Ramsey reached him he was dazed, scraped raw on his face and along his arm, lying in the grass.

"Don't tell my daddy what happened," A.G. said as Ramsey knelt down to him. "I just fell, that's all. Don't tell him they got the best of me."

"I wouldn't," Ramsey said. "Anything broken?"

"Naw. I'll be all right. And I'll get mine."

"Sure you will. Hey, cock. I know what. Let's get you cleaned up and go get us some cock."

"Where we gonna get some?" A.G. did not say that he did not really want any, that he wanted more than anything to be home. But that would be a defeat. He had won the race, after all.

"We'll go over to Big Ruby's. How 'bout it?"

"Sure," A.G. said.

A.G. never did enjoy going to Big Ruby's that much. It seemed an alien place to him, over in what everybody called coloredtown or niggertown on the other side of the creek, but Big Ruby's was where all the boys went. It was either Ruby's or some slut or other, because the girls you dated were not like that. By the time he had two or three shots of Ruby's bootleg whiskey, though, he felt a lot better. He and Ramsey sat at the table with the two black girls, and A.G. talked about how he had won the race by a mile but the horse had been too god-damned squirrel-headed and ought to be put out to stud, period. Then he took one of the girls into a bedroom and tried to go right at her, but it wasn't any good.

"Slow down, honey," the girl said. "We got time. What in hell happened to you anyhow? You're all cut up."

"I told you, I got throwed off, that's all."

"You're A.G. Kruger, ain't you?"

"That's right."

"Well I feel real privileged. You think I'm pretty?"

"You sure are." A.G. found it difficult to look at a black girl the way he would a white. Everybody said how good black ass was supposed to be and how you hadn't done anything until you'd split black oak. She had small hips like a boy and thin legs that might not win the Miss Oklahoma contest on a white girl but that appealed to him a lot. He figured he was too worn out to be aroused. This sure was a great idea Ramsey had, he thought. What a way to end the day. Shit.

"I know a guy in Tulsa," she said. "He don't know I does this. I got cousins over in Tulsa and he'll pick me up there and take me all kinds of places. I just do this for extra cash, you know? He takes me all over. Real expensive restaurants. He took me to Jamil's. You ever been to the Tulsa Club? He took me there. I guess you can't get no more high-class than that. He must of spent a hundred dollars. Maybe more. He thinks a lot of me."

"Well you deserve it." A.G. could not imagine anyone taking a black woman to the Tulsa Club. If the guy did, he must have some kind of stupid guts. It did not make sense and he figured she was making it up. She was a lying little whore, and realizing this made him feel more like screwing her.

"Does that feel good?"

"Yeah."

"Just relax," she said. "You're gonna kill yourself tryin so hard. You know, I am just like a priest or a doctor. I'm gonna go to New York City and make me some real money. You wouldn't believe the married men. I bet I've saved more marriages."

"Business pretty good?"

"Sure it's good. I got all I can handle. And I got a sister in New York City, she says business is real good there, too."

"Why is that?" A.G. asked, thinking that once he was married, he would have no time for whores.

"I'll tell you why," she said. "Because white women don't respect their mens."

"Is that right? I never noticed that. My mom respects my daddy."

"Sure she does. She's the old-fashioned kind, honey. You take these new white women. Specially city women. You listen to 'em. Why they will tear into their man right on the street, front of everybody, haven't you heard it? No wonder they comes to see me. My sister says it's the same in New York City."

"I'll be damned."

She had been stroking him the whole time and now he felt moved to touch her, and he noticed that the hair on her parts was very sparse.

"How old are you?" he said. "You're practically bald down there."

"Old enough. You know what they say. You can't grow grass on a racetrack."

A.G. rolled over onto her and finished it.

A cigarette butt floated in the toilet. A.G. aimed for it, saying to himself that if he could make it split apart, he could be through with whores and he would find one fantastic girl that he could love and marry and make love to all the time. Images of women came to him as he stood there, actresses, girls from *Playboy*—there had been one in February with a red fishnet draped over her; he had almost written her a letter. He imagined a gold woman on a stage driving men wild. Rich bankers would throw money at her and bark like dogs for her. He would find a girl with blueblack hair streaming like tears and show her his favorite spots along the creeks of the Sunrise and make love to her under an elm. He would fly her to New York and Paris and buy her anything she wanted, lie with her on the beach in California, surf with her, sleep through the day with her in a posh hotel. Everybody would want her but he would have her for himself and tell her everything. He felt better, watching the sogged paper disintegrate and the shreds of tobacco drift outward.

FIVE

"Hit 'em another lick!" Earl Kruger shouted at the TV. "Get that son of a bitch! That is some goddamned linebacker, sitting on his ass."

They were in the big red living room, the Krugers and Ramsey, watching Oklahoma beat Colorado as usual. Every twenty minutes or so, Edward would appear bringing Earl a fresh drink on a silver tray.

"That's it! Hit 'em! Hit 'em!"

"I sure would like a drink," Margaret said in the third quarter. "Is that Colorado boy going to be all right?"

"They sent him for X-rays. I knew we'd get him sooner or later. You don't complete four passes in a row against us and not expect to get hit. Edward! Where in hell is Mrs. Kruger's drink?" Earl picked up the lucky walking stick he liked to keep by him when he watched O.U. games or any game he had money on and waved it around. "I'm gonna give that nigger a whack! Stop him! Stop him! That's it. They got to punt. That Colorado kicker ain't worth a damn. I told you we was gonna beat 'em. Sure we started slow, but goddamnit, church ain't over till they sing. Lousy kick. Lousy! Look at that. We got the ball on the forty-five and here we go again! Now pass, damn it, pass! Pass their asses off! Hey! Edward! That is one of the slowest niggers I ever seen." He waved his stick. A.G., sitting nearby, inched back.

"Edward's a good boy," Margaret said. "Don't be too hard on him."

"I'm not. He gets paid. Eats a bellyful. But he is one auger-headed nigger if I seen one."

"We're lucky to have what we have these days," Margaret said.

"Civil rights and all," A.G. said.

"Commie rights is more like it," Earl said. "Some people can't abide peace. They will stir things up. You don't have to ask what their purpose is, do you? That Edward is one auger-headed nigger."

O.U. scored a touchdown and Earl leapt out of his chair.

"I told you we'd do it! I told you we'd whip their asses! We're gonna whip those goddamned Horns next week, too! Boys, we're gonna bring this baby in!"

Earl, Ramsey and A.G. all gathered in the center of the room, grabbing hands and hugging each other and hollering.

"I wouldn't trade Wynema for all the cooks in Paris France," Margaret said.

"What does that have to do with it? Look at that. If they'd of gone outside they'd of had six points. She's seventy-five if she's a day. That's it right there. They might get a three-pointer out of it. These new ones. I tell you, it'll happen here sooner or later. Dr. Martin Luther Jungle Bunny. You live by the sword, you die by the sword. You let these nigs loose and they revert to the jungle. I mean, what do you think? These other immigrants, at least they come from civilized countries." Edward brought Margaret's drink. "What do they expect? Turnin savages loose. They taken 'em out of the jungles, they made 'em into slaves, I admit that, and then they set 'em loose. It's the law of the jungle all over again. There is no question there is nothin in the Constitution said we had to do that. It was not intended."

"Education . . ." Margaret began.

"Education bullshit," Earl said. "There is three things you can't give a nigger: a black eye, a fat lip, and a job!"

Margaret was reminded of something she had been meaning to bring up. She would have a couple more drinks and wait until dinner to mention it, because Earl was always too excited when he watched an O.U. game. By the time they had dinner, he would maybe be in a mellower mood. She looked over at A.G., who was absorbed in the game. Lately they had had some good talks, almost as in the old days, except that now A.G. seemed most interested in asking her questions about her early life, before she had married, growing up on the small farm, watching her mother die, watching her father begin to go under, meeting Earl at a dance. Margaret had been touched by her son's curiosity, something he had always had, and when he had said to her, "I want to make something of myself. I want to find the right girl and I want to make something of myself. The Sunrise, sure. But maybe I should do something. Maybe someday I will run for the Senate, too, like Bob Kerr"—when he had said these things, Margaret had begun to think that maybe A.G. should be given the chance to go to college in the east or in California or in someplace different, just to give him the opportunity to see things and have his own experiences, before coming back to the Sunrise. And to have the best education. She knew what O.U. was, or enough about it, and its value did not lie primarily in the education it offered. She had even heard that the daughter of one of her friends had described the university as a jock hole. A boy like A.G. deserved the best chance. It struck her that A.G. had mentioned Senator Bob Kerr. There was a man who had made his fortune and had ended up doing great things for his state, building dams and lakes. In a few years, because of Bob Kerr, there would be no more floods in Oklahoma. A.G. could become such a man. He had continued to do well in school: Margaret liked to think that this was her influence. Earl could not be expected to be as involved as he was in the ranch and care about education too. Earl cared a lot more about how A.G. did on the ranch or on the football field than in the classroom, and the reason he wanted A.G. to go to O.U. was that that was where Earl had gone and that was where everyone went. But what harm could it do for A.G. to see a little of the world?

"Wynema," Earl said. "You are the best cook in the state. I'll take another heap of them cheese grits."

They sat at the long oak table, Earl at one end, Margaret at his right and A.G. and Ramsey on the other side. Ramsey was living with his mother during the school year but would usually come up to the Sunrise on weekends.

"I guess that Kennedy's doing a pretty fair job," Margaret said. "Looks like he's settling in."

"He's an arrogant snot-nosed little kid," Earl said. "And somebody ought to kick his brother's ass. We haven't had a good President in this country since Teddy Roosevelt. Ike was all right. At least he knew what it was to look down the barrel of a gun. That Kennedy, every time he talks, it's like hearin a fat baby poop."

"He graduated Harvard University, I believe," Margaret said. "He's an educated man, anyway."

"Wynema!" Earl shouted toward the kitchen. "This steak is the pure Dee! What difference does it make he went to Harvard? Like plenty other assholes. There is a certain lawyer in Tulsa went to Harvard, you know and I know. I wouldn't go to small-claims court with that fathead."

"All I meant was, whether he's doing a good job or not, that's one thing. But probably going to Harvard, that probably helped him a lot, don't you think? To be President. And a Senator before that."

"Bob Kerr didn't go to Harvard."

"That's true."

"And you know what got Kennedy to be President, don't you? Don't everybody? Well if you don't know, I'll tell you. His daddy bought him the nomination, that's what. Pure and simple. Now I don't blame old Joe Kennedy one bit. That's what a father does for his son, if he can. But anybody tells me that kid would of made it on his own, he don't know the score. Old Joe is all right."

"I'm sure you're right about the Kennedys," Margaret said.

"I was only thinking, sometimes I kind of get the idea, it might be an advantage for A.G. here maybe if he spent a little while at some place, a famous university."

"He is," Earl said. "He's goin to O.U."

"I meant out of the state. In the east or in California."

"You what?" Earl asked, putting down his knife and fork and staring at Margaret, an unchewed piece of steak resting on his tongue. There was a pause, and then Earl asked Margaret to repeat what she had said. She did so in the most conciliatory tones she could manage, pointing out how well A.G. had been doing in school, how they always wanted to give him the best of everything, how they say that travel broadens a person. He would meet all kinds of different people if he went somewhere else, and then, when he came back, he could bring all that experience to bear and know a lot about a changing world. He could make a lot of contacts, too. If he went east, for instance, he could meet eastern bankers, or the sons of eastern bankers, and that could be useful for everyone someday.

"Eastern bankers?" Earl asked. "Eastern bankers? Do you know what eastern bankers have done to this state? Do you know what J.P. Morgan did to E.W. Marland? Are you finished, woman? Do you have anything more to say?"

Margaret continued, repeating herself, looking over from time to time at A.G., who sat staring at his plate. She had discussed all this with her son, and she had got the idea that the more she explored the matter with him, the more he seemed intrigued by it. She had suggested to him that he go to the library and check out books on colleges and universities, so that they could investigate things together and go over the possibilities. He had not, but she had thought that if she could get Earl to come around, A.G. would feel freer to think about all the advantages of his going away for a spell. Margaret had never gone to college, and like most people without a degree she figured she had missed something. Life on the Sunrise was all she wanted, but she often thought that without her reading, which took her anywhere she wanted to go and told her about

people she would never meet, she would probably get bored
from time to time. Every Sunday morning at eleven she
watched "The Lewis Meyer Book Shelf" on television, a half
hour of advice on the best in new books. Mr. Meyer owned a
bookshop on Peoria in Tulsa, and he had been recommending
books every Sunday morning since the beginning of television
in Oklahoma. Margaret would watch with pencil and paper at
the ready, marking down the best sellers and the other titles
Mr. Meyer would tout, and about once a month she would
drive into Tulsa and buy the books from him. When Mr.
Meyer was on, the other channels featured evangelists, and it
occurred to Margaret that Mr. Meyer talked about his books
with the same enthusiasm that the evangelists talked about
Jesus. He ended every program with a verse from the Bible
appropriate to his "book of the week" and with the suggestion
that his viewers recite with him his motto, "The more books
you read, the taller you grow." Margaret liked Mr. Meyer. He
had recommended so many wonderful books for A.G. in years
past. She felt indebted to him. If A.G. could benefit as much as
she thought he had from Lewis Meyer, think what he might
learn at a great university. That was it. She did not want A.G.
to be far away any more than Earl did, but the boy might be a
better man for it. He almost surely would.

"I just want A.G. to have every opportunity," she said to
Earl. "I know you do too."

"I'll tell you somethin about opportunity," Earl said. "You
see all that?" He pointed out the window. "That's opportunity.
And you know what made the opportunity? We did. What do
a bunch of Yankee professors know about opportunity? This is
the future, right here. We have had bad times and good times,
and from now on it's gonna be the good times, and that boy is
gonna be part of it."

"Nobody said he wouldn't."

"He can run away if he wants to. If he does, he's no son of
mine." Earl stared at A.G.

"I don't really want to go," A.G. said. "It was just an idea."

"I have a better idea," Earl said. "You want to see the world, join the army."

"I sure don't want to join the army," A.G. said.

"Why would he want to join the army?" Margaret said.

"Well I am gonna set out the options," Earl said. "As a matter of fact, the more I think about it, the better I like it. He can join the goddamned army."

"I don't want to join the army."

"Hold it, son." Earl pointed a finger at A.G. "I'm robbin this train. I wasn't askin what you wanted. Your mother here, she thinks she knows what's best for you. She thinks you oughta see a few things. Well, fine. I get the idea there'll be plenty to look at in the Far East pretty soon. You register for the draft yet?"

"I will this summer."

"How'd you like to get drafted? I could get you drafted in a New York second. You could learn a hell of a lot in the infantry, seems to me. They might teach you to shoot worth a damn." Earl poured himself a full glass of wine and drank it down. "Funny thing about some people. They don't even know how the world's run. You'd think somebody at this table would know for instance I got an arm on every goddamned member of that draft board. Now, hypothetical, what do you think would happen if I told 'em, 'Boys, I think this boy should go into the army at this time.' Or supposin I said, 'This here boy's time is up. This boy is ready for that army. Now.' What do you all think would happen? You think it would take a hell of a long time for that goddamned draft board to make up their mind? How long do you all think it would take?"

"A.G. won't have to go into the army," Margaret said.

"Well I said I'd lie out the options," Earl said, "and I will. He can go to O.U., he can join the army, or he can go to one of them Yankee universities you seem to think so much of. Course if he does that, he's no son of mine. The more I think of it, maybe the army is what he needs. He might find out what life is all about." Earl bore down on Margaret. "Tell you somethin, this boy of ours, he's a fine boy, but he's got some work to do, I have noticed. He's at half speed, you hear me? That boy is at half speed. He is at half speed on the football field, he is at half speed on this ranch, he is goin at half speed and I want him at full speed! He ain't goin nowhere in the world at half speed and I know it and you know it and goddamnit he better know it!"

"We were just talking about it, that's all," A.G. said. He wished his mother had never brought the subject up.

"It was just an idea," Margaret said.

"I always thought I wanted to go to O.U. anyhow. Hell yes. We were just talking."

"You talkin," Earl said, "you better talk to me."

"Sure," A.G. said.

"You know that well enough, Earl," Margaret said. "You're his father."

"I wish it never came up," A.G. said.

"Well son," Earl said, "why don't you wish in one hand and shit in the other and see which one fills up first."

In thinking afterward about this dispute, if that was what it was, between his parents, A.G. cared more that it had been resolved than about the merits of the arguments. He hated to see them disagree about anything, and they so rarely did that it had especially pained him to see himself the center of their opposition. It was his father's way, of course, to have strong opinions about everything: it had always been Margaret's way simply to soothe Earl. "Sure, he barks, and he bites too," she used to say, "but I know him like nobody else and underneath he's just an old softie. He's soft as a grape. I know how to gentle him down." And she did. So A.G. was glad when Earl got his way about O.U. It would never have occurred to A.G. to think about going anywhere else to college had his mother not brought the matter up, and the names she conjured, Harvard, Stanford, meant nothing to him. It was true, he had

confided to Margaret that he had secret ambitions to make
something of himself even beyond the Sunrise, but he had no
idea what that might be, yet, and nothing he could imagine
would require that he go so far away from home so soon. So it
was that A.G. went to O.U. He finished out high school and
then one September day he left—not alone, precisely: Earl
hired a bus with a bartender and the three Krugers arrived on
campus in style and "tighter'n three ticks on a hound's ear," as
Earl liked to recall afterwards.

Ramsey drove the Thunderbird down to O.U., and he and
A.G. went to a coffee shop to talk over the future.

"I guess you'll come up to visit on weekends sometimes,"
Ramsey said.

"Sure. And there's Thanksgiving and Christmas and Easter.
And the whole goddamned summer. It's not like I was away
really."

"We'll be pals," Ramsey said.

"Always."

SIX

Ramsey had wondered what it would be like on the Sunrise with A.G. away, and he found out soon enough how different it was for him. He still took his meals with the Krugers, but other than that he began to feel like just another cowboy, and he got itchy feet. Had he won a football scholarship to O.U., he would have gone to college himself, but that had not panned out. Couldn't he simply wait for A.G.'s return? He had thought so, but as the weeks passed, four years began to seem like a very long time. A.G. would probably get married anyhow, and things would not be the same.

The idea of California appealed to him. He thought about it every time he visited his mother, because she had a small aquarium with tropical fish in it, and the brightly colored, strange-looking little fish swimming in their heated water always made him think of California and the Pacific Ocean. He had never seen any ocean at all, and he felt that a man ought to see that. He thought of girls lying on the beach in bikinis the colors of tropical fish, loose, athletic girls who were always asking you to rub suntan oil on them. Girls waving from surfboards and convertibles who would invite you into their apartments with refrigerators chock full of beer and be happy to let you do anything you damn well pleased to them. And the movie stars. You could go to Disneyland or even just some dumb hamburger place and see movie stars. And oranges. Every time somebody went out to California they always said they would send back some oranges. Evidently there were oranges everywhere you looked. Sunkist.

He started dropping hints of his Californian impulses to the cowboys.

"I might give it a try," Ramsey said one day when the boys were sitting around during a break from digging post holes.

"I don't know," one of the boys said. "I don't guess an Okie would stand much of a chance out there with all them pricks."

And another of the boys said: "I see where they let some guy out of jail in California the other day. Killed his wife with a goddamned chair. But seems like the police, they didn't let the son of a bitch call his mother up, when he was arrested. Judge let him go. Sounds like a hell of a state."

Sam sensed an opening for a story.

"There was this good old boy," Sam said, "was out in California drivin a semi. He didn't know his way around real well, so he stops in this fillin station and he asks directions. He says he wants to know the way to Valley Joe. Valley Joe? the other guy says. Valley Joe? You mean Val-lay-ho. V-a-l-l-e-j-o, right? Where you from? And the good old boy, he says he's from Oklahoma. I thought so, the other guy says, and he says, mister, out here, in California, we pronounce the 'j' like an 'h.' It comes from the Spanish. So the good old boy, he says, is that right? Well I'll be damned. And the California guy he says, how long you gonna be out here, Okie? Oh, the good old boy he says, I don't know, I reckon I'll be leavin round about Hune or Huly!"

But after everybody stopped laughing Sam went on to say that he thought Ramsey ought to give it a try. Things weren't like they had been in the 'thirties. There were jobs out there, Sam said, even for a cowboy. Ramsey might even latch onto something in the movies. Lots of Oklahoma boys had, good times and bad.

"Think about it," Sam said, hunkering down and rubbing his jaw. "There wasn't nobody ever made it bigger than Will Rogers. Number-one box-office star, is what they say. God-damnit, old Will Rogers, he used to come back here to over in

Claremore ever damned year, pick up his stories. Made him a
fortune, and his sons ain't doin so bad neither. And what about
old Gene Autry? And don't forget Ben Johnson. His daddy
used to manage that ranch over near Pawhuska. Well Ben
Junior, they still calls him Son, he done pretty damned well for
himself. What I heared was Son he went out to California with
his daddy's horse and he ended up a goddamned movie star.
Buddies with Duke Wayne and all the rest. Then there's Jim
Garner, that *Maverick* fella, he's from over down in Norman.
One hell of a smart feller. I hear he's sharper than a dog's
pecker."

The litany of Oklahoma names who had made it big in the
movies tantalized Ramsey. By God, he thought, there's a
chance.

"Hell," Sam added for icing, "half the goddamned cowboys
in them old Hollywood days come from up there near Ponca
City, the old 101 Ranch, them Miller Brothers. Talk about
Tom Mix. Hell, they arrested him for horse stealin in Dewey.
Where it all began."

"I ain't no actor," Ramsey said, looking at Sam, who had so
many stories you had to figure he knew something. "I might
end up on skid row. I could starve out there."

"Ben Johnson weren't no actor neither," Sam said, spitting
out a neat thin stream of Red Man, missing his boot by an inch
and a half. "Son sure could ride though, and they spotted that
right off. What the hell, Ramsey, everthin else go bust, you
could find some job on a ranch. I understand they's cows in
Californy. Funny thing about cattle. They don't change much
from place to place."

"Well then, hell, I might as well stay put."

"Up to you."

"I don't know, goin out there not knowin nobody."

"You'll meet some. A man's got to take a chance. And listen,
boy, one thing you'll learn, you don't know how to gamble till
you been all the way down and almost out. Once you figure

out you been all the way down, and you survived, that's when you learn how to gamble, 'cause that's what gives a gambler his nerve. A man's got to learn, he can lose it all and still get by. Then he don't mind losin it and he'll take a chance. You get down lower than snail shit, you learn how to gamble."

What Sam said made a lot of sense to Ramsey, although he had never known Sam to be much of a gambling man. Sam had been around the Sunrise longer than anybody. It was about the only job he had ever had. Still, Ramsey thought, you could understand about things without actually doing them, probably.

"But maybe you got the right idea, Sam," Ramsey said, "stickin close to home."

"I had my reasons. Had a wife once, you know. And I ain't young no more like you. Ramsey, you remind me of the guy was so scared on his weddin night, he didn't know what he was supposed to do. So he asks his friend, and the friend says to him, 'Son, just take the hardest thing you have and put it where she pees.' So the poor son of a bitch, he throwed his bowlin ball into her toilet! Course we got a Oklahoma version of that."

"Go on."

"The Okie, he throwed his shoes into her back yard! Ramsey, just take a deep breath and git. You can always come on back."

"I don't know," Ramsey said.

"You got any ambition?"

"Seems like I must. Ever since A.G. left, I got to thinking, I gotta do somethin. Only I don't know what. Guess I could sit around forever makin up my mind. I could just lay down and die right here, makin up my mind."

"Well," Sam said, "if you died, you might come back as somebody else. Or somethin else. I wouldn't count on it, though. You believe in reincarnation?"

"What's that?"

"That's where you die and come back somethin else. A frog or anythin. I remember one time, I heard these old boys talkin about it. They was askin each other what they'd like to come back as. So this one old boy, he says he'd like to come back as a stud horse, so's he could run around and do some fuckin pretty near all day long."

"Sure."

"This other old boy, he says he'd as soon be a rabbit, on account of they is supposed to do more fuckin than anybody. Then this other old boy, he says he'd like to come back as one of them sperm whales."

"A whale?"

"That's right. A sperm whale. Well, the other old boys, they asks him, why in hell would you want to be some kind of a goddamned fish? What's the matter with you? And he says, I ain't so dumb. Don't you know, them sperm whales, they got a five-hundred-pound tongue and a hole in the top of their head they can breathe through."

"I'll be damned."

"Well Ramsey, chances are that reincarnation is bullshit. I tell you what. You wanta be somethin, you better take off."

One mist-chilled November morning Ramsey made the familiar rounds of the Sunrise, gulping air to clear his head from the farewell bash of the night before. He said goodbye to everyone, laughing and gossiping, putting off departure as long as he could. He looked into a drain and thought of how many times he had cleared it, and he wondered whether a spring afternoon would ever find him clearing it again. He walked near a stand of trees and remembered how he and A.G. had found a wasps' nest there so many years before and had run shouting and laughing in escape across the fields. He had polished his boots but the wet morning grass polished them again with dew, and he thought of how he had bought this pair to impress a girl in town he would probably never see

again, or maybe not, maybe so. He had announced to everyone
he was leaving, and he knew he could not back out now. That
was why he had told everyone, so that he could not possibly
stay. By the time he had reached Tulsa and boarded the bus
for Los Angeles, he was choked with regret, feeling that he
was banishing himself into the world for reasons he did not
understand and that there was something about this land, his
country, that he would never know again. But he had to go.
Didn't everyone? It was as Mr. Kruger had said, every man has
to find himself in his own way, and you don't find anything
sitting at home with the blinds drawn.

The bus trip took two days and a night. Ramsey stared out
at the treeless red earth of New Mexico and Arizona and felt
lonely. At night, when he wasn't dozing, he contemplated his
reflection in the window, wondering whether he would look
like a hick to Californians, feeling the life he knew and everyone in it growing smaller and smaller as the miles multiplied.
He bolstered himself with thoughts of all the good things that
might be going to happen to him out there. They said the
women were fast and wild. They said there was money to be
had if you were smart enough to grab it and not let somebody
cheat you out of it. He would do the best he could moving and
hustling, and he had Ben Johnson's address. Ben Johnson must
be a powerful man by now, Ramsey reasoned; surely he would
lend a hand to a good old boy if it came to that. But with luck
he would not even need Ben Johnson. With luck in a few
months he might be driving a new car, hitting all the spots
with some starlet. He remembered a guy in the eighth grade
who had started a fan club for a starlet named Susan Gordon,
and Susan Gordon had even gone to the trouble to telephone
the guy personally to thank him and had sent him some auto-
graphed pictures. They couldn't be all bad out there. One of
the photographs, Ramsey remembered, showed Susan Gordon
standing in hot pants beside a palm tree. It would be something to see those palm trees.

He hit L.A. with eight hundred dollars in his pocket, three hundred saved from his pay and five hundred the Krugers had staked him, and since he was going to stay with Cousin Carl Dean Hogan for the time being, he figured he had plenty to last until he found out what kind of a job he could get. Cousin Carl Dean had come out to California after World War II and had stayed on and become pretty prosperous, from what Ramsey's mother had said. Ramsey had seen a snapshot of Cousin Carl Dean's swimming pool. It was good to have a cousin to rely on at first. Carl Dean could show him the ropes.

He had nearly two hours to wait for the bus that would take him near Carl Dean's house, so he decided to wander around downtown Los Angeles for a bit. There were palm trees all right, plenty of them in a place called Pershing Square, but beneath them lolled not starlets but winos, and on the streets Ramsey was surprised to see more Mexicans than anything else. The signs on the shops were in Spanish, and most of the movie theaters he strolled past were showing Mexican films. Main Street was littered with drunken bums and ragged men leaning against storefronts and lampposts. Ramsey tried not to let any of this nor the foul air bother him. He knew that every town had its back end, although that was usually not called Main Street.

He was disappointed in Cousin Carl Dean's house, however, a low-lying Medallion home in Pomona, forty miles east of downtown. He had not expected the Sunrise, but obviously his mother's idea of Carl Dean's prosperity had been inflated. There was a swimming pool, but it was smaller than it had looked in the photographs and it took up the entire backyard, so that you had to be careful not to fall into it when you stepped outside. Inside there were two small bedrooms and a living room–dining room decorated with rubbery plants and a big color television set in Early American style. Ramsey noticed that the ceiling glittered.

"You're just as handsome as your picture," Rita Hogan told

Ramsey. She was Carl Dean's third wife, a Bakersfield native of forty-five who favored halter tops and shorts that permitted glimpses of her bottom. "We're awfully glad to have you. I cleared out the other bedroom. Carl Dean, fix some drinks. You want to take a swim first, Ramsey?"

"I didn't bring any swim trunks."

"That's all right. We believe in body language, don't we, Carl Dean?"

"That's right," Carl Dean said.

"I'll just get cleaned up," Ramsey said. "That was some long bus ride."

"Did you see the Petrified Forest?" Rita asked.

"I didn't see nothin.'"

"I've been trying to get Carl Dean to take me to see the Grand Canyon and the Petrified Forest. He doesn't do it soon, I'm going myself. Or get somebody to take me. There's fresh towels in there for you."

Carl Dean barbecued some steaks in honor of Ramsey's arrival.

"I'm going to take a picture of Ramsey eating his dinner," Rita said. "He looks so cute I can't stand it. I adore red hair. Carl Dean, where's the camera?"

"I'll get it."

Rita took two Polaroids of Ramsey and his steak and had Carl Dean take a couple more of her posing with Ramsey. Ramsey noticed that there were many framed photographs of Rita scattered around the house. She was attractive for her age, Ramsey thought, a little hard maybe, very tan with white teeth and dark impenetrable eyes that had a tendency to pop. Ramsey noticed the way Carl Dean followed her every move. Obviously he was in love with her. Ramsey wondered what had happened to Carl Dean's two other wives. He knew there were some children from one or both of them.

"Are you really a cowboy?" Rita asked.

"Guess that's what you'd call me," Ramsey said. "Cowboy out of a job. Come to California to try my luck."

"Good," Rita said. "I didn't think anybody lived in Oklahoma anymore."

"What's that?" Ramsey felt a mild surge of adrenaline.

"Didn't everybody move away? I mean there's nothing there, is there? Just dust and old cars?"

"No, ma'am. It's real pretty where I come from. Maybe not like California, but it's nice." He was going to say more, but he figured he was a guest.

"You look like you're in touch with yourself," Rita said. "Where did you get those jeans?"

"Veach's in Tulsa, ma'am."

"Well they're a perfect fit. I've been looking for a pair like that."

"Just plain old Levi's."

"I don't believe that for a minute. And those boots. I bet they're custom-made."

"Huh-uh. Just bought 'em."

"I bet you don't have problems relating," Rita said.

"Carl Dean's the only cousin I have. Seems like my mother and my daddy they both come from real small families."

"I hear where you're coming from," Rita said. "Do you think about death a lot?"

This woman talks like hammered shit, Ramsey thought to himself, but he said: "Death? My daddy died when I was real young."

"And you haven't had a male figure to identify with."

"I guess it was God's way of tellin him to slow down."

"I've made some avocado dip. We'll have it with the drinks. Wow! Those boots! Far fucking out!"

"Eighty-three bucks," Ramsey said, thinking that he was sorry Carl Dean had ended up with a woman who used language like that.

After dinner Rita went to bed to watch the Sunday Night Movie and the men sat down to talk.

"I can't tell you what a difference that woman has made in my life," Carl Dean said.

"She's a fine-lookin woman," Ramsey said.

"That's not the half of it. Rita's got a head on her shoulders. I tell you, I was lost till I found her. She knows about things."

"What things?"

"Just everything. She helped me switch jobs. I thought I was happy in the other job, but she made me see I wasn't happy at all. Wasn't going nowhere. How about a beer?"

Carl Dean told Ramsey that coming to California was the greatest thing that had ever happened to him, next to meeting Rita, and that Ramsey would never regret his decision. There were no tornados here. Your heating bills were next to nothing and if you opened the windows at night you didn't need air conditioning. There were hardly any flies in California. Everything was within reach, the mountains, the desert, the ocean, pro football and big-league baseball. He had come out penniless and in a few weeks he had landed a job selling cars, and after that there had been no looking back. Ramsey said next to nothing. He never said much of anything anyway, but with Carl Dean there was no need to. The words tumbled out as the beer poured down, and it was a tale of right decisions and relief and satisfaction. The time years ago he had watched the Rams beat Detroit and Bobby Layne. The time he had seen Koufax and had been surprised by the curve ball—everybody knew about the fast ball. The time he had sold six cars in one day, and how by next year he would probably get himself a GTO. To tell the truth, there had been some rough times. His first two marriages had not worked out. But Rita had put an end to all those miseries. He had met Rita three years ago and he had been pretty low at the time, but she had pulled him out of it and had made him realize that it was not the end of the world that he hardly ever saw his children anymore. As Rita said, life-styles had altered. It was a new order. People were getting in touch with themselves. They needed their own space. He and Rita had each other, and that was what counted. Rita had taught him about self-space.

"The what?" Ramsey asked.

"Space. Self-space. You have to realize your self," Carl Dean said. "I never knew that, and I owe it to her. I won't go into it now. Listen, Ramsey, you got any plans? What kind of a job you looking for?"

"I don't know. I figured I might try latchin on with the movies or TV. Handlin stock, maybe, at first. I understand Ben Johnson did it. There's this fella called Sam on the Sunrise, knows about everything. Told me about all the Oklahoma boys has made it big out here. Them Okies, they was in it from the start, Sam says. Say, you wouldn't know this Jim Garner, would you?"

"No. But did you know I met Tom Mix's wife once?"

"Is that right? I'll be damned."

"I'll never forget it. I don't remember rightly which wife she was, but there was one time, this was quite a few years back, I was drinking at the bar in the Hollywood Roosevelt Hotel. The Cinegrill. Well there was this woman there, and she told me she was Tom Mix's wife, one of them. She had a cane with her. She was sort of crippled. But you know, she told me she lived right there in the hotel and she had a bottle of Scotch up in her room, and why didn't we drink that instead of wasting our money on bar drinks. So you know, I went up to her room with her, don't get the wrong idea, we didn't do nothing or anything. But we polished off that bottle of Scotch and had one hell of a talk. I'll never forget it. How are things back in Oklahoma?"

" 'Bout the same, I guess."

"I haven't been back for years," Carl Dean said. "No reason to." He was into his second six-pack now. "Last time I went back was to see my daddy. You know, he was working in a church in some little town or other, I forget which. I told Rita about this. I think she understood. Anyway, I went to see the old man, he was working in this church, and you know, he said it was the best job he ever had. He was the janitor in this church. And I said, 'Daddy, how come this is the best job you ever had?' And he said, 'Well son, when I don't feel like workin, I can just sit here in one of them pews and think. I work as hard as I'm supposed to, but you know somethin, to tell you the truth, He ain't pushin me very hard.'" Carl Dean looked at Ramsey. "The old man had a point, don't you think?"

The later it got and the more beer he drank, the more Carl Dean wanted to talk. He confessed that he was having a hard time making ends meet, what with heavy alimony and child-support payments. They would never get through the month if it weren't for Rita's job as a receptionist at General Dynamics, and for that matter he would never have made it through emotionally had it not been for Rita. It wasn't that she was so kind and understanding and all that. It was that she was the sort of woman who didn't stand for any bullshit. Oh, they had their disagreements. About drinking, for instance. Rita didn't understand that every once in a while a man has to let go. He had never met one yet that understood. He guessed there weren't any. But sure, there was always a way around it, if Ramsey knew what he meant.

"Come here, Ramsey. I wanta show you something," Carl Dean said. His tone was conspiratorial.

He led Ramsey out the front door and around to the side of the house, where a garden hose lay coiled beneath a bush. He picked up the hose, twisted the nozzle and held it up to Ramsey.

"Try some of that. Just tilt back your head and open your mouth."

Expecting water, Ramsey sputtered and coughed as his mouth filled up with vodka.

"Don't waste it, for Christsake," Carl Dean said. "That's my insurance. I found out you can pour a quart in there." He took the hose from Ramsey and drank down a long draft, then screwed the nozzle shut again. "This way I can take what I want and nobody's the wiser."

Back inside, Carl Dean went on about Rita. She was the most attractive woman in the world to him. He knew damned well that every man who met her wanted her, but that didn't bother him, because after all, he was the one who lived with her, wasn't he? That made him the envy of everyone, the way he saw it.

Ramsey dropped off to sleep sitting there.

For a few days Ramsey was inert, unable to decide how to go about making contacts, and then he started riding in to work with Carl Dean, who was now the manager of the Thrifty drugstore at Sunset and Vermont, in Hollywood. Ramsey would wander around all day, trying to get the feel of the place. He thought the people looked pretty freaky, and Holly-wood seemed to be mostly bars and adult bookstores, but he did find the entrance to Paramount Studios. He would station himself at the gate, watching people drive in and out. Once he got up the courage to ask the guard whether he could go inside, but the guard told him that if he wanted a tour he should go see a travel agent. He asked Carl Dean how to connect with movie people, and Carl Dean said he had no idea. Lana Turner had been discovered in a drugstore. There was a job at Thrifty for him, if he wanted it.

"I might just take you up on that," Ramsey said. "I think I'll look around a while longer first."

One Saturday, after Ramsey had been in Califrnia for three weeks, making no progress and coming around to the view that he would have to try something different, meet some different people somehow, Rita and Carl Dean told him they were going to have a party that night.

"Who's coming?" Ramsey asked.

"We don't know yet. That's what's so exciting," Rita said. "I think you'll enjoy it. I'd stick around if I were you."

Rita showed him an advertisement she and Carl Dean had placed in the classified section of a paper called the L.A. *Free Press*. The ad said:

COME TO OUR PARTY
Straights only

This was followed by a date and the Hogans' telephone number.

"You can meet some of the most interesting people this way," Rita said. "And besides, it brings in a little extra cash. You see, everybody pays ten dollars apiece to come to the party. We supply the drinks. Everybody has fun and you meet new people."

Ramsey thought this was a peculiar way to give a party, putting an ad in a newspaper, but he figured he would have to get used to California ways, and he did need to meet new people. Somebody there might know something about the movies or TV. He asked Rita what "straights only" meant and she said that having homosexuals to these parties complicated things too much. Ramsey said that if he were giving a party he probably wouldn't want any queers around either.

When Carl Dean started taking snapshots of Rita over the kitchen counter that served as a bar, Ramsey began to wonder about the party. These pictures were different from the photographs of Rita that decorated the rest of the house. In these she was either partially or completely nude.

"You like them?" Rita asked, giving him a nudge in the ribs.

"They're something," Ramsey said. He didn't know what to do with himself. He had noticed that Rita was not particularly modest. She would often walk around the house with her bathrobe falling open and her bikinis showed almost everything, but this was different, having nude pictures of herself put up. And what did Carl Dean think? Hell, he was arranging the pictures himself.

By nine o'clock six couples and one single man had arrived. They were all in their forties or fifties and to Ramsey they appeared overfed and underworked. The women wore pants and high heels and the men's shirts opened to the waist, displaying necklaces and chests. They stood around introducing themselves, sticking to first names, exchanging information about occupations in an unspecific way. Carl Dean seemed to keep mostly to himself, fixing drinks, vaguely smiling. The guests looked past him to the photos of Rita akimbo, Rita scrutinizing her breast, Rita recumbent poolside, but they did not comment. The party went on demurely until suddenly two of the men announced that they didn't care what anyone else did, they were going swimming. The stripped off their clothes in front of everyone and jumped in the pool, laughing and shouting like children.

Rita, proclaiming her admiration for people who took the initiative, disrobed and dived in, and soon everyone was in the pool except Ramsey and Carl Dean, who kept to his post by the bar.

"You ain't goin in?" Ramsey asked.

"Naw. I just like to watch. That Rita's really something, isn't she?"

"Sure is."

"I'll tell you confidential," Carl Dean said. He lowered his voice and breathed: "Rita's had hundreds of men!"

"Is that right?"

"Hundreds!"

"I'll be damned. Say, give me a refill, would you?"

He took his fresh drink, went into his room, closed the door and lay on his bed thinking of the parties the Krugers used to throw on the Sunrise. People flying in from everywhere. Music and drink tents and more food than you could imagine. Things could get pretty wild at those parties. There was usually a fight or two, glasses thrown. Couples were always sneaking off somewhere. But nobody sure as hell paid to get in, and he would like to see the day when Earl Kruger pasted up naked pictures of Margaret. These people here must be pretty desperate. Funny thing was, he had always heard that California was free and wild but this was something else. The thought of poor old Carl Dean standing out there watching his wife make a whore out of herself wasn't very inspiring. And the people weren't even good-looking. Rita was all right, if you liked the type. They say the closer the bone the sweeter the meat but it sure seemed a whole lot more appetizing to eat off your own plate. Ramsey managed to shut out the noise and go to sleep.

He was up early Sunday morning and was making his way through the debris to put some coffee on when he chanced to look out at the pool through the sliding glass doors and noticed a human form outside, curled up on the narrow strip of concrete between the pool and the house. It was Carl Dean, still dressed in his clothes of the night before, asleep, one foot dangling in the water, his head resting in his arms. Drunk, Ramsey thought, and wondered whether he ought to wake Carl Dean up. The poor son of a bitch might fall in and drown. He decided he would keep an eye on him and made the coffee.

Carl Dean began to stir when the sun hit him. Ramsey watched him sit slowly up, rub his head, take his foot out of the water and empty his shoe. He took some deep breaths and crawled over to the glass doors. He got to his knees and tried to slide the doors open, but they were locked, and he started to slump down again, evidently resigned, when Ramsey opened them.

"That's nowhere to sleep," Ramsey said. "Come on in."

"Shit."

"How'd you get locked out?"

"Oh me and Rita we had a little argument. Nothing special. Coffee smells good." He crawled onto the couch. "Do me a favor would you podnah and get me a beer. Hey, we got some good football today. The Rams is televised from New Orleans. Gotta clean up this mess before Rita gets up. Shit."

SEVEN

The party convinced Ramsey that he had better move on, so
he made up some bull about having a job offer, drove in to
work with Carl Dean for the last time and said goodbye in the
Thrifty parking lot, telling his cousin to be sure to give Rita
special thanks for her hospitality.

"Keep in touch now, Ramsey. You know you always got a
place to stay."

Ramsey had figured that it would not have been too many
more nights before he discovered Rita crawling into bed with
him and that this was more than he was prepared to pay for
room and board. He walked along Sunset Boulevard with his
suitcase, found a motel, checked in, counted his money and
contemplated a plan of attack. It might be time to contact Ben
Johnson, but Ramsey decided to try it on his own for a while
longer. He would knock on every door he could find.

He did not find many. After another week of no progress,
with the motel bill eating into his cash, he hitched a ride out to
Ben Johnson's place in Thousand Oaks. It was late when he
got there, and all the lights were out, so he curled up on the
doorstep. When Johnson opened the door in the morning to
get the paper, there was Ramsey.

"Mr. Johnson?"

"How you doin. Must of been pretty cold."

"I'm Ramsey Hogan. I been workin for the Krugers on the
Sunrise Ranch."

"Sure. I heard of old Earl. He run you off?"

"Nosir. I just come to California to try my luck. Seems like so far I haven't had much. I thought maybe you could give me some advice or somethin. I do hate to bother you."

"No bother. I been there myself. Come on in. Meet my wife and have some coffee."

Mrs. Johnson cooked a big breakfast that made Ramsey think of home, and Ben acted as though he had known Ramsey all his life.

"I'll do what I can for you, Ramsey, but there's a lot of luck to this business. You gotta remember, ninety-six percent of all the actors in Hollywood are out of work."

"Is that right."

"I got lucky and I've stayed lucky. Jack Ford and the Duke, they were good to me. But there ain't many makin westerns nowadays."

"The Duke's a good guy?"

"Never met a finer gentleman in my life. Can't say the same for everybody out here. If I was you, I'd buy a ticket back to Oklahoma and hang onto it, just in case. There's actors here livin in their cars."

"You get back to Oklahoma much?"

"Every chance I get. Hell, I still get homesick. I make it to that rodeo in Pawhuska near every year."

Ramsey and Ben talked about rodeo and ranching all morning. Ben's father had been a champion roper and the foreman on the Chapman ranch, a spread even bigger than the Sunrise, although Earl Kruger would never admit that. Ben said that as much as he was grateful for all the success he had had in Hollywood, he sometimes wondered if he would not have been better off just staying put, like his dad, and someday he thought he might go back, sit on a porch and watch the grass grow. He said this in so many ways several times, and Ramsey got the idea that Ben was trying to discourage him.

But that afternoon Ben made a couple of phone calls, and within a few days Ramsey found work as an extra on *Gunsmoke* and was promised extra work on *The Virginian*. He telephoned Ben to thank him.

"You buy that ticket like I told you to?" Ben asked.

"Yessir. Well, not yet. You still think I should?"

"Might be a good idea."

But Ramsey had strong hopes. He wrote to A.G., telling him that he was thinking of joining the Screen Actors Guild and that things were going great. A.G. wrote back that O.U. was one big party after another, that he had dated the Miss O.U. Beauty Queen and that the Texas-O.U. game had to be seen to be believed. It made Ramsey homesick to hear from his friend, and he decided not to write again until he was really established.

But the work came in spurts and in a few weeks Ramsey was having money troubles. He had moved from the motel into a twenty-dollar-a-week room way up on North Western Avenue in an old fleabag of a hotel called the La Paula, a relic with slight chance of being declared a historical landmark in a neighborhood of pawnshops, porno shops, bars, and motels with hourly rates. It depressed him to go to his room, but he spent a lot of time there, waiting for the phone to ring and knowing that even going out for a beer meant spending money he didn't have. Lying on his bed, he thought about the duck-hunting season he had missed and he found himself dreaming about certain high school girls. The girls he met around the TV studios didn't seem to be interested in two-bit extras. Maybe my only chance is to marry a rich woman, he thought. There didn't seem to be much prospect of that.

Whenever he did have a few extra dollars he would spend the evening in Slick's, a country-and-western bar on Cahuenga, where the music would make him feel at home and the bargirls were pretty to look at. After three or four beers Ramsey could almost imagine himself back in Oklahoma. It was even better when he could get there during the Happy Hour, when Jacks and water were sixty cents apiece.

One evening at Slick's Ramsey was switching to beer after four bourbons and feeling pretty good. He had not felt very good coming in but the drinks had raised him up just enough, and as he sat there he congratulated himself. He could hardly call himself a success but, goddamnit, he was surviving, and if he could just survive a little while longer, his chance would come along. The band, Barbara and her Country Gentlemen, had not come in yet, but somebody had put Marvin Rainwater singing I'm gonna find me a bluebird, let him sing a song for me, on the jukebox, and Ramsey was feeling almost good enough to sing himself. Every once in a while the thought would flash through his mind that when he got back to his room he would feel lousy again, but he managed to keep that thought at bay, and besides, he knew that if he could get shitfaced enough he wouldn't feel anything at all by the time he had to go home. The girl who was bringing him his drinks was awfully pretty and friendly. He made up his mind that the next time she came over, he would say something to her. He could use a little female contact, even if he was broke.

"Thank you. What's your name?" Ramsey asked.

"How're you? Kitty."

"Well hello, Kitty."

Cute was the word for her. She had a turned-up nose and a little pointy chin and teeth just buck enough to make her lips stick out in an appealing way. She was wearing tight jeans, and as she walked away Ramsey thought that he had not seen an ass like that on a white woman since he could remember. She was definitely high-assed. Ramsey thought how nice it would be to sink his teeth into that.

"Kitty, I'd like to bite your butt and pray for lockjaw," he said when she came around again.

"You're bad," she said, but still friendly.

"You're so pretty. These California girls is supposed to be so pretty, but a lot of 'em I seen's as ugly as a splatterboard on a gut-wagon."

"You do talk," Kitty said. "Where you from?"

"Oklahoma."

"Thought so. So am I."

"You don't say. How long you been out here?"

"Almost three years."

"Tell you what, Kitty. Buy you a drink?"

"After I get off?"

"You're on."

They ended up at Kitty's apartment because Ramsey didn't want to take her to his dump and he had no money left to take her anywhere else. Ramsey was loose and he told Kitty how much he liked her looks.

"I like a jimmyjawed woman," he said.

"What's that?"

"You don't know that?"

"No. What is it?"

"Well jimmyjawed is a woman with a nice little pointy chin, like you got."

Kitty felt her chin, a bit doubtful.

"You know what they say about a jimmyjawed woman, don't you?"

"What do they say?"

"They say a jimmyjawed woman's got a pussy no bigger than a mouse's ear."

Kitty was in no way offended. After they made love and Ramsey confirmed the truth of the adage, Kitty said:

"Meow."

"What was that?" Ramsey asked, cuddling her.

"Meow. That's how Kitty says thank you."

They made more love after that and in the morning, when they were sitting around comfortably, Kitty told him how great it was to meet someone from home. She confessed that she had actually been in California almost six years. She was twenty-five going on twenty-six, and she had come out, sort of like Ramsey, thinking about the movies, but not much had happened. She had some nice friends, though. Ramsey would have to meet them. Some of them would maybe seem a little weird to him but they were nice.

"The thing about you," she said, bringing him more coffee and throwing an arm around him, "you're a real man. You don't even wear a mustache. I hate mustaches and beards. Everybody out here wears them. I think men wear mustaches to hide the stretch marks."

Ramsey asked her what she meant by that but Kitty did not answer. "Look at you," she said. "With that red hair. You're warm as a fireplace."

Ramsey and Kitty got close. They began seeing each other every day and after a couple of weeks Ramsey gave up his room and moved in with her.

"I was feelin pretty lost before I found you," he told her. "Didn't know what was going to happen. I felt like a turd in a punchbowl."

Kitty's apartment was not grand but there were two rooms and a halfway decent bathroom and Ramsey figured he had made some progress. Between the two of them they seemed to have barely enough money to get by month by month, but Kitty had some way or other of coming up with what was needed just when things appeared to get desperate. She was a little on the loony side, Ramsey could see that, but it seemed to work out for her.

"I don't know how we're gonna make it to the end of the month," Ramsey said one time.

"Don't worry," Kitty said. "October's only got about twenty days in it, isn't it?"

"You're thinkin of February. It's got twenty-eight, most years."

"I know about February, silly. But October's got even less. You'll see."

"You're not careful, we'll have to get you locked up in the goon garage."

"Trust me," Kitty said.

The only thing Ramsey did not care for about Kitty was her friends. They mumbled rather than talked, and as far as he could tell they did nothing with their lives except collect welfare and smoke pot. At first he tried to be open-minded but they got on his nerves, lounging around getting high with the stereo blasting. They seemed to have no homes or families. One of the girls was tattooed. He told Kitty how he felt, and she said that she understood, but he had to realize that these people had been kind to her when she first arrived, had taken her in and fed her and done all kinds of favors for her. She said that after he was in California a little longer he would understand them better and appreciate them. They had opted out, was all.

"It's the counterculture," Kitty said.

"The what?"

"Counterculture is what they call it, I heard them say."

"Over the counter or under the counter?"

One night about a year after they had started living to-gether, Ramsey was sitting alone in the apartment, sipping a Lucky Lager and watching *She Wore a Yellow Ribbon* on the TV, half dozing but waking up whenever Ben Johnson had a scene. He noticed how often Ben was shown riding and he reminded himself that he had to try to get some stunt work, because it was the riding that had really given Ben his start. The movie was beautiful to look at but all those shots of the desert gave him a pang of longing for the lush grass of the Sunrise. He had begun to think, since his homesickness never really went away, that if he could just make a small score he would grab it and run back and maybe buy himself a few acres. He and Kitty could get married. He was willing to bet that the Krugers would even help him get started. Certainly A.G. would. Maybe he could swing some sort of a deal with Earl, work for him part time in return for a loan. He would not have to score that big in Hollywood if the Krugers would help him out partway. The old man was mean but he was loyal to family, and Ramsey could not help but think of himself as family.

Then came the knock on the door. He wondered who it was.

Kitty's friends were not in the habit of dropping by when she was out. He opened up and found a plainclothesman and two uniformed officers waiting for him.

"You Mr. Hogan?"

"Yessir."

"Can you show us some identification?"

Ramsey brought out his new California driver's license. It showed the address of Kitty's apartment.

"We'd like to come in and look around," the plainclothesman said. "If you don't mind."

"Sure."

Ramsey would later regret letting them in without a search warrant. It was one of many things he would wonder about, trying to figure out where he had gone wrong. The police turned the apartment upside down and discovered a large cache of pills and a sugar jar with a pound of cocaine in it. Like any good cowboy, Ramsey liked speed, but he preferred drink over anything else and rarely popped a pill. Speed to him was only something to keep you from dropping off a cliff if you had started drinking too early in the day. He hardly ever needed it and certainly he had never sold it. And as for the cocaine, he had never taken it and could not imagine how Kitty had the money for such an amount.

But he said nothing as he was hauled off to jail and booked. At first he wondered whether Kitty had set him up, but when she came to see him where he was being held she managed to convince him that it had not been her fault. A couple of her friends had been using her apartment to store their supplies. She had been afraid something like this would happen, but she said that her friends had plenty of powerful connections and they would spring him in no time flat. They never did. He was given from two to five years for possession with intent to sell.

Kitty came to see him regularly at first, and they even talked about getting married after he got out and got his career off the ground again. When they learned that he would be sent to

Chino, she told him that he should consider himself lucky. Chino was not so bad at all, she had heard. Parts of it didn't even have fences, and since it was obvious that he was basically a good guy, they would never lock him up in maximum security. It was much better than Folsom or Soledad.

But they did, to begin with. They took him to something called the Youth Reception Center, California euphemism for maximum security, and Kitty never came to see him after that. It hurt him badly, her running out on him. He wrote her daily for a while, begging her to come, but finally gave up, realizing that she had her own life to live and that she could hardly be expected to be loyal to a man behind bars. Well, he had hoped she would be. People were supposed to be loyal if they loved each other, weren't they, and she had told him that she loved him, but maybe she hadn't loved him so much after all, or maybe they had not really had enough time to get to love each other to the point of absolute loyalty that you were supposed to reach. He puzzled over these things in his cell. Oh shit, he would always conclude, and he would remember what the one cowboy had said about not standing a chance in California with all those pricks. Maybe it was not in any way Kitty's fault. It was probably those friends of hers, the beards-and-beads set. Poor Kitty. She was simple, that much he knew. He resolved that whatever else was going to happen to him, he would never again be a fool.

After a few months they did move him into the minimum security section, called the California Institute for Men, but Ramsey never did decide whether he liked it better there than in the Youth Reception Center. At least in the YRC you never forgot where you were, but the minimum security part was just pleasant enough that every once in a while you would forget that you were in prison at all, and when you woke up and realized you were, it was doubly depressing. There were no locks on the cell doors, you could watch television a lot, and they had regular programs to help you get a job when you got out, because everyone in that part of the prison was going to get out before too long, if they didn't run away. It was a kind of bribe, Ramsey figured. They dangled getting out in front of your nose and in return you stayed put.

He had his choice of working in the furniture shop, where they made tables and chairs for the entire California prison system, or in the cow barn, where they produced milk for the system, or in the dog-grooming school, where you could learn to trim poodles for rich people. Everyone advised him that poodle trimming was the best option to take, because there was getting to be such a demand for it on the outside, but Ramsey chose the cow barn, because he felt more at home in it. He had to laugh. He had gone from a good job, totally secure, on the Sunrise, to milking cows for murderers and dope pushers and thieves in California. Every few days he would sit down to write A.G. a letter about it. He would try to be jocular, saying things such as you should see me now, old buddy, or if you ever want to open up a dairy farm, I'm your man, but he found that writing to A.G. made him unbearably sad, and he always tore up the letters before he finished them. He would get to thinking about the Sunrise and about A.G. tooling around Norman in his T-bird, probably with the girls hanging all over him. Sometimes he would catch himself feeling envious of A.G. and would have to stop himself from that, because A.G. had always been kind to him and had shared everything with him, and he knew that if he had not been stupid enough to throw it all over to go to California, if he had simply waited for A.G. to come back from college, everything could have been the same again, or almost, or certainly better than the fix he was in now. He found himself missing old man Kruger's gruff commands and old lady Kruger's gentleness and sometimes he missed his mother, had visions of her standing at the blackboard telling the students about the virtues of hard work and perseverance.

There was even a swimming pool in the minimum security

section, and, lying beside it, Ramsey would think, well old Carl Dean, you ain't got nothin on me. I am even gonna have one hell of a California tan before I get outa here. He had not contacted Carl Dean and Rita because he was afraid that they would let his mother or somebody back home know where he was, and that would be the last thing he wanted. As the months wore on he began to think that the best thing for him to do when he got out was to head back to Oklahoma immediately and not tell anyone anything, just try to pick up where he had left off. He could make up some story about where he had been and what he had been doing. He had had to re-register for the draft in California and had been shipped out to Vietnam, where he had spent two years loading bodies into plastic bags. One of the other prisoners had told him about that. The duty had upset the guy so much that he had not known what to do with himself when he finally got out and he had ended up in Chino on an armed robbery charge. I can tell some story about Vietnam, Ramsey thought, and everybody will believe it, unless I run into somebody who was actually there. Then I'll keep my mouth shut.

Ramsey noticed that most of the prisoners he talked to had plans, big plans, for when they got out, and most of them sounded like bullshit. One guy was going to be a millionaire evangelist, another was going to write a book and go on the Johnny Carson show. But a lot of the prisoners in this wing were just white-collar guys who had fouled up one way or another, some little embezzlement here or missed alimony payments.

"I knew a guy over in Sand Springs once," Ramsey told one of the alimony jumpers. "He owed his wife like I don't know, maybe eighty-five thousand dollars in payments. So she's in Arizona, see, and gets the authorities there, they start telephonin around, lookin for him, and by God, one day he is in the sheriff's office, who happens to be a buddy of his anyhow. And the phone rings, and it's the guy in Arizona, askin the sheriff to arrest this guy, he owes eighty-five thousand in back payments. So the sheriff, he puts his hand over the phone and tells this guy what's goin on, and the guy, he hands the sheriff a C-note, or maybe it was only ten dollars, and the sheriff gets back on the phone and he says, 'Well, he used to live around here, but I understand he's somewheres over in Wagoner County now. If I do see him I'll sure get him for you.' And that was that."

"Maybe I should move to, where'd you say it was?"

"Sand Springs," Ramsey said. "Maybe you should. You'd get some cooperation, I can tell you that."

Ramsey figured that these white-collar prisoners were worse off than he was. They could never go back to what they had been doing. You couldn't embezzle even a little bit and expect them to hire you back. That was the thing, he told himself over and over again, no matter how bad off you think you are, there is always somebody who is in a worse mess than you are. In some ways he wouldn't want to trade places with Carl Dean.

EIGHT

A.G. was rather lonely at O.U. until, in his junior year, he met Claire Gladstone. It was not that he spent all of his time alone. From one angle you could say that for him O.U. was just plain party time, especially after he joined the Phi Delts. But when he was not partying he was often in his room alone, not sure exactly what to do with himself, looking often at the calendar to see when it was that he would be going back to the Sunrise for a visit. And when he did go back, he would spend hours riding around the place, listening to Sam, enjoying the meals with his parents and always, come Sunday night, reluctant to drive back down to Norman.

He thought often about Ramsey and wondered what his friend was up to. His last letter to Ramsey had been returned "Addressee unknown." When he had first heard that Ramsey had left, he felt a little envious. There was something appealing about hitting the road for California. Not that A.G. shared any of Ramsey's ambitions. Their situations were so opposite. But to be free of ties for a time—it was an exhilarating idea. Hit L.A. with a big bankroll and see what was happening and shake things up. It occurred to A.G. that maybe in some ways Ramsey was better off than he was, having to take a trip into the unknown. The women he would meet. Ramsey was probably sitting on some golden beach nuzzling a golden girl. And besides all that, he just plain missed old Ramsey. They had shared everything, and from habit A.G. wanted to keep on sharing things with him and to have him around as he always had, checking things out, always there like a reassuring partner.

Even the Sunrise did not seem the same without Ramsey,

although A.G. never really felt at home anywhere else, whatever people thought. He knew that everyone had the impression that A.G. Kruger, who had learned to act every inch Earl
Kruger's son, would be at home anywhere, the life of a party
on the moon. He drove his T-bird like a Heisman winner running through linebackers, with a girl at his side and a drink in
his hand and his hat set back on his head. He built a reputation as a hell-raiser and a free spender. It came to be known
that when A.G. Kruger was around, it was time to let loose.
A.G. would buy the booze and A.G. would lead the parade. He
might end up passed out, but everybody would know he had
been there.

In truth he did not drink any more than a lot of O.U. boys,
but that standard covered a lot of territory. Like most of them,
A.G. had learned to put the stuff away at his father's knee. His
real initiation into partying, apart from the bashes held every
couple of months at the Sunrise, had come when he was fifteen
on the weekend of the O.U.-Texas game. Earl had chartered a
plane, left Margaret at home and taken A.G. and Ramsey
along. They were not among the five hundred people arrested
in Dallas in Baker Street and at the huge state fair held next
door to the Cotton Bowl, people having a hell of a time just
whooping it up, boozing it up, throwing up, pushing and
brawling till the dawn of the game. But by prearrangement
Earl had run into some cronies and after dinner and a blurry
tour of the fair, they ended up in Earl's hotel suite with three
or four bottles and plenty of ice.

"Have another, son, now's the time. This is the big game,"
Earl kept saying, and the next day A.G. experienced for the
first time the pleasures of sitting in the sun watching the Soon-
ers, nursing a hangover with beer. That night the celebrations
or the lamentations had to go on and on, and Sunday there
was brunch with bloody Marys, so by the time they got back
to the Sunrise, A.G. had had a pretty good initiation, and by
the time he was actually enrolled at O.U., he was already an
old hand.

A.G. became known for the wild ride, the impulsive bustout. Sometimes he would bring one of the family Cadillacs down from the Sunrise and take a couple of his fraternity brothers and their dates out to dinner in Oklahoma City or drive all the way up to Tulsa, about a hundred miles, and back in the same night. On one of these expeditions, they had finished dinner at a Tulsa restaurant. A.G. wanted to unwind the girls a little bit, so he drove over to the Live and Let Live on South Sheridan to watch the topless dancers and sip a few more. The girls had never seen anything like it, or said they had not, and A.G. went kind of wild, pouring down the drinks and carrying on. As he said later, he was drunker than seven hundred dollars. His date was flattered to be out with him but did not care much for his behavior. When she told him she thought he had had enough to drink, he told her to find her own ride home if she didn't like it, and she started to cry. Then he got remorseful and solicitous. He ordered more drinks, apologized over and over, and told her he bet her tits were twice as good as the ones up there on the stage. Everybody except his girl thought that was pretty funny. When they were finally ready to leave, A.G. called the waitress over and said:

"Gimme the check and give us go-cups."

The waitress brought the last round in plastic cups and they all took their drinks to the car. It was a crazy ride back to Norman, with A.G. driving and finishing off his go-cup and his date's and one of the other girls' too. He rarely took out the same girl twice.

But when he was not being wild, he had trouble knowing what to do with himself. Now that he was in college, there did not seem to be much point in studying, because he knew he would be back on the Sunrise soon enough. The only course that interested him was one in Oklahoma history. He got on good terms with the professor, who took to inviting him over to dinner, and A.G. enjoyed those evenings, looking over the professor's library and talking about how the state had emerged from wilderness to Indian Territory, through the land

runs and the oil booms and the Depression to its present condition of prosperity and rising expectations. The professor was
especially taken with A.G.'s account of his childhood encounter
with the Cherokees and with his narration of the legend of the
white snake. He suggested to A.G. that on his next trip home
to the Sunrise he ought to stop at the Gilcrease Museum in
Tulsa and look at some of the paintings and artifacts there. He
could get some material for a term paper that way.

A.G. never did write the term paper, but he did visit the
Gilcrease collection, and he found himself taken with the Rem-
ingtons and Russells but especially by the George Catlin paintings of the plains in the 1830s, the Indians in their elaborate
costumes, the expanses of bright-green prairie with strings of
buffalo stretching into the infinite, the buffalo hunts in the
snow, with Indians on snowshoes sneaking up for the kill. He
lost himself for hours in the Catlin paintings, imagining himself dressed in buckskin exploring the wild prairie, regretting
that he had not visited the Cherokees since that July night
years before. The inscription under a painting of a Mandan
village struck him: "A small tribe of 2000 souls, living in two
permanent villages on the Missouri. This friendly and interesting tribe all perished by the smallpox and suicide, in 1837,
three years after I lived amongst them, excepting about forty,
who have since been destroyed by their enemy, rendering the
tribe entirely extinct, and their language lost, in the short space
of a few months!" Why them and not the Cherokees? A.G.
wondered. Was it chance or fate? Had they failed to follow the
right way? More often than not, he supposed, it was every man
for himself in the world. Later his professor explained to him
that whites had brought the smallpox and that Indians committed suicide when they felt that they had lost their place in
the world as they had known it. Whites were more adaptable.

The professor was angry with A.G. for not writing the
paper, angry enough to send him a note expressing grave disappointment. A.G. had a good mind, the note said, and it
was a disgrace that he didn't use it more. The professor had

given freely of his time, not to speak of his whiskey, and he
had expected A.G. to produce something fine and notable.
Someday A.G. would be an important man in the state, and
the state could use men who thought deeply about things and
had an appreciation of what was valuable in their region. A.G.
tore the note up without showing it to anyone. He tried to be
indifferent, but he was ashamed, and he avoided the professor
from then on. Then he met Claire, and it was easy to forget
about everything else.

When he had first seen her, it had been one of those moments that occur once in a lifetime or maybe two or three
times to the odd few souls who canter through life on a romantic streak. He watched her from the other side of the room
chatting with some of his fraternity brothers. He lost all sense
of where he was and just stared, until he caught her eye and
turned away. Why had he chickened out? Ordinarily he could
stare a girl right out of her slip. Looking at her, it had been, he
thought later, almost like the feeling you get when you aim
down the barrel of a gun, when there is nothing there but you,
the gun, and the target. He went to get himself another drink.

It was the Phi Delt Spring Howdy, which everybody
agreed was about the best party of the year. A.G. looked like
who he was in his tailor-made beige western suit and hand-
tooled boots with stovepipe tops and the outline of the state of
Oklahoma on their sides. The boots made him almost six feet
tall, and although his face showed signs of that old whiskey
puff, he made quite an impression, his skin fair and his hair
dark. He had not bothered to bring a date. He seemed to have
used up the girls on campus who he thought might interest
him and had decided to take his chances on what might stray
by, or he might just get drunk. A few of the brothers, A.G. not
among them, specialized in corralling abandoned dates, waifs
needing comfort in their loss or girls angered into heat and
ready to take revenge in the time-honored way. Surefire, or so
they said.

The party was no more than an hour old when A.G. spotted

Claire. Here was news. Here was something definitely unusual. A.G. observed her long neck and the graceful arms with small wrists that curved into gestures as she talked. Her coloring, dark with light eyes, drew him. He thought of a hickory tree blazing in autumn. He was not sure which brother she was with, but he decided it didn't matter. He had to meet her.

"I'm A.G. Kruger."

She gave no sign of recognition but only showed him her eyes, bonafide green ones. A.G. was put off balance by her evident indifference to his name. He was used to the acknowledgment that was almost a giving in.

"Get you a drink?"

"I'm fine."

"Well. Who are you?"

"Claire Gladstone." She was not cold, but she was not as warm as her looks.

"I'm A.G. Kruger."

"I know. You told me."

"Well, Claire. Where you from?"

"Tulsa."

"Is that so. What part?"

"Brookside."

"Well. You go to high school in Tulsa?"

"Yes."

"Which one?"

"Monte Casino."

"Oh. You're a good Catholic girl."

"A lot of girls go to Monte Casino who aren't Catholic."

"Is that right. They say you can get lost in Tulsa. The streets are all kattywampus."

"They're what?"

"Kattywampus. Crooked to each other. You know. There's kattycorner and then there's kattywampus. I'm just a country boy."

"Sure you are. I know who you are."

"You do? I didn't think you did."

"You can get me a drink now."

"Great. What are you drinking?"

"Orange juice and sloe gin. Plenty of ice."

"Orange juice and sloe gin. What do you call that?"

"Some people call it a slow screw."

A.G. was put off by the remark, but then he was not. She was playing him like a violin, he knew, but he kind of liked it.

"You hadn't heard that before?" Claire said. "Oh, God, that's so old. I thought A.G. Kruger would've heard everything."

"I guess not," A.G. said. "Be right back."

He responded to her playing games with him by not even trying to take her away from her date, but he managed to talk with her quite a bit that night and to dance with her. She went on kidding him, getting close and then edging away, letting him believe she was falling for him and then making him think she didn't care a damn for him, but when she finally walked out the door with her date she threw a look at A.G. that kept him awake most of the night thinking about her. He found himself lying in bed smiling, feeling a little foolish, and at four in the morning he leapt out of bed and looked up her pictures in the previous year's yearbook. He took her for coffee the next day and they went out together on the weekends left in the semester. He drove her around; they went to the movies and out to dinner; they kissed at curfew on the steps of her sorority house and A.G. said to himself that those long kisses were better than anything more that he had ever had; and then the school year was over. She was to spend most of the summer with relatives in San Antonio. He would be working on the Sunrise. They would keep in touch and see each other in the fall. Their parting was awkward: they spent most of the time speculating on whether O.U. would be number one in the nation next year. It didn't seem likely. Gomer Jones had just been fired as coach and not many people thought the new

coach would last long. It wasn't like it had been in the days of
Bud Wilkinson. There never would be anyone like Uncle Bud.
Uncle Bud had made O.U. number one.

A.G. thought of little but Claire all summer. With Ramsey
gone, he spent most of his free hours by himself, dreaming of
her mouth or of what he had not seen of her, hearing her voice
and carrying on imaginary conversations with her. Something
told him that she was the girl who could understand everything about him, and he conjured up scenes from the coming
year where they would be parked by the Canadian River, say,
on an Indian-summer night, touching each other and getting
closer and closer, and at some point he would be able to say
things to her that would bind them together forever. He did
not even know what he would say but he imagined himself
saying it anyway, something that would reveal himself to her,
his soul, all of his impulses, his doubts, the very qualities whatever they were that made him himself; and she would see
those things and love them and embrace them and take them
into her and make them a part of her, too. She was strong, he
could see that; but she could be sweet and yielding. She
seemed somehow to be self-sufficient in a way that he admired,
and he sensed that were he joined to her and her to him he
would need nothing else. Yes, she could be like his mother,
kind and understanding, but she could be like his father, too,
because she had one hell of a will. When she did not want to
do something or go someplace, she said so, and just when A.G.
had thought that he preferred girls who went along one hundred percent with his way, he found himself liking Claire's
strength. He wondered whether she was thinking of him as
much as he was of her. He was not going to be the one to give
in and write the first letter. Finally by the middle of July he
could stand it no longer and he wrote her:

Dear Claire,
    I am not much for writing, but I've been thinking a lot

of you and missing you. I am working hard and the ranch
looks good. Last Saturday Mom and Dad threw a big
party and I thought of you. I swear, everybody in the
country must have been here. I got pretty smashed and
went and soaked my head in a creek. One couple flew in
from Dallas and landed on the new airstrip we have had
put in here and I said to myself why couldn't that plane
have Claire on it? Let's get together real soon in September.

Love,
A.G.

He used stationery with the Sunrise brand on it.

After a couple of weeks he received her reply. He combed
the letter for personal things, but it was all about a quarrel she
had had with her mother over whether one of her bathing suits
was too revealing, and this had the effect of making A.G.
spend hours trying to imagine what the bathing suit looked
like and how much of Claire could be seen in it, but it also
made him wonder who had been looking at her. The envelope
flap did have S.W.A.K. written on it, and that gave him hope.
He was angry with her for not writing something about her
feelings for him, but he found himself writing her letters that
alternated between pique and passion. He tore them all up.

But there was another letter that summer, and for the moment it took A.G.'s mind off Claire. A letter from Ramsey:

Dear A.G.,

First and foremost when you recieve my letter I hope
you and your family are in the best of health and spirit,
with an exceeding state of mind. Mainly a open mind so
that you will comprehend me to the fullest. for me, the
fumes of germs that ramish my health from inhaling so
much bitterness and frustration does indeed cause me an-
noyance and a touch of intimidation yet and still I maintain my hope in order to survive, A.G., my old buddy and

pal as I truly believe you still are. I have a wonderful and exciting pleasure remembering all the good times we done have of an evening or of a day in the old times with you and youens. I would give anything to be out some of these mornings with the old shotguns after birds. Some guy here who is from down in Lawton tells me the wild turkies have been seing many of them again. But not to keep you in suspense any longer. I am incarcerated. That's right in the pen. Its a wonder I'm not on a nut farm by now to tell you the truth because I was alright to start with for the first year even and I was supposed to come up for parole after a year but there was some kind of a screw up red tape and the like and I didn't get out. I was so frustrated you see I had made careful plans to hightail it right back to Oklahoma and pick up where I left off which the more I thought about it the more it did sure enough seem like a fine place to pick up. I just sat around brooding for days or weeks and finally this guard who started to get on me of which he is really not a bad guy at all and I think he was trying to do me a favor to shock me out of being so depressed, I let him have it. I know what I was doing. Taking my frustrations out. Thank God I didn't kill the son of a bitch but he was hurt bad and they thought he was paralyzed, he did recover. But the long and the short of it was that put me in a different category of prisoner. They moved me back into the maximum security, I spent time in solitary and just about went nuts and even now they watch me more than before. I won't bother you how I got in here in the first place. It was a woman as you might suspect isn't it always the case though I don't believe it was her fault I was framed you might say for drugs but I don't know to this day which it was I was framed or just plain unlucky, after all these years considering myself one lucky sob especially knowing you and your fine family. So here I am but the point of this is this, including just to say hello after all these years, I believe I have another chance for parole in a few years—excuse me! I mean months! You see how you get to thinking in here! In a few months they tell me I have a chance for parole. But the thing is, I will have a much better chance for getting out if I have somebody to sponsor me like. I thought naturally of you and your folks. Do you think you could do me a favor? You wouldn't have to take me on really if you didn't want to. I know you have taken on ex-cons in the past but I know they were trouble sometimes like Dale Worth who shot that guy down in Vian and your Dad went to a lot of trouble about that. But maybe you know me well enough. I am not all that changed deep inside I promise you. Still a good guy. Would like to knock back a few beers Jesus I can taste it, and nothing better than sitting out in a pasture with a few cool ones. If you can do this I would much appreate it for the rest of my life. If you can see your way clear then you can write me at this address and I can give you the rest of the information.

> Your friend,
> Ramsey (Hogan)

P.s. Please don't mention anything to my Mother. Thanks.

A.G. read the letter over and over. It was written in a very neat hand with no crossings-out, obviously the result of several drafts that had taken him days and days to compose, and it was not lost on A.G. that Ramsey had begun to confuse days with weeks and months with years. Obviously Ramsey had gotten himself messed up on something or other out in California. A.G. went straight to Earl with the letter.

"I wish the dumb son of a bitch had of wrote sooner," Earl said. "I'd of had him sprung in nothin flat."

Earl was sitting in the big red living room, and once he had read the letter, he reached for the phone. He dialed the private office number of one of the Oklahoma United States Senators.

"Well things is just great," Earl said into the phone. "I got a little problem out in California, though. . . . No, it ain't no oil deal. It's a friend of mine. And a real close friend of my son A.G. got in a little trouble, was framed it sure looks like to me.

. . . That's right. . . . You got it. . . . No. . . . I don't give a good goddamn about that. . . . That's right. Name of Ramsey Hogan. Chino prison. Some kinda hoked-up bullshit drug charge. I want this here Ramsey Hogan out *tomorrow.* . . . Don't give me that bullshit. Listen, you asshole. I own this Ramsey Hogan. Just like I own *you.* . . . Right. Well that's just great. I'll send A.G. out to pick him up."

"So it's all set?" A.G. asked as soon as his father had hung up.

"You're damned right," Earl said. "Some of these politicians, they get elected, they forget for a minute who got 'em elected. Takes a little remindin. They get into the goddamned Senate, they think they gotta have a clean ass. Hell, I ain't wiped my ass for three days."

"You sure got fast action," A.G. said.

"Just remember somethin, son. Like they always say, don't be shitty to nobody. You don't be shitty, everybody will like you. Now, nobody will remember you, but they sure as hell will like you."

Earl arranged for A.G. to take a plane to L.A. two days later. Earl said that he wanted to give Senator Dick-around time to get his circus organized. There was no point in rushing things. Within seventy-two hours A.G. and Ramsey were sharing a quart of Scotch at the Beverly Wilshire Hotel.

"I cain't hardly believe it," Ramsey said. "This place sure beats hell out of Chino."

"I noticed you had a swimming pool," A.G. said. "Maybe I oughta check into Chino for a rest. Ramsey, I met the goddamnedest girl at O.U."

A.G. and Ramsey had a blue-ribbon reunion. There was a little trouble when A.G. wanted to take a drink out on the street from the Pink Pussycat Club on Santa Monica Boulevard, but fifty dollars took care of it.

NINE

Ramsey watched as Wynema prepared her special chili with nine spices. He was home on the Sunrise, out on parole after the pen, and he felt he had never been so happy in his life. It was as if the California nightmare had been wiped out. Everyone treated him as though he had simply been away on vacation, except there were a lot of jokes about his being an outlaw just like Pretty Boy Floyd. Everything on the ranch seemed newborn to him, and he woke up each morning so exultant that when no one was watching he would buckleap, clapping his heels against his butt. In prison he had often daydreamed about Wynema's cooking, the ribs barbecued for six hours over hickory and mesquite, the jalapeno soufflés, the chili especially.

"Get on outa here, Ramsey Hogan," Wynema said. "You know this recipe's a secret. Ain't nobody can do it right but me."

"Aw," Ramsey said, watching her cut up the meat. "I had chili better'n yours."

"The hell you say."

"Sure. Course yours might be as good if you had the right kind of meat."

"Go on. What kinda meat's that?"

"Well, it's championship chili meat, and I know how to get it."

"Sure you do."

"I do. Matter of fact, I get it and I sell it to all the chili champions."

"Rattlesnake meat?"

"Huh-uh."

"Squirrel chili? I make that."

"Huh-uh. I'll tell you how I get it."

"Well go on, big mouth."

"Well," Ramsey said, "you seen me goin out at dusk, haven't you?"

"Sure."

"And you seen me goin out at dawn?"

"Yeah."

"Well where I go is, I go down to the highway and I look for these dogs and cats that's been run over. And I got to go down there and find 'em after they been run over three or four times. You want to get the meat when it's about this thick." He held his thumb and forefinger about three inches apart. "If you wait till they're much thinner than that, all the flavor's squashed out, see."

Wynema ran him out of the kitchen and he took off howling and happy. The other cowboys told him that the only change they noticed in him was that he seemed to have gotten pretty windy. He didn't seem to be able to stop talking, and the way they remembered him he had been a pretty silent type. Ramsey explained that if you were locked up for four years in the pen with hardly anybody to talk to, you'd be pretty windy too. They wanted to hear about his brush with show business, and he told them what he could, although he would have preferred not to remember anything about the past three years, and then Sam said that he knew one about show business:

"There was one day this show-business guy and the Pope, they dropped dead on the same day. No foolin. The Pope and this show-business guy dropped dead and they both of 'em ended up in front of the pearly gates together. And this big old Cadillac limousine comes along and the guy says, 'Get on in the car. That's St. Peter drivin. He'll take you where you all is gonna live.' So St. Peter he takes off and they drive to this big neighborhood where all the houses is mansions and they cost five hundred thousand apiece. But he don't stop there. He keeps on a-drivin and they get to where the houses is only a hundred thousand apiece, then on down to where they is fifty thousand, and twenty-five, and finally St. Peter he has taken 'em to where there's nothin but little shacks made outa boards and tin roofs and trash everwhere and old Chevies in the yards and what-all. "Okay, Pope," St. Peter says. 'Get out here. This is where you gonna live.' The Pope he says he is very grateful, and he acts real humble, and he gets out and goes into the shack and shuts the door and they take off again. And the show-business guy, he thinks, Jesus Christ! If this is where they put the Pope, where they gonna put me? I might of been better off in hell. But St. Peter, he turns the Cadillac around and heads back the way they come. Back through the hundred thousand and so on, till they get to the biggest damn house on the nicest street in heaven. I mean it is a real mansion. And St. Peter says to the show-business guy, 'Okay, out you get. This is where you live. The key's under the mat.' So he gets out, but then he leans in the window and he says to St. Peter, 'Look, can I ask you somethin? It's botherin me. The Pope, you put him way over there in that shack, and I'm just a show-business guy, how come I get all this special treatment? I don't think I deserve it.' 'Listen,' St. Peter says to him. 'Yes you do. Don't you know, we're up to our arseholes in popes here. You're the first show-business guy what ever got in!"

"He didn't deserve it, neither," Ramsey said after he had got over laughing. "All them show-business guys is crooked sons of bitches. Except for Ben Johnson." Ramsey said he was damned happy to be out of show business. He had found out something and had finally learned something, that the best thing in the world was sitting around with the boys drinking beer and swapping stories.

"Don't forget the ladies," someone added.

"Maybe," Ramsey said.

When A.G. telephoned Claire back on campus in September, she acted as though there had been nothing at all remarkable in their having exchanged only one letter apiece and she

accepted his first request for a date. He took her to the 700
Club in Oklahoma City for dinner and afterwards drove to a
spot he knew by the Canadian River and parked.

"Well, a great thing happened," A.G. said. "We found out
my old best friend Ramsey, you remember I told you about
him?"

"Yes."

"My dad got him out of prison in California."

"Was he guilty?"

"Hell no. Total frame-up. You should have heard my dad.
He called the Senator, by God that guy danced."

"Really," Claire said.

They were silent for a while.

"Well I don't mind admitting it," A.G. said. "I missed you."

"I missed you too. You know, I used to think about you
when I was going out with other guys. They all seemed pretty
creepy."

"You go out a lot?"

"Not too much. I mean, God, you have to do something. I
couldn't spend all summer talking to my mother and uncle and
aunt."

"So you really didn't like any of the guys?"

"No. There was this one guy who was really putting the rush
on me. Even asked me to marry him. Can you believe that?"

"Amazing. Well, he's got taste anyway." A.G. thought to
himself that he would like to find the guy and stomp him.

Parked by the river, they had got pretty warm with each
other and she had not hesitated at all to take him in her hand
and give him rubs and squeezes that would bring him right to
the point, but then she would shut things off by some irrelevant
remark about a song on the radio or the moon or San Antonio
or how when she had been in high school all the boys from
Cascia Hall had been after her from freshman year on, but she
had been rather shy, really, and known as very particular or
maybe even a snob, although she had certainly never been
that.

"About the worst time I can remember," A.G. said, "was when I got on this big black horse. We had these rodeos, you know, and well, that horse just never would stop. I won the race, all right. But that horse kept on going. We hit a fence. I was lucky I was alive."

"The most trying time in my life," Claire said, "was when my daddy died."

"I'm sorry to hear that."

"He committed suicide."

"He did?"

"Shot himself."

"He did?"

A.G. reached over instinctively and held Claire close by the shoulder, but his thoughts went to his own father. He could not imagine Earl killing himself. It was the most unimaginable event. He knew that his grandfather had done it, but the idea of Earl's doing it was beyond possibility. He tried to imagine it but realized it was impossible. Then he was able to think of Claire again. He hugged her.

"I'm sorry," he said. He was glad she had confided in him.

"My mother was never the same after," Claire said. "We had some insurance, though, thank God."

"Really awful."

"Some people aren't strong enough for this world."

"I guess not. I guess, I don't know."

Claire told him that when her uncle, her mother's brother, had jumped off the 21st Street bridge in Tulsa, that had been upsetting too, but he had only broken his back. She remembered her father as loving and kind but she guessed he had given in to something or other or maybe it was bad luck or bad genes.

"You don't look like you have bad genes to me," A.G. said.

"Still, I believe a woman needs a man to protect her."

They kissed for an hour after that.

A.G. decided later that, considering that they had not seen each other in over three months, the evening had gone pretty

well. He came away believing that Claire looked up to him,
although if the truth were known, he thought, he looked up to
her. She seemed like a girl who had been through some things
and could be counted on. And she was so pretty. No, beautiful.
And so intriguingly changeable. She had a proud look, an almost haughty bearing when they were in public, and sometimes in private, too, but then she could get all cuddly.

They went to the home games together, and A.G. was proud
to be with her. The other guys would come up to him and
express their envy. They would ask him, of course, whether he
was screwing her, and he would be noncommittal, letting them
think what they would while giving the impression of being a
gentleman one way or the other. He would certainly like to
have been sleeping with her but he had decided to let things
take their natural course. He knew Claire well enough already
to sense that she liked a strong man but was not the type to be
bullied into anything, and he admired that about her. He admired so many things about her, from the way she dressed,
never sloppily but never too formally either, so that she
seemed to be ready for anything no matter what, to the way
she talked, not overly feminine like some of the more Southern
kinds of girls but not overly loud or aggressive either. At one
party at the fraternity house after a game, A.G. was sitting
with her in a window seat. He had brought his flask to the
game and they were warming themselves now with a couple
more drinks. A.G. thought he was in heaven with the closeness
of her, her color heightened by an afternoon in the autumn air,
the top two buttons of her blouse undone so he could glimpse
hints of dizzying undulations the color of heavy country cream,
the air full of whiskey, tobacco and her perfume, and without
thinking about it for even a second beforehand he leaned over
to her and whispered in her ear, an act that always made her
shiver and raised goosebumps on her arm,

"I think I love you."

"Maybe I love you too," she whispered back. "Look at you."

She ran a hand over the curved back of his head. "The big tough rancher." She touched his face. "You're just a little boy. Aren't you."

"Maybe sometimes," he said. "I'm tough too, though."

"Would you be tough with me?"

"Sure."

"And a little boy too?"

"I guess I would."

They kissed for minutes. She sucked on his tongue till it hurt. "Oh, A.G.," she said. "Those kisses."

"Come on," he said and led her up to the second floor, where there was a room set aside for private encounters. After a while she was half undressed and he was protruding, and A.G. thought the moment had come, but when he pressed the point, she said,

"No. Not here. I don't want it to be here. It has to be someplace special. With us."

There was always plenty of diversion around Norman. If it wasn't a game or a frat party or sorority event, there were the drinking clubs, where you could get in if you knew someone, and there was the river. Once in a while on a Saturday night A.G. and Claire and one or two other couples would take in the Trianon Ballroom, a huge place in Oklahoma City where folks would come in from the country to dance. These were the days when thanks to Elvis and Buddy Holly and others rock and roll had become white music, too, but you never heard any rock and roll at the Trianon. It was strictly country music, a band of veteran guitars, mandolins and fiddles playing the old favorites for people who went on dancing in the old ways, twirling and dipping, skimming the floor in elegant swoops. A.G. and Claire went there often enough to recognize the same pairs, energetic old men and women, or to youth they seemed old, and single men with great, horny hands who would occasionally make bold to ask one of the girls to dance, saying things like:

"Pretty girl, would your husband knock me down if I asked you to dance?"

"He sure would not."

"He wouldn't? Well why not?"

When they weren't dancing, A.G. and Claire would sit at a table with their bottle of Scotch and speculate about the dancers, whether this one ran around on her husband, whether that pair were really married or just out on a fling. There was one couple, they must have been in their fifties, who were called the Dippers because they specialized in the most dramatic dips imaginable. She would hook one leg around his thigh, hold one arm up in an arc behind her head, and he would bend her back so low that you saw plenty of her legs and wondered what principle of physics kept them from falling over. The rumor was that the Dippers drove down from Guthrie every Friday night, checked into a hotel and drank and fought all night and all day Saturday, arrived at the Trianon loaded and ready to tear at each other, and then dipped away their differences until by midnight they were lovers once again. A.G. and Claire liked to hold hands, enjoy the music and wonder about the different things that people did to keep their marriages together. They did not get quite to the point of discussing marrying each other, but they agreed that for them, whomever they married, it would be for keeps. The last dance at the Trianon was always a slow one, something like "Silver-Haired Daddy of Mine" or maybe a country version of "Harbor Lights," and A.G. would be feeling very romantic by then, bringing his hand in so it rested with hers on her breast, catching sight of the other couples through a wisp of Claire's hair and wishing secretly that years and years later they would still be dancing together.

What was it about Claire? What was it? Her looks, the way she seemed to understand him, the way they could go anywhere together and enjoy it, even a place like the Trianon, especially the Trianon? He was beginning to feel that he could rely on her, that no matter what lay ahead he would be able to face it and triumph over it as long as she was there. For a time, after he had gone to college, he had thought that he would have to face many things in life alone, that even after he returned to the Sunrise it would be different from before, because he would be a man, his parents would get old, and he would have to deal with the world himself, and he admitted to himself though certainly to no one else that the prospect frightened him. Now there was just the chance that the loneliness was already over. Claire's beauty was out of this world, but she was down to earth, too. She was the sort of woman who would stand behind you and yet be able to take you down a peg, when you needed it, as when she reminded him as she was so fond of doing that he was just a little boy inside.

Flying across the floor with her, he imagined dancing with Claire on the Sunrise after he had made the ranch his own. It might be a big party out on the lawn or they might even be alone in the red living room. His parents would love her, she would be a second child to them. She would be his inspiration and everything he did would be for her. He could not yet conjure up all that he would do, but it would be something and many things. The music, mournful but full of life, told him so, and this light, warm form in his arms told him so. Ramsey should see him now—he would be jealous but happy for him, too.

She seemed to respond to his movements before he dreamed them up, leading him even as he led her. If he had not been afraid of sounding like a fool, he would have told her that he had never been so happy in his life.

What did it matter that he had not proposed to her? That would come in due time. He could hardly imagine that she would refuse him. He may have had his doubts about himself and about life but these did not include whether any girl in Oklahoma or anywhere else would want to marry him. It was simply a question of finding the right one. He was surprised that it had happened so easily—all it had taken was a look. He knew he wanted to marry Claire. They had something together, and when he married her everyone would know about it and that way they would never lose it.

Claire's mother had moved into an apartment in Norman, and A.G. did worry about that. It was not merely strange, it was downright irritating. Why couldn't some parents leave their kids alone? He figured Mrs. Gladstone had come down to chaperon. Didn't she know this wasn't South America where the unmarried women all had nursemaids? A lot of parents were after their sons and daughters to make more frequent visits home, but he had never heard of any who actually moved to Norman from September to June. Did she think she was going to keep Claire from getting knocked up or what?

Claire tried to explain how insecure her mother had been ever since her father's suicide and that she found it tough to cope with life alone in Tulsa.

"Well I'll tell you what," A.G. said. "I'd like to meet her. Set the poor woman's mind at rest."

"You sure about that?"

"Of course I'm sure. And one of these days, you'll come on up to the Sunrise. Meet my folks. And my buddy Ramsey."

"My mother's just got this little apartment," Claire said.

"I'd like to meet her. Fix it up."

"She'd like to meet you, I know that. I told her about you."

So one evening A.G. arrived at the apartment building where Claire's mother lived only a couple of miles from the university. It was a tacky new place called the Lanai, and as A.G. made his way up the stairs he could smell half a dozen dinners cooking and hear Bob Dylan behind one door and Paul Anka behind another.

"I've heard so much about you," Vivian Gladstone said. "What would you like to drink?"

"Pleased to meet you, ma'am. Scotch and soda would be fine."

"Claire, fix Mr. Kruger a Scotch and soda. I'm sure you know the way he likes it. Mr. Kruger, I'm glad you agree, there is nothing like a Scotch and soda. I'm having one too. Just one, unfortunately. I've had to cut down. It's a battle, but I'm a battler!"

"I wish you'd call me A.G."

"A.G., I've known you since you were a baby. I mean not really known you, of course, but I remember I saw the announcement in the paper. My goodness, that was a special event. I remember your parents had quite a celebration up there on that wonderful ranch of yours, which of course I have heard about for years and years. They are great, great people. I mean, everybody knows, there's no better people than the Krugers. Here's to your parents. Two of the greatest people. Really. I must say, I'm honored to have you in my home, such as it is. We do have the home in Tulsa, you know, but I declare it is worth living here in this silly little place just to have the honor, the real honor, of meeting you. So sit down."

As soon as he saw Mrs. Gladstone, A.G. figured that Claire must look like her father, because Mrs. Gladstone was short and thin-lipped, and her skin was so pale that you could see veins all over it. She kept her pale eyes on A.G., asking him about his parents, saying they were almost a legend, that his father was a man who commanded respect. She had scarcely encountered people like his parents in her own life, but she did remember when she and Gerald, her late husband, had got their first Cadillac.

"How many Cadillacs your family have, A.G.?" Mrs. Gladstone asked.

"Three. Then there's the Lincoln."

"And what do you drive?"

"I have my T-bird. I wouldn't trade it."

"Well, I suppose you'll have a Cadillac soon enough! I'm having such a good time," she said, sipping her drink. "A little Scotch and soda never hurt anybody. Scotch whiskey cannot harm the human body, did you know that? Scotch has saved many a nation from going under. I tell you, I am having the best time. I can't remember when I've had such fun." Her ebullience was confined to speech. She sat immobile except for the lifting of her glass, and she never removed her eyes from A.G.

"You know, there is one thing about money," Vivian Gladstone went on. "Claire, I think A.G. is ready for another. How about it, A.G.?" He extended his glass, trying but failing to catch Claire's eye. "There is one thing about money, which it is not everything, as we know, but what they do with it. My God! To think the opportunity! Now your parents, look at what they have done. They have built something that anyone would be proud of. The Sunrise Ranch. Why, it sends shivers down my spine just to say it. Some people, they have money, they don't know what to do with it. You take my Gerald, God help him."

"Mother," Claire said.

"My Gerald was a wonderful man. In many ways. A saintly man. It could be said. He killed himself."

"Mother."

"Did you know that, A.G.?"

"I had heard it, yes ma'am."

"Yes, he killed himself. He put a gun to his head and shot himself through the temple. About shot his head off to tell the truth. I don't know, I don't think you ever get over something like that. You are too young, but. There are some things. I climbed the stairs—"

"Mother!"

"It's all right," A.G. said. He was beginning to get interested.

"A.G. should know these things. I climbed the stairs, and the light was on and I thought he is reading in bed again or he has passed out and forgot to turn the light. You can imagine. There he was. I had been out you see to a bridge game. I climbed the stairs and there he was. You can imagine. Blood absolutely everywhere. I had to throw everything out. It was on the drapes. You can understand, A.G. I can see it in your face. You are a very understanding young man. Why don't you have another Scotch and soda?"

"It's all right. I'm just starting on this one."

"As I was saying, there is one true test of a man, and that is what you do with it if you get some money. Now my Gerald, he was not very good at getting it. That was the trouble in the first place. He was with the Bureau of Indian Affairs, you know."

"Is that so."

"I am all for honesty, but you can take it too far. The fact is, everybody else in that office came out a rich man. Not Gerald."

"Not Gerald?"

"Frankly he was a fool, in my opinion, in that respect. Not that he did not have his good points. In my judgment. He was a loving father. Of course, what kind of a father is it that kills himself? When I think about it, I get so distressed, I wonder where is that old gun, anyhow? I think I'll dust it off and see if it still works. Well one time we did have something saved up, a few thousand, and it was our anniversary. The tenth, as I recall. We had the baby-sitter for Claire and we decided we would have dinner at the Mayo and celebrate. Kind of a second honeymoon."

"Nice idea."

"Well just wait. This was ten years ago and we had the best dinner, you know. A French wine. We ate very, very well, I promise you. And do you know what happened? The check came, and the bill for that dinner must have been near seventy-five dollars, what with the drinks. Well, we got back to the house, and do you know what he did?"

"No, what?"

Claire got up and disappeared into the kitchen.

"Claire doesn't like to hear this but I'll tell you. Gerald got home and threw up that dinner. Right in front of the babysitter! Thank God the child was asleep. He threw up that dinner that we had paid for. Now that is what I call a waste of money. Have you ever heard of such a waste of money?"

"That's some story," A.G. said.

Claire called them to the table.

Over dinner Mrs. Gladstone talked about what a wonderful girl Claire was. Claire had a temper and once in a while she could be hard to handle, Mrs. Gladstone said, but she had been pretty well-behaved as a child on the whole. She had been a daddy's girl when she had had a daddy, but after the tragedy she had pitched in like a trouper and had always done her share. And she had always been pretty. Everyone had always noticed those beautiful green eyes and after she had developed, well, that phone had started ringing and hadn't stopped since. Her figure was very attractive, didn't A.G. agree? A.G. did agree. And her complexion was picture-perfect: she had never had pimples, never any trouble with her skin at all, it was remarkable, her skin. Very nice legs. Her thighs especially were firm and shapely. Claire could have won any beauty contest had she chosen to enter. In fact she had urged Claire many a time to enter the Miss Oklahoma contest but she never would. Mrs. Gladstone talked about Claire all the way to dessert.

They were having coffee and after-dinner drinks when Claire, who had hardly spoken all evening, said suddenly in a very firm voice: "Remember your bridge date, Mother."

"Oh I wouldn't forget that. I was just finishing my coffee. I thought I might have a little more brandy in it. There's time."

"It's getting late," Claire said.

"There's very few things I like to do more than to play bridge," Mrs. Gladstone said. "One of them is meeting such a fascinating person as yourself, A.G. I do enjoy that so much. Having you in my home. Another is to shoot. Do you like to shoot, A.G.?"

"Yes ma'am, I do."

"I certainly do like it. Did Claire tell you I am a member of a gun club?"

"No she didn't."

"Yes. Every Saturday for years. Aim and hit, aim and hit. There is nothing better than to aim and hit. Hit and hit and hit. Hit that target. I do enjoy it, aim and hit. Why I like it so much, if I am driving along and I see an old paper cup just laying there in the street, I will take aim at it and swerve my car if necessary. Hit it. Crush that old cup flat. I just love it. Aim and hit hit hit."

"I know what you mean," A.G. said.

"Most of the time it's just target practice, you know. But every once in a while we go out and get doves. Aim, shoot that dove, then cook it up and eat it. Pan-fried in butter. Very delicious."

"You're going to be late, Mother," Claire said.

"Of course you're right. I'll get my things. Now you two just enjoy yourselves. Make yourself at home, A.G. Help yourself to anything you want. Stay as long as you want. These bridge games can last forever."

After Mrs. Gladstone left there was a long silence. Finally Claire said.

"I'm sorry. She was at her worst."

"She wasn't so bad. She just likes to talk, is all."

"I hate her."

"Don't say that."

"Don't tell me what to say."

Claire picked up a heavy ashtray and hurled it, not at A.G., but against a wall. It made a hole in the thin plaster and shattered.

"Holy shit!" A.G. said. "What you do that for?"

Claire slumped down and started to cry. A.G. went over to her and put his arms around her and asked her what was the matter.

"I'm just embarrassed," she said, "and I'm so mad I can't even stand it."

"Don't be embarrassed. Not with me. I love you."

"You do?"

"Of course I do."

"Even after that? God, it was bad enough, all that stuff about Daddy. But then when she started talking about me. I thought I was going to die. Or kill her. I felt like I was up on the auction block."

"I didn't think that."

"All that stuff about my body."

"You are beautiful."

"That's not the point."

A.G. took her in his arms and kissed her. He wiped away her tears and kissed her again. It moved him to see and feel her this way. She was usually so self-assured. Even though her mother had done all the talking, A.G. had sensed in some way that Claire was in control of the situation. After all, when she had told Vivian that it was time to leave, Vivian had left. Now she felt fragile in his arms. A.G.'s heart began to thump and he was conscious of growing hard. He made sure that she could tell that.

"I have a wonderful idea," Claire said.

"You do?"

Claire led A.G. by the hand into her mother's bedroom. He knew what was going to happen. There was no way that it was not going to happen now. He sat on the bed and watched as she undressed slowly and deliberately. Here was this girl who a moment before had been crying in his arms and now she was peeling off her clothes as though she knew exactly what she was doing, as though she had done this many times before, this girl who had been crying and taking comfort from him. I have never been so excited, he said to himself. He wanted to lunge at her and fill his mouth with the flesh of her bare stomach as she stood there before him in her bra and panties. She stood as though she wanted him to look at her carefully and appraise her, so he did, digging his nails into his palms as he examined the flesh not three feet from him. The bedside lamp was on. It cast just enough soft light for him to scan every inch of her as she pulled down her panties and stepped out of them. That she had done that before removing her bra excited him still more. Wasn't it usually the other way around? Didn't that gesture say something about how ready she was to have him, after all the kissing and petting and groping? He stared at her tidy dark crotch. She stepped another foot toward him and took off her bra so he could see her round breasts that made him think perfect, perfect.

"Get naked," she said.

He wanted to go right ahead but she slowed him down, taking hold of him, flattering him, telling him that his penis was beautiful, a perfect shape, that she couldn't wait to feel it in her but that she wanted to savor it. She whispered to him that next time or the time after or the time after that she would take him in her mouth but not this time.

"You would?"

"Yes. I want to."

"Have you done that?"

"No," she said. "But I want to with you. Because you're so beautiful." She held his penis and ran her fingers over it as though it were delicate and valuable. "But you know what we're going to do now." Then she lay back and guided him in.

A.G. lost himself in her and when he came he heard himself shout. She came just after him, thighs gripping him with a strength that surprised him. He drew back his head as she thrashed and he watched her face contort. They held onto each other for minutes. As he lay there with her, smelling her shoulders and neck, he thought that there could not possibly be anything to equal this in the world, ever. He remembered that every other first time had been flawed in some way. He said to himself that this must be what being in love does to you.

And he had not even thought about getting her pregnant.

When he mentioned it, she put a finger to his lips and said there was nothing to worry about. He was soon excited again but they decided that they would let it happen just once, this first time, because it had been so perfect.

"Mother will be coming back," she said later. "We'd better go."

He looked at the little white plastic alarm clock beside the bed. "Christ," he said. "It's after curfew. How're you going to—"

"Don't worry about me," Claire said. She turned on him a slow, faintly derisive smile that said poor little fellow. "You're not worried about breaking a few rules, are you?"

"Me?" he asked. "Me?"

"I didn't think so."

TEN

They made good use of Vivian Gladstone's bridge nights after that. A.G. figured he must be the luckiest guy on earth. The more he saw of Claire the more absorbed he became by her. When he was alone he would telephone her and tell her that he loved her and wanted her. He started dropping hints about her to his parents, and he told her that soon he would take her up to visit the Sunrise. He looked forward to that. It would be like showing her a big part of himself that she could not possibly know or understand until she saw it. The grass would be lush by late April and they could ride out by themselves and see his favorite spots. There was one hill especially he wanted to show her, not too far from the big house. They could ride up there and see for miles in every direction, all of it the Sunrise. On a spring night it was so peaceful up there, and you could look back and see lights burning in the house. He thought of how he would lean over in his saddle and kiss her, just as they do in the movies, and the smell of her would mingle with the spring night smells, grass and hay and the hint of a storm on the wind.

It took some doing to get Earl to agree to entertain this girl he had never met, but with Margaret's help he finally came around. He was annoyed to discover that A.G. was already thinking of marrying somebody unknown to the family. What did A.G. know of her background? A.G. told what he knew, but that hardly satisfied Earl. He wanted to know what Claire's track record was with other boys. What had she been like in high school? What did A.G.'s fraternity brothers know about her? A.G. had heard rumors about Claire, that she had been pretty wild, but he chose not to believe the rumors and did not pass them on to his father. He chose also, when Earl asked about Claire's parents, not to mention for the time being her father's suicide. He was afraid that Earl would conclude that Claire came from weak stock. Of course there was the case of Margaret's father, a parallel act. But A.G. held the information back. He did not want to get things off on the wrong foot from the start. He knew that he and Claire had something almost sacred together, and he was not going to compromise it.

He tried not to worry too much about his father's stubborn resistance. Surely once he saw her and got to know her, he would approve. When at last he drove her up for the weekend, he did take her riding up to his favorite hill on a spring Saturday night luminous with moonlight, a strong, warm wind hurrying clouds and their shadows. When he leaned over to kiss her, the thought came to him that he would do everything to make this girl happy and he would succeed. He had finally found what his goal in life was, and that was to make Claire happy. Everything else he did would be toward that goal. It was all so simple. It made sense out of everything. Looking out at the land with her that night on the hill, he knew that he knew where every tree was; he had practically counted every blade of grass on the tens of thousands of acres; he knew everything that had to be done on the place, every job; he knew the name of every cowboy and their families' names too, if they had families; and now he would make Claire a part of it all. Someday she would be mistress of the Sunrise, and together they would be happy. Certainly if anyone could make her happy, he could. She had a streak of temper in her, and sometimes she would get moody and angry for no reason at all that he could see, but she had not had it easy. What she needed was the peace and security he could give her. And the passion.

Up on the hill, after he had kissed her, she was silent for a while and they listened to the wind together. A.G. looked over at her, her dark hair tossing, her figure erect on the horse, and he thought to himself that if this wasn't heaven, he didn't care what heaven was. He had everything, or was about to. He was trying to put this thought into words that did not sound foolish when she said:

"Your father doesn't like me."

"What makes you say that?"

He had noticed, but he was ignoring it. He was determined to make the weekend work and he was convinced that time would take care of Earl's resistance. Between Margaret's warmth and the excitement of being there with Claire, it had been possible to push Earl's belligerence off into a corner of his consciousness, although every once in a while he would be aware of his father, start to worry, and then forge ahead because that was what he had to do. It had been Kentucky Derby Day and after lunch they had sat in the big red room drinking mint juleps, waiting for the race to start. Edward brought in a steady succession of juleps in pewter mugs with fresh mint and silver swizzle sticks that were miniature Sunrise branding irons. Claire, A.G. had noticed, had been particularly subdued and polite and appreciative, and he liked that. It was obvious that she was trying her best to make a good impression. She had asked one by one about the paintings of family members on the walls, about the Indian rugs, the hunting and livestock trophies. To him she had been just the right combination of politeness and dignity, because she had a core of pride that he loved and that she never lost. Certainly she had acted every inch the grateful guest. When the Derby came on television, she joined in the excitement, rooting for the same horse as everyone else, the horse that Earl had put money on, and when it won, she said something to Earl about its being nice to know that somebody knew how to back a horse, and she asked Earl whether he had ever considered owning racehorses.

"Yes I have considered it," was all Earl had said. Perhaps

there had been something a little irritable in Earl's tone, but again, A.G. tried to ignore it. Earl was so often irritable that it was hardly worth noticing, wasn't it? As far as A.G. was concerned, the whole weekend was going as well as he could have hoped or better.

He tried to take the edge off her statement about his father's attitude toward her. What could have given her the idea that Earl didn't like her?

"I have that feeling. I'm always right about these things."

"I think you're imagining it." His voice sounded hollow to himself.

"No. I'm not."

"You're just not used to him," A.G. said. "He's crusty, but it's just like my mother always says, underneath, he's just an old softie." A.G. thought to himself that he had heard Margaret say this so many times that it had become an article of faith with him. But he was not sure that he could prove it.

"Let's go back," A.G. said. "Ramsey's waiting for us. I want you to meet him."

Ramsey was having a snack in the kitchen. He had had to work and so had missed the Derby.

"I understand you all made a few dollars today," Ramsey said, rising to meet Claire. "I sure am glad to meet you. This son of a gun here cain't talk about nothin else."

"He talks a lot about you, too," Claire said. "I understand you're his oldest friend. That must have been a terrible ordeal you had in California."

"It's all over now. Course I'd probably still be in there, weren't for A.G. and his dad. And I'm on parole till God knows when. They gotta watch me pretty close around here."

"I can't imagine you getting into trouble," Claire said with a coquettishness that pleased A.G. She liked his friend, he could see.

"You know, I thought that filly was gonna win that damn Derby," A.G. said. "Glad I didn't bet on her."

"You don't never bet on a filly in the spring," Ramsey said. "They's always in love, didn't you know that?"

They joked and laughed for a while longer and then Claire excused herself to go up to bed. A.G. and Ramsey sat down to talk with a couple of beers.

"You like her?" A.G. asked.

"Am I a sissy, or what? A.G., any man didn't like that had better hang 'em up. Now I understand what you been talkin about."

On a Sunday morning of bright spring sun and heavy air, they set off again on horseback, after a breakfast of ham and eggs, sliced tomatoes, biscuits and cream gravy. A.G. noticed that Claire was a pretty good horsewoman for a city girl. Was there anything wrong with her at all? They covered a lot of ground. He showed her the old water well and the foundations of the old house, and he told her stories from his childhood as they rode along, how he and Ramsey had discovered this creek or that, how they had once come upon the Cherokees.

"He seems nice," Claire said. "You two were really close, weren't you?"

"Sure. Like that. Didn't you have a girlfriend you were real close to?"

"Not really. I always liked boys better."

"I bet you did."

"I don't imagine Ramsey has much trouble finding women."

"No, he sure doesn't. Old Ramsey does all right in that department."

A.G. led the way into some woods that he said his father had once talked about clearing for more pasture land but had never done anything about. In among the brilliant dogwoods and the redbuds they dismounted and drank from a creek. They lay down with their backs against a tree and listened to the birds.

"We could be a thousand miles from anywhere," Claire said.

"You like it, don't you, the ranch and everything."

"It's paradise."

A.G. decided this was the time.

"Last night," he said, "after we were in bed. I was laying there in my room. And you. You were down the hall. In your room."

"Yes?"

"And I wondered what you were thinking."

"I don't know. What were you thinking?"

"I was thinking that it sure would have been nice if we'd been in the same bed."

"You know what I was thinking?"

"No, what?"

"I was thinking I wished you'd sneak out and come into my bed."

"You were? Really?"

"Why? Does that shock you?"

"I thought of it," A.G. said. "But I didn't." He picked up a small stone and tossed it into the creek. If he had known she had been thinking that, he might have done it. But then again he might not have. "I might have woke up somebody," he said.

"Not if you'd been careful. We could have been quiet."

"Well, I was wishing we were in the same bed anyhow. Just like you."

"It's not enough to wish sometimes," Claire said. "You have to do it. A.G., I want you to be the kind of man who does things. I know you are, really. I know you're going to do great things."

"I think so too," he said, thinking that finding her would make it possible for him to do almost anything. That there was something about Claire that made you realize that, to keep her, you couldn't stand still. Whatever it was that had made her single him out, he would always have to strive to keep her. He liked that. Maybe that would prevent them from ever getting tired of each other. And it would be just the catalyst he would need to fulfill his ambitions. He was not even sure what his ambitions were yet but Claire would spur him to them.

"You're very quiet around your parents," Claire said.

"Am I?"

"Yes you are. You do a lot more listening than talking. Not like when you're around your friends. Or with me."

"Well, I'm comfortable around them."

"Not with me?"

"That's not what I meant. What I mean is, I don't have anything to prove around them. Well, in a way I do. But I already have, really. Oh, I don't know."

"You don't think you have anything to prove around me, do you?"

"Do I?"

"Of course not."

"You're pretty quiet around your mother, too."

"That's different."

"Why is it different?"

"Because she's crazy, and besides, I don't want to get into it with her when you're around. I don't think you should have to listen to that."

"You really let her have it when you're alone?"

"You bet I do. Let's not talk about it."

"Tell me what you say to her."

"Let's put it this way. I know she doesn't really love me, and I don't let her get away with pretending she does."

"I'm sure she must love you."

"No, she does not. And I also don't let her get away with running my life, which believe me she would like to do."

"How does she want to do that?"

"Oh, A.G., let's not talk about it now. I really don't want to talk about it."

"O.K.," he said, and fell silent. There was a strain in Claire's voice that made him concerned for her. She must have suffered a great deal. Imagine if your father killed himself and you believed your mother didn't love you. But as he thought about it he realized that what he felt for her was not pity at all but admiration. She was proud, independent, vivacious in spite of all this or because of it. She was someone he could look to as an example of personal triumph. Someone else under the same circumstances would be spilling it to a psychiatrist three times a week for years or the rest of her life. Claire simply faced it, spat on it and went ahead. She seemed the sort of person who could overcome anything. If the world came to an end, Claire might just be the last one there atop the rubbish heap with her fist clenched. He imagined what sort of a mother she would be. No one would touch her child and come away unscathed. It was funny to think that here was this city girl who seemed to have all the virtues of the land. City people were weak, divided, confused, and generally fouled up under the banner of progressive thinking. That was what Earl had always said and Earl was right. But Claire was the exception. Claire was a woman you could count on.

"Claire," A.G. said after a while listening some more to the birds and a rising wind that was making the temperature drop. "Claire, I wish something else. I wish you'd marry me." He felt his face flush as he said it. When he uttered it to her, the word "marry" had a mysterious force to it. He waited for her to reply and had the idea that he could feel the trees growing in the interval.

"That's a beautiful wish," she said and rolled up against him.

"Well. Will you?"

"I'll have to see," she said. She dropped one hand onto the front of his jeans.

"See what?"

"I don't know," she said. "Kiss me."

They got their jeans off, spread them on the ground, and made love there in the woods, squirming off the blanket of jeans and onto the ground and not noticing when the rocks and twigs dug into them. They clutched and struggled for a good long time. A.G. managed to open her shirt as he thrust at her and to glance down to wonder at her breast exposed to the air, and as the moment came he kissed her hard again, crushing her head back against the tree trunk. She gasped, tore her mouth away and breathed at him, "I'll marry you, I'll marry you, I'll marry marry marry marry marry you, A.G., marry you!"

As they lay entangled, quiet, A.G. thought he felt a drop of rain or two, and he looked over to see the surface of the creek puckered with drops.

"Starting to rain," he said. "We better go."

"Can't we just stay here and drown?" Claire asked. She shuddered as he pulled away from her.

"Come on," he said.

They were nearly a half hour's ride from the big house, and by the time they were halfway the storm was on them. Veins of lightning flashed to the west against a black sky. A.G. began to think tornado, but he had little doubt that they would make it back safely, so he did not try to go at full speed, for fear that Claire might fall. As they rode through the open pastures the sky was a swirling vault of light and color above them, moving, changing, the light around them purple and then a luminous orange, then purple again, then gray. They arrived drenched but in high spirits, and after hot baths they settled down in front of the television in the living room to watch the weather reports with Earl and Margaret. There was no point in trying to drive back to Norman with this storm. They would stay another night. Tornado watches and warnings were out in all the neighboring counties. One did hit Salina that night, killing seven people, and in parts of Tulsa families climbed to their rooftops to escape the flooding.

But on the Sunrise everyone was safe. Snug inside the house with a fire blazing, they stayed up half the night listening to the storm reports, with Edward supplying hot toddies. Earl dozed a lot and Claire managed to have a long talk with Margaret, who told her what it had been like in the old days during storms, before the big house had been built. They had lost a barn once twenty-five years before, but other than that they had always been spared. Margaret told Claire about all the hard work and the dedication and how they had raised A.G. to appreciate what had to be done to build a place like this and keep it going. She could see that Claire came from strong stock, too.

"My daddy killed himself," Claire said.

"That doesn't matter," Margaret said. "So did mine. Sometimes we women have to be stronger, just so the men can be as strong as they can be."

"You think women are stronger than men?"

"I didn't say that. I didn't say that at all. Looking at you, I can see you know a lot. I can see you weren't raised on a pile of logs."

"Well, Margaret, what do you think a woman should do? I mean, what's the best thing a woman can give her husband?"

"Loyalty. Loyalty first and last. With a man, it's the same, only a little different."

"How different?"

"A disloyal woman, she's loose. She's a slut, is what she is."

"Isn't that a double standard?"

"Of course it's a double standard! And it's what makes things work!"

"But Margaret. Isn't there such a thing as a male slut?"

"Yes, dear. A male slut is a man who goes to bed with other men."

Claire had to laugh a little at this, and she asked:

"Then what do you call a man who goes to bed with other women?"

"Why, Claire," Margaret smiled, "that's a Don Juan. With his sword flashin and his .45 a-blazin!"

"Well this certainly is a happy occasion," Vivian Gladstone said. Claire and A.G. had become formally engaged, and the

Krugers and the Gladstones were celebrating with a dinner at the Summit Club in Tulsa. Earl was a member there. He also belonged to the Tulsa Club and to Southern Hills Country Club, both of which were more exclusive than the Summit, but Earl had decided that the dinner should be at the Summit because, as he said to Margaret, "Those two bitches are climbers if I ever saw one. Well let them wait a little." Vivian Gladstone had been hoping for Southern Hills, the place where oil deals were made on the fairways. There had been a time when the dream of the day when Gerald would be able to get a membership at Southern Hills had sustained her, and she had brought the matter up with him again and again, because she knew that having a membership there would solve all of her entertaining problems and would put her on a par with anyone. After Gerald had shot himself she had realized that to hope for a Southern Hills membership from a man who worked for the Bureau of Indian Affairs had been totally unrealistic, but you have to dream, don't you, she told herself, and if fate had dictated that she marry a man who just was not enough of a dreamer and a go-getter, she would have to learn to accept it. She would never have a membership at the Temple, as Southern Hills was known, but she could pass on her dreams to her daughter, and by God, it looked now as if the dreams were about to be fulfilled. Gazing around the dining room at the Summit Club, she noticed a U.S. Senator and the minister of the First Presbyterian Church, and she felt wonderful. Claire had made her swear not to tell the story of Gerald's anniversary dinner, had told her that if she breathed one word about it or about anything sordid and degrading she would walk out and see to it that never again after that would Vivian be allowed any contact whatsoever with her new relatives and that for that matter Claire herself would never speak to her again, ever, but Vivian found that she had plenty to say, marveling at the view from the thirtieth floor.

"I admire this view so much."

"Isn't it wonderful," Margaret said. "It's heaven."

Through the huge windows the Arkansas River swooped in shining arcs below, past the refinery that glittered like a miniature city through the night, a shimmering, spidery lighted metal network of prosperity. Beyond the refinery lay shadowy wooded hills, with television towers atop them, blinking. You could sit having a couple of drinks at the Summit Club, take in that view, and feel that you were ascending toward the stars on a mountain of cash.

"There is something about this city that is so bright and cheerful," Vivian said. "I have always loved Tulsa."

"You find a few billion barrels of oil and you can build a pretty fair city," Earl said. "It's not like cattle, that you have to work at it."

"I wouldn't trade the Sunrise," Margaret said. "And now with A.G. coming back and Claire joining us, it's gonna be so great. Don't you think so, Earl?"

"Sure." He ordered another double Wild Turkey and soda.

"I certainly would like another Scotch and water," Vivian said. "There is nothing like it. Scotch cannot—"

"I'll have another one too," Claire said.

"Another round," A.G. said. "And let me see the wine list."

"Order what you want, son," Earl said. "This is your party."

A.G. ordered two bottles of Montrachet to begin with and followed up with two bottles each of Lafite and Haut Brion.

"I never cared much for wine," Vivian said.

"Try some," A.G. said.

"Well, that's pretty good. If you all don't mind, though, I'll stick to my Scotch and water."

As they made their way through oysters, snails, salmon, steak with peppers, even Earl mellowed. He was involved in the wine as deeply as anyone but he had also taken the precaution of a steady supply of booze. Now, with the last mousse cleared away and the Rémy Martin and Grand Marnier flowing, Earl managed to rise and propose a toast:

"To the best goddamned son a man ever had. And to a beautiful young woman who'll be a credit to the Sunrise and bring us grandchildren."

Applause, applause. A.G. then toasted Claire, his parents, and his new mother-in-law, and he presented Claire with a diamond ring. "My God," Vivian said, "it's almost knuckle to knuckle." Claire toasted A.G. and their love. Finally it was Vivian's turn. She protested that she was not much at making speeches, but everyone insisted and urged her on.

"I don't know what to say," Vivian said. "I'm really at a loss for words. I, well, I can't tell you all what this moment means to me. My daughter here, Claire, we have been through some rough times together. My late husband, Gerald—" Claire gave her a good kick. "Gerald would have been so very proud to see this. And I want to include him in this toast. He was a saintly man, in many ways." Another kick from Claire. "But there is no use dwelling on the past. I always tell my students, as you know I have done substitute teaching for some years, I always tell my students that today well lived makes every yesterday a dream of happiness. And every tomorrow a vision of hope. I live by that and I know you all do too. Otherwise there would not be such a place as the Sunrise. And this boy here, he is a fine young man. Everybody knows it who meets him when he walks into a room. And he is marrying a fine young woman who frankly could of won any beauty contest." Kick. "I do say that if a woman has a choice in the matter, which they don't, then why not be attractive and beautiful? They say that the eyes are the windows of the soul, so you can look into my girl's eyes and see a beautiful soul. When my parents came to Oklahoma it wasn't even Oklahoma and times were tough. They lived in a log house in the west and they were just plain farmers. Well that didn't work out too well. Gerald's parents, they were educated from Pennsylvania and how he developed this thing about the Indians I don't know. I don't believe I ever did see an Indian until I met Gerald, and then they were all over, he would invite them into the house. That was all right. They never did steal anything, though I kept an eye out. And I kept Claire out of sight, you can believe that. It may be Gerald learned to drink from the Indians for all I know. I don't know how it got started." Claire had given up now. She finished off her Grand Marnier and poured some of A.G.'s cognac into her glass. "But we all have our faults. Even Claire has her faults though they are not of a kind that would interfere with a long and happy marriage, I don't mean to imply that. I believe in marriage. I believe in the institution of marriage. I also believe that no one is perfect. A little rain must fall. The test is whether you endure it and get on with it. Human is by nature frail. We all fall off the beaten track once or twice. There is a fling here, flung there. By God sometimes it may be it does a person good. I am not one to cast stones." Vivian took a deep breath, placed her hands under her breasts and gave them a vigorous upward push. "What I mean to say is"—and here she faltered, her eyes filling up—"I am so happy to be here, so happy for my beloved Claire, and I say it with tears streaming down my eyes, God love you all." And here she collapsed back into her chair.

The Krugers all said they loved Vivian too. Earl called for the check, and A.G. helped Vivian into the elevator.

ELEVEN

The wedding was so much an expression of the power and the glory of the Sunrise that the bride and groom seemed almost irrelevant. Nearly a thousand guests, bankers, ranchers, politicians, cowboys, oil men and ordinary people from that part of the state swarmed over the great lawn on the Sunday afternoon. The Political Chief of the Cherokee Nation, William Keeler, who also happened to be the chairman of the board of Phillips Petroleum, was there, and the governor of Oklahoma and the O.U. football coach. It would have been a good day to do some business. No one enjoyed it more than Vivian Gladstone, who said to Claire that if only Gerald had lived to see it, he would never have killed himself.

An altar of sorts, candles and flowers and white ribbons, was set up under a sky blue and dotted with little puffy clouds hanging like cottonballs. Before the altar stood U.S. District Judge Byron Burroughs, of whom Earl was fond of saying that he liked and respected a man who had the courage to do what was right and not worry about the legal niceties. Vivian would have preferred a minister, but when she asked Earl about it, he said simply no, Judge Burroughs would perform the ceremony. The groom and his best man, Ramsey, marched to the altar. Billy Parker's Western Swing Band struck up the music, and Claire, radiant in a white gown paid for by the Krugers, swept down the aisle on the arm of her uncle. Her beauty set the crowd to murmuring. When she was just a few yards away, Ramsey whispered to A.G., "You lucky son of a bitch."

It was a brief service. The judge made a little speech on the subject of marriage, happiness and responsibility, punctuated by "As ye sow, so shall ye reap"; the couple exchanged their deep-sworn vows; and then there they were, joined, kissing, a good, long kiss that evoked a few cowboy whoops from the guests.

The receiving line took over an hour, and by the time A.G. was able to step aside for a chat with some of the boys, he was well past nervousness and full enough of champagne to say:

"I don't feel much different. Drunk feels about the same married or single."

"It's divorced drunk feels different," Sam said. "My case, I been happily divorced twenty-two years come my next divorce anniversary."

"This one is for keeps," A.G. said.

"Tell you what," Ramsey said, "you ever decide to split with Claire, I got first dibs. Aw, hell, she's too high-class for me, ain't she. She's gotta have a high-toned educated asshole like my buddy here, right?"

"You may be ignorant," A.G. said, "but I can still take you arm-wrestling."

"The hell you say!"

In a second A.G. and Ramsey had stripped off their tux jackets and were on the grass, locked in arm-combat. They both looked dead serious, grunting, veins bulging. Ramsey could not figure out why A.G. had challenged him on this day, because Ramsey almost always won these battles, but just as he began to feel A.G. weaken, he decided to let him win, just this once. And when it was over, Ramsey said:

"Hell, A.G., you must be feelin pretty good. I might have to try this marriage stuff myself."

"Where's my bride?"

Claire was less impressed by the extravagance of the reception than by the way A.G. was treating her: attentively, solicitously, just what she needed. In the previous months she had had trouble keeping straight her own interest in him and her mother's interest in the Krugers, and there had been nights when she had lain awake wondering what she was getting into. Vivian had been enthusiastic about A.G. before Claire had. That first summer after they had started going out, Vivian had gone on every day about how A.G. must not be let to slip away and how she thought it would have to be her duty to move to Norman to make sure that nothing went wrong.

"You do that, we're going to have a knockdown-dragout," Claire had said.

"I wouldn't do anything to upset you," Vivian had said. "Still and all, I believe I am free, white and twenty-one the last time I looked and I ought to be able to move anywhere in the state I choose to or in the world for that matter."

When A.G. had written to her, that letter that she had found simple and touching and rather naive, she had been more or less inclined to write back, but she had delayed just to defy Vivian. She was not at all sure how she felt about him then, and she saw several other men that summer in San Antonio, and not only to get away from her relatives, as she had told A.G. She was not ready to be tied down. She had done very well in school and had considered transferring east to finish her degree, because as long as she had declined to be a football queen she felt she was wasting her time academically at O.U. She read a lot and had even toyed with the idea of not getting married for a long time. She thought she might want to try her luck in the world. The idea was not popular with her mother or with anyone else she knew, so she kept it to herself. She thought about it when she read books by women writers. So many of them seemed to be about the horrible effects of marriage on women. And as for A.G., when she had first met him she had not cared much for his blustering and drinking nor even that much for his fast driving, although she knew he thought she did; but there was another side of him, she began to see, and the more she went out with him the more she began to appreciate that other side, the gentleness, the sensitivity, that side of him that appreciated her and that grew

more and more devoted to her, that side of him—she began to
believe it was the only true part of him—that she could join
herself to and that she might even be able to help to shape or
to form or perhaps to lead, if that was the right word, in
directions that would be so good for him and of course for her.
That was one certainty about A.G.: he was unformed, in many
ways. Not to deny for a minute his virtues. His sensitivity, his
intensity in relation to her. Physically he was very attractive to
her, especially when they were alone. But his being in other
ways unformed and she had to say it downright ignorant about
most things outside of his world presented all sorts of possibilities and challenges that were even more attractive to her than
his wealth and future power, whatever her mother thought.
Sometimes she was so overcome with feeling for him at the
thought of all she might be able to do for him that she wished
she could never have to let go of him, could carry him around
kangaroo-style. He was like beautiful marble that she could
chisel into shape or soft clay that she could plunge her fingers
into and press and squeeze into perfection. She sensed that his
love for her was so complete and almost frighteningly unselfish
that he would gladly, eagerly let her show him things he would
otherwise never know.

Once, not long after she had begun to sleep with A.G., she
had called up one of her old boyfriends and had gone to see
him and had slept with him in his room after he had got his
roommate to leave for the night. It was not that she was in any
way attached to the old boyfriend, she was not, that was just
the point. She would never have told A.G. because he would
never have understood, but she and the old boyfriend could
share a casual and emotionally uncomplicated sort of sex that
A.G. either could not understand at all or, probably, associated
with whores. She and the old boyfriend, who knew who A.G.
was but was not a friend of his or a fraternity brother, so there
was no danger of his ratting on her, had hardly had to speak.
Each knew what the other wanted and each was more than

willing to give it and take it. You could say that the sex with
A.G. was more intense not merely because it was newer but
because it was emotionally deeper. She would not forget the
look on A.G.'s face the first time he had made love to her, there
in her mother's bed with the framed picture of Gerald Gladstone in his army uniform staring at them mildly from the
bedside table. A.G. had looked like a creature possessed. He
had a wild look and when he had come he had groaned and
opened his mouth, stared at her with wide eyes almost as
though he was being stabbed in the back, and she had actually
been able to feel it spurt inside of her, seven or eight strong
spurts, and she could not remember feeling that before, or
never so strong and so much. You would have thought it was
Genesis or something and she remembered thinking thank God
I am on the pill, that would have been it for sure. The little
escapade with the old boyfriend had simply brought herself
back to herself, given her back her self-reliance when A.G., she
had begun to worry, was overwhelming her with passionate
intensity.

Claire of course had never had money, but neither had she
ever had reason to doubt her attractiveness to men, not once
the blooms and rhythms of adolescence had taken her over.
Before that, after Gerald's suicide, she had gone into a kind of
retreat for a couple of years and had rebuffed the first tentative
gropings of young little males, had created for herself the reputation of a frightened prude who would just as soon slap you
as give in to a kiss when kids gathered in a garage or in
someone's vacant house for initial explorations. In those days
she had fed herself on romantic novels of the sort that never
quite allow anything to happen before your eyes but imply it
sufficiently so that delicate or reluctant sensibilities can be titil-
lated but never offended. She wanted to be like the heroines,
wanted men to be unable to resist the sight of her on a stair-
way or in a room, but she saw herself as plain and at the ages
of twelve and even thirteen was resigned to a life of looking

on, of never being Scarlett but rather her younger sister, and she was vaguely conscious in herself of a combination of self-deprecation and resentment, sometimes sharp, against boys for ignoring her and not realizing that beneath her barely discernible breast beat a heart big enough to encompass a man and not only a man but a castle or a plantation or a fashionable house on Fifth Avenue along with him. But if boys were that unperceptive, she would avoid them and someday get back at them some other way. She did not bite her nails or pick at scabs or cut off her eyebrows or do any other of the nervous things typical of young girls, but she did sometimes disappear into the woods that still existed then in Tulsa beyond 31st Street and take off her clothes to run around, she imagined, like a nymph looking for Pan or a young woman abandoned by a cruel lieutenant who had promised to carry her off but had cast her off his horse, stripped her, inflicted stinging slashes and puncture wounds with his rapier and instructed her to seek for her salvation a secret underground passage beneath a certain charmed oak tree, a passage that would lead her after several days' journey back to her bedroom where she would be protected by stuffed animals. She was to speak to no one and not comment if anyone should look upon or attempt to touch her naked body, nor was she to attempt to cover herself with leaves.

Going to Monte Casino high school was a help to Claire, she always thought. On the very first day there she was taken with the statue of Jennifer Jones that the nuns had placed in a little grotto lit with blue lights. It was Jennifer Jones as St. Bernadette in stone, and during the first week of school the nuns showed the movie called *The Song of Bernadette*, with Monte Casino's most famous alumna in the starring role, and after the movie Claire was even more fascinated by the statue, because a couple of the nuns and some of the girls told her she looked just like Jennifer Jones. Claire was pleased, not only because she was flattered by the physical comparison but because she

knew that she had already achieved an established place at
Monte Casino. She preferred Jennifer Jones in some of her
other roles, *Love Is a Many Splendored Thing*, for instance,
but it was fun having a statue and a grotto dedicated almost to
yourself.

Claire came from mixed Protestant stock. Her mother had
sent her to Monte Casino for the education rather than the
religion, and Claire was only once or twice seriously tempted
to convert. There were a number of Protestant girls at the
school and the nuns soft-pedaled the proselytizing. But Claire
enjoyed the mystery of Catholicism and she did envy the girls
who could go to confession, because the idea of climbing into a
darkened chamber and whispering sins to a man appealed to
her. She also liked the flowers and the statues and the golden
chalice in the chapel at Cascia Hall, the boys' school, because
it was almost like owning them to be able to go into the chapel
at any time and see them; and she liked the boys at Cascia. It
seemed just right to have them over there in the other buildings across the lawn, beyond the Jennifer Jones statue, not in
the same class but available. You would see them in chapel
and at dances. They began asking her out. The nuns were very
good teachers and she was happy at Monte Casino. It seemed
ideal to be advancing her mind, to have just enough of the
beauties of Catholicism, and to have the Cascia boys and her
feelings inflamed toward them by the nuns' cautions against
them. Occasionally the nuns would have a priest in to warn the
girls about boys. There was one priest especially, a handsome
man with dark hair and pale skin who probably had to shave
twice a day, who told the girls that being alone with a boy was
like throwing cayenne pepper into chili and having too much
beer along with it. This was in her junior year, when many of
the Cascia boys already had cars, and that evening after the
sermon she sat with her date in his car on what was known as
the social row at Pennington's Drive-in and ordered a large
bowl of chili. She liked the boy well enough and when she had

finished the chili she asked him whether he knew where they could get some beer. They got a six-pack and drank it parked by the river. High school was full of pleasant incidents like that. She always had a lot of boyfriends and never let any of them think that she was in love with them. If a boy got too close, emotionally, she felt smothered.

That was the one trouble about marrying into the Kruger family. To A.G. that first weekend they had spent together on the Sunrise had been idyllic. To her it had been almost so, but something else besides, possibly a lesson in her limitations or possibly a lesson in their limitations, she could not say which. She had felt dwarfed by the scale of Kruger life, but then maybe it was that they, with their ways so established and set and invincible, could not accommodate someone like her, who had her own ideas and her own sense of herself. It had been enough of a battle to keep her mother from running her life. Was she to surrender it now to someone else, to another family, to what amounted to an empire? Through Monte Casino and Cascia she had known several rich Tulsa families and had heard about a lot of others, but it had been, she supposed, not too different from growing up in any other city of comparable size in America. Oh there had been the guy who had decided to have a beach party at his house and had ordered tons of sand delivered to his back yard; and she had heard about Hobby Day at Cascia when Charles Campbell had had his black chauffeur spend three days setting up his model trains in the gymnasium. Things like that. And at O.U. the oil rich were always flying in and out. But the Krugers were different. Visiting them was like visiting the Oklahoma you read about in books and that everyone thought was dead. Certainly it appealed to her. The ranch was beautiful and grand, the obvious money and its power awesome, but there was something raw about it all that put her off. The old man, especially.

He had done nothing overt, but she had felt his suspicion,

even his scorn, like a razor. What was it? Didn't she look
enough like a pioneer woman? Did he want his son to marry
someone who knew how to slop hogs? You could certainly say
that the Krugers were genuine, genuine articles, whatever that
meant, but you could also say that they lacked a certain refine-
ment. She had been shocked by the way the old man shouted
at the servants, though they didn't seem to mind it. The Krugers seemed to have very little culture, well maybe Mrs.
Kruger did, but she would be willing to bet that the old man
had never heard of Beethoven, let alone William Faulkner.
Claire had had ideas of marrying a famous writer or someone
successful in the arts. A.G. had a lot of sensitivity but it was
obvious what he was going to do with his life.

She had to admit that seeing A.G. on the Sunrise was a
pleasure. Obviously he was at home there in a way that she
had never seen anyone at home, and for the first time Claire had
a sense of what it meant to own land and to feel a part of it.
She had read about how small farmers in Oklahoma had clung
to miserable plots of land during the Depression as if to leave
would be to die; of how others had gone to California and
come back; and of course she had read about the furious
mania that had come over people when the chance to stake out
Oklahoma land had been offered during the land runs in the
1880s. Seeing A.G. on the ranch had made her understand
more. He had an ease and a sure-footed enthusiasm there that
he had nowhere else. It might be that as his wife she could
acquire that for herself. After all, the whole place would be
theirs someday. She did not care for A.G.'s obvious and, to her
mind, extreme deference to his parents. She would have to
work on him, build him up, make him feel his own man, bound
to her, so that when and if the time came he would have the
backbone to buck his parents. She could give him a lot if she
gave him that. And that way she could maintain her own
independence and integrity and even power. For weeks before
actually visiting the Sunrise, she had had doubts about what

she was getting into. She knew that A.G. was intelligent but he could not be called her intellectual equal, simply because he didn't seem to care about those things. She had actually had serious doubts about him right up to the moment under the tree when he had asked her finally and formally to marry him and they had made love. There was really no going back after that. Good God, woods and streams and fields and making love and thunder and lightning. Who could resist it?

Now, on the day itself, surrounded by hundreds of guests, watching her mother fawn, feeling trapped between Earl's indifference or coldness and Margaret's warmth, she was grateful for A.G.'s attentiveness and overt pride in her, and she felt so drawn to him that she wondered whether it had been love she had felt for him until then. She even whispered to him that she loved him, and that was rare for her, because usually she told him that she loved him only in response to his declarations, and as she said it she was aware of what a difference there was between the phrases "I love you" and "I love you too." The first could be passion and the second was mere courtesy. For good measure she whispered the first again, and she could tell that it penetrated his heart, and she thought to herself, it will work, it will work, A.G., if you put me first, always.

TWELVE

Claire drank a lot of champagne at her wedding. When she and A.G. finally got into their new Cadillac to drive off to Colorado, he was sober and she was pretty far gone. She felt as though she had just fallen in love with him, and only a fierce impulse to self-concealment prevented her from expressing a weirdly abject gratitude to him. I am drunk, she said to herself; I won't feel this way in an hour or two. But she started sobbing. A.G. pulled the car over.

"What's the matter, Claire? What's wrong?"

"You're just so good, that's all. You're a good person. I don't think I'm worthy of you." She wished she had not said that. She was not at all sure she meant it, but it had come out. She would have to find some way of correcting it, of righting the balance, later. He could take advantage of it and it didn't make sense. She fell over toward him and put her head in his lap. "I don't care about the Sunrise." She blubbered on, unable to stop herself. "I just care about you. I don't think you even know how good you are. You think you're tough sometimes. I want you to be strong. You're just good, that's all."

"Well I guess I'll do. But you'll love the Sunrise. I promise. We'll make it even better. We will together." He squeezed her hand. She dried her eyes.

"In a way, you know," Claire said, "I wish we could have run off together. Just you and me. And gotten married somewhere where nobody knew us."

"You know what they say. Weddings are for the parents."

"I know. But imagine some little place far away. In Switzerland maybe. Imagine getting married in some little church in

Switzerland and then spending our honeymoon in a little chalet in the Alps with a fire going in the bedroom. We could get snowed in. Wouldn't that be romantic?"

"Yes. We can do that sometime. I hear the Broadmoor is nice, though. I think you'll like it. I was there with my parents once but I was too young to remember."

Claire began to hum "Isn't It Romantic." Then she tried the radio, could not find anything to her liking, switched it off.

"I wonder what we'll do tomorrow," A.G. said. "I understand there's a whole lot to do there. Swimming."

"I want breakfast in bed."

"You'll get it."

"A.G.?"

"Yes?"

"There's only one thing that bothers me."

"What's that?"

"Your father doesn't like me. Why doesn't he like me?"

"You're imagining that. My mother told me, he just wants to protect me, that's all. When he gets to know you."

"Why do you care what he thinks?"

"Why?"

Claire sat up and looked at him.

"Yes," she said. What had felt like unfathomable love a minute before was turning into something else. "Why do you care what he thinks? About me or about anything else?"

"I don't know what you mean. I don't know that I do. Care that much. I mean, I'm the one who loves you."

Claire was silent for a moment. Her head bobbed slightly from front to back. She bit her lip and clenched one fist, as though trying to get hold of something.

"You disappoint me," she said.

"I disappoint you?"

"Deeply."

"I disappoint you deeply already? Well ain't that the shits."

"You don't understand yourself."

"Jesus Christ Almighty. Here we are just married going on our goddamned honeymoon for Christsake and you pick this time to tell me I don't understand myself."

"Is there anything to drink? Is there any more champagne?"

"There's a bottle of Scotch under your seat."

She reached under for the bottle and took a good long pull out of it. A.G. took it from her and drank from it himself. They stared at each other, then fell silent for minutes. Claire moved away from him, settling near the door, her arms folded.

"Why are you making trouble?" A.G. said. She did not respond. "Damnit. Talk to me! What's eating you?"

"You! I'll tell you why your father doesn't like me. Because he knows you're Daddy's boy and he wants to keep you that way."

"Claire."

"He can take one look at me and know I'm trouble, as far as he's concerned. As far as keeping little A.G. under his boot is concerned. You are so under his boot, I suppose you told him you weren't the first person I ever slept with and asked his permission if it was all right to marry me anyway."

A.G. felt so much assaulted by the accusations that he had one reaction and then another and they canceled each other out. He felt welling within him an impulse to hit her but he also felt stung and numbed by everything she was saying. He had never discussed her past love life in any detail with her. He had preferred not to know about it or to believe what he wished to about it or to leave it for some time in the future when they could talk about it in the best of circumstances, in front of the fire maybe, in an atmosphere of love. He wondered why she had suddenly called him a daddy's boy and he resented it. It occurred to him that if you had a failed father and a mother like Vivian then maybe it was hard for you to understand why somebody with parents like his might love them and respect them and want to do everything he could to continue earning their respect and to live up to their expectations of him. What expectations did she have to live up to, anyway? Considering her relative disadvantages made him think that perhaps he was not being fair to her. He was beginning to swerve toward feeling sorry for her and was thinking that this was maybe one of those times that putting your arms around someone solved a lot of problems, when she began again:

"You think that just because you were born on the Sunrise you know anything about life? You don't know how people live. You don't know how people suffer and die." She took the bottle from him again and swigged from it. "You know why you don't know? Because you're a daddy's boy! You're Daddy's boy and you do everything Daddy says and you don't make a move without checking with Daddy!"

"Claire."

"Shut up!"

This time he did slap her on the side of the face, but immediately he regretted it. It only spurred her on.

"Sick! What kind of a man is it that hits a woman? You think you're some kind of a cowboy, Daddy's boy? What century do you think this is? What do you know about anything? What have you ever done? Your daddy got you out of Vietnam. Fine. Just as well. What good would you have done?"

"Shut up."

"All right. Sure. You don't want to hear it. You don't want to hear anything and you don't want to do anything. Because you can't do anything. You can't even ride a horse."

"What are you talking about?"

"You can't even ride. All right, you can. Why not? Your daddy taught you. Why not? You can drive a car, too, and you know how not to pee in your pants. What else? You couldn't even teach school."

"Why the hell would I want to teach school?"

"Because you have to know something to teach school, and what do you know? Nothing."

"Teach school and starve to death."

"Money. All you care about is money because that's all you have, Daddy's boy. Soft face. Write a check. That's it. A problem comes up, write a check. Go on. Write one. Write me off. Put me on the accounts. Debits. Would have been better you'd gone in the army. Stand on your own. You could use a little basic training. How to be a human being. How to be a man. You're going to be one of those men never look their age. And you know why? Because you've never done anything and you never will do anything. Tulsa's full of men like you. Failures with a bank account. Don't think I don't know plenty of them. Maybe you should open up a hot-dog stand. Maybe you should get a job cleaning urinals in the Mayo Hotel. Shine shoes. Be a barber. Do something. Learn a trade. *Call Daddy.* You know what? There's even a word for men like you. You know what it is? Silver spooner."

A.G. could not believe what was happening to his wedding day. Neither could he make sense of the avalanche that was coming, nor did he want to make sense of it. Claire had turned gray.

"You look like you need to puke," A.G. said, not without pleasure.

She looked at him defiantly for a moment and then banged her head against the window. He started the motor to work the electric windows, pushed the button and lowered her side. She stuck her head out and he tried to make a fast getaway in hopes that the wind might carry off what she was letting fly, but some of it was blown into the back seat and the rest splattered over the rear side window and down over the car. Shit, A.G. thought, that stuff will eat right through paint. He drove fast toward Colorado, hitting ninety, half hoping he would be stopped so the cop would comment on her condition and the mess she had made.

Claire passed out and A.G. kept on driving. Her fury had erupted so suddenly that she had not really given him time to catch up to her. Even when he had slapped her he had been conscious specifically of doing it to silence her, and he had been able to calculate the exact force of the blow. Maybe if he had hit her good and hard she would have shut up. But that would have been an even better way to start their marriage, wouldn't it, beating her up. He went over what he could remember of her tirade and tried to make some sense of it, failed, and began to wonder in a vague way whether he had done something wrong, or had failed to do something. Certainly she could not have erupted out of nowhere. The more he thought about it, the more he felt wounded, with that particular frustration that comes from feeling that you have offered someone everything you knew how to offer and that somehow they have come to hate you for it. He remembered his father saying that the reason you don't loan money to people even when they need it is that they end up hating you for it. Even if they get on their feet after that, looking at you reminds them of when they were down, and they hate you. A man had to make enough enemies in the world without going around inventing them for himself. Was this what was happening with Claire? Did she hate him for giving himself to her? He didn't know what to do. He could not help loving her. He would love her even after this, he knew. What was the answer?

He glanced over at her. She looked helpless and innocent. Maybe he had not taken into account the pressures that must have been on her. Her mother. Coming into a family like his. He had tried to protect her, and he had simply ignored what he knew to be his father's doubts. That was certainly not being a daddy's boy. He told himself that he absolutely refused to feel guilty about the Vietnam business. His father had said that by this time anyone who went over there was either a nigger or a fool, and A.G. agreed with the sentiment, although by now he would have phrased it differently. He reminded himself of how he really felt about Claire. Her strength and independent-mindedness drew him toward her as much as her beauty, and as for that, he was as excited by the underside of her arm or behind her knee as by any of the obvious features, and that was one way he knew it was love. He remembered how he would gaze after her when he let her off at the sorority house. He knew he loved her. What the hell was the matter with her? Him?

"Where are we?" She was stirring. It was dark.

"Almost to Colorado," A.G. said. He wished he could see her. "How you feelin?"

"All right. What happened?"

"You just had a couple too many drinks is all."

"I'm sorry. I said some mean things, didn't I?"

"I'll say you did. What the hell were you runnin on about, anyhow?"

"I'm sorry. I didn't know what I was saying. I don't know when it was the last time I got that way."

"Forget it."

Things went better after that. The next morning they walked out from the Broadmoor Hotel for a stroll through the woods, chasing each other in and out of the pine trees, and they picnicked at the foot of Cheyenne Mountain. A.G. dug a little hole in the ground, made some mysterious signs over it and covered it up again.

"What was that?" Claire asked.

"I just buried our argument," A.G. said. "Right at the foot of Cheyenne Mountain. It's an old Indian custom."

"Bull. You're making it up."

"So what if I am? It's buried, isn't it? You don't know. It may be the last argument we ever have."

"That's unrealistic."

"I don't care. I'm not a realistic guy. I believe anything can happen. Look at us. Who would've thought?"

Claire spent a lot of time looking around the shops at the Broadmoor. Her favorite was Montaldo's and there was a two-hundred-and-fifty-dollar dress there that she eyed. Finally she told A.G. that she would like it.

"Sure," he said. "Try it on."

"Maybe I should have said 'May I have it.'"

"What? Go ahead. Try it on."

She bought the dress and two others. A.G. put them on the hotel bill and told her he couldn't wait till she wore them.

"There's an Abercrombie's here," Claire said. "Let's go over there and get you something."

"I don't really want anything," A.G. said.

"Come on. We'll just go look."

She was taken by certain shirts and A.G. finally agreed to get one, then changed his mind and ordered twenty.

"Would you like those monogrammed, sir?"

"Monogrammed? Well sure. I tell you what. Put the Sunrise brand on 'em."

"I don't know if we do brands, sir. Initials."

"You can do a goddamned initial, you can do a brand. For Christsake, I bought twenty."

"Which brand was that?"

"Sunrise. You mean you don't know what the Sunrise brand looks like?"

"I'm afraid not."

"Well, I don't suppose you'd know one end of a cow from another anyway. Here. I'll do a goddamned drawing for you."

"You think your seamstress or whatever she is can do that?"

"I hope so, sir."

"Well here's another twenty dollars says she can."

That night they had a dinner full of whispers under the chandeliers in the Penrose Room. Claire wore one of her new dresses and A.G. said he had never seen anything like it. She asked him several times whether it really looked all right. She had never worn let alone owned a dress that expensive. She could see that she looked elegant and striking in it. She could tell that the Penrose Room had quieted when she had entered and it was obvious that she was making a good impression. A.G.'s reaction and even something in the waiters' manner told her that. But she could not help feeling somewhat ill at ease at the same time that she was proud and ready to take on the manner of her new station in life. She was keenly drawn to A.G. that evening and thought to herself how well he handled the ordering and how pleasant it was to be with someone who knew which wine to choose and did not have to ponder the bargains. Up in their room, when she finally slipped the dress off and they threw themselves half-drunkenly into bed, she went after him in a frenzy, and when they lay there sweaty in each other's arms and A.G. suggested ordering up a bottle of Rémy Martin she said she thought it was the most wonderful idea she had ever heard in the whole world.

After three days at the Broadmoor, Claire began to get restless. When they weren't in bed there was not much to do, and although A.G. seemed content to do nothing with her, she got fidgety. Neither of them played golf, she didn't play tennis well at all, and they had done as much walking around as they could. It did seem silly to spend their honeymoon playing cards. Claire had been disappointed when Earl and Margaret announced that the honeymoon would be at the Broadmoor, but she had decided not to say anything and to make the best of it. A.G. had accepted the decision as though it had been foreordained or as though he had made it himself, and to tell the truth, the wedding itself had been such a big event and had involved so much planning that neither Claire nor A.G. had worried much about what would follow. A couple of weeks at a grand hotel in the mountains had seemed great to

him and would have been perfectly acceptable to her had
either he or she thought of it.

But now she began to feel depressed. She could not quite
put her finger on the exact cause, but something was wrong.
She did her best to conceal it, but on the fourth morning she
told A.G. to go ahead down to breakfast without her, she felt
like staying in bed. When he came up again and got back into
bed with her, she turned over on her side, facing away from
him, making it plain, she thought, that she was not in an
amorous mood, but when he told her that she was almost the
color of the coffee he had drunk with cream in it and pressed
himself lightly against her buttocks, she thought the comparison a bit trite but was moved by his enthusiasm at least
enough to accept him into her in a rather passive way and to
enjoy a slow, lazy morning lovemaking that made up in
warmth what it lacked in frenzy and that, as she lay there
quietly and silently with him still inside her, made her think
that there was enough between them for her to be able to
confide in him and to speak her mind.

"A.G.," she said, disengaging him and turning over to face
him, "you know something?"

"No, what?"

"I don't think we should waste any moment."

"Well, I don't either."

"Not a single moment of our lives."

"No."

"I want to tell you something, and I don't want you to take it
wrong. Promise?"

"Sure. I promise."

"Well, I don't know whether I should say this, but I think
we're wasting our honeymoon."

"You what?"

"Don't misunderstand me. I feel so much closer to you now
than I ever have. That's why I know you'll understand when I
say this."

"Go on."

"Tell me honestly. Do you really enjoy this hotel?"

"Well sure. It's a great hotel."

"I know it is. But do you really, really enjoy it? I mean, is this the one place in the whole world you would pick to have your honeymoon if you could pick any place in the whole world?"

"I hadn't thought about it like that."

Claire had come to realize that she had been thinking about it like that since their honeymoon plans had first been made. She realized that without even knowing it in full consciousness she had hoped that they would go to someplace truly different or exotic and exciting, someplace she had dreamed of going to. She realized that she had been disappointed that with all the money in the world available to them they had ended up only a few hundred miles away at a hotel that was luxurious and beautiful and more than satisfactory in every respect but that was, after all, only in Colorado. You had a honeymoon only once, at least that was the way it was supposed to work. I'm no different from anyone else, she thought. There is nothing wrong with wanting perfection or at least striving for it. So many people waste their lives settling for less than they might have. Her mother had done that, although God knows the truth probably was that she drove the man to drink and suicide. Claire did not like to think about it, but she had even wondered from time to time, always suppressing the thought as best she could, whether Vivian herself had pulled the trigger on Gerald, out of sheer exasperation or disappointment; whatever the truth of that, her father was killing himself slowly anyway, so it was merely a question of timing. People do die of disappointment.

All I'm asking for, she thought, is what a lot of other people would grab at if they could get it, a yacht sailing in amongst the Greek islands with me sunning myself and making love on the deck with a warm breeze blowing not caring who was watching, or a trip around the world, riding an elephant or a camel, or Paris, London, Rome, Naples, Marseilles, a country inn in France where a family would serve them dinner on heavy white and blue plates, or a drive through the Irish countryside where they had wild fuchsia bright red against the green. Someone had told her once that her eyes were green as Ireland, one of the nuns at Monte Casino it was, and somewhere she had read in a poem that the stars in the sky washed up from Ireland out of the Atlantic. She thought she would like to see Normandy in the leafy yellowness of October, ticklish with cider and reminiscent of World War II. She was not sure where these thoughts came from, books and movies she supposed, but she was sure they had a reality. Like Mexico. The idea of it. Green peppers and men in elegant rough linen shirts and intricate sandals that showed the toes. Didn't she have a right to that as well as anyone?

Let's face it, she said to herself, every night it just gets duller. She wanted everything to be right and everything was getting wrong—that was too harsh, she was sure, but why couldn't they be in some hotel in Paris with the right amount of champagne? Her mother had never had the luxury she wanted. It was not that her father had not tried. He simply hadn't had the means. She remembered him always promising a better way of life. He had blown whatever savings they had on an oil deal that had collapsed. That was going to be their salvation. He had brought the samples of rock home and let her smell them. They had smelled like oil all right, and that was supposed to be the real test, that and the taste of the stuff, but apparently whatever oil was there was in those rocks, period. Well, at least he had tried. Better to try than never risk at all. She made up her mind that she was going to try everything with A.G. and not reach old age wishing that she had.

"There's an idea I'm cooking up in my brain," she said, becoming rather kittenish, kneading A.G.'s shoulder blades.

"You have to promise you'll listen to it and consider it carefully and not get mad."

"I won't get mad."

"What if . . . oh, I don't know if I should say it."

"Go on, go on," he said, cheerfully.

"All right. What if we left this silly old hotel right now and
flew to Europe."

"You're kiddin."

"No, I'm just romantic, that's all. Didn't you know that?"

"I guess I did."

"I am the most romantic person in the whole world. But you
are too. That's why I love you. Now listen."

She explained to him all the reasons romantic and logical
that they should be in Europe at that moment instead of in
Colorado. The need to start their marriage on the best possible
note. The wonderful possibilities of being in a really strange
place together. The need to take advantage of the time they
had now because they might not have the time later when
A.G. got deeply involved in the ranch as she knew he would
and wanted him to. And the best reason of all, which was that
there was no reason, that it was just a crazy impulse and that
they had to do it because that was what made life exciting and
worth living.

A.G. had no comeback. He was attracted by the current of
energy that was running through her. He could see that and
feel it. He had sensed that something was going wrong, because she had been growing somewhat distant and distracted
in the last couple of days, and he had noticed that she sometimes wasn't listening to him when he talked. In the dining
room last night she had been more involved in eavesdropping
on conversations at other tables than with him, and it was not
that he had been offended but that it had occurred to him that
something was out of kilter between them. He liked the idea
that he could set everything right by agreeing to crazy impulse,
as she put it, so he did. The only thing that bothered him was

having to call his father to make the arrangements. He suspected that Earl would not be too enthusiastic.

"Tell you what," A.G. said, knowing that he was about to
make Claire extremely happy, "I'll call home and make the
arrangements."

"Oh A.G.! I love you."

"I'll go downstairs to make the call. Might have to do a little
persuading. I think I know how to handle it."

As Claire lay in bed waiting for A.G. to return she was so
happy she touched herself. She realized now that she adored
him. He had not made any fuss at all. Anybody else would
have hemmed and hawed and made her feel like she was
asking for the moon when all it was was a warm, loving impulse that, given the resources of the family, would inconvenience no one and would bring her and A.G. closer together.
She couldn't imagine that Earl and Margaret would object,
and if they did, well, too bad. She could sense that A.G. would
stand up to them and take what was rightfully his. He was
going to pass his first test. Her nipples had stiffened. She felt
them and wished A.G. would hurry back because she wanted
to make love to him again, badly. It occurred to her that they
had not settled on just where in Europe they would go, but
that could be taken care of.

"It's all set," A.G. said as he closed the door. Claire ran to
him, hugged him and jumped up and down like a child. "Look
at you," he said. "It doesn't take much to please you, does
it?"

"I never said it did. Oh A.G., where will we go?"

"That's all set too. I've got it all taken care of."

"You have? Really?"

"Yup. It just so happens that my parents have these friends
who live about fifty miles from London. We can stay with
them."

"Oh. Well why can't we just stay in London? In a hotel. I
understand the hotels are fabulous. Haven't you ever heard of

Claridge's? You haven't? I can't believe it. Everybody's heard of Claridge's. Don't you think we should stay there?"

"It'll be better this way. We can use their car and go anywhere we want. They're great people. Used to live near Seminole."

"What are they doing in England?"

"Oil. Some kind of a deal he's got with Getty. You happy?"

"Of course I am. I knew you'd come through."

THIRTEEN

Earl had been furious when A.G. telephoned him. What was the matter with the Broadmoor, he wanted to know. It was good enough for everyone else. Wasn't seventy-five dollars a night good enough?

"Son, level with me. Was this your idea or hers?"

"Both of us. We both thought of it."

"Bull. Since when did you care jack-shit about goin to god-damned Europe? Son, you got a line of shit longer than the Chisholm Trail, and just as crooked. Tell that woman of yours to stick her highfalutin notions where she can't find 'em. You don't teach her right quick, you're gonna have a heap of trouble on your hands. That little bitch crawled out of the same bar-ditch as her mother."

But A.G. insisted that it had actually been his idea first and pointed out that Claire knew a lot about Europe, and it would be a shame to let all she knew go to waste. He didn't get very far with Earl until Margaret came on the other line and took his side, softening Earl up as only she could. It was Margaret who thought of their old friends Judd and Nellie Rackley who had been in England for two years and had invited them over for a visit numerous times. Judd and Nellie would be delighted to have A.G. and Claire visit, and that way all the trip would cost would be the air fare and a few incidentals. Earl gave in.

Then A.G. called Ramsey.

"Guess what," A.G. said. "We're going to Europe."

"You are? What in hell for?"

"Claire's idea. She's always wanted to go."

"I thought you all were stayin in that hotel in Colorado."

"We are. But now we're going to England."

"What're you gonna do there?"

"Well, there's a lot of stuff she wants to see."

"Castles?"

"Yeah, I guess."

"Well, what's the matter? Ain't they got no beds in that hotel? Or you all fucked out or what?"

"I'll see you when we get back."

"Maybe the beds in England is special. I guess she might know something. You tell me she's real smart."

Claire was not as happy with the arrangements as she let on, but she decided to keep quiet and handle the situation her way once they got to England. On the airplane, she resisted the impulse to suggest, strongly, that they go directly to a hotel and skip visiting the Rackleys altogether. It did annoy her to think that after all the trouble she had gone to saving their honeymoon from tedium, the bitter irony was that they might end up wasting her first trip to Europe sitting around with people from Seminole, of all places. Seminole was just east of Norman and was apparently such an attractive place that no one she knew in her life had ever been there, but then again it might be all right. If someone had told her that a mere cattle ranch could be beautiful and luxurious before she had seen the Sunrise, she probably would not have believed it. But she could not help feeling a vague irritation as they settled into their seats on the Pan American flight from New York. Even the champagne and caviar they served on first class seemed lacking in something, and when A.G. started touching her under the blanket after the cabin lights went out, she responded only to humor him.

But the Rackleys, who were renting a manor house on the edge of a village fifty miles from London, were entirely accommodating.

"Of course you'll want to tour the countryside and be alone,"

Nellie Rackley said, and she instructed her driver to take the Krugers anywhere they wanted to go. They could tour for five days and then come back before they flew home. There would be a big surprise for them on their last night.

Claire had in mind a survey of literary landscapes and landmarks, and A.G. said that was fine with him. He enjoyed the prospect of giving her free rein. He had begun to sense that there was a certain restlessness in her, some determination to impose herself on life that he did not quite understand, but he knew that this was a large element of her attractiveness to him, and he felt sure that letting her have her way and be herself in a place she knew from books and he knew but little of would make her happy. And it would make her grateful to him. For him it was enough to sit in the back seat of the Rackleys' Daimler near her, watching her react to the sights, looking forward to crawling into bed with her later, or almost enough: he had to push from his mind his own discomfort in the strange environment. He caught himself counting the days until their return and imagining the satisfaction he would feel settling into his seat on the return flight. And he looked forward more to establishing their room together in the big house than to all this travel. He wondered whether he was after all more domestic than she, an odd thought, because wasn't it supposed to be the other way around? He decided that their differing attitudes were all owing to the difference in their backgrounds, his settled and secure, hers one uncertainty after another after her father's death and even before that. She had told him that she had lived in ten different houses in Tulsa, and that made him feel sorry for her. Once they established themselves on the Sunrise together, she would change. No one could have the Sunrise and want anything else.

"There are so many things to see," Claire said. "I don't see how we're going to do even a little of it in five days. I mean there's the Hardy country, there's Oxford and Cambridge, Jane Austen, the Brontës, the Lake District. My God, what about

Shakespeare? Are we going to leave him out? Oh, A.G., if only
we had two weeks instead of just one or not even one. Is there
any chance, do you think, we could stay two weeks? Is there
any chance at all?"

"We better not," A.G. said, with a hint of firmness. "It
wouldn't be right. I've got to take charge of some things on the
ranch, you know."

"I thought cows pretty much took care of themselves.
They're not going to miss you that much, are they? I mean, the
grass doesn't need you to watch it grow, does it?"

"You don't understand now, but you will. We'll have to be
satisfied with what we have."

"There's not a chance? Even a small chance?"

"Not really. It wouldn't be right."

She pouted but dropped the pleading and determined on
Shakespeare, Wordsworth and the Brontës. They would have
to leave London for another time. Maybe for our silver wedding anniversary, she said a little peevishly and then laughed
to soften the dig.

Stratford-upon-Avon reminded A.G. a little of an amuse-
ment park or a reconstructed ghost town, and he was bored to
tears by a production of *The Taming of the Shrew*, but he held
his tongue, because Claire seemed to be enjoying it all im-
mensely. He quickly learned to order triple Scotches, wondering how the English ever got drunk on their minuscule mea-
sures. The Lake District called to mind eastern Oklahoma
except that there were more people and there was a tame,
worn quality to the landscape that made him feel constricted.
But it was fun making themselves warm in a featherbed in
Cockermouth, putting the name to good use and laughing in
the morning as the maid burst in on them with bacon and eggs
and cold toast.

It was raining steadily when they arrived at an inn near
Haworth in the Brontë country.

"Doesn't look like there's much to do here," A.G. said. He

was examining a placard tacked up on the wall of their room that bore the title "Local Walks." "Let's go down to the bar."

"You go on down," Claire said. "I'm going to rest and freshen up."

In the bar A.G. found Hugh, their driver, and sat down with him, glad of some male company. They chatted through two drinks and then Hugh revealed that he had not always been a chauffeur but the life he had been leading was no life for a man getting on in years, and he had had to find something quiet and steady.

"What were you doing before?"

Hugh leaned in close: "I was a mercenary, if you want to know," he said in a low voice. "There's good money in it. But it takes its toll."

"A mercenary?"

"Mercenary soldier. I was in the Congo. Working for the Belgians. That did it for me. I've got a strong stomach but I don't go in for raping nuns. If you want work of that kind, I can give you a number in London to ring." He winked.

A.G. asked Hugh about the adventures of a mercenary and Hugh launched into his life's narrative—how he had started out in Korea with the British army, screwing Korean women who had a peculiar smell. Every nation's women have a different smell, Hugh said. He could write a book about it if he had half a mind to. Then he had taken up as a soldier for hire. He had fought in Algeria and in the Congo, against blacks and against U.N. troops, Irish and Indians. The Congo was the worst. His experiences in the Congo had made him decide to be a chauffeur. Hugh told A.G. a lot about what had gone on in the Congo, and by the time Claire came into the bar, scrubbed, perfumed, radiant, A.G. was into his third triple Scotch.

"Hugh here has had quite a life," A.G. said, rising and clapping Hugh on the back.

"Well, that's enough of that now," Hugh said.

"A.G.," Claire said, "did you see that little dog in the hall-way? Out in the lobby?"

"What dog?"

"Oh come see! You've got to."

Claire took A.G. by the hand into the lobby where, beside a coal fire, a pug dog napped.

"Isn't he adorable?" Claire asked.

"What is it?"

"It's a pug. Isn't it cute?"

"It's the ugliest thing I ever saw."

"I know. But it's so ugly it's cute. It stood up before and it has a curly tail."

"Like a pig."

"Don't be cruel. It's adorable. Oh, A.G., I want one. I want a pug dog from England to take home."

"We must have fifteen dogs on the place already. Good hunting dogs. We don't need another dog. Not one like that anyway."

"The Royal Family has pugs."

"What do I give a shit what the Royal Family has? The Royal Family's got the clap for all I know." He was surprised by the sharpness of his tone. Something about her asking for an ugly dog had irritated him. "Let's go on in to dinner," he said, trying to sound as cordial as he could.

It was a difficult, mostly silent meal. A.G. could feel the tension and he drank a lot of wine to try to banish it. He tried to start conversation several times but Claire cut it short with dismissive remarks. Finally, over coffee, she brought up the pug again.

"You didn't have to be so mean about the dog. What's wrong with my wanting an English dog?"

"Nothin."

"Well what were you so mean about?"

"I just think it's ugly, that's all. What good is a dog like that?"

"I don't know what you're talking about. It would be nice for me to have it around, that's all."

"Well, forget it. They wouldn't let a thing like that across the Oklahoma state line."

Claire put her napkin down carefully, got up and left the room, leaving A.G. to sign the bill. He went from the dining room into the bar, hoping to find Hugh. But Hugh had left. He drank three brandies before going to bed.

There were single beds in their room and they slept separately that night, not speaking. A.G. lay awake for a long time, his brain heated by the drink, suppressing alternately impulses to apologize and to attack. One moment he was ready to crawl into her bed and heal the breach in the time-honored way, to find the path to her heart down there, and the next moment he had the urge to shake her awake and tell her that she might think he didn't know anything just because he hadn't read the same books that she had, but the truth was she knew nothing of life as it was lived in the real world. The truth was, he would tell her, that Hugh the chauffeur knew more about life than she did because he had killed and seen men killed and seen soldiers buried alive with their balls shoved into their mouths. He had the impulse to tell her these things at the top of his voice, to wake up the whole hotel and shout them, and then his anger would subside, he would feel remorseful, then confused. Finally he fell to sleep.

In the morning they made up. Claire did not mention the pug dog when they passed it in the lobby and A.G. did not say she could not have one. They took a walk on the moor in the rain, holding hands, and she told him about the Brontës. Hugh joined them for a drink in the Black Bull tavern and suggested they try whisky macs, Scotch mixed with ginger wine, because of the cool weather and the rain. The whisky macs made everyone feel warm and jolly, and later in the car A.G. held Claire and told her he was happy to be with her and did not know what had been bothering him.

"You're not bored?" she asked.

"Bored? With you?" He kissed her.

When the Rackleys told them that the special surprise for their last night was going to be a dinner party with a duke, Claire was delighted and A.G. figured he could endure anything since they would be going home the next day, so he pretended to be pleased. He even told himself that he ought to be more enthusiastic, but his personal exhortations were not entirely effective. He decided that the thing to do was to get just drunk enough to try to enjoy whatever was in store. He was able to get a head start when Judd Rackley suggested that the men have a cocktail together in the library while the women were dressing. Judd told A.G. about the deal with Getty and about the tremendous tax advantages he was reaping, living abroad for a while. He would prefer to be home himself, but Nellie loved it, and businesswise it had turned out great.

"How'd you meet this duke?" A.G. asked.

"I haven't met him, exactly," Judd said. "I've talked to him over the phone."

"And he just invited us all to dinner? Just like that? Pretty friendly guy. I didn't think the English were supposed to be that friendly. You got some kind of a deal goin with him?"

"Not exactly," Judd said. "Nellie and I have been wanting to do this for months, and we thought having you all here would be the perfect opportunity. You see, the deal is, with the tax situation the way it is here on the English, estate taxes and income, some of these dukes get pretty hard pressed. They don't want to lose their property, but they can't pay the taxes. So what this guy does, and a lot of others, is he has people take tours of his estate, for a fee. That brings in some. But once a month he gives a dinner party. All you have to do is call him up."

"And you pay."

"That's right."

"How much is it?"

"Don't worry about that. You're our guests. Have another drink."

"Make it a double," A.G. said.

It was the way the duke talked about the wine that finally made something pop in A.G.'s head. The tour of the house had been impressive enough, and A.G. had almost been able to get caught up in everyone's admiration of the paintings and the furniture. The scale of the house made the big house on the Sunrise seem small by comparison, and when the duke pointed to this or that portrait and reminded the Americans that when his ancestors were saving England, America was still inhabited by savages, A.G., like everyone else, took the point in good humor. But when the duke, sitting at the head of the long table, china and crystal glittering in the candlelight, held up his glass and began a discourse on the virtues of the 1929 Château Petrus, A.G. wanted to let out a yell or throw a glass or do something to break the place up.

"He has been a friend to me for many years," the duke said, holding up his glass and looking at it. "He has lain quietly in my cellar, patiently awaiting this moment. How often have I passed him, noting the dust covering him, knowing that one day I would raise him up, gently pull his cork, and decant him ever so carefully by the light of a candle." A.G. tried to catch Claire's eye, but she was staring at the duke. "And now the moment has come." The duke inhaled, dropping his large nose over the edge of the glass. "The scent of crushed violets," he said. "Exactly so. No, you have not disappointed me, old friend. Not yet, not at all. You have given me the bouquet you promised. Thank you, old fellow, thank you. And now . . ." He drank, closing his eyes and rolling the wine around in his mouth, finally swallowing and then going on and on about how the old friend had proved loyal and true.

A.G. had taken the precaution of bringing his flask with him, and after the duke's speech he excused himself, went into a bathroom and took several healthy swigs. By the time he sat down at the table again, he was on his way to insensibility.

After dinner everyone was supposed to retire to a drawing room for coffee, cognac and chamber music, but A.G. slipped quietly outside and lay down on the lawn near a lily pond. The music drifted out to him. His head spun as he tried unsuccessfully to see stars through the mist. He wondered what Claire was making of the evening, and he wished she would come outside and join him on the lawn. Maybe they could take a swim in the lily pond together. Lying there quietly, he was able to think clearly enough to realize that he had overdone it with the flask, on top of everything else he had had, and he decided that the the thing to do was to try to sober up, because after all, he told himself, he did not want to embarrass Claire and the Rackleys, who were probably wondering where he was. He did not want to have a fight with Claire on the last night of their honeymoon. But what could he do to sober up? He took deep breaths, but these seemed only to make him dizzy. He contemplated running around on the lawn but felt he did not have the strength for that. A glint of light off the lily pond attracted him and it occurred to him that the solution was simple. Why hadn't he thought of it before? He would take a quick dip in the pond. That would clear his head and he could return to the party and get through the rest of it. If he could clear his head, he could even have another drink.

He stripped off his clothes and waded into the pond. The bottom was slimy. His foot skidded in the slime and he fell, splashing into the cold water, immersing himself totally. For a second he was frightened that he might turn into a frog or be eaten by giant frogs; then he realized suddenly that he felt weak from the shock of the water, and he began struggling to get up and out. That will do the trick, he told himself; that will sober me up quick. The thing to do now is to go on in and make some conversation. He staggered out of the water, shivering and stumbling toward some stone steps, against which he promptly tripped and fell, hitting his face on a sharp stone edge.

He came to his senses and realized that his mouth was bleeding because he could feel the warmth and taste salty blood. I am not going to let a little thing like this beat me. I am going to see this thing through. You don't let one mistake beat you. He got to his feet and lurched toward the lights and the music.

When A.G. appeared in the doorway of the music room naked, dripping, shivering, blood trickling from his mouth, bloody teeth showing through a smile, the musicians stopped playing, Claire screamed, and Judd Rackley rushed to his aid. As for the duke, he acted as though nothing unusual or untoward were occurring at all and ordered the musicians to resume playing. When they did, A.G. shouted, "Hey, let's dance!" to Claire as Judd helped him out the door.

It wasn't until they were on the plane that A.G. attempted an apology. He said he realized that he had let it get out of hand, but didn't she agree that the duke was a squirrely old bastard? He couldn't have let the duke get by with all that bull without saying something or doing something. He had just let things get out of hand. It was a case of overkill.

"It doesn't make any difference," Claire said. "Nothing makes any difference."

"Well, we had a lot of fun anyway, didn't we?"

"It doesn't make any difference," she said. "I don't suppose England was everything I thought it was anyway. I don't suppose anything is like you read it in books."

FOURTEEN

Like most unspeakable events, the climax of the honeymoon was forgotten or at least repressed, except when A.G. was out of Claire's earshot. Then he actually enjoyed recounting the dinner at the duke's.

"Hell of a start," Sam said when he heard the story. "I'd say you made it pretty clear what you thought of that old duke."

"A.G.," Ramsey said, "I don't believe anybody could of done a better job of it than you. I'd say you did one hell of a job. I'll tell you one thing, I never been that drunk yet."

"You know," Sam said, "you can get into a heap of trouble in them furrin countries. You couldn't get me to New York City for no money. But that reminds me. Did you hear about them two priests what went down to Mexico?" They had not heard. "Well, these two priests, they went on down to old Mexico to do them some fishin. The fishin was real good, they heard. So they's out in this boat, and they got 'em a Mexican guide, you know, and right away one of the priests he lands him one hell of a fish. Must of weighed two hundred pounds and he damn near drownded haulin it in.

"So they get the fish in the boat and the priest, he says, 'Pedro,' he says to the guide, 'Pedro, what kinda fish is that there?' And Pedro, he says, 'It's a beeg son of a beetch.' And this other priest, he says, 'You ought to know better than to speak to a man of the cloth like that. This here cloth is respected all over the world. Don't use foul language to a man of God.'

" 'Padre,' old Pedro he says, 'Padre, I don't mean no disrespect. That is the name of the feesh. We call heem a beeg son of a beetch.'

"So the priests, they accept that all right, and that night, they's fixin to have a big fish dinner with this fish. And there's a third priest is invited, a young feller just fresh outa the school for priests, you know. And when they serve up some fish to this young priest, he says, 'That's real good. What kind of fish is that?'

"And the priest what caught the fish, he says, 'It's a big son of a bitch.' 'That's right,' the other priest was fishin says, 'A big son of a bitch.'

"Now the young priest, he looks a little shocked at the other priests usin such foul language, but then the young feller gets a big old grin on his face, and he says, 'You know, when I come in here, I thought maybe you fellers was kinda stuffy and uptight. But you know somethin? You motherfuckers are all right!' "

When the laughter had died down, Sam added a moral:

"That's what you gotta watch out for in them furrin countries. They can be trouble. They's like a broken rubber and a rattlesnake. You don't wanta mess with any one of 'em."

"I tell you, Sam," A.G. said, "I wish I'd had you along in England. You might have kept me out of trouble."

"Don't count on that," Sam said.

A.G. and Claire had everything. All they had to worry about was happiness. They settled into the routines of the ranch, with A.G. up early every morning to begin his rounds of checking on the work and pitching in and Claire trying to figure out what role was hers to play. After she had fixed up their bedroom to her liking, she found that there was not much that she had to do, since all the cooking and cleaning were taken care of by servants; even the planning of the meals was out of her hands, although Margaret would consult with her. Vivian, who had had the idea that her daughter's marriage would bring instant riches, was dismayed to learn that Earl had put A.G. on a salary of five hundred dollars a month and that any extra purchases had to be cleared with Earl. The shopping sprees Vivian had envisioned in Tulsa or Dallas or Kansas City would have to be postponed.

Claire herself was not pleased with A.G.'s salary and lack of financial autonomy, but she listened to his long explanations of how it was still necessary for him to prove himself and how eventually he would take over more and more of the operation. Earl could not be expected simply to abdicate.

"How are you going to prove yourself?" Claire asked. "You already know all there is to know, don't you? At least he could make you a partner."

"Not yet," A.G. said. "You'll see. I'll make my mark."

"Well what am I supposed to do in the meantime?"

"Be patient."

She tried and did a fair job of it, even biting her tongue when Earl would bait her by saying things such as how he knew damn well that what Claire would really like to do would be to run off to Europe or Neiman's every other day but that she would have to learn to accept things the way they were. She had plenty to eat and plenty of clothes on her back: she ought to be grateful. She lived in a big house and was waited on hand and foot. It seemed like she might act a little more cheerful and appreciative. When Claire started running up phone bills calling her old friends in Tulsa, Earl would show her the charges and wonder what she had to talk about to anybody for twenty-five minutes. Hadn't she heard of writing a letter, or was that out of style? She had a few things to learn. Maybe her father had run his business differently but as long as Earl Kruger was running the Sunrise, things would be done his way.

"I am running the son of a bitch. And I built it up. Don't you forget it."

"I'm sure I'll learn how to act," Claire would say, putting

some effort into sounding convincing and not entirely succeed-
ing. She would complain to A.G. about these encounters, and
he would try to mollify her. "You'll learn to love my father
when you really get to know him," A.G. would say.

"Is it absolutely necessary that I have to try to love him? I
don't think he's very lovable."

"Watch my mother. She knows how to handle him."

"I'm not your mother. Maybe you better remember that."

Their best times were on Sundays when they would take
rides together and A.G. would do his best to make her enjoy
the country life.

"I'm sure I could love any life with you, A.G., country or
city, I don't care. Sometimes I wish we could move somewhere
and live by ourselves."

"Give all this up?"

"No. I don't know. It's hard, living in the same house with
your parents. And you're away all day. I don't even have anyone to talk to. Of course I love Margaret but we're not exactly
the same generation."

"We're just starting out," A.G. said. "We got to put in some
time. We'll go along with the old ways for a while, then we'll
have our own, you'll see."

She wanted to believe him. During the long days alone she
took again to reading and wondering whether she was pregnant. If she were, that would change things. Could they possibly go on living in the same house once they started their
own family? It seemed to her that for years the thing she had
cared most consistently about was having control over her own
life. Was she going to surrender it now? Something would
happen. In the meantime she would preserve herself by reading and by holding onto thoughts that no one, not even an Earl
Kruger, could take away from her. One day she had the impulse to start writing her thoughts down in a diary or a notebook, and it occurred to her that she might take advantage of
all the free time she had by doing what so few people have the

time to do, writing. She went into town and bought a hand-
somely bound notebook with thick, unlined pages in it and an
assortment of pens and pencils. She decided she would not
start writing that day but would wait until the morning, after
A.G. was off to his work, when her brain would be fresh and
perhaps filled with thoughts germinated and nurtured during
the night. She was in a cheerful, expectant mood that evening,
even managing to draw old Earl out at the dinner table by
kidding him about what must have been his wild bachelor
days, and when she made love to A.G. that night she felt an
unusual kind of freedom, conscious of him yet afloat and lost
on the oceans of her own feelings.

When she sat down at the table in her bedroom to write the
next morning, she felt that something good was going to happen, and the first sentence came easily. It was "The jonquils
were blooming." She did not know what the next sentence
would be, so she paused and admired the first one, trying to
tease forth the vague idea that she was probably going to end
up writing about a funeral. She pictured the jonquils in her
mind and she liked the sentence, until she realized that she
could not quite picture the sentence because she was not exactly sure what jonquils looked like. She was fairly certain that
they were yellow but not absolutely sure, and she began to
wonder why she had chosen jonquils. Maybe because of the
sound of the word, but was that a good enough reason? By the
time she was convinced that she could not produce an accurate
picture of a jonquil if her life depended on it, she had lost the
idea of the funeral or wherever it was that she was supposed to
be going on the page, and she began to get depressed. She
knew there was no point in writing about her daily life because
it had become so uneventful. The view from her window never
changed, except for seasonal changes. There was a tree by the
window but the tree seemed to have no special point to it. She
had not planted it nor watched it grow. Perhaps she should
write about some major event in her life? Her wedding, honey-

moon? She banished those thoughts. Her mother? Why ruin
the day? Her father? That was a possibility, but she felt she
had never really known him. The more Claire thought about
how little she had to write about, the more depressed she
became. The Brontës, she knew, had sat around dreaming up
romances, burning up from the dreaming, dying young. She
did not believe herself capable of doing that, she was too much
of a realist. Obviously she had sat down to write without a
clear enough idea of what to write about. Or was it that she
had nothing to write about? What was the point of it? She was
not interested in being famous, and she would never lack for
money now. Did she lack a theme? Weren't books and stories
supposed to have themes? What was her view of life? She
thought about this last question for a while, decided that it
was too broad a question but that if she had a view it was that
people went ahead and did things because they thought they
were choosing, but they were really being chosen. Yet she
fought against this view, remained determined to choose in her
life and to do so with her eyes open. After all, she had been
aware of the complications of marrying someone like A.G. but
had gone ahead anyway, in full knowledge. She stared at the
paper for a while longer and then lay down on the bed,
drained, enervated, hoping she would come up with another
idea soon or sometime. By the time A.G. came home, her mood
was the reverse of what it had been the evening before, but
when he asked her what was wrong, she could not answer.

She did not wish to give up the writing so easily, so she kept
at it, and one afternoon Margaret came in as Claire was lying
on her bed staring up at the ceiling.

"What's wrong, dear?" Margaret asked. "You're looking a
little drawn."

"I'm just tired."

But Margaret pressed her and Claire confessed that she felt
rather useless. She knew that A.G. cared for her, but she did
not think her presence in the house mattered one way or an-

other. Maybe it had been a mistake for them to come and live in the same house. Maybe she and A.G. should have a place of their own that they could build up, just as Margaret and Earl had done. As it was, she wasn't sure what to do with herself. Margaret said she understood how Claire felt, but it wasn't necessary to do anything that drastic. Claire had to remember that being married was a big change, and that it took some adjustment. There were things she could do to help Claire. Christmas was coming, and that would take a lot of preparation. There were the cards to get out. They always made up special gift boxes for the cowboys. There would be the Christmas shopping to do, and she and Claire could do that together. So much would change when they started raising their own family.

"I know that, but what about now?"

"We'll take care of it. You'll see."

But Claire became more listless. She would get up with A.G. at six and then go back to sleep and not get up again until lunch. After trying and failing to write A.G. a poem about how she loved him but felt that she was drowning, she gave up on the writing entirely. She even lost the energy to read and spent long hours of the day lying on her bed watching soap operas, sickened to realize that one way or another she could identify with many of the situations. Nothing much seemed to happen on the programs: people sat around drinking coffee and agonizing over their problems. That was the way it was with her, and the more she thought about it, the more she knew what the problem was and the less she thought she could do about it. She was trapped. She felt she was no longer Claire Gladstone: she was A.G. Kruger's wife, period. Perhaps soon she would be the mother of A.G. Kruger's child; at least then she would be two things. But she would never be Claire Gladstone again. Do you love A.G.? she would ask herself. The answer was always yes. Yet he was disappointing her. If she was going to identify herself as someone's wife, she wanted to be proud of him, and somehow the fact that A.G. was being a model son, doing everything his father asked of him, was not making her proud of him, was even causing to grow in her a kind of impatience and contempt that she tried to deny but could not. She had known A.G. as a hell-raiser, and while she had thought that there had been something a bit compulsive about his behavior, she had to admit that she preferred it to the A.G. she saw at the ranch, off every morning at the crack of dawn, home just in time for dinner, exhausted from his exertions, quiet at the table. Dinner conversations seemed to consist mainly of A.G. reporting to his father about how this fence had been mended or that hay field mowed.

Every once in a while A.G. would make a suggestion for an improvement—a new barn, woods cleared—and Earl would always veto it, saying things had gone on just fine for a long while and he wasn't about to mess it up now. And A.G. would nod, agreeing, acquiescing, playing, from Claire's point of view, the servant's role. After dinner the four of them would usually watch television together. A.G. wasn't drinking much, and it was strange about that. After the honeymoon Claire was going to suggest to him that he had better cut down on the drinking or he was going to have a rough time not turning into an alcoholic. But once he had started working he seemed to care about the booze hardly at all, and at the same time he had become much duller as a personality. It was the old man who really put the stuff away. A pretty good setup for him, Claire thought: the son comes back to work like a mule so the father can sit in his house boozing away the rest of his days. Was that what sons were for? And paying A.G. a lousy five hundred a month? God, her mother made more than that teaching school part-time.

"A.G.," she said to him one night in bed, "I'm going to tell you something. You might not like it but I'm going to say it anyway. I've thought about this a lot. I know I haven't been in a very good mood lately. Ever since we moved in here, really, and I've thought a lot about it. First I thought it was me. I felt guilty because, you know, we had such great hopes, and I didn't know why I didn't feel more enthusiastic. I was afraid I was doing something wrong."

"You haven't been doing anything wrong."

"Well, whatever, I've decided we have to have our own house."

"Not now."

"That's just it. Now is when we have to have it."

"No."

"Now wait. You can't just say no like that."

"How the hell are we supposed to build a house or buy one and I'm makin five hundred a month?"

She was silent. That was the dilemma. Her whole point was that A.G. and she had to be on their own more. But the only way to be on their own was to ask Earl for more money, and that would make them even more dependent on him. For the moment she could not see a way out, but she went ahead and told A.G. what she had concluded, that it was ridiculous for him to be working like any other cowboy on the Sunrise, earning what the rest of them did or only a little more, and the only difference she could see was that he lived in the big house with his parents. She could even see that the rest of the cowboys were better off than she was and he was. At least the married ones had their own houses. At least the others could be by themselves when the work was done for the day. She and A.G. were stuck with the boss day and night.

"It's nothing new, Claire," A.G. said. "You've said it before. I don't want to hear any more of it." And he turned over and went to sleep.

But A.G. was troubled too. He knew there was truth in what Claire was saying, but he did not want to face it because he did not know what to do about it. She made him angry by harping, but he could not wholly avoid that after all she was being reasonable. He had married her, had fallen in love with her, precisely because of her pride and independence. He had thought that together they would make a perfect partnership, but he could see that they had somehow to be more on their own for her to flourish. Yet the whole direction of his life had been the Sunrise, being groomed for it, waiting to take it over; he could not throw that away and he was not equipped to chase after anything else anyway. He did not want to go ask Earl to build him a house: he knew what Earl's reaction would be and even if he could make Earl give in, the price in anger and resentment would be enormous. He would have to figure something out. In the meantime he did not want to hear any more about it from Claire. The next time she brought it up, he told her to shut up, and she went to bed crying.

Ramsey of course became A.G.'s right-hand man, implementing his orders and giving advice when asked. It was nice, Ramsey thought, that nothing much had changed between himself and his friend, except that A.G. had this beautiful wife. He stole plenty of looks at her but rarely conversed with her, although he had his traditional place at the family table. He could not quite figure her out. She seemed distant. She would often come in a little late and was generally the first to leave the table, sometimes saying she had something to do but often departing without saying a single word. A.G. would talk to Earl, Ramsey and Margaret would talk a bit, usually reminiscing, and Claire would eat quietly. Sometimes when he would glance at her Ramsey would see what he thought was a trace of anger on her face, and sometimes she looked as if she were holding back tears. The more he noticed how much emotion she was evidently suppressing, the more he wanted to ask A.G. how the marriage was going, but when he was alone with his friend during the day they spoke of nothing but ranch business.

One day A.G. and Ramsey drove to the Tulsa Stockyards to sell some heifers and look over a Charolais bull. It was early afternoon when the business was done, and they decided to head for a bar, the Wheeler Dealer's out on 26th and Harvard. It was A.G.'s favorite bar in Tulsa, dark with a good jukebox, the sort of place where if you didn't know anybody when you walked in, you knew almost everybody by the time you got out. At the Wheeler Dealer's they kept the Christmas decorations up all year round, and if you thought your drink was too weak, you could send it back and the bargirl would juice it up with a smile and no charge. Old Mr. Wheeler, who looked ninety but was fifty and owned the place, was usually there, either sitting down at the end of the bar or standing over the toilet spitting blood. Mr. Wheeler had cirrhosis but had vowed that it would not beat him. He would get his insides pumped out and be back at his post day after day. His patrons—truckers, laborers, the occasional insurance man, oil-field veterans, women dragging themselves from marriage to marriage—made bets on how long Mr. Wheeler would last, and his endurance gave the place its special morbid cheer. When A.G. entered, Mr. Wheeler managed to gesture to him and told the bargirl that A.G.'s and Ramsey's first and last drinks would be on the house.

"My dad got old Wheeler out of a scrape once or twice," A.G. said as they sat down in a booth.

"I sure wish I'd of had the sense to contact him when I was in trouble," Ramsey said.

"Why didn't you?"

"Ashamed, I guess. Then I thought this girl Kitty would help out. Said she would."

"She frame you?"

"Naw. She ain't got the brains. I kinda liked her though."

"Loved her?"

"Maybe. I did think about her in the slammer."

"Well what else would you do?" A.G. laughed. "Jesus Christ, you must've jerked that thing raw."

"It ain't no joke, that long with no pussy."

"I bet you're makin up for lost time."

"I'm doin all right. But you got it all. That Claire is some good-lookin kinda woman. You got it all, A.G. Ninety-proof bourbon, hundred-proof woman, and fourteen-karat gold."

"Let's have another round," A.G. said. "I wanta tell you about some of the plans I got cookin."

A.G. told Ramsey that he had great plans for the Sunrise. Ramsey said he didn't see how the place could be any better than it was, but A.G. said that you could not stand still, not the way things were today. He was telling Ramsey some things in strictest confidence. He was not even going to tell Claire, yet, because she was an impatient kind of woman and would want him to move too fast. She had her virtues, that was for sure, and he even found her impatience attractive, because it was part of her having a lot of life in her, but he did not want to be pushed too fast. It was too soon to make a move yet. Earl was still very much in charge, and that was the way it should be, didn't Ramsey agree? Ramsey agreed completely. The ranch was the old man's baby and should remain so as long as he wanted it that way. A.G. told Ramsey that there were tremendous possibilities for improvements on the Sunrise. It would take a big investment at first, but that would pay off in increased profits in the long run, and the long run was the thing to think about. Earl did things in the old ways, hardly even keeping books, but someday the old ways were going to catch up with the place—not next year and not for a while, but eventually—and A.G. wanted to be prepared for change. What he had in mind, the gist of it, was that the Sunrise should become completely self-sufficient. They should grow all their own feed, to start with. They would have to clear a lot of land to do that, and they would have to have a big grain elevator, and that would cost a bundle, but it would pay off. If they grew all their own feed, they could produce cattle cheaper than anyone else, and the profits would be bigger. As long as the price of grain kept on rising, the better off they would be raising everything themselves. They had the land to do it.

"Makes sense to me," Ramsey said. "Ain't nothin more expensive than clearin land these days, though."

"We're gonna improve the hog operation, too. Double it. Maybe triple it."

"When you gonna start on all this?"

"Don't know. Not now. I got plenty of time to think about it. I plan on takin out most of the bluestem and puttin in Bermuda grass, too. Higher yield per acre."

"I heard some of the ranchers tried that, they had a hell of a time gettin the Bermuda to grow," Ramsey said.

"We'll lick that problem. I'll have it all figured out by the time we get goin on this. Are you with me?"

"Sure."

"We'll have another round."

Their spirits rose with the whiskey. Ramsey could see that A.G. was very excited by his big plans. They seemed very ambitious to Ramsey, but A.G. had obviously read up on it a lot and must have talked to people. At any rate, they were talking about things that were years away. The girl who was bringing their drinks was making sure that they were good and strong. Ramsey complimented her on the service and on her perfume.

"That's just me, honey. That's the way I smell." She leaned down so that Ramsey could get a whiff of her where her neck met her shoulder. "I'm from Houston."

"Is that right," Ramsey said. "Well, you smell like Houston."

"What does that mean?" she said. "What does Houston smell like?"

"Money," A.G. said. "Bring us another round."

When the girl returned with the drinks, she asked them whether they had ever seen what she could do with a bar towel. They said they had not but would certainly want to see that, so she went back to the bar, dampened a bar towel with water, and returned to their table. She smoothed out the towel on the table, folded it in half, then in quarters, and started folding down the corners of one end in a complicated way until the end of the towel began to rise up like a cobra, or what looked at first like a cobra until you saw that the end of the towel, quivering, knobbed and streaked with bar slop, looked exactly like a big thick penis.

A.G. and Ramsey applauded along with a few other customers who had gathered to see the trick. Ramsey gave the girl a gentle squeeze on her breast and told her that she had made it stand up better than anyone he had ever seen.

"My husband doesn't like to see me do that," she giggled.

"He doesn't?" A.G. said. "Well call up the cocksucker. Get him in here. We'll knock the shit out of him."

A.G. was in an exalted mood now and went on about his plans for the Sunrise, asking Ramsey again and again for declarations of loyalty and matched enthusiasm. The Sunrise was great, everyone in the state knew that, but they were going to make it greater. They were going to make it the goddamned General Motors of the cattle business with an operation so big and so unique and so invincible that not one son of a bitch in the country would be able to touch it. It was going to be what it had always been but more so. With the Bermuda grass you could get one cow on three acres, or maybe it was only two, but anyway not the six or eight acres it took now with the bluestem.

"We're gonna pull this baby through, aren't we?"

"We sure are," Ramsey said. "I know you can do it, A.G."

"We're gonna knock everybody on their ass and make everybody proud. Claire won't even believe it. You know that? Claire won't even believe it when she sees it. She won't even believe what I got in my mind. But that's all right. We'll show her, won't we?"

"We sure as hell will. Say, how's married life treatin you anyways? Pretty good?"

A.G. grew very serious. His thoughts were racing but his speech had begun to slow. He felt he had something important to say to his old friend but he was not precisely sure what it was.

"I wanta tell you something," he began, and then fell silent. "We better have another round."

He took a long swallow of his fresh drink and tried to organize his thoughts. He wanted to convey something broadly philosophical about the complex relations between men and women, but when he finally opened his mouth what came out was: "I love her. I'd do anything for her. That's what counts, isn't it?" He swallowed. "The thing of it is, if she knew what I had planned, she wouldn't be so impatient. There's some friction. My old man."

"I could see that."

"But where would we be without my old man? I ask you, where would be we?"

"Right. I know where I'd be. Back in the pen."

"Right. So get your priotease—" His voice forced itself through a belch. "—priorities straight. That's what I tell her."

"Right. She'll come around."

"I know that."

"Let's get outa here."

A.G. went over to Mr. Wheeler, who was slumped at the bar. His face was ashen and his wispy hair looked as if it had been sprinkled with ashes. It was awkward for him to rest his elbows on the bar because his belly was so distended. He held onto a beer with one hand.

"You're a great son of a bitch," A.G. said to Mr. Wheeler. "A great son of a bitch."

"Give the boys go-cups," Mr. Wheeler managed to wheeze.

Ramsey seemed the less drunk of the two, so he drove the Eldorado back to the Sunrise. Their go-cups were paper malt cups so there was enough to keep them going, through the twilight, the radio blasting KVOO your award-winning country-music station. As Ramsey drove A.G. listened to the songs of love lost, won, betrayed, destroyed, revived, and formulated in his mind a way of conveying to Claire the importance of all he had planned. If only she could understand that, he reasoned, she would be more than willing to put up with present inconvenience for the sake of future triumphs and glories. She was a spirited woman and that was why he was in love with her but deep down he knew that she was an understanding woman too, wasn't she? She had handled her mother. He knew Claire was understanding. The comprehension of how understanding she was made tears well up in his eyes, and he turned toward the window so Ramsey would not see them.

When they arrived at the big house A.G. went straight up to his room, or almost straight up, stumbling on the stairs. He found Claire as he so often found her these days, lying on the bed staring at the ceiling. He went over to the bed and reached out to take her hand.

"You're drunk," she said.

"No."

"Look at you. You're so drunk you can hardly stand."

"Not really. Ramsey and me, we had a few. Real good cattle sale."

"Go take a shower."

"No. I have some very important tell you."

"Well, you better take a shower, because I have something very important to tell you, too."

"I want to hear what I have to say."

"You can't even speak."

"I can too. Wait till you hear it. I'm gonna make this place the General Motors of cattle business."

"You're what?"

"Bermuda grass. Elevator. We are gonna clear them damn woods that always. You'll see! Believe in me, Claire!"

He crawled onto the bed and she inched away from him.

"Listen, sot-face," she said, "you listen to me for one minute."

"I'd listen to you for one minute. An hour. Two days. I'd listen to you for the rest of my life. What you think I want to do, listen to you rest of my life. It's true, I listen to you a lot. You got to admit that."

"Oh Christ," she said, turning over and burying her face in the crook of her arm.

"Now what's the matter? Something's always the matter. Fuck it!"

She sat up. "I'll tell you what's the matter. I'm pregnant."

It did not register.

"I'm going to have a baby."

He was lying on the bed fetus-fashion, asleep.

FIFTEEN

That night A.G. dreamed that he was afloat on his back, fully clothed, on a phosphorescent bubbly river, borne along feet first. He was pleased to notice that although he was in the river, his boots and jeans remained dry. The river seemed to be flowing through a friendly jungle. Big leaves hung over the banks and brushed him as he passed and wild animals looked out friendly and immobile. He saw the big white diamondback snake: it was asleep in the sun, unmoving. At last the river flowed out from the jungle and passed into a flat, dry country that looked like west Texas or New Mexico, with red bluffs and a lot of dust. The bubbles disappeared from the river and it became red and muddy and finally dried up, leaving him sitting in the middle of a hot, dry wash. He climbed up the banks of the wash and found his father standing there, motioning to him to hurry up. "We got a long ways to go," Earl said. Earl looked as he always did except that he was wearing a heavy gun belt studded with cartridges and a big ivory-handled .45 Colt revolver. He followed Earl over the desert. He became weary but forced himself to carry on. At last they were in a little town and A.G. took the opportunity to rest by leaning against a plate-glass window in which he could see his own reflection and his father's. He was watching his father's reflection when all of a sudden he noticed that his father was drawing a gun. Earl drew the gun slowly and the nickel-plated barrel flashed in the sunlight. "You have let me down," he heard Earl say, "you little son of a bitch. I should of done this years ago." A.G. turned toward his father and, as he did, Earl started firing at him. The .45 bullets made huge holes in the plate-glass window all around A.G. as he tried to dodge and looked for cover. He was still dodging the bullets, hearing the gun explode and the glass shatter, as he woke up.

"Jesus Christ!" Claire said. "You almost threw me out of bed."

"I'm sorry," he said. "Dreaming. Look, I'm sweaty as hell."

"What were you dreaming about?"

A.G. said that he could not remember. In fact he could remember most of it but he did not feel like talking about it. He sensed that Claire would not understand, or maybe she would.

"You were drunk last night."

"Yeah. Me and Ramsey—"

"I don't care if you get drunk. Just don't bug me when you are. You should have heard yourself. You were ranting on like a candidate for Menninger's."

"Not really."

"You don't remember." She leaned over to him. He was pleased and surprised that she did not seem hostile. She seemed almost concerned. Most of the time, especially since the honeymoon, she would get pretty angry when he got drunk, and he was glad he had not felt like drinking that often. He and Ramsey had just got carried away. It had to happen every once in a while.

"I remember what I was saying," he told her.

"Come on. It was whiskey talking."

"I was telling you my plans, Claire. It's true. I got big plans. Maybe it's too soon to tell you."

"I don't know how you can talk about such big plans when you won't even get us a house of our own."

"That'll come. You'll see. We got to time it right. We don't want to get on the wrong side of the old man. That would screw everything up."

Claire said nothing for a while. She sighed and lay back on her pillows. When he took her hand she left it limp.

"What's the matter?" he asked.

"You don't remember what I told you last night, do you? You remember your big plans but you don't remember mine. Or ours. You didn't hear me, did you? You were too drunk."

A.G. racked his brain. He could not remember her saying anything.

"I told you I'm pregnant."

The news produced a double reaction in him of pleasure and fright, but he suppressed the fright, took her in his arms and said all the right things, fending off the thought that kept trying to impose itself on him that if only they had waited a little longer to let nature take its course, things might have been a little easier. The more he held her and thought about what was happening inside her, the more thrilled he became. He told her how wonderful it was to think that they would be forever together and that the child would live on after them. When he had quieted down, she brought up what else was on her mind:

"You know what this means, don't you? We've got to get our own house."

They argued for an hour, A.G. saying that there was really no need for it yet, that there were enough rooms in the big house to raise three families, Claire adamant, growing angry, then silent. It was not resolved between them.

Claire began to see that if she was going to get what she wanted, she would have to act on her own. She had hoped that the confrontation would not come so quickly. They had been married for less than a year. But now that they were going to have a child, she had to act. To her the worst thing that A.G. had said when they were arguing was that she really had no idea whether she was pregnant or not until she went to a doctor and had a test. She was absolutely certain that she was. Any woman who knew her own body well could tell when she was pregnant: it was like telling someone that she didn't know whether she was hungry or not. And it was almost as though

A.G. wished that she were not. She had not cared for that at all. There was a limit beyond which she would not pamper or put up with his insecurities. And she had begun to see that if she was going to get what she wanted from Earl, she would have to deal with him herself.

She started playing up to Earl, dropping subtle little compliments about the ranch, even flirting with him, and when the doctor confirmed what she already knew and they broke the news to Earl and Margaret, the old man began warming up to her. Claire knew it was because she was carrying his grandchild, and she did not like Earl any the better for that, but she held her tongue and buttered him up. As for A.G., he was so grateful for a relaxation of tension that he became even more attached to her. Now that she was getting on with his dad, his regard for her came to border on worship. He would come in from his day's work and go immediately to find her and throw his arms around her. He figured that when she would simply stand there with her hands at her sides, unresisting but not exactly reciprocating, it was because of the pregnancy. He knew that things would change for the better after the baby was born, and he knew too that his time would come in a few years when he was able to start his great plans in motion. I guess I have turned out to be a bit of a philosopher, he said to himself. It's not everyone can take the long-range view. But what could make a better combination than Claire's impatience and my restraint? It's like the polar principles of electrical energy.

Claire pushed quietly ahead with her own scheme. She took to long talks with the old man when she could find him alone during the day. She would get him going by asking him questions about the old days, and Earl would open up about the great floods of 1927 and the hard times of the 'thirties when nine hundred thousand Oklahomans were on relief. That was all changed now, he liked to say with pride. It was the rest of the country that was going to hell now, and there would come a time when all the Californians and Honyawks would look to the real America to bail them out, but it would be too late. They would be too far gone in debt, perversion, LSD, topless dancers, phony sophistication.

It got so that the more Claire listened, the more Earl opened up. She would find him of a morning drinking coffee in the big red room, going over cattle sales receipts or fuel and feed purchase receipts, on the phone to Kansas City or Tulsa to see what the prices were doing, contacting his friends on the Board of Trade in Chicago to get predictions on commodity prices. She would come in and sit down and just listen to his conversations, and she could tell that he was beginning to enjoy her as an audience. Sometimes she would catch him glancing at her out of the corner of his eye as he exploded at somebody over the phone, and she got the idea that at least part of the performance was for her benefit. One morning she caught Earl in a relatively quiet mood, for him.

"I'm beginning to think you might just understand what it's all about, someday," he said to her. "When you first come up here, I wasn't so sure. But you're beginnin to act more like a real woman. Sometimes I think you might do all right. Just take care of my boy." He said that often. "Just take care of my boy."

"I'll do the best I can," Claire said, swallowing the impulse to spit out, "He's my boy now, Earl. You better get that straight."

"He's a good boy," Earl went on, "and everything we done was for him. And whatever family he would choose to have. Otherwise, what's the point? Do you get me?"

"I think so."

"What's the point? What else do you fight for? You fight so you get yourself in a position, you don't have to answer to nobody. Let me tell you somethin. The rest of these poor sons of bitches, they go through life until it's too late. They think somebody's gonna take care of 'em, God or the government,

and what the difference is between those two I'm beginnin to
wonder. They go through life, they think if maybe they're nice
to everybody or kiss enough ass or go to church every Sunday,
then everything's gonna work out for them. And you know
what happens? They get their ass kicked in, that's what. And
they wake up, maybe around the age of forty, and they look
around, and they see that it's all over. They're finished. Maybe
they got a pension to look forward to and maybe they don't,
and maybe that pension isn't gonna be there anyway, 'cause
some crooked union boss is already fat on it. So they get to
feelin real sorry for themselves, and the wife she looks at this
sorry son of a bitch and thinks Jesus, what the hell kind of a
sap did I end up with, so she starts screwin around, and pretty
soon the whole world has collapsed on him, and he's got
nothin. He's finished. You can write him off. And you know
what?"

"No, what?"

"It's his own damn fault, that's what it is. His own damn
fault. Because he didn't wake up soon enough and early
enough to see how the world's made up. This country. It used
to give people the chance. Still does, if people would take
advantage of it. Shit, there's sons of bitches right now makin a
fortune drillin oil right in this state, and some jerk in New York
City says it's all over, we gotta have socialism. Well I tell you,
let them talk. We will go right on protectin ourselves and doin
things our way. Let the rest of the country go to hell. We will
be all right. Because some of us woke up a long time ago and
figured out what the world was all about. Fight for it, get it,
and hang onto it. For your family. And fame don't mean
nothin. Some idiot, he thinks if he's famous and gets his name
in a gossip column and his picture in the paper, it means
somethin. It don't. You can be famous and reach down into
your pocket and scratch your knee. That's fame. Because just
as sure as God made little green apples, you let your guard
down just once, and some son of a bitch is gonna take it away

from you. All these people preachin brotherhood and share
and share alike, all they are is openin the door for someone
else who wants to get fat on what we already got. They may
not know it, but that's what they're doin.

"I tell you, I always wondered how the Commanists would
do it if they ever did it. I used to think, they would come in the
back door. Sneak up on us and catch us nappin. But hell, you
know what they are doin, don'tcha?"

"No, what?"

"They are comin in the front door! I thought they might
sneak in the back door, but they are comin right in the front
door! In plain daylight."

On another morning, Earl discussed foreign policy:

"You know one of the stupidest goddamned things this country has done over the last twenty years?"

Claire said she didn't know what that was.

"I'll tell you. It has been the belief that people around the
world would like us better if we gave 'em a livin. Gave 'em
millions and billions of dollars. Now anybody with half a sense
of how the world works and how human nature works knows
that exactly the opposite is true. You give somebody somethin
for nothin, and they hate you for it. They hate you and despise
you for it, because every time they look at you, it reminds
them of how nothin they was until you gave them somethin,
and they got a choice, to hate themselves or to hate you, so
naturally they hate you and they have contempt for you and
they will be the first ones, the very first ones, to line up on the
other side when push comes to shove. You don't go through
this world tryin to be loved. You go through it gettin respect.
And bein feared. It may not be pretty, but it's true. Which is
why a woman always hates a man what crawls to her. I had a
woman say to me once, and she meant it, she said, 'I'd rather
have 'em beat me than whine.' There's a whole lotta human
truth in that."

"I guess I would just as soon do without either," Claire said.
"The beating or the whining."

"Sure you would," Earl said. "And good luck to you. I tell you one thing, ain't no man is gonna make it in this world with a bitch wife who don't know what it takes to get to the top. It ain't gonna work. I saw some half-assed TV program the other night, it was how in Chicago I think it was or some damn place, this couple, they decided they was both gonna make it, separate, and they was gonna share and share alike on everything else. That was some damn bullshit."

"Why was that?"

"Because it won't work, that's why. Plain and simple. You can't tell me that some son of a bitch is gonna make it when he has to worry about the diapers, are you? Don't get me wrong. I'm not as blind as you think. Some woman wants to make it, fine. But then she better not get married or she better marry some faggot who likes housework. You can't have it both ways. And you don't get nothin for nothin."

"Maybe you're right."

"Well you weren't thinkin of runnin off for some career, was you?"

"No," Claire said.

She did not know what she thought about a lot of what the old man was saying. Listening to him was like hearing a tornado approach—you weren't about to argue with it. Sometimes she decided that what he was saying had been right for his generation but did not apply to the modern world, and sometimes she wondered whether he was just plain evil, and yet at other times she entertained the possibility that he was speaking in general, uncomfortable truths. But how could they possibly apply to herself and A.G., when everything they had was being handed to them if they could only get their hands on it? She was determined to persuade the old man to build them a house of their own, but he seemed obsessed with his you-don't-get-nothing-for-nothing argument. What were they supposed to do to get it? A.G. was already working as hard as he could, and for a lousy salary; she was growing a baby inside of her. She could not see anything else that they could do, but she refused to accept the prospect of raising her child and others that might come after in the same house with Earl and Margaret. She would suffocate, she already was suffocating. It was one thing to give up as she had all thoughts of a career for herself, it was another to give up herself. She would have to discover, through guile, some approach to him.

She decided she would try to get to him through his unborn grandchild. She began by asking Earl how it was that he and Margaret had come to build such a beautiful big house, and of course he leapt to expound on that subject: how he had selected every stone, how they had wanted it to be a part of the country they lived in and not some phony import. A lot of these rich oil men in the old days, Earl said, they had decided that the thing to do was to live in some goddamned Italian palace or what-have-you and they would build something to make themselves look like they'd been to school or come from some damned royal family, but his and Margaret's idea was, the house would be big but it would be comfortable and it would have the feel of the west and of cattle in it, because that was the sort of folks they were.

"You have wonderful ideas on things like that," Claire said. "If I ever built a house, I'd want to ask your advice on every nook and cranny."

That was how she got him started. She got him to say that if he built a house today, he would do it the same way, and then she began to add some random thoughts on the importance of raising a child in the close bosom of his immediate family. She discussed her ideas on the overriding role of mother love, and how she believed that it was important for a child to spend time alone with its parents, introducing this last theme gradually by degrees. At the right moment she brought Margaret into the discussions, and later told A.G.: "If you just go along with me, and keep your mouth shut, I am going to get us a house of our own."

"What're you going to do?" A.G. asked, fearing that Claire

was about to explode with her demands and ruin everything.

"Leave it to me," she said. "You'll see. You just let me handle it."

Eventually she was suggesting to Earl that if A.G. and she could build a house for themselves, near the big house but far enough away to give everyone a little breathing room, it might give them a sense of the thrill that he and Margaret had and it might even increase their sense of commitment and responsibility. And of course Earl would have complete say-so over the design. He might even get some pleasure out of putting a new roof over his grandchild's head. It was just a thought, just an idea.

"I'll think about it," he said.

She knew she had won when Earl said that, and just to cement the deal she backed off for a while, telling him that it would probably be too big an expense, though exciting to think about, and that maybe she was only envious of the life that he and Margaret had built up and that perhaps she was just pipe-dreaming.

"Dreams made this country," Earl said. "I like a woman with vision. Margaret had it."

"I suppose it would be all over if people couldn't still dream," Claire said, and for a moment she thought old Earl was going to cry. They hugged each other like father and daughter.

So it was that one night at the dinner table Earl announced that, in honor of the impending birth of his grandchild, construction would begin soon on a new house for the next generation of Krugers.

"I've thought about this," he said. "I've decided it's right. And so, by damn, we'll do it."

SIXTEEN

A.G. was torn between admiration for Claire's diplomatic triumph and the feeling that somehow he should have been the one to bring off the deal, but he allowed his admiration to overshadow his resentment. The house, a smaller replica of the big house, was built in a little over a year, and they moved into it when their baby, Earl Gladstone Kruger, was a year and a half old. The house came equipped with five bedrooms and three servants. When Claire announced that she was pregnant again, Earl added a swimming pool.

Good years followed. From time to time the thought would come over A.G. that something had gone out of his romance with Claire. He would occasionally feel useless, because what was he, he asked himself, provider? Not really. Lover? Well, they made love, but in an increasingly perfunctory way, and it was clear that Claire put her babies, little Earl and Margaret Vivian, first.

One afternoon A.G. and Ramsey took off from work to shoot some 8-ball down the highway at Sweeney's bar. They were the only customers, and after a couple of games they sat down at a table to sip some beer and talk. They drank red ones, beer and tomato juice.

"I tell you," Ramsey said, "that old man of yours, he never stops."

"He just screwed old Joe Kestner out of another two hundred acres."

"Damn right. Hell, Kestner's on his last legs anyhow."

"Tell me something, Ramsey, you gettin along all right?"

"Sure I am. I look sickly or somethin?"

"No, I don't mean that. I mean financially. You need a raise?"

"Hell no. Long as I got beer money, what the hell else do I need? You all give me the Ford. And I got plenty to show some gal a good time. When I get the urge. Which is probably more often than it oughta."

"One thing I was wonderin," A.G. said. "When are you gonna get married?"

Ramsey showed an embarrassed grin.

"It just might be," he said, "I could leave the marryin to other folks. Course you got a good deal, I can see that. But most times it seems like a man's givin up more than he's gettin."

"Yeah. But you want children, don't you?"

"Maybe. In time. I don't have much to give a child right now. I tell you one thing, I marry, I ain't marryin for pussy. There's always pussy. It might be I'd find some good woman sometime would take care of me and some kids. But I ain't marryin for pussy."

Was that what I did? A.G. wondered to himself. Did I marry for pussy? No, Claire's mind had been as attractive to him as her body. Whatever problems they had right now would work out. That was what marriage was supposed to mean, wasn't it? Getting through the good times and the bad.

"Well, here's to marriage," A.G. said. "It suits me."

"Right. Here's to marriage."

It was difficult for A.G. to make the transition from lover to father, but as his children grew he loved them more, and as always he thought of the future, the future, the day when he would come into his own and mark out his own place in the world, the day when, as his father had always told him, a man becomes a man and takes orders from nobody. They had a pleasant life. He was still on salary but it had tripled, and his parents had begun to put some stocks and even a few hundred acres of land in his name. And each year, when their birthdays came around, his children would receive from their grandparents a few more acres of land in their names. A.G. noticed that these gifts never entailed an actual loss to Earl's personal holdings, because the old man always managed to increase the Sunrise by a couple of thousand acres a year at least.

Even with the servants, there was plenty for Claire to do with the babies when they were young, and A.G. had his ranch work and Ramsey to talk to and occasionally get drunk with, usually to celebrate a big cattle or hog sale. On weekends they would gather in the big house to watch football and have a few drinks, and every couple of months they would throw the big, traditional parties on the lawn. There would be a lot of pretty women at these parties. A.G. wondered at himself that he never really felt much of an urge to go after another woman. Even in his fantasies it would always be Claire. She had been careful to get her figure back after the babies, and it remained enough for A.G. to see the glint of sunlight on her dark hair or to watch her lying out by the swimming pool to realize, he guessed, that he was a one-woman man. Or almost. Once, drunk at the Wheeler Dealer's after a cattle sale, he and Ramsey had taken one of the bargirls into the car after closing time and had sat there drinking go-cups while she had sucked them one after the other and back and forth, but A.G. had felt kind of stupid and dirty afterwards and he wondered whether he had gone along with it as much to impress Ramsey as anything else. At least he was proud of himself that he had had the good sense not to confess to Claire.

Yes, they were good years, peaceful ones, more or less free of argument, except when Vivian visited and made clear her resentments at not yet being treated like a queen. Mostly she took it out on the servants, ordering them around, asking for food and drink in the middle of the night, criticizing the cooking, trying to get Claire to believe that the wife of a big-shot rancher deserved more than this. Claire would take it on a Friday night, lash back in small ways on Saturday, and on

Sunday even Vivian would be glad she was going back to Tulsa.

On a summer's day, one day shy of A.G.'s thirtieth birthday, old Earl and A.G. were taking a tour of the Sunrise in one of the pickups. On the way back to the house through twilight they drove across the grass on up to A.G.'s favorite hill. They got out and surveyed the vista, saying nothing at first, father and son sharing the immense beauties of a land possessed and repossessed year after year by its grass, its water, animals, insects, reptiles, birds, people, its owners.

"This is the best spot of all," A.G. said. "You can see everything from here."

"I've always felt that way," Earl said. "I'll tell you something. When I die, I want you to bury me right here."

"That'll be the day," A.G. said. "You'll make a hundred, easy." And he halfway believed it. Nor did he care, down deep, that his father's life postponed his own ascendancy. It was the right rhythm of things.

But Earl did not last through that year, his seventy-third. At the dinner table one night he was in an unusually jovial mood, exuberant over pheasant, telling Claire that she and A.G. ought to eat dinner in the big house three or four nights a week instead of only two, as was now the custom.

"Tell me the truth," he said to her, downing some wine. "Your Eula ain't half the cook Wynema is, now is she?"

"She's learning," Claire said. "Not everybody can have the best, Earl, you know that."

"Well by God, you deserve," he started to say, and then his eyes took on a strange glaze and the fork dropped from his hand to his plate, clattering. A rivulet of wine ran from the corner of his slack lower lip.

Claire was the first to his side.

"He's having a stroke," she said, holding onto him as he swayed in his chair.

"What?" Margaret said, rushing to her husband. "A stroke? How do you know?"

"I just know! Ramsey, call an ambulance. A.G., call Dr. Atwood."

But he suffered two more strokes in the next forty-eight hours, and not even Earl Kruger could stand up to that. The night of the first stroke they rushed him to St. John's Hospital in Tulsa. He seemed to be recovering the next morning and managed to curse whoever was responsible for sending him to "a goddamned Catholic hospital," but the second stroke took away his speech forever and paralyzed his left side. Margaret leaned on A.G., and he managed to appear strong and to comfort his mother, but inside a terrible panic grew. He tried to absorb the sight of his father, Earl Kruger, speechless and immobile, lying there, but he could not. He thought ruefully of how in his semiconscious mind he had sometimes hoped for this moment, because it meant his own passing into power, and he did not feel that it was the right moment yet, he did not want Earl to die, he needed so much to talk to him more and to learn more from him so he could ready himself. He did not feel at all ready. He felt ignorant, unfit, caught short. He realized how happy he had been, once Claire had the new house and the babies to occupy her, just going on with his work and enjoying life in the same old way. It had almost been like recapturing childhood, these last few years. Childhood was about over. Thank God he had Claire.

Toward the end of Earl's second day in the hospital, Margaret, A.G. and Claire went in to visit him. He was conscious but that was all. His ruddy face had paled to yellowish green, and for the first time he looked his age. He had not had time to waste away, so there was something incongruous about this enormous bulk lying helpless. For those who knew him his presence still filled the room, and they somehow expected him to rise up suddenly and start screaming orders, but he did not.

They took chairs around the bed. Margaret held one of his hands, telling him that he was going to be all right. An hour passed. He kept looking at each of them in turn and seemed to want to speak to A.G. but could not. Suddenly he began to shiver, then convulse. His face sank toward blue. A.G. started to run for a nurse but he was not out of the room before old Earl, in a last explosion, drew in his breath and, rasping like an old bellows full of angry wind, blew it out again, vomiting with such projectile force that a fist-sized knot of slime shot out from his mouth and splattered against the window opposite. He subsided, gone.

It was an open funeral, and it seemed that half the population of Oklahoma was there, but the actual count was about three thousand people, cowboys, ranchers, oil men, the governor, both U.S. Senators, businessmen and bankers from Tulsa, Dallas, Kansas City, ordinary folk from hundreds of miles around. A riderless horse, its stirrups turned backwards, led the procession from the big house, where Earl had lain in state on the dining-room table, on up to the hill. Later a marker cut eight feet high in local stone would be placed above the grave.

Earl had decreed that his was to be a nonreligious burial. A.G. would not have dreamed of going against his father's wishes, nor had he any specific beliefs himself other than that there were many things he did not understand about the purpose of life, yet he could not bring himself to put his father into the ground without some custom or ceremony. He knew that certain prominent evangelists would horn their ways in anyway, in order to be photographed, and he would not call on anyone from their ranks, but he wanted someone to dignify the day. It was his father had died. And something even more than his father. A.G. felt not only the filial loss but something of what Americans would feel later when someone representing themselves yet beyond themselves, a Bing Crosby or a John Wayne, would pass from the scene. The father's death had brought back in vivid pictures all the life of the son, and from these A.G. chose or was chosen by an image of Chief Red Bird Smith speaking to his people of their history and ritual. He managed to contact the old Cherokee, who was of the same generation as Earl, and it took no persuasion to get him to agree to eulogize a man whom he had never met and who, A.G. knew, had had no great regard for him.

Chief Red Bird spoke in English in the heavy August heat, beside the grave on the hill, the family gathered near, A.G., Claire, Earl Gladstone, Margaret Vivian clinging to her mother, Margaret, Vivian, Ramsey. The servants, all of them black, next formed a ring, then the cowboys, and the other guests spilled over and down the hill. Chief Red Bird was brief. He had never met Earl Kruger, he said, but he had met his son long ago, and he was certain that the son would carry on the great work of the father, who had tamed the land and had used it well and had provided work and subsistence for many men and their families over long years. Some men were chosen to be leaders, like Indian chiefs. Their responsibility was thrust upon them by the Spirit, by history and by the will of the tribe. Others made themselves leaders, and such a man was Earl Kruger. The land that he had tamed and called Sunrise would live after him, as would his son, and his sons and daughters after him, on the land that had been good to the father. That was the lesson to be learned and learned again and again forever.

A.G. stole looks at his family as Chief Red Bird spoke, and he had the impulse to reach out to each one of them and ask for their help. But he kept his panic inward and concentrated on presenting an image of strength worthy of his father. He glanced at his own son, now six, who was standing bravely in highly polished little boots, and A.G. was proud of him. Would he be as good a father to young Earl as the old man had been to him? Would he now carry through his great plans for the Sunrise, or were they only fantasy and should he simply try to

keep things as they had always been? No, that would be fatal,
he knew. Old Earl would want him to go forward. Maybe that
was what Earl had been trying to tell him on his deathbed, or
was he trying to tell him not to do anything rash? Surely not.
Surely he was trying to tell him to be strong and bold and to
set a goal and go for it, never looking back, never apologizing
and never explaining, never taking no for an answer, all the
things he had always told him.

They lowered the coffin into the ground and began shoveling
dirt over it. A.G. imagined his father moving restlessly inside
and he had the crazy impulse to pry it open just to check one
more time. It was hard to imagine his father in there, still. At
least he had gone quick. A.G.'s panic grew as the loose dirt
piled up. Wait, Daddy, my daddy, he wanted to say. There's
one more thing. There are a hundred more things you didn't
tell me about, I don't know. Am I doing the right thing? Did I
marry the right girl? It's too late now. At least you and Claire
got along at last. Wait, wait. I'll climb in there with you and
you can whisper to me a last secret.

He felt conspicuous. He felt that as his daddy disappeared
three thousand pairs of eyes were on him. His shoulders had
slumped, and he straightened up, sucking in the warm air,
smelling the fresh earth and the grass. Then it was over and,
knees shaking, he led the procession back to the lawn of the
big house, where tents had been set up and tables heaped with
food and drink.

He was in a daze, not hearing the mechanical things he
replied to people, downing three Scotches in no time at all. He
knew he was the center of attention but he felt entirely alone.
He lost track of Claire, of his mother and of his children. He
was standing on the lawn but he felt he was still with his
daddy up on the hill, and he kept looking up toward the grave.
It was as though gravity pulled him there. He imagined himself trading places with his father and wished he could, open
up the coffin, pull Earl out, climb in himself, and let old Earl

come down and enjoy the party. They would welcome the old man back like Jesus Christ and no one would miss the son for five minutes because after all, what was he, his father's son, that was all. Well, he would have to be something else now. Or he would call on his father's spirit to inhabit him and instruct him. One way or another he would have to become his father and make everyone proud. Of him. Of the new Sunrise. Somehow.

He spotted Ramsey chatting it up with some woman and went over to him, feeling the effects of the liquor but trying not to show it.

"Ramsey, I got a couple things I got to go over with you," he said, ignoring the woman.

They went around behind the house and sat down on the back steps.

"You all right, A.G.? Christ, you look tighter'n the bark on a tree."

"I'm all right."

"I know how you must be feelin."

"We can't worry about that. We gotta make some moves. I need another drink."

Ramsey took his glass and came back with refills.

"You are my number-one man," A.G. said.

"You can depend on me. You always know that."

"We gotta make some moves."

"Right."

"First thing tomorrow, we're gonna start."

"I got you."

"From now on, you're in on everything. I am gonna make you very glad you stuck with me, if you do."

"You know I will," Ramsey said. "You know I'm with you."

"There aren't many people a man can trust. Maybe nobody. Are you with me?"

"You can trust me, A.G. You always could."

"Well, what do you think?"

"What do I think about what?"

"Can I make it?"

"Of course you can."

"I'll need your help."

"You got it."

They sat in silence for a while, listening to the low hum of the crowd. A.G. was tired and his brain whirled.

"We been through a lot together," A.G. said.

"We sure have."

"Remember that time the big horse threw me? Ran into the fence?"

"Sure I remember."

"You picked me up. And you." He broke into a semi-hysterical cackle. "You took me to Big Ruby's, you son of a bitch! Why'd you do that?"

"I figure, hell, one thing gets messed up, you gotta remember there's always others can take its place."

"Ramsey, you dumb son of a bitch, when did you get to be a philosopher?"

"I reckon I had plenty of time to think in jail."

"Maybe I should have gone to jail."

"I don't recommend it. Nosir."

They sipped their drinks, sweating, staring at the ground. Ramsey picked up a pebble and threw it against an elm. A breeze brought the low hum of mourners' conversation.

"Ramsey, do you think my daddy was a good man?"

"The best. Oh, he was mean, but that's the way they made 'em in those days. That's how they survived. He would've killed anybody tried to mess with you. Or your mother."

"I think he even got to like Claire at the end, don't you?"

"Sure he did. He just had to test her, that's all. That was his way. That was the old ways."

"I got a funny feeling, you know," A.G. said. "All my life I been following my daddy around, you know, even when I was real young. We'd ride out to a pasture and look things over, and I'd be right behind him. I followed him to O.U. Followed his ways. Learned to shoot. But you know? I got a funny feeling. I got the feeling he's behind me right now. And he will follow me every step of the way from now on and help me whichever way I go. Can you believe that?"

"Sure I can," Ramsey said.

"Tell me something," A.G. said after taking in some deep breaths. "Is there anybody on this place I can't trust?"

"Not that I know of."

"Is there any of the boys might be disloyal?"

"They's all good boys, far as I know. Oh hell, they get into scrapes, you know that, just like everybody else. But far as I know, they's all good boys."

"Do they like me?"

"Sure they do."

"Ramsey, do they respect me?"

"Course they do. You're A.G. Kruger."

"I know that. But how do I know it?"

"Well."

"Goddamnit! Fuck it!"

"What's the matter?"

"I want to know," A.G. said, "do they like me and do they respect me?"

"Come on, A.G. You're their meal ticket. Don't forget that."

"Well it would be nice if they thought more of me than that. I tell you what." He managed to get to his feet and he struck a determined pose, pushing his hat back on his head. "I am gonna show those boys what kind of a feller I am, right off."

"That's a good idea," Ramsey said.

"I want everyone fired. Will you do that for me?"

"What?"

"Run 'em all off."

"You don't wanta do that."

"I thought you were on my side."

"Now wait a minute, A.G. Sam and everybody?"

"No, not Sam, of course not."

"Let me get you a refill, A.G. And sit down. You're runnin off nuttier'n a peach-orchard boar."

When Ramsey returned with the drinks A.G. said:

"Maybe you're right. I just want to be sure I can trust everybody, that's all."

"Tell you what." Ramsey pulled out his billfold and extracted a one-dollar bill. He pointed to it and said, "Who is that guy?"

"It's George Washington."

"You got it. Well let me tell you somethin. He is the only guy in the whole damn world you kin trust. And Lincoln and Hamilton and a couple others if yer lucky enough to meet up with 'em. Just remember that. And don't worry, they is good boys and they respect you. Hell, they know you're richer than ten feet up a mare's ass."

"Maybe. We got to get an accounting. The old man kept it all in his head. I don't know what all we got. Shit. My mother knows next to nothin."

"You'll figure it out."

"I gotta do somethin for the boys. Let 'em see what."

"Don't worry about that."

"No." A.G. got to his feet again, pretty unsteady by now. "I tell you what I'll do. I'll show 'em what I'm made of. From now on, you tell the boys, they can charge all the beer they want down at Sweeney's or Five Corners. Charge it to the Sunrise. Charge it to A.G. Kruger."

"You don't really have to do that."

"I know it. You don't have to do nothin. It's like my daddy always said, 'You can't make a comeback if you ain't been nowhere.' So I am doing it. You can implement that order tomorrow."

"All right. There may be some fellers, they might take advantage of it. We got some pretty fair beer drinkers on this spread."

"Number one," A.G. said, "I can handle it. Number two, they better know quick, they abuse the privileges, they're out on their ass. I mean out. Down and out."

"Right."

"And show up the house first thing in the morning. We're gonna make some moves. I'm gonna show you some stuff. Knock your dick in the dirt."

"Sure thing, A.G."

SEVENTEEN

Although Earl had left everything to A.G., with the stated assumption that Margaret would continue to receive whatever she needed for the rest of her life, A.G. and Claire decided to stay on indefinitely in their own house. They visited Margaret daily and at dinner she was often at their table or they at hers. She had been through enough in her life not to be crushed utterly by the sudden loss, and she managed to switch her attentions to her son and his family. Inside she knew that with Earl gone there was little left for her to do but to wait for death, but her desire not to be a burden was too strong for her to show that.

A.G. tried to adjust to what had been given him. His accounting showed that he owned, in addition to the land, one Cadillac De Ville, one Cadillac Eldorado, one Cadillac Fleetwood, one Lincoln Continental, one Ford station wagon, one Jeep station wagon, one International Harvester four-wheeler wagon, twenty-three three-quarter-ton Ford pickup trucks, three John Deere tractors, four Massey-Ferguson tractors, two John Deere lawnmowers, six International Harvester 400s, three John Deere tandem disks, five International Harvester tandem disks, and seven International Harvester grain drills. Nothing was owed on any of the cars, trucks and farm equipment, because it had been Earl's policy, since he had escaped the Depression, always to pay cash. Nothing was owed on anything, as far as A.G. could see, and the ranch land itself was valued at over twenty million dollars, exclusive of the buildings on it and the twenty thousand head of cattle and the twelve hundred hogs and the chickens and pheasants and quail and other game that grew fat on it.

It struck A.G. as ironic that the Sunrise had all this farm equipment and very little land that had been cleared so as to be suitable for farming. This would be the key to the expansions he would make, and he would make them in the modern way, by using someone else's money. He wondered why his father had bought all the harvesters and tractors. You did not need anywhere near that many to keep the pastures clear and to take care of what hay the Sunrise grew. It must have been, A.G. reasoned, that Earl himself had planned just what A.G. had in mind but had not yet put anything in motion. Certainly Earl had never talked about it. But it made A.G. feel better to think that he might indeed be going ahead with something his father had already scheduled. It made him feel that even with his father gone, he would be carrying out Earl's wishes, though as far as anyone would know the new Sunrise would be his own dream come true.

He took Ramsey out to survey some wooded land.

"All this is going," A.G. said, his hand sweeping the treetops.

"You looked into the cost yet?"

"No. It's going, that's all."

"I'd say you better get the costs down pretty exact 'fore you start in. Then you gotta figure out what sorta investment gettin that soil ready will be. I'd work it out real careful."

"I know one thing," A.G. said. "We get it cleared and planted, it will pay off, big. Not right away, but eventually. And the thing is, I don't have to put a penny in myself. Borrow the money, pay off the loans with the profits."

"How far off you figure the profits are?"

"There isn't a corporation in this country," A.G. says, "improves itself with its own money. We'll get the money at prime rate or lower, you'll see things happen fast."

"Well, I guess you know more about that than I do. You get the money, I'll keep countin cows in the meantime."

Clearing land was expensive. It cost half a million dollars to clear a thousand acres, and A.G. had in mind at least six times that. He would also go ahead with replacing the native blue-stem with Bermuda grass on more thousands of acres, and he had no idea what that would eventually cost, but he was going ahead with it. I am in the position, he told himself, that my daddy was in forty or fifty years ago. I'm facing a frontier, it's just a different kind, that's all. My motives are the same, security for my family forever. And a name for myself, oh yes, there is that, but what man ever did anything that didn't want to make a name for himself? And what woman ever loved and respected a man who didn't? And what children ever looked up to a father who didn't?

He would need to borrow millions, and he was going to do it, he hoped, without mortgaging any of the Sunrise land. In his position, he could borrow a hell of a lot without collateral, but not enough. He discussed the situation with Ramsey. Ramsey knew what was needed to carry through the plans, what new buildings, a huge grain elevator, practical things, and he knew that they said that the best way to clear land was to use some of the new defoliants the army had been using in Vietnam, but Ramsey knew nothing about money. So A.G. started talking to bankers. He sounded them out in Tulsa and Dallas, old associates of his father's and some new people he dug up himself, at first not actually asking for money but whetting their appetites. He would stride into an office or a hotel room for a meeting, put his boots up on a chair or a table, and spit tobacco juice into a paper cup he carried with him. The chewing tobacco was something new. He thought it gave him extra color, a suitable western air, and the manner of a son of a bitch who didn't give a damn what anybody else thought because he did not have to give a damn. Claire did not care for the tobacco and said so, but A.G. told her with an arrogance that surprised himself that there might be a lot of things that she wouldn't like but that she was going to have to get used to

them, because that was the way they were going to be. He
believed that in the long run, this was the way he would take
charge and that she would admire him for it. She told him that
he was acting like a fool, but he looked at her so menacingly
that she shut up.

She did not know what he was up to, with all the trips he
was taking to Tulsa and Dallas, but he refused to confide in
her. Underneath, he longed to tell her everything, to ask her
advice, to share his plans and hopes, but he felt that he had to
accomplish everything on his own now. Everything he had
heard and read told him that a man had to do that. He was
going to test himself and by God he was going to pass the
test.

It seemed to work. Taking things into his own hands, seizing
responsibility, did great things for him and for his self-confi-
dence and even for his marriage. He would work steadily all
week, and sometimes he would have to be away on weekends,
but when he was home on a Sunday he and Claire would take
to lying in bed together past noon. On one such Sunday she
said to him:

"You seem happy. I like seeing you this way."

"All I needed was a chance."

"I always knew that."

"Did you? Sometimes I wondered."

"No. I've always had faith in you. I admire you, the way
you've taken over."

He touched her breast. She had not lost any of her attraction
for him and he loved these Sundays when they could talk to
each other and touch one another leisurely, not worrying about
anything, luxuriating in each other. Her new respect for him
heightened her appeal because it acted on him like a transfu-
sion of power from her to him. She was lying with her back to
him, he with his arms around her, his hand smoothing her
breast, kneading it, and he grew hard against her. She drew
open the scissors of her legs and he slid along the crevice of

her buttocks and entered her from behind, holding her by the
hipbones now, driving at her and pulling and pushing her back
and forth along his length. He felt tenderly toward her but he
felt powerful, too, pulling and pushing her like that, and he
leaned back with the upper half of his body so that only his
groin was attached to her and their legs entangled. They were
separate and joined all at once. He could not see her face but
he could hear her make little groans, and he roamed over her
back, her neck and her dark hair from his vantage point, pushing and pulling. Then when it was over he freed himself,
turned her around and kissed her as though they had never
kissed before, and she sucked hard on his tongue. They held
each other and fell asleep in each other's arms, awakening half
an hour later, warm, content, not wanting to let each other go.
It was like that on many a Sunday. Later he would play with
his children, throwing the football with little Earl or taking
everyone out for a drive and maybe a picnic, happy and proud
as part of his family and as head of it. He could feel Claire's
eyes on him all the time.

He got to feeling playful. One night after the children were
asleep he and Claire sat in the living room talking about how
they had first met, rehearsing their first responses to one another.

"I thought you were the most beautiful girl I'd ever seen."

"I thought you were so handsome, but I didn't want you to
know that."

They brought out some snapshots that Claire had carefully
placed into albums and shared stories inspired by the photographs, laughing about how much fun it had been to run
around Norman in the old T-bird and go dancing at the Trianon. They were having a couple of drinks and A.G. thought
to himself that he had never felt better, not as a kid, not when
he had first been married, not ever. It was an unpleasant truth,
perhaps, but it had taken his father's death for him to begin to

come into his own, not a truth that he enjoyed facing, because he knew that he owed everything to Earl. He thought about Earl every day and he had concluded that while Earl always had his heart in the right place, he was simply the sort of man who didn't want to let you make your own mistakes. It had to be his way. A.G. did not want to handle his own son the same way, but then you could go wrong in the other direction, too, as millions of totally screwed-up American kids proved. Claire had good sense. He could let her handle the children, and when little Earl was old enough he would teach him things just as old Earl had done for him, and Ramsey could help with that.

Claire turned to some snapshots of their honeymoon and they were even able to joke about that, the ups and down of it.

"I got to admit I wasn't on my model behavior," A.G. said.

"Why do you suppose that was?"

"Don't know. Just being an asshole, I guess."

"I just don't think you knew what you were doing," Claire said. "I think you were lost."

"Maybe so."

"Maybe we can go to Europe again someday."

"Soon as I get these projects going. Sure we can. Listen, if things happen the way I think they will, we'll buy a Lear jet and run over there anytime you want."

"We could go once a year. We could see a different country every year. You could take time off for that."

"Sure I could. Once I get off the ground, is all. Anything."

He put Hawkshawe Hawkins' recording of "Dial LOnesome 7-7203" on the phonograph and sang and danced by himself in the middle of the living room, making Claire laugh and tell him he was nuts. Then he fell into an easy chair, pulled off his boots, socks, jeans and underwear and sat there in his shirt, grinning at her, beating time to the music, acting plain silly.

She came over and eased herself onto his lap and they hugged each other.

His ebullience carried over into his business dealings. Many people advised him that normally it took eight to ten years to convert any sizable sort of operation to Bermuda grass, but A.G. said that while that might do for other places, this was the Sunrise, and he was going to do it in two to three years. How the hell long did it take a bunch of grass to grow, anyhow? He felt sure that Earl wouldn't have taken any ten years for a project like that. Earl would have made up his mind and that would be it. A.G. felt in tune with his land now. He was at one with the land and with the weather, which in this part of Oklahoma was something you could not count on to be anything but different, so you just lived with it and lived like it. You made decisions quickly and you acted on them, so that no one could keep up with you any more than they knew whether April would bring snow or heat or whether when you walked out in the morning with a fur-lined jacket you would come back in the afternoon in your undershirt. It didn't matter a damn anymore what the weather was now that eastern Oklahoma had more water than they knew what to do with. That was one of the big reasons A.G. could put so much confidence in his plans.

Clearing the pasture land was one thing, but the woods were another. A.G. could not have the cowboys working rooting out trees, eliminating acres and acres of thickets, so he took bids from contractors and finally settled on one guy who had not submitted the lowest bid but who promised to get the job done quicker than anyone else. Ramsey was in on the negotiations, and he was not as satisfied as A.G. was that A.G. had made the right choice.

"I don't know about that guy," Ramsey said. "To me, he looks slick as cat snot on a doorknob."

"He screws it up, we fire him," A.G. said. "The son of a bitch says he can do it, we'll give him the chance. He knows enough not to mess with the Sunrise. He better know. I tell you one thing, he looks like the only guy knows his ass about these new defoliants. We'll give him a shot."

But Ramsey did not like the look in the contractor's eye, and so he did a little private investigating, asking around in bars, dropping the man's name and waiting for a reaction. First he found out that the man was a Texan, and that made Ramsey more suspicious. Then he discovered that the man had been indicted in Kansas for land fraud. The charge was still pending, so nothing had been proved, but Ramsey took the information to A.G.

"I tell you what," A.G. said. "The way I look at it, maybe somebody would find out you were convicted in California on a drug charge, they wouldn't want to hire you. Now we know different, but that's not the point. You get me?"

Ramsey said he did, but inwardly he was angered by A.G.'s reference to his bogus conviction and he was alarmed by the way that A.G. had ridden over his objections. Did he want advice or not? A.G. had also pointed out that his father had always used some convict labor, because they would take lower wages, and they had always done a pretty fair job anyway; but Ramsey did not see that there was any comparison between using a convict for ordinary ranch chores and risking a contract worth tens of thousands of dollars on someone who might not know his ass from his elbow about what he was doing and who might be a con man to boot. He considered making his case again, more forcefully, but A.G.'s manner made him see that it would be futile. A.G. seemed obsessed with having made the right decision. He was acting, Ramsey thought, like a man in a poker game who held a couple of tens but was determined to see his way through to the pot no matter what. You could lose that way. You usually did.

The contractor began his spraying program. The idea was to kill the trees by spraying from the air, so one day three planes appeared over the ranch. They continued the spraying for a couple of weeks. Then after a period the bulldozers were supposed to come in, but before they reached that stage, Ramsey began hearing complaints.

He was sitting in Sweeney's one day having a red one, worrying about the spraying. His latest doubts came from having found out that the defoliant they were using was considered dangerous by some and that there was talk that it was going to be banned because it did more damage than it was supposed to. In fact some people were saying that you would have trouble making anything grow at all for years and years after that defoliant did its job. Ramsey had brought this matter up with A.G., too, but A.G. had said it sounded like a lot of bureaucratic bull to him. If it did too much damage, they would have to find some way of fixing the damage, that was all there was to it. Ramsey swallowed his red one, ordered another, and turned to see a neighboring rancher come in. Ramsey knew the man and started to greet him, but the rancher ostentatiously ignored him and sat down at a table with his back to him. Ramsey wondered what was up. There was no feud between this man and the Sunrise that he knew of. He went over to the rancher.

"How's it going, Jed," Ramsey said. "Hot day."

The man said nothing. So Ramsey just sat down at the table with him.

"Somethin botherin you, Jed? Wife all right?"

"If you don't know what's botherin me," the rancher said, "you must be the only man in these parts what don't. Or is everybody on the Sunrise got deaf and blind."

What the rancher told Ramsey was that the defoliant was falling on neighboring lands. It also appeared to be contaminating the water supply in several creeks. There was going to be a meeting of local ranchers that night and they were going to see what could be done about it.

"I swear to you, Jed," Ramsey said, "we didn't know nothin about this. Listen, I'll get on this right away."

"It may just be too goddamned late."

"We'll figure somethin. Listen, buy you a beer?"

"Buy me one after you get that boss of yours to cut out that goddamned sprayin."

Ramsey went straight to A.G.

"Looks like we got some problems. Some days those guys were sprayin, it seems like there was a pretty good wind and that damned spray it carried a lot further than we figured. Seems like it carried over into other people's land."

"So what?" A.G. said. "We did 'em a favor. They get their land cleared for free."

"No. Pasture land, a lot of it. They got grass dead. They even say some cattle sick. Maybe dead. Some of these little ranchers, they're pretty mad. One guy he even took his shotgun and tried to shoot down them planes. I reckon he'd like to shoot us now. The story is, they're goin to court."

"I'll handle it," A.G. said.

Once the other ranchers began to realize what had happened to a lot of their land bordering the Sunrise, they got into an uproar and organized. They had hated Earl but had heard that the son was a different kind of man, somebody you could get along with, someone who would play fair. Now he was looking like a worse arrogant ruthless son of a bitch than his father. When the dispute got into the Tulsa *World* and the Tulsa *Tribune*, A.G. decided to take action. He was not going to have a little thing like this foul up his plans. There was more spraying to do, and the ranchers might be able to get a court order to stop it.

He sent out word that he would meet with the disgruntled on a Thursday morning in front of the big house. He was up all the night before planning what he would say to them. By ten o'clock they had gathered on the lawn, some fifty farmers and ranchers, the Sunrise cowboys hanging around on the fringes, everybody acting friendly enough, but A.G. peered at them through the window and felt nervous. They have nothing

to fear from me, he thought. They have no reason to hate me.
There have been some miscalculations and maybe that contractor got a little overenthusiastic or maybe he didn't know
his ass from his elbow but there is nothing that has happened
that cannot be fixed. There is no problem that cannot be
licked. He poured himself a small whiskey and stepped out
onto the front steps, glass in hand.

"I understand some of you gentlemen have a few complaints," he began. He looked out at the attentive faces, trying
to gauge the level of hostility and seeing only a mass of expec-
tation. He felt like a beautiful girl surrounded by eager suitors
and like a girl he felt the pressure to give something. "I understand that there is a problem here," he went on, "and the one
thing I want you to know is, A.G. Kruger can handle it. Because A.G. Kruger is not gonna let some petty-ass little thing
like this come between neighbors. Now I am gonna ask you,
one by one, what is the complaint, and by God, we will work it
out."

For an hour A.G. heard about pasture land ruined, cattle
sick, dying and dead, trees falling over, watering ponds
poisoned. He listened and had Ramsey write everything down
on a big legal pad, and when it was all over, he said:

"I tell you what. I am gonna tell you what kind of a man
you're dealin with. Ramsey Hogan here has noted down every
one of your complaints, and I tell you what, I am gonna make
good on every one of 'em. I will pay you for every dead head
of cattle and I tell you that if your land is fouled up by my
spray planes, I tell you what, I'll pay what it takes to get it in
shape again. Or I will buy it up from you if you want to sell it
at five hundred dollars an acre, which I believe you'll agree is a
pretty damn fair price. So you all decide what you want, and I
will come across. I'll be good for it."

It took months to settle the claims, and when it was all over
A.G. had increased the holdings of the Sunrise at a cost of a

million and a half dollars for three thousand acres, and he had doled out nearly that much again in damages.

Ramsey said nothing about the deals, but privately he wondered about the eagerness of his friend to buy peace. The old man would have done it differently. The old man would have told the other farmers and ranchers to stick it, to go to court if they wanted to, and then he would have had the judge's pecker in his pocket. Making peace seemed to make A.G. happy, but it sure was a different way of running a business. A.G.'s ways with the cowboys were beginning to bother Ramsey, too. All the free beer, and A.G. had raised the wages, and he never seemed to care when a cowboy took off for a day or a week—discipline was breaking down. You make it too soft for people and they will take advantage of you, Ramsey believed, and he knew that Earl had gotten the most out of his men just by being so damned mean. Well, if A.G. was so set on doing things his way, let him. Maybe it would pay off in the long run, you never could tell. Hell, it was his ranch.

But problems multiplied. And the only approach that A.G. seemed to choose was to borrow more money, buy more equipment, fly to banks in distant cities, buy more, borrow more. The Bermuda grass was being terribly slow to take, Ramsey believed. He worried about that and about his friend, who seemed to have begun to confuse being frantic with forward movement. One day A.G. came to Ramsey and announced that he had all the problems solved.

"What's the answer?" Ramsey asked.

"I found out with life insurance, you can borrow on it. The deal is, pay the first premiums, borrow on the insurance, then you can pay the next premium with what you borrow."

"Is that right," Ramsey said. It sounded like witchcraft to him, but he did not say so. "How much insurance you get?"

"I did it up right," A.G. said. "I went first class."

"How much?"

"I got one policy for two million. Unbeknownst to those guys I got another for six million. And another for three million. Hell. My life is worth eleven million bucks! Not bad!"

"Keep your health up," Ramsey said.

EIGHTEEN

One morning months later A.G. hit the road to Bushyhead, a little town less than an hour's drive from the Sunrise. His destination was the Bushyhead National Bank, where an old family friend, Roy Twyman, was president. "Roy," A.G. had said on the telephone, "I'm comin over to see you tomorrow. I got some things I gotta go over with you, and I need some advice from somebody I can trust." "Come right on over," Roy had said. "Always glad to see a Kruger. How's your mother?" A.G. had decided to call on Roy Twyman because he had not been getting the responses he wanted from the big Tulsa banks. He had borrowed plenty from them already, but he needed more, and he could tell they were getting a little cool. Not that they had turned him down, but he did not want to run the risk of getting turned down flat, so he had decided to go to Roy Twyman because you were better off dealing with family friends anyway.

And there was nothing wrong with a country banker. The truth was, country bankers were smarter than city bankers and they weren't so fouled up with red tape and looking over their shoulders at a dozen vice-presidents that they couldn't give you a straight answer.

A.G. had taken the Eldorado because it was the most expensive car he owned, and when he pulled up in front of the bank on Bushyhead's short main street he felt properly conspicuous. He had picked out his wardrobe carefully, simple jeans and a shirt to show he was just one of the boys, but a new Resistol hat and Lucchese boots to show that if he wanted to, he could buy and sell anybody.

It was a one-room bank and A.G. walked straight to Roy Twyman's desk in a back corner. Roy came out and grabbed A.G. by the neck and twisted his hand and told him that he had stayed away too long. Roy was a short man, fat like all country bankers because obesity suggests prosperity, with a reddish head that had a dozen hairs on it brilliantined and carefully combed. He wore what he always wore, a brown suit with a brown vest and brown squarish shoes. He looked as though he might have been managing the carpet department at a Sears store, but A.G. knew that he was as shrewd a man as you could meet and that his one-room bank had millions in assets. Country people liked to let their money sit in the bank and several big men from Tulsa used the Bushyhead National almost like a Swiss account: it was a good place to put money you would just as soon nobody but Roy Twyman knew about.

They sat down together at Roy's desk and shot the breeze. Weather. Not much snow this winter. Warm spell. Rains to come. Gossip. Going price of a headright up in the Osage. Insurance scandal in Tulsa. Indians hiding some rapist down near Fort Smith. Whether a certain high school prospect would go to O.U. or jump to Texas.

A.G. let the small talk go on as long as it might because as he sat there, conscious of the other bank employees who could hear every word, he knew that he would have to find someplace to talk to Roy Twyman in private, and he found himself becoming apprehensive about what he was going to say. That was the trouble with borrowing. It had been fine at first, but the more he borrowed, the more he felt he was putting himself in an inferior position to the lenders. When he had started out, he had known that they needed his business more than he needed them, but the tables had turned, slowly but definitely, and now, as he sat at Roy Twyman's desk, he felt too much like some young slob asking for help on his car payments. Involuntarily he said to Twyman:

"You know, Roy, sometimes I wish I hadn't gotten into this

borrowing business at all. Not that I can't handle it. I can. But it's a pain in the ass, it seems like."

"Well," Roy said, leaning back in his swivel chair and patting his vest, "people didn't borrow, I'd be outa business."

That was reassuring. Roy knew how to put a man at ease.

"Roy, I got some things I wanta discuss with you in private. Is there someplace we could go?"

"Sure thing. Come on back."

Roy led A.G. through a back door and into a kitchenette, but there were two women in there making tunafish sandwiches, so he backed out and beckoned A.G. to follow him through another door. It was the men's room. A urinal, a washbasin, and a toilet stall. Roy leaned against the washbasin and lit up a cigar that quickly filled the windowless room with smoke. A.G. found himself wedged between a wall and the urinal.

"My private office," Roy said between puffs. "What's on your mind?"

"It's like this," A.G. said. "I'll be straight with you. On the one hand, I know it's just a matter of time before these improvements start paying off."

"Damn right."

"On the other hand, at the moment, I got some payments due, and it's not like I can't meet 'em, it's just that I got a cash-flow problem. And I can use the cash I got. What I could use would be some more cash."

"Let's see. How much did you say you got borrowed now altogether?"

A.G. did not want to lie to Roy Twyman. He hedged:

"I didn't say, exactly."

"Well," Roy said, "the way I figure it, it's gettin around the eight million mark."

He was right. But how did he know? A.G. had scattered his debts around so extensively that he had figured no one creditor knew that much about the others. But Roy Twyman knew.

Well, that was because Roy Twyman was one smart son of a bitch. Surely none of the others knew as much.

"Somewhere in there," A.G. said. He spat tobacco juice into the urinal, trying to appear casual.

"You got two hundred thousand here. If I remember right, there's a payment six weeks overdue." He looked A.G. in the eye through the smoke.

"Sure. I'm aware of that. And I can write you a check right now if you want." A.G. broke a sweat as he said this, because he knew if he wrote a check right then it would bounce. His last payment to the Bank of Oklahoma had bounced. Twenty-eight thousand dollars. It had been embarrassing, but he had switched things around and had finally been able to cover the check. But he had just met his payroll, barely, and the well was almost dry. For the time being.

"Naw," Roy said. "I'm not worried about your damn payment. I know you're good for it. We can always refinance if we wanta go that route. Don't worry about it."

Roy is a great guy, A.G. thought. I have nothing to worry about. He has already reassured me about the payment. Now all I have to do is ask him for the cash I need to make the other payments.

"Well," Roy said. "Is that all settled? Hell, you didn't have to come all the way over here for that. I could of told you on the phone. But I appreciate it. I appreciate the courtesy you have shown me, A.G. I know I can rely on you. Hell, your daddy had money in here before you could walk and talk."

"There's one more thing," A.G. said.

"Is there? Well just a minute."

Roy moved away from the washbasin and entered the toilet stall, closing the door behind him. The son of a bitch is going to take a shit, A.G. said to himself. I suppose I have to put up with that. Through the space under the metal walls of the stall he saw the brown shoes turn around and trousers and under-wear drop onto them. The sounds that followed suggested that

Roy had been eating green apples or drinking too much whiskey.

"Jesus, Roy," A.G. called. "It's like I'm locked up in a muffler factory."

"Go ahead, son," came Roy's voice. "What else was it on your mind?"

With the cigar smoke, the tobacco juice and the smells spreading from the stall, A.G. began to feel faint, but he forced himself to speak. He had come in having in mind a further loan of a hundred thousand, but somehow the peculiar circumstances of the interview made him drop his request.

"I need eighty thousand, Roy."

"For what?"

"Just these payments I got. Once I get them out of the way. I can see my way clear, now. That Bermuda grass—"

"This is just a little country bank," Roy's voice said. Then he grunted a couple of times. "I sure would like to help out some more, but I can't handle it."

"You can't help out?"

"I'd like to." Grunt. "But I can't. I got the stockholders to think about." As far as A.G. knew, the only stockholders in Bushyhead National were Roy, his wife and his wife's cousin. He is putting me off, A.G. thought. He is turning me down. Son of a bitch. "The thing is, son, in my private view, which is just a little country banker of which we are a dime a dozen as you know, you are overextended to a certain extent. My advice to you is, pull in your horns for the time being. Consolidate. You might think of sellin off a few acres. I'd be happy to help you out on that, if you want. I know several buyers. I can get you buyers in five minutes. Meantime, you go ahead. I'm real sorry. But you'll be all right. Hell, with them assets? Now you go on. I'll be in here some time. You know the way out, don't you?"

A.G. left without another word. When he got outside he leaned against the Eldorado and breathed to counter his nausea. He spotted a liquor store down the street and bought a bottle of Scotch and sped out of town. As soon as he was clear of habitation he pulled the car off the road, turned off the ignition, opened the bottle and took four or five good swallows. He was trembling. I have to calm my nerves, he thought. I have to get this thing under control and figure out what my next move is. But he did not know what his next move would be. He considered just sitting there in the car, finishing the bottle, passing out and letting somebody find him. He took more Scotch. What in hell has happened? How did I end up like this? No, I am not finished, I just have to get my priorities straight. Back up some. Make a run at it later on. The phrases had no substance for him. They sounded in his head like cheers for a team that had already been beaten. For months now he had managed to juggle his accounts and keep barely ahead, but Roy Twyman's refusal was a blow right on the button, it seemed. He had gone to Twyman precisely because Twyman was a sure thing, the most likely of all the sources he knew. A.G. did not start up the car again until half the bottle was gone. When he got home he went directly upstairs, climbed into bed and pulled the covers over his head.

It had been a slow and invisible process, but when one day about a year and a half into his improvement program A.G. had gone over his accounts with a clear eye, he had felt as though someone had pulled the rug out from under him. He kept the figures to himself, but any way he looked at them he could see that he was in too deep. He had felt some anxiety growing as soon as he had begun to borrow in a big way, and eventually he started concealing some of the loans he had already taken out in order to secure new ones on the most favorable terms, but everyone gets nervous when they borrow, he had told himself. It was unimaginable that the Sunrise could not sustain the burden of debt. But he began to realize that even with all the cattle he had scheduled for the market, he was going to have trouble making the payments, carrying

on with improvements, and just plain paying the bills and
salaries to keep the ranch operating at full tilt.

Roy Twyman's refusal tightened the vise. Not being sure
what move to make next, A.G. became obsessed with his
schemes and found that he could not get to sleep at night
without plenty of whiskey, he would be so keyed up. He
would be out on the land early in the morning, supervising the
new work and the old business of deciding which cattle to put
in which pasture, but all the time the list of his creditors and
the sums he owed them passed through his mind, rolling
through his brain like movie credits on a screen. Often he had
a dreamy, abstracted air and Ramsey would have to speak to
him two or three times to get his attention. He would get back
to the house late, tired out, not feeling like talking to anyone,
not wanting to hear Claire tell him one more time that he
should slow down and that she was not seeing enough of him,
and he would almost always stay up, going over his accounts
and sipping whiskey, long after Claire had gone upstairs. As
his anxiety grew, he found that he had begun to shrink from
intimacy with her. All he had on his mind was the calendar,
the due date for the next payments haunting him. When he
did finally join her at night, they were, as the song would one
day say, sleeping single in a double bed.

At first A.G. had been surprised at how easy it was for him
to borrow big sums, and then it was hard for him to accept it
when it became difficult to make the payments. He knew that
it would take at least five or six years for the improvements to
begin increasing the Sunrise's income, so he had borrowed
more to meet the loan deadlines. Sometimes, after finally managing to get to sleep, he would wake up in a sweating panic
about the loans, but then he would tell himself that he was
sitting on millions of dollars of assets and there was no reason
to think like some poor dirt farmer waiting for the bank to
foreclose. At any moment if he ever got pressed to the wall he
could sell off some of the Sunrise. Although he never would.

That would be a definition of defeat. All great men had been gamblers. Hadn't Harry Sinclair shot off his toes to collect the insurance to pay for his first oil lease? It had taken a gambling shotgun blast to start the Sinclair Oil Company. If you weren't a gambler you might as well pull the covers over your head.

But owing so much money—after a year it was creeping toward the five-million mark—was not something he could bear lightly. Right after his father's death he had attempted to get to know every one of his hands and their families and would often drop in on them at night with Ramsey to chat, sip a few, maybe play a little friendly poker, but then he began to withdraw, preferring Ramsey's company and confidence exclusively. He had radiophones installed all over the Sunrise and in his car, so he could check up on everything without even having to step out of his car if necessary. And he would telephone home throughout the day, telling Claire that he loved her, trying to ignore the coolness of her replies, saying that he didn't know exactly when he would be home but that he would try to make it early, and then always being late. And he could not get the loans off his mind. The ranch's income was not enough to cover them.

"You know something?" he said to Ramsey one day. "I may be worth more dead than alive."

"Don't say that."

"It just might be true. Shit. This deal of ours is turning out to be quite a gamble. But we'll see it through, won't we?"

"We sure will. You know what you're doin, A.G. Course it might be, you movin a little fast."

"Are you with me or against me?"

"Come on, you know I'm with you. It's just that, maybe we should of done one thing at a time. It seems like for instance that Bermuda grass, it's a good idea, but we get some of the land ready, and now we're puttin it in, and if it growed all right we could triple the cows, okay, but it don't seem like it's growin right yet."

"It will."

They were parked beside a pasture, looking at a herd of Herefords. A.G. picked up his radiophone and called home.

"I don't know, Claire. Yeah. Well, I'm sorry about that. How's little Earl? Oh sure, he's in school. Well what do you think, how's he doin? . . . Well, I love you. Bye."

A.G. reached under the seat and pulled out a bottle of Scotch and took a long drink of it. He offered it but Ramsey refused. Ramsey never drank on the job. He might quit work at six and go tie one on and find a woman, but on the job he stayed sober.

"Ramsey, you're my oldest friend, right?"

"Right."

"Matter of fact, you're my only friend. I always treated you good, haven't I?"

"You sure have."

"I mean, if it weren't for me and my dad, you might be out in California and in trouble again and back in the jug, for all you know."

Ramsey did not like the tone or the implications, but he let them pass.

"I'm gonna tell you somethin," A.G. said, "and I'm gonna ask you somethin. Cause I figure you owe me one or two anyways."

"You don't have to think of it like that."

"Well let's face facts. I'm doing all of this for my family, but I can't do this and do the kind of job at home maybe I ought to be doin. The truth is, Claire and me, we're not as close as we were or like we should be."

"They say marriage is ups and downs."

"Too many downs right now. The truth is, she's pretty fed up with me right now. I'm workin hard and drinkin hard and gamblin hard." He spit tobacco juice out the window. "And I'm runnin with a pretty fast money crowd right now. You know I might be worth more dead than alive. But I intend to fight it out and to win."

"You will win."

"You see this?" A.G. opened the glove compartment and pulled out a .38 pistol. "This will make sure I win."

Ramsey did not see the point of the pistol but, as he watched A.G. take another swig of Scotch, he sensed his friend's nerves were pretty stretched and figured that if the pistol made him feel safer, well let him carry it.

A.G. weighed the gun in his hand and said:

"I want you to start carryin one of these, too. You never know. Matter of fact, we're gonna get you one right now."

He floored the Lincoln and headed off at a hundred miles an hour, down the ranch road and out onto the highway and down to a little wooden shack of a store where they sold guns and ammunition. He bought another .38 for Ramsey. Behind the counter a sign said, "The West Wasn't Won with a Registered Gun."

Back in the car, A.G. told Ramsey that he was worried about his children. Everyone knew who A.G. Kruger was, and the way people were, someone might just decide to kidnap one of his children and hold the kid for ransom. He wanted Ramsey to take it as his personal responsibility to see that something like that never happened. He had a gun with him now at all times. If necessary, he should not hesitate to use it.

Ramsey could not argue with A.G. It was true that the children of rich people were always getting kidnapped. Yet A.G.'s manner had become so agitated, so edgy, that it was almost as if he saw ten kidnappers behind every bush. He also did not see how he could protect A.G.'s family if he was out making the rounds with him every day, and he said so.

"I want you to protect me, too," A.G. said. "There's plenty of people would as soon see me dead. We're runnin a high-risk operation here. I'm not afraid to take the risks. I am willin to pay the price. But I intend to keep my eyes open and I want you to do the same."

"A.G.," Ramsey said. "Maybe we should slow this whole

thing down. Know what I mean? You don't slow it some, you're gonna end up a heart attack."

"You sound like Claire."

"Maybe she's got a point."

"She's a woman. You know what women do when they don't like somethin a man's doin, don't you?"

"Hold out on the pussy."

"That's right." A.G. felt a twinge of conscience at what he had implied. He knew his marital problems were as much his doing as Claire's and they would pass. "Ramsey, what would you do if you found your wife fucking somebody else?" He wondered why he had asked this. He had no reason to suspect her.

"I don't know," Ramsey said. "I'm not married. I had it happen once, though, real bad. You remember that Sally I used to run around with?"

"Sure. The redheaded gal. You looked like twins."

"Yeah. People used to say that. The little bitch. You know what happened to me? I was fuckin her one night and I found a rubber in her cunt. And it weren't mine, neither."

"Holy shit. What did you do?"

"Cold-cocked her. And never saw her again."

"You find out whose it was?"

"Nope. Didn't want to. Might of lost my temper."

"Well, I think I can trust Claire, don't you?"

"I'd say that was one loyal woman, A.G. You got yourself a good one there."

Ramsey asked why A.G. didn't hire some guards, if he was so worried about security.

"Sure," A.G. said. "And make everybody feel like they're in prison. No, we can handle it, can't we? I'll tell Claire you're keepin an eye out."

"Right."

"And I know this'll make Claire feel better. Take some of the heat off my back."

"Anything you say."

"Hey! Wait a minute!" A.G. shouted. "What in hell is that son of a bitch doing?"

They had pulled alongside a big scrap heap, piled with old pieces of fence, wire, metal, ranch junk of all kinds. One of the cowboys had his pickup raised on blocks and was taking a tire from the scrap heap. Obviously he was planning to put the scrapped tire on his truck.

A.G. slammed the Lincoln to a stop and leapt out, Ramsey following. He stomped over to the cowboy, who stood there with the tire in his hands, looking wide-eyed but innocent.

"What in the fuck do you think you're doin?" A.G. yelled at the cowboy. And he asked Ramsey: "Who is this son of a bitch?"

"Lonny Waters. Been with us almost a year."

"Well what was you plannin to do with that tire, Waters?"

"Mr. Kruger, I was plannin on puttin it on my truck there. My old tire kind of blew out, total, and I was gonna put this one on. It ain't much, but it's a damn sight better'n the other one. There's the other one over there. She's older'n dirt."

"Yeah?" A.G. said. "Well who gave you permission to take that tire?"

"I figured it was scrapped. Nobody wanted it. Why, Mr. Kruger, nobody'd give a dime for it."

"I'll give you somethin!"

"Yessir?"

"Waters, you have stolen from me. You have stolen from the Sunrise Ranch." A.G. had stuck his .38 in the small of his back. Now he took it out, pointed it at the ground, and fired at Lonny Waters' feet. "And here's another thing." A.G. fired again. "That's right. Dance! And dance your way right off this ranch. You are fired!" He shot again. Lonny Waters ran off down the road and out of sight.

A.G. took more Scotch as he drove off.

"You got to watch these bastards every minute," he said. "They will steal you blind."

Ramsey thought that his old friend was even more disturbed than he had imagined. Poor old Lonny Waters.

When A.G. got home that night he was ready to come unraveled. He was drunk and feeling guilty because he knew that he had taken it out on Waters, but he could not admit that he had made a mistake. Waters would find another job, but A.G. told himself that he had to keep better control. At the same time he hoped that Claire was not in the mood to get on him tonight. He needed to be quiet and to relax.

"You're drunk," she said as soon as he opened his mouth. "I can see it and I can smell it. What the hell is this, A.G.? You're hardly home at all, and when you do get home, you're supposed to be working so hard all day, and you're loaded."

"It's all gonna change," A.G. said. "You'll see. What's dinner?"

Coldly Claire arranged for the cook to serve A.G. his dinner alone. She went up to bed.

A.G. picked at his dinner, trying to eat it because he knew it would help sober him up. He needed something to drink. He decided on a bottle of wine. That would taste good with the food, it would not be too strong, it would let him down gently, and in an hour or so he would feel better. He opened the wine and thought of all the dinners at the family table. Old Earl had always liked wine and always had a big stock of it. Old Earl had been great about that. Other people had wine and were assholes about it, but old Earl just liked it and never made a fuss about it. A.G. sat there eating his dinner, drinking the wine, and thinking about his father and about his mother, over there alone with the servants in the big house. What a loss she must feel. What was left for her? He felt very sorry for his mother and he realized how much he loved her. She was such a good person that you hardly even noticed her. Tears came to his eyes, and he swallowed more wine and tried to think positive thoughts. Eventually it would all pay off, he told himself. If you don't suffer, you never get anything. He thought of his children, asleep in their beds, and more tears came.

This is asinine, he told himself, what I need is a good shot of brandy to shock me out of this bullshit. He poured some brandy into his coffee and sat there contemplating life and the combination of brandy and coffee. It was a good combination, because the brandy was strong and perked you up and the coffee counteracted the effects of the alcohol. A man could probably drink brandy and coffee all night, or almost.

He had tried not to think about Claire, but as always she finally invaded his thoughts. She is the most important thing in my life, when all is said and done, he thought, and he put his head down on the table at the thought of how much he loved her and wanted her. He tried not to think of how seldom they made love anymore. He hardly ever felt like it when he was with her. It was odd that he would often feel the most intense surges of passion for her when he was out driving around on the ranch. That was when he would call her and tell her that he loved her. But when he got into bed with her all he could think of was his plans and his money problems, and he felt no desire, all he felt was the distance between them. He sometimes had the suspicion that the road he was traveling to expansion and success was taking him away from Claire and his children, but he knew that this was a false sensation, because it was all for them, all the hard work and planning and wheeling and dealing. Why else had he taken out such enormous amounts of life insurance but for them? Well, it was to borrow on, sure, but at least if something should happen to him they would be free and clear. Yet something was haywire. He would simply have to have faith in himself, see this thing through and know that in the end he would earn Claire's gratitude and love. He had already given her carte blanche to spend whatever she wanted on herself. She had gone on a couple of shopping sprees and the last bill from Gordon Tay-

lor's in Tulsa was seven thousand dollars for nightclothes, but
he knew that Vivian was the one who liked to run up the bills.
Well, let her. He had bought his mother-in-law a car and had
let her send him the bill for redecorating her house, but these
were piddling sums in relation to everything else, and if it
made the old lady shut up and stay off his back, well and good.
The one thing Claire really seemed to like to spend money on
was the telephone. She must waste half the day talking to two
or three old girlfriends in Tulsa, he thought, and he wondered
what the hell she talked to them about. Him? How unsatisfac-
tory he had become as a husband and father? It occurred to
him that he should have the line tapped. Maybe she was planning to divorce him. Maybe she was asking people for advice
on who was the meanest, toughest divorce lawyer in the state.
More than once in arguments she had told him that she was
fed up and getting out, but from what he could tell every
married couple said that in arguments. No, she would not
leave him. Where on earth would she find something like the
Sunrise?

Upstairs Claire was trying to get to sleep, worrying about
A.G. and about how she was feeling about him. His physical
appearance had begun to put her off. He was bloated from the
drink, whiskey-puffed, and pale and sweaty all the time. His
manner was either bravado-inflated or depressed. She knew
that something was going wrong on the business side of the
ranch, but when she tried to talk to him about it, he either
flatly refused or fended her off with talk of impending great-
ness. He was losing something, that quality of genuineness she
had cherished. Maybe, she thought, she had neglected him for
her children; but every mother had to do that for a time, and
just when she might have been ready to pay more attention to
him, he seemed to have become obsessed with his expansion
schemes. She was bored with hearing about them. She could
not believe everything he said about them anyway.

She had several times been on the verge of asking Ramsey

what was really going on with A.G. Ramsey. She had begun to welcome the sight of him. He had come to appear to her as a sort of beacon in a storm she could hardly define or see, a mist, a fog. There was something calming about him, as though he would remain rooted should others be torn up. She realized that she liked having him to dinner—he was always with them or with Margaret for dinner, unless he was going out. With a woman. He must be a comfort to Margaret, too, she thought. He must be a comfort to these women he sees. He never brings them around or talks about them. Strange, she thought, just thinking about Ramsey makes me calmer, makes me slide toward sleep. If I go on thinking about Ramsey, I may drop off to sleep soon. I bet I could sleep if he were here in this room with me. Maybe he would hold my hand. Hold me. Ramsey, hold me. Ramsey, what is wrong with A.G., will you tell me? Tell me all, Ramsey. All.

Downstairs A.G. decided to have one more brandy and coffee, and as he poured the stuff, the inspiration came to him that it was time to take a few days off from the work and do something for Claire and the children. He knew what it would be. They would go to New York. Or why not Paris? Paris or New York, let her choose. That would be it. He would present the idea to her and let her be the judge. He rehearsed in his mind what he would say to her and imagined what her reaction would be. She would leap at the idea. She would see that he was thinking of both her and the children. She had already said that she was determined that little Earl see something of the world and, like Margaret before her, she was talking about sending her son out of the state to college. A.G. had already decided that he would not stand in the way of that. This trip to Paris or New York would be the first step in a new life for them. And he would be able to begin showing that not only was he taking the Sunrise beyond whatever his father had made of it, he would display himself as a different sort of man from his father, more tolerant, more cosmopolitan, more a man of the world who could hold his own in any corner of the globe.

When he stood up he stumbled and fell, hitting his jaw on the corner of the table. He hoped no one had heard the noise. Nothing was broken. It hurt, but it was nothing. He got to his feet and made a few deliberate moves, checking on his coherence, and, satisfied that he could make it, walked slowly toward the stairs. Slowly he climbed them, holding the banister and feeling each step with his toes before putting his weight on it. He made his way into their room only to discover that he had pushed open the wrong door. It was little Earl's room. The boy lay on his back, angelic, his face illuminated by the soft light he kept on for fear of the dark. Around the room A.G. made out a football, baseball mitt, little Earl's pine-cone collection and rock collection, and in a special glass case A.G. had given him for Christmas, his collection of arrowheads found on the Sunrise. The scene filled A.G. with happiness and gratitude. He had everything. A wonderful wife and two perfect children and the best ranch in the world. What was he worried about? He was so happy that he decided to check on little Margaret. He found her with her head under the covers. Very carefully and gently he folded back the blanket, plumped up her pillow, eased her head onto it, and gave her a light kiss on the cheek before creeping from the room. Everything was right. All was in order. All he had to do now was get into bed without waking Claire.

But when he saw her lying there, curled up with pillows over her head as though to shut out the world, he was so moved and overcome that he went over to her side, knelt down, and tapped her lightly on the shoulder. She stirred, moaned, pulled the pillows tight. He tapped again. She yanked the pillows off and suddenly they were eyeing each other, inches apart.

"Claire." He could tell his voice was too loud, and more softly he blurted, "Claire, my darling. Darlingness. I."

"What are you doing?" She sat straight up and switched on the bedside lamp. "Look at you! Get up!"

"No," he said. "You see, I love you very much." He lay his head down on the bed.

"Get out of here! Now!"

"You'll see. We're going Paris, New York, anywhere you want."

"I want you out of here!"

"Give me a chance."

"I told you, I don't want you sleeping in here when you're drunk. Get out."

"It's my room, too."

"Not any more it isn't! Out! Sleep in another room! I don't want you!"

He inched his head toward her and suddenly he felt her fingers grip his hair and pull back on it. For a moment he felt little and then the pain told him that she was pulling on his hair with all her strength. A tearing sensation told him that she had yanked a clump out by the roots. He grabbed her wrists and dug his thumbs into the pressure points. Then they struggled. She bit into his shoulder and he managed to reach back and crack her across the face, grab her throat, bang her head back against the headboard, screaming at her, "Fuck you! Fuck you! You're ruining me! You ungrateful bitch! Bitch! Bitch!" He grabbed one of her breasts, twisted it, then pushed her back and stumbled from the room, leaving her sobbing.

In the hallway he passed the bewildered figure of little Earl.

"It's all right. Go back to bed. Mommy's not feeling well."

NINETEEN

It took weeks for that one to blow over, if it ever did. A.G., on reflection, decided that he had become a monster, although he reserved for himself the slightly mitigating circumstance that she had rejected him and had pulled on his hair, knowing this to be a childish rationalization but easing his guilt a little with it. The incident sobered him up for the time being. Claire reeled for days between anger and feelings of degradation, most angry of all because little Earl had heard the fighting. She did not have to ask A.G. to sleep in another room, he did so voluntarily, saying nothing about it, and she would wake up in the middle of the night missing him, then glad she was alone, then wanting him, then fearful that something would happen again. When Eula, their cook, had asked about the bruises, Claire admitted that A.G. had cuffed her, and Eula said that she knew that Mr. Kruger was a good man but that he was under a lot of strain and that she guessed a few bruises came with the bargain of marriage anyway. After a couple of weeks, Claire asked him to come back to her bed, and he did, feeling like a punished child, half inclined to stay away, hurt and confused that she did not want to make love, yet somehow relieved as well.

If A.G. wanted Ramsey to keep an eye out for the safety of the family, it happened that Ramsey was able to fulfill this role at closer range than anyone had anticipated. He had been supervising some branding, sitting on a fence watching the action, when the top rail of the fence gave way and he fell, snapping an ankle and searing the side of one leg in the fire, as a calf panicked and ran over him. A.G. drove him to the hospital in Tulsa, cursing the idiots who had let the fence get out of repair. Too many things like that were going on.

"When you get better," he said to Ramsey, who was doubled up in agony on the back seat of the Lincoln, "we are gonna kick some ass. We are gonna go over a list of these sons of bitches and fire every damn slacker in the bunch. Heads will roll!"

Ramsey was hurt too badly to take care of himself, so A.G. set him up in the house, where Claire and Eula could see to him while he recovered. And to make him feel less useless, A.G. reminded him that while he was there he could keep an eye out. "You may be flat on your back, but you can still take a shot at somebody if you have to," A.G. kidded him, and he told Claire that Ramsey had a gun.

Claire wondered about all of A.G.'s talk of safety and protection. How serious was he? What was all this talk about guns? She wasn't happy that A.G. was already teaching little Earl how to shoot, even if that was the way things were done in the country. A.G.'s nerves were getting on her own. What does it all mean? she wondered. What is happening to us? What is the point of having all this if we end up living in a cage and it seems to be driving my husband away from me and into a world obsessed with money, kidnapping, suspicion run wild? On the telephone she would hear how her old friends' lives were going. One was divorced, another contemplating divorce, all were unhappy except for one Catholic girl who seemed to be content bearing her sixth child and living as though women had not even got the vote yet, afraid to go to the bathroom without asking her husband's permission. Is it me or is something happening to the world? Margaret, her mother-in-law, seemed to be getting a bit senile and talked of nothing but old Earl and the old days, her eyes watering when she recalled some dramatic moment from the past, rattling on about Earl had done this and Earl had done that and how glad she was that A.G. seemed to show so much of Earl's spirit these days. If only she knew, Claire thought. Margaret was not an unintelligent woman and she still had her brains even if they were getting a little soft. She had been married for fifty years to a blustering bigot who was hated throughout the state by anyone who gave two cents for honesty and decency and kindness and fair play. And he had made her happy. What was the answer? Her own father had been a good man, a kindly altruistic man, and he had killed himself. A.G. was a good man, underneath the bluster, she knew that, but what was going to happen to him and to them? Whatever, she realized, she had her children. Somehow she would figure out a way to hang on and to see this through and to give them a good life. She would find a way for herself, too, somehow, she didn't know how, and it just might be that A.G. would too. He was trying. That's what Margaret said all the time: "That boy tries so hard. It's wonderful."

She began talking to Ramsey during the day as he lay in his bed recovering. At first she thought she might be able to get something out of him about the financial situation at the ranch, but he either knew nothing or was too loyal to A.G. to say anything, because all he did was reassure her that everything was going great and that A.G. was too smart to go wrong. When she would ask him why he thought that A.G. had become too edgy and didn't he think A.G. should cut down on his drinking, Ramsey would reply only that big plans like A.G.'s were bound to play on a man's nerves and that a man sometimes needed a drink or two to stay on an even keel and to relax. She admired his loyalty, even if it was exasperating, and she began to see that Ramsey had a sensitive side to him even if he was more or less illiterate and rough. She made a point of bringing most of his meals to him and sometimes they would watch a soap opera or a game show together and share a few laughs.

They were watching *As the World Turns* one afternoon. Ramsey was in bed with his foot propped up and Claire sat

beside him in a chair. In the soap opera, which they had been
following for several days, a mother was about to go to prison.
Her daughter had killed a lover whom they had unwittingly
shared, but the mother had confessed to the crime, preferring
prison for herself rather than seeing her daughter locked up.

"Mother love," Claire said during a commercial. "I suppose
I'd do that. I don't know. Having children changes your life."

"I reckon it sure does," Ramsey said. "I know guys I used to
know, they has changed completely once they got a family.
You don't raise as much hell, I can see that."

"But going to prison. I can't think of anything worse. Imagine being a woman and going to prison."

"It ain't no fun for a man neither," Ramsey said.

"You were in prison."

"Yes ma'am. That is the truth of it."

"What did you think about, all that time? What was it like?"

Ramsey told her that the worst part was, you never knew
when you were getting out for sure, and what was even worse
than that had been when he had been scheduled for parole
and then did not get it. That was when he had gone a little
berserk, and that had been the worst mistake he had made.
What he had thought about most of the time was coming back
to Oklahoma.

"You never thought of trying again in California?"

"I saw enough of the place," Ramsey said. "I got to appreciate where I come from. You want my opinion, California is
overrated."

"Why? I hear it's beautiful."

"Maybe it was. The way it is now, it's fine if you like weirdos.
I heard somebody say once, the land tilts west, and all the
lightweights, they rolled into California. Just so's they don't
roll back, it's fine with me. I believe the old ways is the best
ways. I found that out. I heard a girl out there say, if we was
in Samoa, we could do such and such. Well hell, she weren't in
Samoa. She was in a lousy little apartment in Hollywood.

That's the way they think out there. They don't know where in hell they are."

It occurred to Claire that Ramsey was like a gentler version of old Earl. It was not a bad combination. She liked to hear him talk. His rough, low voice had music to it.

When he was able to get up and around a bit he would hobble around the house looking for jobs to do, things to fix, and one morning he volunteered to drive little Earl to school, saying that he was sure he could drive an automatic shift since it was his left ankle that had been broken, and that he was dying to get out. He picked little Earl up at school that day, too, and Claire was pleased at the way Ramsey was making himself so useful. As he got more mobile, he found more things to do, cleaning the swimming pool, working on the cars, and one night when A.G. asked Ramsey when he thought he would be ready to get back on the job full time, Claire interrupted and said:

"He's practically working a full-time job around here. You wouldn't believe what a help Ramsey's being. I don't want him gone till he's really well. He's such a help to me."

"Well, good," A.G. said.

When the weather turned warm, she would spend part of the afternoon sunning herself beside the pool with a book, and without even being asked, Ramsey would fetch little Margaret and play with her by the pool and take her for dips, throwing her up and letting her splash, laughing with her. Claire liked the way Ramsey cared for her children. When he brought little Earl home from school he even went over his homework with him, telling him that he himself had never been much in school but A.G. had, and that a good education was the best insurance a man could buy. "My mother was a schoolteacher," he told little Earl. "She's dead now. I wished I'd of learned some of her lessons better. Oh I do all right, but when it comes to learnin, I couldn't pour piss out of a boot on a hill with instructions on it. You hit them books."

Ramsey did not care for his confinement at all. He liked the children genuinely enough, and he didn't mind a few good views of Claire in her bikini either. A.G. had intimated that he was having trouble in bed with her, and for the life of him Ramsey could not understand why. She was maybe a little aloof in her manner but he would lay fifty to one that she bucked like a bronco in the sack. She had a five-hundred-dollar ass, and her skin, darkening as May slipped toward June, made him think of something slick and slippery, he didn't know what. Once with one of his girlfriends he found himself thinking of Claire and he had tried to banish the thought because it was almost like being disloyal to A.G. even to think about it. Loyalty was why he was doing this dumb job, because as he had feared, a glorified babysitter was what he had become: loyalty and, he supposed, the fact that he was an ex-con beholden to someone. But it would not go on forever. For the moment he had no choice and tried to make the best of it. You could only play whatever cards were dealt.

Often he and Claire dined alone. A.G. would come in later and eat in front of the television or talk about his day, his frustrations with the Bermuda grass, which was not taking, or his meetings with this or that banker. A.G. would always sound certain and optimistic, but Ramsey could tell he was worried and he was sure Claire could see it too. When he was alone with Claire, he found it awkward, and he tried to keep up a steady line of chat about what it had been like when he and A.G. had been young. She seemed to enjoy hearing about these adventures, and Ramsey found that he could make her laugh. Somehow he felt that it made things easier to keep talking about A.G., as long as he was being forced to be alone with his friend's wife.

Claire took to calling Ramsey in a little early and offering him a drink. At first he refused, but she pressed him. She had grown to like him a lot. She appreciated the way he acted, never complaining, wonderful with the children. She made him stop calling her "ma'am."

"Tell me something, Ramsey," she said one evening in the

living room over drinks. "Do you think A.G.'s going to pull off
all these improvements? Do you think he's getting in over his
head?" She knew she knew nothing about the economics of
ranching, and she wanted the honest opinion of someone who
had grown up on it.

"I'm sure he will," Ramsey said. "I never seen that man give
up on nothin. He bites onto somethin, he won't let go. He's got
his daddy's fight in him."

"You don't think he might be biting off too much?"

"No, ma'am, uh, Claire. If anybody knows what he's doin,
it's got to be A.G. I always knowed he was smart."

She got up to freshen his drink for him. She preferred not
having the servants around when she was talking to Ramsey.
She did not want them to get ideas. When she gave him back
his glass, she said to him:

"You know, I'm very grateful for what you're doing for us. It
must be boring for you sometimes. I'm sure you'd rather be out
with everyone else."

"No."

"Not just a little bit? Come on, admit it, it's boring spending
so much time with a woman. And her children. Isn't it?"

"No. I'd do anything for A.G. After all, he done whatever
he could for me, ever since we was kids."

Claire found that the answer annoyed her. She had wanted
to hear something else, or not that. What about her? She was
conscious of her attractiveness. Surely a man like Ramsey got
pleasure just from being around her, didn't he? She could not
ask him that, but she could feel it anyway. Ramsey was very
masculine. More masculine than A.G., the truth of it was.
Ramsey did not seem to have anything feminine about him.
These country boys had a hardness to them that you could not
find anywhere else. None of the boys she had grown up with
had it. A.G. did not quite have it, although his tenderness and
sensitivity had of course been a great part of his appeal. And
always would be, of course. She had seen Ramsey in the pool

and he was strong as a horse. But he was gentle, too. Gentle
with her children. Soft in his speech. Courteous. So courteous.
He was like something from the past. Like something out of a
pioneer story. Imagine, he had been in prison. It had not
seemed to embitter him. He seemed, from what she could tell,
to have waited out his time behind bars, patient as an Indian,
and then to have resumed his life: it had been merely incon-
veniently interrupted. It was as though he knew something.
About life. About patience. Some secret that maybe had been
lost to others.

"Tell me something," she said. "Are you ever going to get
married?"

"I don't know. Not for a while, I can tell you."

"Why not? You like women, don't you?"

"Sure do," he grinned.

"From what A.G. tells me, you like them a lot."

"Well, nobody never called me a sissy."

"Maybe you just like them in bed. Maybe you wouldn't want
to bother with one all the time and put up with a family."

"I got burned once. That might be it. You get burned, it can
stay with you a long time, maybe forever."

"Tell me about it."

He told her about Kitty. He said that he was not sure
whether he was in love with her at the time, but somehow,
after she had stopped visiting him and he had lost track of her,
he believed he did love her. It might have been because he
didn't have much else to think about in prison, he didn't know.
And it might have been because she had given up on him.
Sometimes, he noticed, if a woman scorns you, even a little bit,
you want her more. Like tracking a deer. The challenge. He
wasn't sure. He guessed it was human nature.

Claire noticed a twinge of disappointment in herself when
she heard A.G. at the door.

She found herself lying awake at night thinking of Ramsey.
She tried to banish the thoughts with a book or a magazine,

but when A.G. would come to bed, often smelling of booze, the thoughts would assail her again, and sometimes she would give in to them, remembering the line about how the only way to conquer a temptation was to give in to it. She was not about to give in to the temptation in actuality, there was no possibility of that. She was not, she told herself, some mindless adolescent who never thought about the consequences of an act. But thoughts were only thoughts, and some of the thoughts were so pleasant that she let them invade her and excite her. Sometimes when A.G. was asleep she would lie there, turned away from him, thinking about Ramsey with her hand tucked between her thighs, pressing and teasing herself until the wave broke with warm force. It would all pass, she thought, when Ramsey was completely recovered and out of the house. She would see him, he would come to dinner as always, but as long as he was not around all the time, it would be different.

He was so attractive behind, the way his jeans clung to him, and in front, there was a pale spot on his well-worn jeans where, she knew, his penis rubbed against the denim. What was it like? He had such a reputation as womanizer, it must be pretty damned adequate. She tried to expunge these thoughts by thinking about A.G. sexually, but she could not. He had ceased—it was a momentary thing, a passing thing she knew, hoped, a thing that happens in every marriage—simply ceased to interest her sexually. No, that was not strictly true. When she remembered times past he would come alive to her again. But now when she confronted him, she did not hate him, that was not it, she loved him, but seeing him did not make her heart race or her breathing quicken, and seeing Ramsey did. He would have to leave the house soon, or something might happen. She did not want it to happen, not really, but it might. It could. She would have to will that it would not. He was almost recovered now. He could stand on his ankle and had a new plastic cast that made it possible for him to go in the water. Swimming, that was supposed to be good for him. God, he looked good in his swimming trunks, lean and strong with reddish, coarse hair on him. She found that she did not need much sleep. She would wake up after a fitful night and hurry downstairs to see him.

Sometimes her feelings became so strong that she could not resist accidentally brushing up against him and she was constantly making up some excuse to see him. One day she announced that she simply had to have Ramsey accompany her into Tulsa because she had a lot of shopping to do and couldn't manage all the packages by herself. She said this to Eula, not to A.G. She figured that they would be back before he came home anyway. She knew the excuse was ridiculous because he still couldn't walk perfectly and would hardly be a great help with packages, but she felt she had to get out of the house with him and wanted to be alone with him for a few hours. Off they went.

She invented things to shop for as she went along, starting downtown and then driving over to Utica Square. She felt a little foolish with him and wondered why she was doing this. They were not having an affair. What was the point of being seen around town with a man you were not having an affair with, raising needless suspicions? She hoped she would not run into her mother. Ramsey was ill at ease in the fashionable shops. It had been a silly idea. They would have lunch and go back.

They ate at Nicole's, a place done up like a chic bistro that was very popular with well-to-do professional people and had some of the most elegant food in town and waiters with British accents. Claire had a spinach quiche, and when Ramsey did not seem to know what to order she got the waiter to bring him a big steak that was not on the menu. They had white wine. They did not talk much. Claire could feel Ramsey's discomfort and cursed herself for bringing him there. Everyone in the restaurant seemed to know everyone else and there was a lot of table-hopping going on and a lot of noise, so that when she leaned over to tell him that she was sorry if he felt out of place, he did not hear her at first.

"I said I can see you don't like it here. I'm sorry."

"Steak's real good."

Their knees touched and neither one of them moved apart. They looked at each other, saying nothing. Claire's mind turned with conflicting thoughts, lust, her marriage, the restaurant. She wanted to say to Ramsey that yes they were attracted to each other, that was obvious, but they could not go any further. But she could not say anything to him because the restaurant was too crowded, someone would overhear, it was already idiotic of her to be seen in Nicole's with a man other than her husband, and what if she were able to tell him that they should not go any further and he were to respond as though he had no idea what she was talking about. What was she, some housewife with dreams? No, the way he stared at her, she knew he knew. And there had been other signs. She had caught him staring at her, in her swimsuit, in the negligee she had taken to wearing at breakfast. No, he knew. That was definite. She eased her leg away from his and stared at her salad. Now I will eat the salad, she said to herself, and keep control of myself. I will say nothing to him. We will drive back to the Sunrise, period.

It was all Ramsey could do to keep from lunging at her on the way back. Her perfume filled the Cadillac, he was feeling strong from the steak and the wine, he liked the way her leg looked extended toward the accelerator as she clipped along. She was wearing a beige silk blouse, very sheer, and when the light was right he could see her breasts, nice ones they were, he could tell, but then he had seen more of them by the swimming pool. What a life that would be, he mused to himself, to have a classy woman like that to drive you around in her Cadillac. He resented her for giving him the come-on, he could not take it for anything else, and then backing off. It was torture. But worse, he thought, so much worse to get involved with her. He told himself that he would have to get out of her house as soon as possible, without making it look awkward. Yet when he thought of leaving, when he thought of never having what was almost being offered to him, he felt sharp regret. I'm a fool. I would like to fuck her so bad. I'll bet she has a mink pussy. Ramsey had a trick he liked to pull on girls. He could unfasten a bra without the girl even noticing and slip it out through the sleeve of her blouse. He felt like doing that now to Claire. No, he thought, no, no.

They were off the interstate now, speeding along a two-lane highway. Claire switched on the radio and began going from station to station, back and forth along the dial, not finding anything that satisfied her. Ramsey watched her hand on the radio. It was a slender hand, tan, hairless, and he wanted to touch it. A small muscle in her forearm moved as she turned the dial. He heard her pass by a Ronnie Millsap song, "Back on My Mind Again," that he liked and without thinking about what he was doing he reached out, put his hand over hers, his big fingers over her fingers, and moved the dial back to his song. He left his hand over hers. She moved her hand within his, turning it palm upward. She spread her fingers and gripped him, lightly, then hard.

"Why don't you pull over?" Ramsey said.

He was on her before she had come to a full stop, and she drove the last few feet with her eyes closed, opening her mouth to him. They kissed, the motor running, the song playing, a long, soft, deep kiss that put them both in a dark and dizzy world.

"We should talk," Claire managed to say when they broke slowly apart. But she drew her arms around him and they kissed again. "We should talk," she said again.

"I guess we should." Ramsey cleared his eyes and looked around. Up ahead was a side road that led into some trees. "Pull in there," Ramsey said, pointing. "Why don't you. We can talk better there."

It was all Claire could do to drive the car another five hundred yards. When she had reached the trees and stopped she said there was a blanket in the trunk. Why didn't Ramsey get it? They could talk better outside. Under the trees. She handed him the key.

The air was heavy and hot after the air-conditioned car and they were both sweating by the time Ramsey spread the blanket and they lay down on it together.

"Hot," Claire said.

"Yeah. Sure is hot."

Ramsey ran a hand over her blouse and was thinking of unbuttoning it but as it turned out there was no time nor need for that. The moment they embraced on the blanket they both thought of only one thing, and it happened quickly. She was not wearing any stockings, and as soon as he touched her thigh she arched her back to make it easier for him to get her panties off and she grabbed his belt buckle. Although he could have ended it in seconds, he checked himself, rending her with long, slow strokes, saying to himself, nice guys finish last, not letting himself go until she was twisting, groaning, digging into his shirt with her nails, and then he let himself go like prairie fire, watching her face, her green eyes opening up with wonder.

Remorse flooded him as he flooded her.

"Now we've done it," he said, still holding her.

"Don't say that," she whispered.

"It was wrong. What if he finds out?" He pulled away, feeling miserable, and she let out a small cry as he withdrew.

"Why should he find out?" she said. "I assume we're not about to tell him."

"It always comes out. He'll know."

"No it doesn't. I wouldn't have missed you for anything." She kissed his red hair.

It was not the last time. It might have been, had Ramsey had his way, but he was still living in the house and Claire could not keep her mind or her eyes off of him. Her blood

would not let her stop thinking about him, and two days later
it was the servants' day off and Earl was at school and Margaret asleep. Claire lay out by the pool, trying to read a book
but thinking of nothing but Ramsey. She summoned him on a
trivial errand and told him that she wanted company. Why
didn't he get his trunks and they could take a swim together.
He hesitated. He knew what was going to happen. Again. He
felt that neither of them could be blamed more than the other
for what already had happened but now he was determined to
do the right thing, but she wanted more. Not that he did not
want it too, but he believed he could hold off, if only she
would play it cool. But she would not. She coaxed and kidded
him. "You're not afraid of me, are you Ramsey?" She smiled,
showing him strong teeth shining with wet. Hell, he thought. I
haven't even seen her naked. I haven't even held her naked.

When she brushed her hand against his bottom underwater,
it was all over and he knew that this was going to be the
second time and it would not stop there either. His desire
mixed with anger. He felt led. She took him into one of the
dressing rooms in the pool house and they tore at each other,
never saying a word, falling down on a heap of towels. Ramsey
was no longer hesitating. He straddled her and rammed it
home like a bull, thinking I am gonna jill-flirt this lying bitch,
having in mind what happens to a cow when the bull is too big
and he pulls out her insides with his prick, jamming at her,
thinking if this is what she wants, if this is what she wants to
do to A.G., then by God she is going to get it good, I am going
to hate-fuck her spoiled rich ass off. And look at her. The bitch
loves it. She gives as good as she gets. Goddamn her, goddamn
her.

They met often after that and kept it up even after Ramsey
had left the house. There was always a way to meet.

A.G. had begun to suspect even before it had happened, but
he did not want to believe it, and he said nothing for weeks.
He noticed that Claire's manner toward Ramsey had altered.

She was positively attentive to him, and she would get angry
with the servants if they dared call him Ramsey instead of Mr.
Hogan.

"What difference does it make what they call him?" A.G.
asked.

"It's not right," Claire said. "Ramsey's not a servant, he's a
friend."

"He works for me."

"You mean you don't think it's different? What kind of a
friend are you? Your oldest and best friend?"

Claire always had a way of putting off his insinuations about
Ramsey, and for his part A.G. was so eager to believe that
nothing was going on that he suspected himself of being paranoid. He knew he had become overly suspicious of everyone,
and he tried to control it, but sometimes he began to wonder
whether he was losing the ability to discriminate between
paranoia and justifiable fear. Besides, what was he to do? He
contemplated trying to surprise them by coming home at unexpected times, but what would happen if he actually did
discover them? Would he kill one or both of them? He might.
He probably would. That would finish everything. Wreck his
children's lives. From time to time he would catch himself
fantasizing about Claire and Ramsey in bed together: sometimes the scene would fill him with hate and anger and sometimes with lust and sometimes everything at once. He was
alarmed at himself. When he felt most suspicious of them, he
tried to figure out which one to blame and usually settled on
Claire, imagining himself with his hands around her throat
squeezing the life out of her, but sometimes he thought of
himself kicking Ramsey in the face with his boot.

One night as they were going to bed, together for a change,
A.G. reached out to her as she was undoing her bra and held
her from behind, cupping her breasts.

"I love you, Claire. Do you still love me?"

"Why are you holding me like that?"

"Why? Because I love you."

"I'm cold. Let me get my nightgown on."

In bed, he told her that she was acting very strangely toward him.

"It's almost like you have someone else," he said. "I know you don't, but it's almost like you do."

"You'd probably like that," she said.

"Why? Why would you say that?"

"Get you off the hook. We hardly make love ever anymore. How long has it been? I can't even remember."

"I don't feel like you want to."

"Well, the last time, as I recall, you couldn't even get it up."

"It happens to everyone," A.G. said.

"Well it can happen too often. I can't take it. It's hurtful and insulting. I don't think you want me. You drink too much anyhow."

He thought for a while. He decided to come right out with it.

"Claire, if you were having an affair, would you tell me about it, if I asked you?"

"Who on earth would I be having an affair with? I don't see anyone."

"Ramsey."

She did not miss a beat: "That's insane. I feel sorry for you. Do you know what that's called? Imagining things like that? Insulting someone with that kind of idiocy? It's called latent homosexuality, that's what it's called. Just how close were you and Ramsey when you were young, anyway? Jesus, maybe you are a faggot."

"You'd better shut up."

"Well you'd better not give in to these perverted fantasies of yours."

"Don't call me a faggot."

"I didn't. I just said that if you go around imagining that I'm going to bed with Ramsey, talk to a psychiatrist, not to me."

A.G. was furious enough at her to want to hit her, but he restrained himself, and he lay there trying to decide whether it was preferable to believe that she was betraying him or that he was a perverted lunatic.

Claire tried to understand what she had done and could not. She went on with it, because there did not seem to be any way of stopping it, but she did not know what was going on. She was full of anguish and a regret that stopped just short of self-recrimination, but she continued. She knew she was not in love with Ramsey, that it was A.G. she believed she still loved, but love was buried somewhere beneath the disappointments and the conflicts. Maybe this would teach A.G. a lesson, maybe that was why she was doing it. Or maybe, she speculated, she actually wanted A.G. to find out about it just to see what he would do, to see whether he would accept it or stand up to her or stand up to Ramsey or whatever, choose her over Ramsey, choose Ramsey over her, she didn't know. Maybe it was the only way she had of breathing. Her anxiety told her that the affair would end horribly for everyone, so perhaps she continued because she did not want to face that end. Well, people had affairs, didn't they? It happened to everyone. It was only human and so on, she told herself, not fully believing it, suspecting that there was something different about A.G. or the Sunrise or the entire situation that would mean bigger trouble than she could imagine. If I could dream about it, she thought, I would be driving a runaway locomotive.

And as for Ramsey, there was not a day when he did not arrive at the house determined to take Claire aside and say no, it's over, you are a hell of a woman but this is wrong and stupid and must end. Often they would avoid each other for a day or two but then, finding themselves alone by chance or by design, singular or mutual, they would touch and ignite. Introspection was not one of Ramsey's habits, but even he was conscious of a certain vague pleasure he was taking in getting the better of A.G. for once in his life, taking his property,

showing that you could have all the money and power in the
world but if that old pecker wasn't up to snuff you'd lose your
woman to the better man. He did not like feeling this way, he
was ashamed of it and he tried to repress it, but he was aware
of it. He did not love Claire any more than she loved him. He
did not care for arrogant women, but he had to admit he had
found out that he did not mind fucking them at all. There was
something uniquely thrilling about having an arrogant, rich
bitch lift her six-hundred-dollar dress and beg you for it. It
equaled things out, or better. Once, in the middle of it, he had
asked her whether she liked doing it with a hard-handed un-
educated son of a bitch cowboy, and she had said yes and it
was not at all difficult to tell that she meant it.

Ramsey found it difficult to keep the whole thing inside
himself. He was dying to talk to someone about it, but of
course he had to keep his mouth shut on the ranch. He wondered whether any of the boys suspected. They had kidded
him sometimes about his baby-sitting job and there had been
one or two snide remarks, but he had no reason to believe that
anyone knew anything. Maybe the servants at the house suspected. Once or twice he and Claire had got reckless and
simply locked the door to her room in the middle of the day,
but usually they were more careful than that, using the pool
house when the servants were around or even, as they had
done a couple of times lately, going off on an errand in her
car or in his pickup and heading into the woods. So no one
knew, he was ninety-nine percent sure. But the pressure was
getting to him.

One evening after seeing A.G. come in looking beat and
distraught, Ramsey jumped in his truck and headed for Tulsa
with the single purpose in mind of getting drunk to let off
steam. He started at Little Joe's over on 41st, but there was a
loud crowd in there, some TV comedian and newspaper and
TV people that thought they were pretty hot shit, so he left
and ended up at the old reliable Wheeler Dealer's. He sat

down at the bar between two friendly old boys and chatted with them about chili and football until the subject turned to women, and pretty soon he was ordering doubles and telling them without naming names that he had become involved with a rich woman and didn't know how to get out of it.

"She married?"

"Uh-huh."

"I'd say you was in hot water. Ain't nothin more trouble than a married rich woman. Now a single rich woman, you might get somethin outa that!"

"I can't see how it's gonna end," Ramsey said. "This thing might go on longer than a whore's dream."

And A.G. continued to want to trust Ramsey as much as he wanted to trust Claire. In the financial shape he was in, he could hardly face the loss of his best and only real friend and of his wife too. No, people did not do things like that to each other. Not good people. It was his imagination that Ramsey had been trying to avoid him. He would have to talk to Ramsey. Talking to Claire seemed to be impossible. What he would do, he decided, was to talk to Ramsey plain and simple about the financial situation. That would be a load off his mind, just by sharing all the information he had, and it would open things up between them so that he could confide his suspicions to his friend and lay them to rest. It would clear the air.

"I want to come clean with you," A.G. said to Ramsey, who did not reply but took a long swallow of his beer. "There's some things on my mind. Most of it shit. Sometimes life smells like a vegetarian's farted."

They were at the Wheeler Dealer's after a disappointing cattle sale, sitting in a dark booth at the back which A.G. had chosen so they could talk. At the bar Mr. Wheeler's old stool was empty. He had given in to his cirrhosis and his kidneys a month before, willing the bar to his ex-wife.

"I don't know how it happened, exactly."

"What?" Ramsey said, his voice uncharacteristically weak.

He took more beer and wished he had ordered Jack Daniel's.

"To tell you the truth," A.G. said, drawing in his breath as though seeking strength from the air. "Tell you the truth, we are not in the greatest shape at the Sunrise. Moneywise."

"I know that," Ramsey said, deliriously relieved that money and not Claire was to be the topic of conversation. "But you're doin the best you can. A man can't do more than that." It pained Ramsey that in truth A.G. was doing the best he could and that if he knew what was going on with Claire it would probably kill him. Here is the guy trying to get close to me again, Ramsey thought, and I can't give him the chance if I want to save my own ass and hers and maybe his too. There has got to be a way out, and maybe there is. Maybe it is to tell Claire to go to hell. But every time he had thought of doing that, he wondered whether she would get back at him by telling A.G. He did not trust anything about her except that he did not trust her. A.G. trusted her and look what it got him.

"What would you do in my place?" A.G. asked.

"Like I said. You're doin the best you can. I figure it's a question of hangin on. Things has gotta improve. Someday, you'll look back, you'll say, we had it tough, but we toughed it out."

"Roy Twyman thinks I should sell some land."

"There's them sections down in the southeast corner. They ain't worth much for cattle or farmin neither."

"Yeah. That's just it. I couldn't get much for that land. Maybe I should sell off some good land. But all I have to do is think of it, and it's like cuttin off an arm. My daddy would never have done that."

A.G. went over all his options. There was a drilling company that wanted to buy up some leases. Earl had never allowed drilling on his land, but maybe it was time to think of that. The price of oil was going up. Maybe that was the answer.

"If they find oil," Ramsey said.

They ordered another pitcher and halfway through it A.G. took a deep breath and said:

"What would you do if you thought your wife was fuckin around on you?"

"Claire? You must be outa your mind. There is one loyal woman if I ever seen one." Ramsey was relieved at the sound of his own voice. He had not flinched. He had not hesitated. He took a sip of beer and put the glass down with authority. "Don't let all these other problems foul up your marriage. You've got a great woman there."

"I guess you're right," A.G. said. The steadiness of Ramsey's reply had reassured him for the moment. "But you'd always tell me, if you knew something, wouldn't you?"

"I sure would," Ramsey said. "Hell. What's a friend for?" He despised himself.

TWENTY

"A human being, with his clothes off of him, is just a human being," Oral Roberts was saying.

A.G. sat in front of the television in his bathrobe. It was Sunday morning and he had only just then gone through with the impulse to turn on the set, after sitting in front of it for he had no idea how long. He had awakened early and had lain in bed trying not to move at all because he did not want to wake Claire. If he woke her, he might have to talk to her, to try to find words that might divert them from the sad situation of a man and a woman who were supposed to love each other lying in bed together on a Sunday morning unable to touch each other. As he lay there, his mind gradually registered the specific assaults of booze and fatigue that were, he knew, going to accompany him throughout the day—the anxieties, the remorse, the short temper and the desire to sit in a darkened room and speak to no one or to try to lose himself in six hours of televised professional football that could, with the help of several beers and maybe some whiskeys beginning about half-time of the second game of the doubleheader, get you almost all the way through to dinner. His troubles invaded him. The improvements were ruining him. He had even been tempted to start selling land to meet the payments on his mountain of debts. He had mortgaged his cattle, so that even if he did sell them the money would go to pay off that debt, and he would have no income. He had used up all the sources of loans he could think of and had even started negotiating with some shady characters who were promising a three-million or five-million loan from some unknown source, probably Las Vegas, but he had no reason to believe them. Though of course he kept telling Claire and everyone else that everything was going to be all right. He knew that if he kept on like this Claire would leave him. Maybe she already had, in her mind, and was just waiting for the right moment. Maybe she was waiting for him to get back on his feet so she could take him for more money. He thought of Ramsey. Ramsey and Claire. She had admitted nothing and he knew nothing for sure, but his intuition must be worth something. She seemed hardly to be able to stand being in the same room with him. When she undressed for bed, she was careful not to let him see her naked now, but a couple of times he had caught glimpses of her and had believed he had seen certain sorts of little bruises on her—or was that his imagination? Whenever he confronted her, she made him feel like a paranoid fool and made him believe that he was pushing her further away with his questions. Either he was dumb or she was clever, or possibly she was even innocent, he did not know.

And as he lay there in bed with her, not wanting to look at her, because the sight of her sleeping, immobile, silent, secretly dreaming, always made him want to reach out to her, he was conscious of his thirst, and he started saying to himself, I might as well have a beer now, I will feel better faster. Instead of going through the stupid self-punishing farce of holding off until lunch when the presence of a mere sandwich sanctifies by custom the ingestion of what everyone knew was better for a hangover than anything. He asked himself if it was possible that he might drop off to sleep again. If he did, she might wake up first and be out of the room before they had to face each other. But no, he knew he would not fall asleep again. He lay there a long time, being careful not to breathe too loud, trying to keep away what he could remember from the night before—another argument, another evening when she had abruptly and unceremoniously and without so much as a good-night gone off to bed, leaving him alone on the couch working on a bottle trying to decide whether to endure the humiliation of sleeping on the couch or the humiliation of sleeping in the same bed with her. Pictures of empty pastures invaded his mind. The herd was down to five thousand head, and he had taken to moving them around more than was necessary so as to give outsiders the impression that he had more cattle than he actually had. The faces of the suppliers of feed and fuel, hostile, suspicious, or at best infuriatingly compassionate and loyal, ranged about him. Other faces joined them, bankers, his mother, Earl's ghost, the faces of his children, who still believed in the future and that he would stock it for them with happiness. I had a future, he thought.

He crept out of bed and down to the kitchen, where he compromised a resolve to have coffee by drinking a beer to pass the time while the coffee was brewing. Even the servants weren't up yet. He brought the coffee into the living room, considered what was likely to be on television at that hour of a Sunday morning, and decided to sit and think and drink the coffee and probably two or three more cups after it. He decided that if he drank the coffee slowly and deliberately, there might be a chance of starting the day off right, of giving it some sort of chance.

It worked for a while, and then the prospect of the day began to oppress him, and he let his mind simply drift, let it slide into unconsciousness by way of counting threads in the couch or looking for cracks in the ceiling. He went to get more coffee and on the way paused at the foot of the stairs to see whether he could hear Claire. Nothing. Eula would be up soon. He would drink another beer before that.

Finally he had switched on the television and there was Oral delivering his line about human beings with their clothes off. A.G. continued to watch. The distance between him and Oral Roberts, who was speaking from the television studios at Oral Roberts University, seemed immense. There was Oral with his belief and his money flowing in, here was A.G., who did not know what or whom to believe in and who was trying at a rather late age to school himself in the art of kiting checks. Oral Roberts went on:

"I have been a sick man in my day. I suffered from tuberculosis and there was a time when my mother thought she would lose me, but she prayed with all her heart to the Lord Jesus, and I was healed by the Lord. It changed my life. From that moment on, I knew that I would dedicate my life to spreading the Gospel. I followed Him.

"I had no illusions about my capacities. I did find that I had the gift from God of spreading His word and I had the gift of healing. It was not Oral Roberts' gift. I was and I remain merely the Lord's humble vessel. God chooses humble vessels to carry His spirit. And when people say to me, Oral, they say, Oral, what makes you think you're qualified to be the president of a university? What do you know about art and literature? I say, not very much. I don't know much about art. I like to look at the flowers and the clouds in the sky. My beloved wife Evelyn wishes I would look at pictures more, and I should. But I am merely the humble vessel. I can persuade people to give their money to His cause and through me a wonderful institution can come into being where young people from all over God's creation can come to be educated and to learn to lead good Christian lives. I am His servant. That is why I am qualified to be president of a great university. Because when you believe in the Lord, He can qualify you for anything.

"Through the years I have been sustained by the Lord and by the love of my beloved wife Evelyn, who you all know. Come on out here, Evelyn."

Evelyn Roberts joined her husband on the television screen.

"Evelyn, I believe you have a story to tell the folks."

"Yes, I do, Oral."

A.G. watched and listened as Evelyn Roberts read from the Bible the story of Ruth. A.G. was moved.

"Thank you, Evelyn," Oral said. "No one could have read the

story of Ruth more beautifully, and no one exemplifies better the lesson of that story. 'Whither thou goest, I go.' That has been your motto with me, Evelyn, and you know that without you I would never have gone very far down that road.

"And now I want all of you out there to pray with us. I want you first of all to think of all the people you love in this world and to include them in your prayers." A.G. thought of his family. "And I want you to pray for yourself.

"Something wonderful is going to happen to *you!* A miracle will occur. Yes, it will. God will come into your heart and into your soul and your mind and body. He will take care of you. He will help you with all the problems you have that are besetting you and getting you down. Family problems. Financial problems. He will help you overcome weakness.

"And now, as we pray together, I want each and every one of you to do as I am doing now. Evelyn, take my hand. And you all do likewise. Take the hands of those nearest you. Let us all join hands in prayer." A.G. was conscious that he was sitting alone and he felt alone. "Take the hands of the loved ones that have joined with you on this Sunday morning. Or if you are not at home, if you are with strangers, take their hands. No one is a stranger in the eyes of the Lord.

"Or if you are alone. By yourself. Maybe you are at home alone and are lonely. Maybe you are alone in an apartment or you are divorced and alone." A.G. shuddered. "Or if you are in prison and you feel that everything has gone wrong in your life and you are near despair. If you are alone, take your arms like this and wrap them around yourself, like this, like I am doing now, and hug yourself, tight, and say to yourself God loves me! I am not alone! I am never alone!"

A.G. found himself hugging himself. He hugged tightly, swallowing hard, as the choir began to sing. It must have been for several minutes that he sat there with his arms around himself, praying or at least wishing very hard.

Suddenly he was aware of himself and he felt ridiculous.

Thank God no one had seen him sitting there hugging himself at the command of Oral Roberts. Yet he was somehow grateful to Oral for making him feel better for a moment. Had it been the mere sight of Oral and Evelyn holding hands and looking so goddamned happy? I am such a mess, he thought. Here I am on a Sunday morning with my family asleep—no, he had not even noticed, but the house was full of stirring now; no one had bothered to come find him—feeling sorry for myself going down the tubes.

Out of a sense of being ridiculous and weak he tried to forge resolution. He realized that he had reached a point where he had to overcome or be overcome. He was starting to feel a surge of resolution when the thought of Claire with Ramsey rushed in on him and he felt like picking something up and throwing it. I would probably be better off, he thought, shipping out on a freighter and never coming back, but he knew he could not do that. His rage diminished and some of the resolution came back. I still have a chance, he thought. Maybe no miracle is going to happen to me but maybe I can make something happen. If I am going to go down, I am going down fighting. I am not going to lie here like a bottom sucker.

He shaved, dressed, and took himself out for a walk. It was Indian summer in Oklahoma and the air was dry, neither too warm nor too cool, the grass turning brownish waiting for the heavy rains that would come later. The leaves were not so brilliant this year as they sometimes were, as it had been a dry summer: they merely dried up and fell. But it was a beautiful season. The bird hunting was well under way, and A.G. regretted that he had not had the heart for it. All over the state the hunters would be out, some expensively equipped and some having just as good a time with an old Remington and a bottle of whiskey, shooting away from the back of a pickup.

He walked along trying not to let the worst money problems oppress him yet trying to sort out his thoughts and make some plan that would take him and the Sunrise up and out. He thought that it was like having first down and about thirty

yards to go. If you tried to get it all back at once, you risked
losing everything with a bomb and an interception. You had to
try to get a little back at a time. Nibble away, throw under
the umbrella. That must have been his mistake. He had tried
to gobble it all up at once and then when he had lost it he had
tried to get it all back at once. He would try step by step. Hell,
he had better stop planning and get moving.

Maybe he would even go against his father's spirit and sell
off a little of the land, just enough to finance a new start. He
had walked almost as far as the hill where Earl was buried but
decided not to visit it today. He would take Claire aside, tell
her what the real situation was, and tell her that together they
would pull through somehow. Once she understood how sin-
cere and determined he was, she might just join up with him
again, she just might do that. His heart beat hard at the
thought. He inhaled the sharp clean air and felt almost inclined to run back to the house.

But when he got back he found Claire, the children and his
mother all climbing into the station wagon. Where were they
going? Were they all leaving him? He ran up to the car.

"We're going to visit my mother," Claire said. "I told you last
night. Don't you remember?" Her voice had a taunt to it.

"Oh, sure. Have a good time."

In her rearview mirror Claire watched A.G. recede. He
looked small and pitiful, waving to them. The children were
chattering in the backseat and she told them to be quiet. I
can't let him go on like this, she said to herself. All during the
drive to Tulsa she told herself that it was time for her to do
something, and at her mother's, Claire was nervous. It was not
just Vivian. A.G. worried her, and some of the old love for him
seemed to be coming back. It was true, as Margaret said, he
was trying hard. That was what mattered. He loved her. He
loved his children and his ranch. He had simply gotten in
over his head. His father's death had been so sudden and he
had tried to do everything too fast. She thought about A.G. all

day long, fending off her mother's nattering, and by the time she was driving home, the children and Margaret dozing peacefully, her guilt about Ramsey and the slowly, gently returning feelings for A.G. began to give her resolve. She had to help A.G. and she had to break things off with Ramsey. She felt a power in her telling her that if she helped A.G., he would respond. And if she broke off the affair now, with no one knowing about it, that would be the first important step to getting things back to normal. They had their lives left together and their children's lives. A.G. was suspicious but if she broke off the affair now, he would forget about it, bury his suspicions, because that was his nature, always to try to hope for the best and believe in her and look on the positive side of things. When she thought about how much A.G. always tried to believe in the best of things and in her, almost the way a child believes, she was moved. What if he did lack realism? She could supply that. They could complement each other and make each other and their children happy. I have to believe it's possible, she thought, I do believe it.

A.G. had watched his family drive off and had felt frustrated and alone. He went inside and tried to watch football but could not get involved. It was too late to call in a bet to whet his interest. Through the window he saw the servants from the big house leaving, taking advantage of Margaret's absence, he figured. He went upstairs, opened Claire's closets and looked at her clothes. There were enough to stock a department store. Well, at least he had given her that. And she had such good taste. She had not really changed, even as they had grown apart. She seemed to be the sort of person who would carry on, regardless. He was the one who might crack. He felt so lonely. Suddenly he wondered whether the trip to visit Vivian was just a ruse. Maybe she would dump the others and run off to spend the afternoon with Ramsey somewhere.

He telephoned the big house, where Ramsey now lived in

A.G.'s old room. It rang five times and A.G. was about to panic when Ramsey answered.

"Come on down here," A.G. said. "I got some things I gotta go over with you. What you doin?"

"Watchin New Orleans get their asses whupped."

"Stay there. I'll come on up."

He felt better, sitting with Ramsey in the big red room, and managed to get absorbed by the game. He had planned not to drink but he was feeling more secure, so he broke out a bottle of Scotch and they went to work on it.

Ramsey was nervous sitting alone with A.G. Being with his friend made Ramsey feel nervous now, and guilty, but it also made him feel angry, because he felt trapped. He had been doing a lot of thinking lately about his life, and he had begun to wonder whether he had been trapped from the first, from childhood, when he had first accepted the Krugers' hospitality and generosity. He had become beholden to them from the start. Maybe he should never have come back from California, as much as he had disliked it. Taking the Krugers as the sponsors of his parole had sealed the trap. He guessed for a poor man to accept the help of a rich man was always a noose around the poor man's neck. Ramsey was even capable of anger at A.G. for allowing him to get so close to Claire and the children. A woman is always attracted to a man when he pays attention to her children, it was the oldest story in the world. Here was A.G. in all kinds of difficulty and obviously not getting on with his wife, and he invites another man into his house when he's not there. It was crazy and stupid. If ever there was a case of letting the fox into the coop, this was it. But of course Ramsey knew who would be blamed. To him, A.G. should be blamed, because a grown man should not be stupid and should know one thing at least, that you cannot trust a woman. But everyone else would blame Ramsey, or Claire. Ramsey did not blame Claire. That would be like blaming a skunk for its stripe.

They did manage to get a bet down on the second game—at least my credit is still good with the bookies, A.G. thought—and A.G. won. He felt pretty good. He had a nice high going, not too much but just enough, and he felt if not giddy then pretty damned good. He took winning the bet as a sign that his luck was changing, and he wondered whether old Oral might know something after all.

"I saw Oral Roberts on the TV this morning," A.G. said, carefully measuring himself another light Scotch. "I'll say one thing for the son of a bitch. He looks like he enjoys what he's doing."

"Some say he's a crook," Ramsey said, "but I always figured, if he makes people happy, and I know plenty he does, let him have his head."

"More than one way to skin a cat."

"That's it."

A.G. began formulating a strategy to coax Ramsey out. He had never done anything but good to Ramsey. Surely if he continued to take Ramsey into his confidence, his old friend would be straight with him. No matter what had happened, there must be a way of facing it and resolving it one way or another.

"I've got some new ideas," A.G. said.

"Shoot."

"Well, first off, I feel like the scum of the earth is closing in on us. Some of these characters offering money now, first off, they ain't got it; second, takin it from them, well, it's like eatin shit or signin your death warrant, take your pick."

"I'm with you one hundred percent," Ramsey said. "Run those bastards off."

"Of course it's tempting. One of those groups, they say they can float an umbrella loan for three-four million."

"Bullshit. You paid that one guy, what's his name, what was it, thirty thousand. Gave him your credit card. Expenses he

said he needed? Hell. Hell no. You ran him off, that's one
thing. Run 'em all off."

"Right. You know something? I do believe I am gonna sell
off some land. Not much. But some. It makes sense."

"You got more land than you need," Ramsey said. "That's
certain. I mean, I been thinkin about it. This ain't the old days.
We made some mistakes. Let's admit it. Let's go on from there.
Practical."

"That's what I was thinking," A.G. said. But he was thinking
of something else, too. All right. Let this be the time we all
admit mistakes. If they have been made. Let's go ahead. What
the hell. Dig in those spurs and ride.

"You know," A.G. said, sipping his drink and putting the
glass down very slowly and carefully, as if he were afraid of
making a noise, "I think my mind's gotten kind of screwed up
lately. Sometimes I think my head's been screwed on backwards."

"Is that right."

"I've had some of the craziest notions. And I know they're
crazy." A.G. felt the lump of his .38 in the small of his back. He
reached back and slipped the gun out and placed it on the
table next to his drink. He felt his nerves act up and he took a
deep swallow of the Scotch and studied Ramsey. His friend
was sitting casually in his chair, the big oil painting of old Earl
on the wall behind him.

"Crazy notions?" Ramsey asked.

"Yeah. Hallucinations, maybe. I believe they are." He decided to plunge ahead. This would be a step toward righting
things. "Like for instance," he said, looking Ramsey in the eye,
"I have had the crazy idea that you have been fuckin my wife."

If Ramsey had answered right away, one way or the other, it
might have been different, but he did not. He sat there for
what seemed to A.G. like a long time, in silence, but however
long it was it was long enough for A.G. to reach the conclusion
that yes, it was true, what he had suspected and known but

not wanted to believe was true. Now he had to face the truth. Facing it turned out to be more difficult than speculating about it and torturing himself with possibilities. He had thought about what he might do if he found out but now he wondered whether he had the strength to stay sitting up. Betrayal numbed him. Nothing will ever be the same now. Not with Claire. You will never be able to believe anything she says. Not with Ramsey. Everything you lived for. Nothing. You have been made a fool and you are a fool. Forever. No one will respect you. Not Ramsey. Not Claire. Not your children. Margaret. Maybe she isn't even my child. He felt tiny enough to crawl into the neck of the Scotch bottle.

"See what you mean by crazy notions," Ramsey finally started to say. "You . . ."

"You son of a bitch," A.G. said but without force. He tried to take a breath. The word honor entered his mind. He had to defend it, didn't he? He had to have the strength to defend his honor. If it was his last act. He tried to shout: "You son of a bitch." Louder: "Traitor!"

He started to stumble toward Ramsey, saw the gun out of the corner of his eye, grabbed it and aimed.

"Hold on!" Ramsey shouted, half rising.

"Why should I? Bastard. Traitor." A.G. cocked the .38.

"All right! Yeah, you probably wanna shoot. I hope you're gonna have the nerve to pull that trigger. I hope so. I hope you're finally gonna have the nerve for somethin."

A.G.'s hand trembled and the gun shook at Ramsey.

"Sure," Ramsey said, standing now but not moving. "You wanna hear the whole thing? Maybe it's about time you did. Maybe I'd like to get the whole stinkin thing out. 'Bout time you faced a lotta things, seems to me. Seems like you ain't been facin nothin. Then shoot me. I ain't got no future nohow. Never did, I can see now."

"Talk," A.G. said. "Talk!"

"Put that gun down, I'll talk. Put that gun down, sit down, and I'll talk."

A.G. sank slowly back onto the couch, never taking his eyes off Ramsey. He held the gun in his lap pointed sideways, his finger still on the trigger. I will let him talk, confess, he thought, and then I will kill him for my honor. Kill.

"You're the smart one," Ramsey said. "So listen. First off. You have fucked up real bad. You admit that?" A.G. did not reply. "Admit it? You ought to. Once in your life. You tried to be tough, well it looks like you ain't. You tried to be your old man, well you ain't. You tried, sure, and every time you made a mistake, you went out and made a bigger one to cover it up. You got this place so far in the hole you might never get out. You drug yourself down, you drug your family down. Your children! Ain't you supposed to be a father? Ain't you sup-posed to of growed up? Who is you supposed to blame? Me? Sure, all right, go ahead and blame me. Blame me if the grass don't grow. Blame me you got bills. Blame me you got married troubles. What have you done? Nothin is about right. Take another drink, is all you done."

A.G. had lowered his gaze now. He was looking at the gun. "What about my wife?" he said. "Claire." His voice hoarsened on her name.

"Sure. You drug her down, too! Into the mud. And me too! What about me?" Ramsey's face had turned the color of his hair.

"You? You went to bed with my wife. Son of a bitch." He wanted to say more but found it difficult to form words.

"Me? Sure. All right. It's done. I been dippin my stick in your wife." He started pacing. "Yeah. I been dipping my stick in some company oil! Sure, I been takin care of business with her. Hell yes. And you know what? You know what?" He drew breath and boomed out the words. "I'm the one's been fucked! Ever since I came here! How about the fuckin I been gettin? Youda taken care of her you know damn well she never of gone for me. I been set up! Played a sucker! She's a woman, didn't you know that? Didn't you figure out you married a woman? The two of you! What do you give a damn about nothin! And I tell you somethin. Nobody never bothered wearin a rubber on *me!*"

A.G. leaned forward, elbows on knees, unable to sit up.

"You want it spelled out more?" Ramsey shouted, shaking. "I could tell you! I could say how she set it up! I could tell you how she went fishin! She ain't no dummy, you know that. Me I'm a country boy maybe I don't stand no chance with a smart woman like that. And you know what else? I could tell you! She liked it! That's what! Couldn't get enough! I cain't see why you ever gave it up!"

Ramsey watched A.G. His friend sat slumped, shrunken into himself, puffed and pale. A.G. looked as though he had scarcely the energy to keep his eyelids up. Ramsey's anger ebbed.

"Hey, wait a minute," Ramsey said. "I'm sorry. I went too far. We all did. You don't know how shitty I feel about it. I'll leave, A.G., I'll go away." He took a step toward his friend, beginning to wish he had handled it differently. A.G. looked whipped. Beaten. I have never seen a man so down, Ramsey thought. I never saw nobody in prison that down. What have I done? He is my friend. What have I done?

A.G. managed to raise his head and look up. His eyes showed terror and an unbearable sadness. His mouth dropped open and formed a silent O and then, suddenly, he let out a long, horrible scream, primitive, reasonless, terrible, the scream of an ape.

"A.G.!"

But in one quick jerk, in a split second that Ramsey would relive again and again for the rest of his life, A.G. raised the gun to his mouth and pulled the trigger.

TWENTY-ONE

Ramsey had rushed to grab A.G. the second the gun moved, but the shot went off before he reached him. The blast sent Ramsey springing back and onto the floor. He sprawled at his friend's feet and looked up.

A.G. lay twisted on the corner of the couch, blood flowing like a swollen creek from what was left of the back of his head, twitching. At first Ramsey believed that the twitching meant signs of life, but then he knew, death registered. "Oh, A.G.," he heard himself say, "don't tell them what I done! Don't tell them what I done!" Hearing his own voice as from a distance, he wondered what he meant. What am I saying? I gotta do something. I know what I meant. I meant I killed him. I killed him by telling him. If I hadn't of told him he never would of known. Oh, yes, he would. He already knew. Had to. Or she would of told him sooner or later. You know that. They would of had a fight some night and she would of told him. Spit it out. It always comes out. That's what I told her. Maybe she did tell him. Maybe he was just tryin to see if I'd come clean. His friend. No. I don't think he knew. Oh, A.G.! The one thing I didn't know how bad off you was! I should of come and told you. I could of explained to you how it was. How she—no. You might of killed her. Your kids. It's no good. It never was any good. Lord God help us all. I got to do somethin. Call an ambulance. He's dead. Somebody should come and help.

Ramsey sat on the floor unable to move, staring at the body. Later he could not figure out how long he had sat there. He passed into a state of waking unconsciousness. The telephone rang. He heard it but it did not occur to him that a ringing telephone was something to be answered. It rang and rang.

Claire was annoyed when Ramsey did not answer the phone. She had thought he would surely be up at the big house, and she felt that she needed to talk to him right away. When she had returned from her mother's to find A.G. conveniently out of the house, she had invited Margaret to stay for supper and had gone up to her bedroom to telephone Ramsey. When no one answered, she continued to let it ring and looked out the window toward the big house. She was sure she could see his truck parked outside. Why wasn't he answering? She didn't want to let another night pass without starting to patch things up with A.G. She wanted to be able to talk to A.G. without the constant worry that she would make a slip of the tongue. She wanted to turn her own house back into something fit for her children, no longer a house of lies, hostilities, evasions. Each ring of the telephone irritated her more.

A dreadful thought came to her. What if Ramsey were with A.G. and they were talking about her? She put down the phone. If they were having that kind of conversation, they might not answer the phone. She panicked. Men were like that, weren't they? Male friends? They stuck together. She knew Ramsey felt guilty, much more than she had until now. Maybe he would be just stupid enough to blurt it all out. Confess to his friend to save himself? He might think that way. She had to stop him. She had no idea of what A.G. might do. All of her good resolutions would be wrecked.

She hurried down the stairs, told Margaret she would be right back, and started walking briskly up the road to the big house. It was almost dark. There was a light on downstairs, she could see. And yes, that was Ramsey's truck. Somewhere in the silence a dog barked. Were they in there, talking about her? No, no, they probably just got drunk watching football. If only

Ramsey would be there alone. She could finish everything in two sentences.

At first she saw only Ramsey, sitting on the floor staring, and she started to speak when she saw A.G.

"No!"

Her cry broke Ramsey's trance.

"No! No!"

He got to his feet and stopped her as she ran toward her husband's body.

"Let me go! I have to help him! I have to help him!"

Ramsey wrapped his arms around her and pulled her from the room.

"What are you doing! I have to help him! He might be dying! Let me go! You shot him!" She tore at him.

"No," Ramsey said. "I didn't shoot him. We'll call an ambulance."

TWENTY-TWO

"Tell me again why my daddy killed himself."

Claire put her book facedown on the arm of the couch.

"Have the children at school been saying things to you again, sweetheart? Earl. Tell me."

"Yes."

"Well, you can't expect them to understand. Come here."

She held out her arms and the boy went into them and settled on her lap. Even if she had decided that it would have been the right thing, Claire had not had the option of lying to her children. Her daughter was small enough not to understand yet much of what had happened, but in the three weeks since A.G.'s death the event had been played up on television and in the newspapers and was dinner table talk at every house in that part of Oklahoma. Despite the efforts of his teachers to intervene, little Earl was questioned, even taunted, at school. A lot of people wanted to believe that it had been murder. When A.G.'s debts had become public knowledge, it was not hard to find a motive. But the coroner had ruled suicide, and when the widow accepted that and failed to file any insurance claims, everyone was satisfied that A.G. had done himself in. He had not been able to handle the pressure of his debts, they decided. At the inquest Ramsey told of hearing the shot and coming upon the body. He testified that, yes, his boss had been distraught about debts and had taken to drinking heavily just before the end. No, he was unaware of any marital difficulties. As far as he or anyone else could tell, A.G. and Claire had got on real well. Margaret and the servants said the same. As it was, the ambulance driver said, when the ambulance came they found A.G. with the gun gripped in his hand.

It did occur to Claire that had old Earl still been around, the coroner would have said what Earl told him to say and the family would have collected the insurance millions. But then if Earl had been around none of it would have happened. Earl could not have lived forever. Somehow A.G. had never taken his father's mortality fully into account.

"Your daddy was a dreamer," Claire told little Earl, hugging him close. "He used to tell me, when he was a boy he would dream of far-off places and kings and queens and princesses."

"That's nice."

"Yes, it was. And then, when we got married, he dreamed of giving me everything I could ever possibly want. Maybe even things I had never imagined. And . . . when I asked for something, he always tried. He always did. To give it to me. Do you know, when we were married, I asked to go to England on our honeymoon. And you know what? He took me. That was the kind of man he was."

"Was England pretty?"

"Oh, yes."

"Did you see the Queen of England?"

"No, but we saw a duke and had dinner with the duke in his castle."

"I'd love doin that."

"Maybe some day. But one trouble was, your daddy sometimes dreamed too much. It was because he . . . well. It was because he had too big a heart."

"Too big a heart?"

"Yes, I mean his heart was so big that—it could be that he loved everybody too much and tried to do too much for them. He loved you so much, and your sister, and I think he wanted you to have more than any little boy and girl ever had. So he tried so hard that he got worn out."

"He needed to take a rest."

"That's it. He did need to take a rest. He was tired out and very nervous."

"Maybe he killed himself to take a rest."

Claire could not answer right away. Then she managed:

"One thing you must understand is that Daddy didn't mean to kill himself."

"You told me that."

"Yes, but I want you to understand it. I don't think you do, yet. He didn't mean to kill himself. He loved us all more than any other daddy in the world, and he wanted to be with us. He wanted to see you grow up and . . ." She had trouble with the next phrase because of its associations but she went ahead with it. "And take over the ranch. He really wanted that. But he got so tired and so nervous, and then, that afternoon. It just happened."

"Was he playing? Playing and dreaming? And then it happened?"

"Yes. That's a good way of putting it."

"But playing and dreaming are all right, aren't they?"

"Oh, yes. You can play and dream all you want. But when you get older, sometimes you can't play and dream as much as before. That's what growing up means."

"Then I don't want to grow up. I don't want to grow up. Why do I have to? Why can't my daddy just grow down?"

Claire held him and rocked him.

After one of these sessions Claire would lie in her bed in the dark and try to keep from falling to pieces. She would tell herself that she was lucky that her own father had killed himself because that way she had her mother's example to strengthen her. Her mother had never stopped bad-mouthing her father since the day he had shot himself. Claire vowed never to say a critical word about A.G. to anyone, lest her children get wind of it. They had to believe that their father had loved them. The minute Vivian had heard what had happened, she had wanted to move onto the ranch and take over, and her first words had been, "I knew he was just like Gerald." Claire forbade Vivian to come to the ranch for the time being, though of course she had been there for the funeral. Claire had kept the funeral private. She did not want anything approaching the extravaganza of Earl's burial. She even asked the cowboys to stay away, all except Sam, and Ramsey. She stood there on the hill holding her children's hands and watched A.G. being lowered into a grave next to his father. She held herself together by worrying about the children and about Margaret. At first she had been afraid that this blow might be fatal to Margaret, but Margaret arose from her devastation to play the grandmother's role with all the strength she had left. She comforted Claire. She fussed with the children. She managed the house with quiet efficiency. From that time on, Claire loved her as she never had before. Margaret reduced the loss of her son to something personal, a private grief.

What mattered was that the grandchildren went on. Margaret became an example to Claire.

Lying in her bed after trying again to explain to little Earl what could not be explained, Claire tried to push away guilt. If only I could talk to someone, she thought. At least if I'd become a Catholic I could go to confession and tell the priest. But she could tell no one and she did not want to talk to Ramsey, except about business, and she knew she had to do that soon. The creditors were giving her the courtesy of her mourning, but before long they would begin to circle about. She was not sure yet of the extent of the debt but she had begun to realize that it was far worse than she had imagined. If only A.G. had confided in her more! Surely that would have helped him and helped their marriage? Maybe not. That was not the way his father had done things and that was not the way he would do them. She had never in her life imagined how rigid these people could be about the old ways and the old codes. To violate them was death for them. Had her violation of the marriage bed really been the thing that had brought A.G. down? I cannot believe that and what is more I cannot afford to believe it, she told herself. I betrayed him. I did. I can't deny that. But what marriage remains pure? If he had had an affair, would I have killed myself? Of course not. Worse than that, she thought, if he had had one during the past year, she would not even have cared. He must have known that.

If only she had been able to reach Ramsey in time! Tell him that everything was finished and that she and A.G. were going to make their marriage work again. Ramsey had haltingly described to her how he had confessed at gunpoint. I should have let him shoot me, Ramsey had said, rather than tell. But then the truth would have come out anyway, for what other motive would A.G. have had for shooting Ramsey? No, Claire thought, the only thing that might have saved it would have been if I'd been able to reach Ramsey in time. But I did not. Is there no one I can talk to? She thought of calling up one of the priests she had known at Monte Cassino even though she was not a Catholic. She even dialed the number a couple of times but hung up when the receptionist answered. Old friends from Tulsa telephoned and wrote letters. She gave them all formal replies. She considered finding a psychiatrist in Tulsa who would listen to her and advise her. But no, she concluded, this is not a problem for a psychiatrist. I am not crazy, not yet. I know enough about them to know what one would say. You must go through a period of grief. You must not blame yourself. Maybe, God help them, my poor children will be seeing a psychiatrist some day but I have to work this out on my own, for now.

She kept close to the children, feeding little Margaret, playing with her, talking to her for hours, trying to give little Earl what a boy would want. She did not wish to ask more than was necessary of Ramsey, so she had Sam help the boy with his riding. One day she wandered out to the stables to see how Earl was getting on and found Sam telling him the right way to cinch up a saddle. The boy was not strong enough yet to get the cinch tight, but Sam had him try anyway, showing him how to brace his knee against the horse's ribs for leverage.

"All right now, boy, let's see us a fast mount. Remember, grab that old mane. Show your Mom how you can do it."

Earl hooked his boot in the stirrup, grabbed the mane and the reins with his left hand and managed to haul himself up in one motion without so much as touching the saddle with his right hand. He smiled down at his mother and she applauded.

"That's it!" Sam said. "Now, put her into a high lope."

Earl dug in his heels, and the horse went right into a lope around the corral. The boy's butt stuck to the saddle.

"Look at that boy ride!" Sam said. "He's got that mare knowin who's boss. By God, the way he rides, reminds me of his granddaddy."

Claire felt some of the torment in her head slip away.

And this sustained her: the thought that she was a mother. The ambitions of her youth and A.G.'s ambitions seemed trivial to her now. Maybe, she thought, being a mother is not the most important thing in the world, and maybe it is, but it certainly is the most important thing to me now. What else counts? For what? For vanity? For what is said behind my back? I may have been a very imperfect wife but I still have that chance, for them. In private I will have my memories and guilts. I can think about A.G.'s kindnesses and cry. And yes I can remember how grotesque he could be and make myself feel better with that. But what I need to do now is to be a good mother. She was able to welcome the dawn because it meant that the children would be needing things done. And Margaret's example helped.

Finally, a month after A.G.'s death the telephones at the ranch stopped working, Claire had to face the financial chaos. The unpaid bill was over six thousand dollars. She met with Ramsey and two lawyers to go over everything. A.G. had left it all to her, saying that he knew she would make proper provision for his mother and the children, but what did it all amount to? Five thousand head of cattle—all mortgaged, no income possible from them. Bills and loans amounting to nearly nine million dollars.

She sat with the three men in Earl's old office off the room where A.G. had killed himself. The lawyers pieced together from documents a narrative of what had happened, step by step. The figures seemed unbelievable to her. What had A.G. done? He must have been crazy, Claire thought, completely mad. For the first time since his death, Claire was angry with A.G., fiercely angry. As the lawyers droned on, she found herself half wishing that Ramsey had killed him. That way she would have been rid of both of them and the insurance money would have paid the debts.

"Well," one of the lawyers said finally, "I guess you haven't got much choice, Mrs. Kruger. You're going to have to sell the Sunrise."

"Sell it?" she found herself saying. "I have no intention of selling it. I intend to run it." No other alternative had even occurred to her. Did they expect her to give up that easily? What would she do, go to Tulsa and become a schoolteacher like her mother?

The lawyers met her statement with silence. She could feel their doubt. She even sensed what she guessed was their contempt.

"Mrs. Kruger," the lawyer said, "even assuming there's some way out of these debts, running a ranch, it's a heck of a business. The know-how. It's—"

"I need some time to think," Claire said. "I believe there's a way out of this. Got to be." She was tempted to add that she thought she could probably run the place as well as her late husband had, but she did not.

"There's over a million in past due payments."

"I'm aware of that. I'm aware of everything, now. I'm sure a few more days won't make any difference."

After the meeting she asked Ramsey to walk her back to her own house. He had told her that he wanted to leave, and she wanted him to go. But she had asked him to stay on until things were sorted out. She did not go so far as to say that she needed him, but that was understood between them. Soon he would be free to go and try to pick up his own life. When they reached her house, Margaret was in the living room watching television. She switched it off and the three of them sat down to talk.

"I know one thing," Claire began. "I didn't see one thing in all those papers that said that the land doesn't belong to me. To the Krugers. It must be worth something."

"Sure it is," Ramsey said.

"How much is it worth?"

"I don't know for sure. I could find out easy enough."

"Because that could be a way. If it's worth enough. I mean selling off some of it."

Margaret stood up: "Earl would never have done that!"

"No, Margaret," Claire said. "Earl isn't here. A.G. isn't here. We're here."

"Tell you the truth," Ramsey said, "A.G. thought of it. I told him I thought he ought to think about it, too. But I just guess he couldn't bring himself to do it. It's the first principle, you know. Never sell land."

"It's how we built the place," Margaret said. She was agitated. She sat down again and looked at Claire as though her daughter-in-law had spoken heresy. "Everybody else sold out. Earl just bought and bought."

"A lot of things have changed around here," Claire said. "A lot of things will have to change."

Claire did not yet know whether her hopes were realistic, but she felt stronger for them. From the first her understanding of the nature of A.G.'s debts made her wonder that all this

money had been borrowed and not one parcel of land had
been sold. There was not even a mortgage on the big house.
Surely not all of the land was equally valuable? She would find
out. She tried to keep a rein on the anger that she felt for
having been kept in the dark. She told herself that much of it
had been her own fault. If A.G. had been acting so erratically
in every other way, swilling at all hours, depressed one minute
and bubbling with fantastic promises the next, how could she
have believed that he had known what he was doing in business? She had escaped with Ramsey the way A.G. escaped
with the bottle and his grandiose schemes. They were all to
blame. But now she would have to find a way. Well, she
thought, I guess it isn't even going to be enough for me to be a
mother. I am going to have to be a few other things too.

Several days later Claire drove to the Bushyhead National
Bank. As soon as she walked through the door, Roy Twyman
got up from his desk and came forward to greet her. He was
dressed in his usual brown suit.

"Mrs. Kruger. I am so pleased to see you again. By God, I do
believe I haven't seen you since your weddin day. Terrible
tragedy. I'm just as sorry as I can be."

"I met you at my father-in-law's funeral," Claire said.

"Why, yes. Sometimes the bad luck does pile on. Come sit
down."

"Mr. Twyman, I believe you advised my late husband to
think about selling off some land."

"Yes, that is correct. I'm surprised he mentioned it. I never
did think he had any intention. Just like his daddy. Sellin land
to them was goin backwards. I appreciated their sentiments.
Most folks around here feel the same way. They would sooner
go broke than sell. Had to fight so hard to get it, you see."

"Well, I'm not of the same mind."

"Is that right. Well, times is tough. You gonna sell the Sunrise? It's probably the best way. A shame, but sometimes you
got to bite the bullet."

"I don't intend to sell the ranch. Just part of it."

"What you gonna do with the rest? Lease it?"

"No. Run it."

Roy Twyman looked out the window. Then he said:

"I understand, you don't mind my sayin, as we are talkin business, you been losin some of the help?"

"I can't pay their salaries at the moment."

"Well then, how you gonna run a ranch without help?"

"Look, Mr. Twyman," Claire said. "Can you help me find some buyers or not? I'm thinking about the southwest corner. Twenty thousand acres or so. I've done some asking and I understand the land is worth four or five hundred an acre."

"You really think you can go on runnin the Sunrise? After all what's happened?"

"I do, yes."

"What makes you think so?"

Claire looked him in the eye, leaned over toward him, and placed a delicate hand on his pudgy, hairy one: "Because I don't think there's any great mystery to it. Because if it was profitable before, it can be profitable again, maybe not as much so, but it can work." She tightened her fingers on Twyman's hand. "Because I want it for my children. And because my father-in-law bought so much land that even the mistakes that were made can't ruin the place." She released him. "You see, I know what the debts are. I've got two choices. Let them overwhelm us. Or realize that there is a great deal left, and that it is in my name now. And go on from there."

Twyman took a big breath. "You're a very determined woman, Mrs. Kruger. I can see that."

"Yes, I am."

"Why, I can see you've dug in your heels like a government mule! I tell you, I'll see what I can do."

"I figure there'll be enough left to make it go."

"They say only old Earl knew how much he had."

"About sixty-five to seventy thousand acres."

"Is that right?" For the first time he smiled at her. "I tell you, Mrs. Kruger, you figured pretty close."

"I haven't been idle."

"Still, you'd have to run a pretty slick operation. It wouldn't be what it was."

"Nothing is."

In a week Roy Twyman came to the ranch with a plan for Claire. He had arranged for bids on the southwest corner and he expected that Claire would be able to pay off all of A.G.'s loans. They sat in Claire's living room and went over everything.

"Mrs. Kruger," he said, "I think what we got planned here is gonna suit you fine as wine and sweet as a nut. I believe you think positive. And I asked around and got two applications here from boys is wantin to be your ranch manager. They is both of them fine boys." He handed her résumés of men with experience in Oklahoma and Colorado.

"My lawyers are still advising me to sell it all."

"Aw, hell. Lawyers. I can see you got that spirit which it is I always said we could use more of it. You know, sometimes I think this country's goin to hell. That brings me to one other little thing. We get this land problem straightened out, I got somethin else for you to think about."

"I can tell you, Mr. Twyman, I've got plenty to think about."

"Hold on. I'll just mention it. You know, old Earl, he wouldn't allow any drillin on his land. He was supposed to, but he kept it off. A.G., he was the same way. But you might consider it. You might consider sellin off a few leases, for a start."

"There's oil on this land?"

"You never know. I tell you one thing, I got some people is pretty interested in findin out. The thing is, times is changed. The price of oil, people think it'll go to fifty-seventy dollars a barrel before too long. It can pay drillin on land like this, where it didn't pay before. You think about that."

"I will certainly think about it."

"You might consider, some of those people in Washington, I sometimes wonder is they lackin a few bricks to make a load. But you and me, why in hell should we be takin orders from them A-rab towel-heads and camel-jockeys if we got oil right here? It might be, anyways."

Claire took to riding out with little Earl on the diminished Sunrise. Now that the land was hers, it meant more to her than it had when she had thought of it as A.G.'s. She had come to think of the Sunrise as her appointed place. She visited every corner of it with her son, and she was proud to have saved it for him and for her daughter. Unlike the men before her, she had no wish to expand the Sunrise. It would raise her children and that was enough. She hoped that they would want to stay on it, but she knew that she would not try to stop them if they wished to leave. At least they would know that it was safely theirs.

And sometimes she would ride out alone. She found that it calmed her to guide the horse where she chose and to be alone on her land with her thoughts. It was when she was riding alone that she realized that she had come to believe in ghosts or to understand what ghosts were. The graves of Earl and A.G. were always there. She could not ride over a hill or through a creek without hearing A.G.'s voice and feeling his presence. Certain places she avoided—the tree under which they had made love on her first visit was one. When she came on it by chance she hurried away.

At first the work of saving the ranch had buoyed her spirit, but now life settled into something duller than it had been, more peaceful certainly, but less alive. Or was it simply less fantastic, more substantial? Her feelings wavered. She became aware of what she missed about A.G., the sense that something was going to happen, the lift that his extravagant thoughts could give, the belief that the Sunrise was the best of all possible worlds. It was merely a cattle ranch now, a pretty place to live but a business like any other—facts and figures, balance sheets and purchase orders. She could not say that she missed the disappointments that A.G.'s failures brought. She had to replace his trust in the future with her determination to hold things together, day by day. She did not throw parties, nor did governors and senators come to call. Nor would there ever again be anyone to love her as he had, this she knew, and this: that she had been another of his failures.

Yet I am luckier than most, she would tell herself. And when she would ride back to the house to find the children playing, she would say to herself that she felt almost happy.

—Tulsa, 1978–1981